YESTERDAY'S
TIDES

T0006230

Books by Roseanna M. White

LADIES OF THE MANOR

The Lost Heiress
The Reluctant Duchess
A Lady Unrivaled

SHADOWS OVER ENGLAND

A Name Unknown
A Song Unheard
An Hour Unspent

THE CODEBREAKERS

The Number of Love
On Wings of Devotion
A Portrait of Loyalty

Dreams of Savannah

SECRETS OF THE ISLES

The Nature of a Lady
To Treasure an Heiress
Worthy of Legend

Yesterday's Tides

YESTERDAY'S TIDES

ROSEANNA M. WHITE

BETHANY HOUSE

a division of Baker Publishing Group
Minneapolis, Minnesota

© 2023 by Roseanna M. White

Published by Bethany House Publishers
Minneapolis, Minnesota
www.bethanyhouse.com

Bethany House Publishers is a division of
Baker Publishing Group, Grand Rapids, Michigan

Printed in the United States of America

All rights reserved. No part of this publication may be reproduced, stored in a retrieval
system, or transmitted in any form or by any means—for example, electronic, photo-
copy, recording—without the prior written permission of the publisher. The only
exception is brief quotations in printed reviews.

Library of Congress Cataloging-in-Publication Data
Names: White, Roseanna M., author.
Title: Yesterday's tides / Roseanna M. White.
Description: Minneapolis, Minnesota : Bethany House, a division of Baker
    Publishing Group, [2023]
Identifiers: LCCN 2022034204 | ISBN 9780764240010 (paperback) | ISBN
    9780764241338 (casebound) | ISBN 9781493440641 (ebook)
Subjects: LCGFT: Novels.
Classification: LCC PS3623.H578785 Y47 2023 | DDC 813/.6—dc23/eng/20220831
LC record available at https://lccn.loc.gov/2022034204

Scripture quotations are from the King James Version of the Bible.

This is a work of historical reconstruction; the appearances of certain historical figures
are therefore inevitable. All other characters, however, are products of the author's
imagination, and any resemblance to actual persons, living or dead, is coincidental.

Cover design by Dan Thornberg, Design Source Creative Services
Cover model photography by Ildiko Neer / Trevillion Images

Author is represented by The Steve Laube Agency.

Baker Publishing Group publications use paper produced from sustainable forestry
practices and post-consumer waste whenever possible.

23 24 25 26 27 28 29   7 6 5 4 3 2 1

To Aunt Pam,
who loved Ocracoke long before I discovered it.

1

TODAY

MAY 11, 1942
OCRACOKE ISLAND, NORTH CAROLINA

The first light of sunrise turned the water of the Pamlico Sound to gold, the clouds to rose, and the dark to morning, promising Evie Farrow that today would be just like yesterday. Just like tomorrow. Just like every other day on this tiny island in North Carolina's Outer Banks. She could fight it, or she could embrace it.

But there was fighting enough going on in the world, and Evie had always preferred the way of peace. So she drew in a long breath filled with her favorite perfume—yeast, sugar, and cinnamon—and slid the still-warm sweet rolls into her basket. She paused one moment more to stare out the window of the kitchen, toward the view of the sound that had always, always soothed her. Later, she'd walk its shores. Perhaps even circle around to where the Atlantic joined its tamer sister with heightened waves and currents. She'd take her familiar path. She'd search for shells and sea glass. She'd pray for everyone she loved most.

Too many of them were on the other side of that ocean now. Too many of them were caught up in the war that made the ocean a harbinger of enemies instead of friends. But then, they had always been capricious, those waters. They stole as often as they gave. But she loved them.

A light hand touched her arm, and Evie spun around, smiling at Grandma See, who held out a cup of steaming coffee. Evie touched her fingertips to her mouth and then lowered them away from her in the second sign she'd ever been taught. *Thank you.* She slid her fingers into the familiar handle and lifted the mug for a fortifying sip.

Grandma See smiled, too, and made a series of quick hand movements. Her usual morning greeting: *Time to race the sun.*

Evie chuckled and leaned over to smack a kiss onto the familiar feathery-soft cheek. "I'm going, I'm going." No need to sign those words—though Grandma See wouldn't hear them, she could read them well enough, and knew to expect them. It was their daily script.

With the basket's handle looped over her arm, Evie stepped out into the spring morning. Just as she had done yesterday, just as she would do tomorrow. Walked the familiar path toward the Coast Guard station, as she'd done every morning for the last six years. As she would likely do for six more, for ten more.

Forever.

She drew in a long breath and reminded herself, again, that she'd chosen this. Chosen to make Ocracoke not half her home, but her whole home. She'd chosen to relegate her other ties to visits and holidays.

So why did she find herself missing so much lately?

A silly question. How could she not? The biggest part of her heart was stuck an ocean away.

"Morning, Miss Evie."

Evie's gaze swept over, upward a few feet, to where her closest neighbor stood on her porch, her own mug of coffee in hand. Evie frowned. Miss Marge wasn't usually out this early. "Morning, Miss Marge. How'd you sleep last night? Your back still bothering you?"

At the mere mention, the old woman rubbed at her lower back and heaved a sigh even the doves on the newly strung electrical wires probably heard. "Gave up—you know I ain't much these days. Figured I'd sit out here on the pizzer for a little while, then maybe stretch out on the couch. You hear them noises last night?"

Evie didn't slow her pace, but she did change her trajectory and aim for the porch's steps, shifting her coffee to her already-burdened arm so she had a free hand. Ever since Mr. Mack had died last year, Miss Marge was always hearing noises, and she refused to believe they could all be from the antics of the neighborhood's feral cat colony. "Nothing out of the ordinary." She reached into the basket and pulled out one of the cinnamon rolls, sticky with icing.

That sticky icing on her fingers was one thing that *would* change, and soon. According to the report on the radio last night, sugar would soon be rationed. Then what would she offer to the boys at the station? She'd have to get creative. Or start bringing them something savory instead. Thanks to the local chickens and hogs, she had plenty of eggs and bacon. Her garden would soon be producing vegetables. Her lips twitched as she considered what they'd say if she showed up with a lovely French quiche instead of pastries.

"Here, Miss Marge. Something to enjoy with your coffee." She handed over the roll with a smile.

Miss Marge's eyes lit up, making Evie chide herself for letting three days slip by since her last baked good–laden visit. The lady didn't get around well enough anymore to spend much time on her feet in the kitchen. "Well, I do thank you, Evie girl. You inn ladies are the best bakers on the island." She closed her eyes and held the roll under her nose for a long whiff. Then opened them again, worry within the rheumy depths. "You be careful walking alone, now. Won't be hardly daylight under the trees yet, and there are Germans in those woods, you know. Pretty young thing like you can't be too careful."

Evie frowned and reached out to tuck one of Miss Marge's wispy gray curls back under her faded kerchief. Last month it had been an escaped bobcat supposedly prowling the woods, having swum to the island from . . . somewhere.

There was no use arguing with her—or trying to reason her into seeing that there could not possibly be Germans here. No point in reminding her that Ocracoke was probably the safest place in the world to live—and that Evie was hardly a "young thing" anymore. She may still have three years to go before she hit thirty, but she'd lived enough life to feel as ancient as the live oak at the corner, gnarling its way heavenward.

No point in saying any of that. But she'd be whispering an extra prayer for sweet Marge as she walked. "I'll be careful. And I'll stop by again later, okay? You try to get some rest after your breakfast."

Armed with Miss Marge's nod, Evie left the porch and returned to the road, picking up her pace now to make up for the detour. She always tried to arrive at the Coast Guard station in time for the shift change, so both groups of men were there.

A hum found her throat as she walked, "Sunrise Serenade"

10

seeming an appropriate companion as daylight won a few more degrees. She saluted a few more early risers with her coffee mug, though the greetings they would shout later in the day remained unsaid in deference to the sleepyheads around. A few fishermen—stragglers, those—were hurrying toward the docks that wreathed Silver Lake. A few housewives were scattering corn for their chickens. But mostly she had the walk to herself.

Her to-do list wanted to crowd her mind, all the things she had to tend for the sake of the inn: checking the reservation book, sending out reminder postcards, maybe placing a few advertisements in mainland magazines to try to get more guests, like Stanley Wahab was doing for his new hotel. Then she had to make up some more sachets of yaupon tea for the two checking out today to take home with them, air out the garret room for next week's hunting party—if they came—and hopefully still find some time to spend in her studio.

But all those thoughts were for later. Now was for the sweet silent prayers of morning. The call of the birds. The ever-present lap of water on shore. The distant rumble of . . . thunder?

She paused and looked out toward the horizon, but the clouds were only puffy, isolated things that she could see. That didn't mean a storm wasn't just over the horizon, of course, but the meteorologist had predicted clear skies today. Which meant it might *not* be thunder. It could be something far more sinister—and increasingly familiar.

Her prayers tripping over themselves now, Evie turned her stroll into a run. From hard-packed road to loose sand, up the weather-worn wooden steps, and into the Coast Guard station a few minutes later, Evie dashed. She slid her now-empty mug onto the porch banister and came to a panting halt inside the doors, where the expected well-ordered bustle was indeed underway.

She nabbed one of the Coasties by the arm. "Herb! Was that an explosion?"

"Hey, Evie." Rather than stop, Herbert O'Neal took her hand and tugged her along with him. "Must have been. Torpedo Junction living up to its name. We're preparing for a search and rescue."

Evie's stomach tied itself into knots. She bit back the words that wanted to spring up—*Be careful! There are German U-boats out there!* They were unnecessary, and if she gave them utterance, she'd sound like Miss Marge. These men were trained to be careful . . . and were well aware that it was the U-boats wreaking such havoc on their shipping lanes. Lately, it seemed like at least once a week the islanders were hearing those rumbles, sometimes seeing plumes of smoke from out at sea.

Who had died this time? What ship lost? One of theirs? Or had one of the ships that England sent over to help protect America's vulnerable East Coast struck a blow against the Krauts this time?

And how many of the Coast Guardsmen would come back from this mission? Thus far the U-boats hadn't targeted the Coast Guard cutters, but could they really assume they never would? In the best of times, theirs was a dangerous job. No one knew that better than she did.

In *these* times . . .

Herb was sending interested glances at her basket, so she opened it up again so he could snitch a roll. He was part of the daylight shift, which meant he'd be on the cutter heading out to investigate the explosion. He'd need all the fortification he could get.

12

She wouldn't let herself say *Be safe*. But she did give him a tight smile and said, "Go with God, Herb."

He nodded. "Always. You be praying, Evie girl."

"Always." Even when it didn't seem to help. Always the Lord was with these men, she knew that—but He didn't always deliver them safely home again. Sometimes He took them Home instead.

She tried to remember that it was better for them. That they died with a purpose. She tried to remember her great-grandmother's voice as she whispered her own prayers, beads in hand, assuring Evie that death was just a veil between heaven and earth. A curtain. So thin, so delicate. Not something to fear, because the life after was just as real—far *more* real—than the life now.

Sometimes those words were easier to cling to than at other times, like this. When she wanted to know that all these men who were friends and brothers and fathers and grandfathers to her would be here still tomorrow, clamoring for their breakfast.

She slid her basket onto the usual table and then stepped out of the way as the horde of hungry Coasties descended. They all mumbled their thanks around full mouths as they took off again for their various tasks.

Evie drifted over to the station keeper, who stood, silver-haired and back straight as ever, looking out the broad windows with binoculars raised. "Any idea who it is out there, Liam?"

First Class Boatswain Mate Liam Bryan didn't even glance down at her. "Morning, Evie. Hard to say." When she sighed, he lowered the binoculars and sighed along with her. "We didn't intercept any Maydays. Must have happened too fast. Blasted U-boats."

She folded her arms, clasping hands to opposite elbows.

13

Feeling the warmth from the palm that had been cradling her coffee seep into her skin made her that much more aware of how frigid the waters would be, should any of her friends fall into them. Not quite winter-cold, but a far cry from end-of-summer warm. "If there's anything I can do, let me know."

Liam angled a crooked grin down at her. "Well now. You've got friends in high places overseas, don't you? Ask them if they can get Hitler in line."

She snorted a laugh and let her hands fall to her sides again. "Gee, why didn't I think of that?"

"Always were a thoughtless little thing." He added a wink and reached out to tweak her nose, like he'd been doing since she was a tot. "I'll never forget the first time your mama brought you here. The way your brother was into everything, but you . . . You just climbed up on Johnson's lap and snuggled right in, like he wasn't a bear that kept us all in line from sheer terror."

Evie let her lips tug up. "Teddy bear, maybe."

"With *you*, maybe." But he chuckled and shook his head, then sighed. "I miss those days right about now. When we only had the weather and the currents and the shoals to worry over. Accidents. Not this."

They'd had another war, too, in those days. But it hadn't touched them here on Ocracoke like it was doing now. Not most of them.

A shudder coursed through her. Not every islander had remained unscathed from that Great War. She'd been too young to really remember much of it directly, but the stories still haunted the inn like the Howard Street Ghost was rumored to haunt the Howards.

She took a step back. "I'd better get out of the way and back to the inn. The guests will be up soon, wanting breakfast."

14

Liam nodded. "We were all talking last night after the rationing announcement. Most of us won't have much call for our sugar allotment. Figure we'll send them your way, if you keep delivering it back to us in the form of pastries."

"Well now." She gave him a grin and executed a perfect naval salute. "You have yourself a deal, sir."

When she reclaimed her coffee cup from the railing a minute later, empty basket now on her arm, the morning was already bright and steady, that magical gold of dawn faded. Every day, she marveled at how quickly it turned from rainbows and fire to regular light.

Another metaphor for life, wasn't it? She'd had her flash of fire and gold, too, but that was long gone. Now it was day. An island day that would have its clouds and its sun and eventually its dusk and night. Nothing out of the ordinary, no matter how splendid and special that daybreak had seemed.

That was all right. More than all right—it was what she had chosen. An everyday life. An island life. One in which she would shine as brightly as she could for her neighbors, for her family. She'd gather her shells and sea glass. She'd pray those bits of ocean into baubles and jewelry. She'd do what she could to make life a little sweeter for the people around her. She'd live until she didn't anymore.

Reaching up, she touched a hand to the necklace she always wore. The blue-green glass, the swirls of silver, the circle of white gold. The reminder of her flash. Of her yesterday.

A few minutes later, as she turned onto the lane toward the Ocracoke Inn again, a shadow settled over her spirit so completely that she came to a halt, breath balled up in her chest. She looked around for whatever had cast it, but it couldn't be blamed on a cloud or a tree branch getting between her and the sun.

It wasn't physical.

Struggling to pull air into her lungs, she rubbed a hand over her chest and let her vision go unfocused. It had been years—*years*—since she'd felt this, at least this strongly. This urgency, this darkness. This warning. As a child, it had come upon her all too frequently, but with age and its doubts and its reason, it had lessened. Weakened.

She squeezed her eyes shut, and that was all it took to be back in her great-grandmother's arms, to hear her whispering prayers for protection over her. To see the worry in Mama's eyes as Evie cried over what no one else could see. To feel the warm surety of her brother's fingers woven through hers.

"Lord Jesus . . ." For a long moment, that was all she could say, a cry, a call that lingered on her tongue. Then she managed, "What is it?"

She opened her eyes again and spun around. Miss Marge's porch was empty, as were the electrical lines overhead. No people, no doves, not even any feral cats slinking around to beg a few scraps from her. There were just live oaks and creaking cedars and wild olives, sand and saw grass and certainty.

Something wasn't as it should be. Something more focused than the war that was devouring the world. Something that meant danger for those she loved.

Drawing in a deep, salt-air breath, she straightened her spine and lifted her chin. Hurried back toward the inn. She'd arm herself with prayer, like all the women in her life had taught her.

But she wouldn't forget Daddy's lessons either.

16

2

F*ire.*
Everywhere there was fire—above him, below him, around him, within him, eating him from the inside out. Sterling Bertrand dove into the roiling water, but even then it seemed he couldn't escape the teeth of hell. Fire still roared, belching its way to the surface, using what had once been a ship as its weapons.

He sputtered his way back to the top, unable to make any sense whatsoever of what he was seeing. "Tommie! *Tommie!*" He tried again to make his arms slice through the waves as they'd done so many times before, but his left side wouldn't obey him. And the waves swirled around him, making it impossible to know which way to go. Which was up or down or left or right. Where, in that mass of flames and groaning metal that had once been called the HMT *Bedfordshire*, his friend might be.

Sterling dove under one more time, but his arm still wasn't cooperating, and even under the water, his skin burned. He could see nothing, hear nothing above the roar in his ears.

Where was the crew? The men he'd eaten with, the ones he'd joked with the night before? They had to be here, somewhere, but he couldn't get close enough to make out any of them.

He surfaced again, and clarity lashed over him like a whip for one chest-pummeling second: If he didn't get back into his dinghy now, *he* would die, too, just like his friend. Just like Tommie's crew. He would already be dead if he hadn't been in the small motorized boat, ready to surreptitiously make for the shore. And his strength wouldn't hold out much longer. If he let the Zodiac drift away, he'd spend the rest of his life trying in vain to swim after it.

No. The clouds in his soul fought against that truth. He couldn't leave Tommie and his men to die. He couldn't go about his business. He couldn't abandon them to preserve his own life—how could he? It was his fault. His fault the *Bedfordshire* had been right there, right now. His fault, then, that it was now a sinking ball of fire.

A wave lifted him, pulled him away from the wreckage, sent him within arm's reach of his Zodi, as if that water was the very hand of God, telling him clearly what he was supposed to do. Still, Sterling choked on a cry. No words came out, but all the grief in his heart did.

This wasn't how it was supposed to be. *He* was the one who was supposed to be taking the stupid risk with this "mad plan," as Tommie had called it. To be dropped by the *Bedfordshire* so many miles off the coast of the Outer Banks of North Carolina in nothing but a dinghy, all in the hope of tracking down a German agent that logic said could not possibly be there, even if rumor and gut instinct told Sterling he had better look into it.

"As foolhardy as ever, I see," Tommie had said the other night in Norfolk, where Sterling had tracked down his old friend to ask the favor. He'd looked long into his glass, tossed

back the last draft of beer, and laughed. *"I suppose if I don't help you, you'll charm someone else into it. All right, then. I'll drop you into the Atlantic—and say a prayer, too, that you make it to the islands."*

Sterling wrapped his not-screaming arm in one of the Zodi's structural ropes and used it to pull himself back into the raft. It took every last bit of his energy. He lay there, gasping and panting, staring up at the sky for an eternity. Blue, but for where the smoke, black as sin, billowed into the air.

He'd teased his old friend about the *Bedfordshire* just yesterday. It was a fishing trawler, that was all. Never meant for wartime work. It, like too many men, had simply been drafted into His Majesty's service—but putting a fancy *HMT* in front of its name didn't change its nature any more than welding guns to its deck did. The *Bedfordshire* had been meant to protect America's vulnerabilities, but the sad truth was that it was no match for a U-boat's torpedoes.

And that's what had ripped the world apart five—ten, twenty?—minutes ago. He'd no sooner looked up from his compass, ready to signal his old friend to cut the towline between the Zodiac and the trawler, than he'd seen it—that terrifying line burrowing through the water.

He'd spun back toward the boat. He'd opened his mouth to scream a warning. He'd seen, one more time, that grin of Tommie's. And then it had all exploded.

His fault. All his fault.

He managed now to hook his good arm over his face, though it hurt enough that he regretted it. What was he going to tell Barb? Barb who, heaven help them all, had discovered before Tommie shipped out that she was expecting. What about that son or daughter who would never know their father? How was he ever going to meet his friend's child and admit that he'd watched their father die and hadn't been

19

able to do a thing to stop it? Had in fact been the reason the *Bedfordshire* was in the path of that U-boat?

Then another reality struck: He couldn't. Because he couldn't admit to anyone that he'd ever been on the *Bedfordshire*. As always, his own naval uniform was back at home in London, packed away. Rank and insignia classified. His whole life, classified. As far as anyone could ever know, he was never even on American soil, much less begging his old friend for a tow up the coast. Officially, he didn't see that torpedo or the explosion or Lieutenant Thomas Cunningham vanishing in fire and smoke.

When he opened his eyes again, it was to the sun beating down on him, warming him, burning him. He sat up, groaning at the agony of it, and looked wildly around. No wreckage. No smoke. No flames.

Nothing to tell the tale but his own anguish.

Where was he? He looked around the Zodi for his compass, his chart, his sextant, but there was nothing. *Nothing.* He was adrift at sea, and he didn't even know whether it was morning still or afternoon, to judge by the sun.

"Think, old boy. Think." He scrubbed his right hand over his face and braved a glance at his left side.

His shirt had burned away, leaving only charred bits of fabric behind, stuck in mottled, angry red flesh, despite his time in the ocean. That didn't bode well. He clenched his teeth and tried to tug at the largest piece of cloth, but the pain made his vision swim.

Better stop that, lest he pass out again. He needed his wits about him. He couldn't save Tommie or the rest of the crew, but he couldn't let their deaths mean nothing. His mission couldn't be abandoned. He had to get to shore. Had to track down Gustav Mansfeld. Had to stop him.

Because if one of Hitler's most elite SS officers was really hiding in the forests of the Outer Banks, then it could mean utter ruin for every ship off the East Coast, as surely as it had for the *Bedfordshire*. He could be gathering key intelligence. He could be signaling to U-boats off the coast at set times. He could be undermining England's strongest ally before she even had time to mount a fleet of her own.

That's right, Sterling. Focus on the mission. Focus. Focus.

It only took him a moment to set up an impromptu sundial, and then a few minutes to track the movement of the shadow and thereby determine time of day and east and west. Which at least gave him a direction to point his dinghy. Convincing the motor to start again took more effort—the thing looked as though it had taken some shrapnel and had no doubt flooded in the same wave that sent him overboard and all his instruments to Davy Jones's locker to begin with. But eventually it coughed to life.

He pointed himself to the west. Should he aim it a bit north too? He'd initially been launching himself for Hatteras Island. That was where all his research said Mansfeld was likely to be, if indeed he had infiltrated this island chain. But the torpedo had struck before they were parallel with Hatteras. He'd been about to cut the towrope, yes, but that was because he hadn't wanted any of the crewmen to know where he was actually going. He'd intended to head west and then north when out of visual range of the *Bedfordshire*.

In theory, he could and should still do that. In practice, he was none too certain his spluttering engine would hold out for that long.

West, then. Simply west. Whatever land he saw first, he'd aim for it. And then pray the locals didn't shoot on sight.

As long as the engine, whining though it was, continued to propel him over the water, he managed to focus on it and where he was going and ignore the fact that his side was still on fire. Perhaps the flames were invisible, but he could feel them feasting on him. He could sense the darkness closing in again. He beat it back, blinked, shook his head. *Focus. Focus.* Then, just as a bit of land emerged from the sea, the injured motor gave one last splutter and died.

Silence must feed fire. Because the moment the sound died, his resistance crumbled, too, and the flames roared over him again. With them came everything else, everything that had brought him here.

He saw his mum as he'd seen her last, so tired from years of struggling to provide for him and Ruby, to supplement the pension they'd been drawing since Father died in the last war. Tired, but proud of him. Proud of him, but fearful. So afraid that he, like the father he could barely remember, would be taken from her.

He tried to blink through the haze, tried to form a prayer with parched lips. Not for his own sake—for Mum's. She deserved better than this. She at least deserved a telegram to let her know it if he died, deserved to hear the empty words about him going out as a hero, fighting Hitler.

But she wouldn't receive that, because it would be months before anyone even tried to raise him. Months before they'd realize he'd vanished. And even then, there would be the questions—was he dead, or had he gone radio silent?

They'd warned him of this risk of the intelligence game. He'd signed on anyway. Because, at the time, he'd told himself Mum would understand. That it was worth it. He'd signed on because he'd wanted to see that gleam in Ruby's eyes as he whispered to her what he wasn't technically supposed to tell anyone else.

And oh, how they'd gleamed. For a moment, he half expected her to leap out of her wheelchair and claim that she'd come with him. As if they'd let her—and as if she could ever leap again. But he was always expecting it, somehow. A mind that moved as quickly as hers surely couldn't be bound by those paralytic legs forever.

He'd told his superiors during the recruitment process that he wasn't bound to his family, felt no compunction about leaving them. That they would never distract him from his mission.

Truth and lies both, those. They wouldn't distract him, they never distracted him. They helped him focus. His love for them, his desire to get back to them, simply fueled him to do the best job he could do. But his love for them, the desire to guarantee they remained safe and well and in a land free of Hitler's tyranny, meant he'd sacrifice his life if he had to in order to preserve theirs.

Now all he could do was give them to God. Give himself to Him too. The Lord had always felt just out of reach, but not now. Now Sterling was all too aware of how close He was. How heaven was there, beyond that blur of his vision.

He tried to call to mind his sins, to ask forgiveness for them, but they were a blur too. All his mental eyes really wanted to focus on were the shining things. Mum. Ruby. The way old Mrs. Higgins would press a hot cross bun into his palm every Easter season and remind him of what it meant. The way the voices of his neighbors turned into something more beautiful than they rightly should when lifted up together in song on a Sunday morning.

Forgive the smudges, Lord, I beg you. But was it really so bad to focus on the light, bright things instead? He hoped not. Because that was all he could manage as he collapsed back to the rubber bottom of his boat and let the currents take him. *Mum. Ruby. Grandmum.*

And then another twist of his heart. *Barb and the baby.* She, at least, would get word someday soon. Someone would realize that the trawler had gone missing, put two and two together. Someone would knock on her door, that horrible letter in their hands, and she would press a hand to her lips as tears surged to her eyes. She would grip her rosary in that way she always did when feeling overwhelmed her. She would put a hand on the rounding of life in her stomach and mourn that her little one would never know the man she so loved.

But she was strong. She'd keep marching forward for the little one's sake. She would smile for the baby, and she would tell him or her about Tommie as the years stretched out. Just like Sterling's own mum had done for him and Ruby.

Father. He'd see him soon, as he hadn't done in so many years. This fire would turn him to ash, and the Lord would wipe those smudges from his soul, and he'd hear the angels sing, and they'd put to shame his neighbors.

If he strained his ears, he could hear them even now. They sounded like birds and ocean waves. He let them serenade him as the blur took over his vision. Cocked his head a bit as the accompaniment changed in pitch. Not only water lapping against the sides of his Zodiac but water lapping now against something else. Something bigger. And the wind, the wind joined in, along with a strange rustling, like grass blowing.

An abrupt jolt sent fresh pain slicing through him, and Sterling opened his eyes with a hiss. Above him, where he expected to see sky and scuttling clouds, he saw branches, green with fresh leaves.

But it must be one of the trees of heaven, because there, too, was an angel. A face of perfect beauty that no one on earth could ever attain, her hair a golden halo of curl and wave falling to her shoulders. Eyes as blue as the sky—though they didn't look all that welcoming. Had the fire not purified him enough yet?

He tried to lick his lips, to moisten them, but his tongue felt as dry as his lips. "In . . . heaven?"

The angel lifted golden brows, and a new sound invaded his peace. A click he knew all too well. When he blinked, the barrel of a gun was between him and her perfect face. "No—the Ocracoke Inn. And most guests choose to arrive by the lane."

Focus. He didn't need to call it down this time—it crashed back on him, bringing with it all the pain and the horror and the weight of his mission. He lifted his hands, though his left one screamed in protest. "I'm an Englishman. An ally. A naval officer."

But he was in civvies, as he always was. Or had been, before the fire turned them to smoldering ash. For the first time in his career, he found himself wishing for his uniform, for its neat, orderly rank there on display. Maybe then the angel would soften.

As it was, she didn't look impressed, and her smile was the strangest contrast to the pistol she kept leveled at his face. "Swell. We have a long history of serving Englishmen here."

Funny how that didn't sound the least bit welcoming.

3

YESTERDAY

MAY 11, 1914
OCRACOKE ISLAND, NORTH CAROLINA

L ouisa Adair leaned back against the rough bark of the live oak and held the postcard with near reverence, tracing one chipped fingernail along the picture. From the bottom, where the feet of the Eiffel Tower planted themselves among the city below, all the way up to the sky itself, where the tip seemed to kiss the clouds. Never in her life had she seen anything so high, not even mountains. The tallest things on Ocracoke were the cedar trees, and even when she'd gone with Mama to Elizabeth City, the tallest buildings weren't much higher. She didn't even know how to imagine it.

The Eiffel Tower. Paris, France. One of the places she and Celeste used to dream of seeing together. They were going to stroll through the streets arm in arm, chatting in the French that Louisa's Grann had taught them—even if it was more the Creole version than the Parisian one, it would surely do—and pretend that they belonged there. They were going to buy a baguette from a sweet little bakery. Sip café au lait. Louisa was going to badger Celeste into touring the museums with her, even though Celeste had never cared a fig for such places. And Celeste was going to badger *her* into all the high-end boutiques, even though pretty clothes had never been high on Louisa's list of things she'd like to have.

Best friends, sisters, fellow explorers. That's what it was supposed to be.

A small smile tugged up the corners of Louisa's lips. At least *one* of them was living the dream. At this point it didn't look like Louisa would ever get off Ocracoke. Her hopes of attending a teaching college and coming back here to help educate the next generation seemed as out of reach as Paris itself. She hadn't even brought it up to her family—she didn't dare. She knew very well Mama, Grann, and even Uncle Linc would move heaven and earth to give her dreams to her, if she but gave them voice.

But how could she ask that of them? She saw the ledgers, she knew how much the inn brought in, and it was just enough. Just enough, always, to keep them afloat. Not enough to send her to school too. And she couldn't ask them to pay for her dreams when they'd already given so much.

She'd have to work her way to education, saving up as she went. It might take a whole lot longer that way, but dreams were worth sacrifice. Garret had taught her that, hadn't he, scraping and saving as he'd done for so many years? And now he was enrolled at a university, studying to become a doctor. If he could do that, surely she could make her way to a teacher's college.

She flipped the postcard over only after she'd memorized every detail of the photograph. Celeste's familiar handwriting made her smile bloom bigger, even before she read the words. It was tiny and tight, trying to crowd as much as possible into the small space, like every other postcard she'd sent in the last three years since her mother had remarried and Celeste had been swept off to Europe with Miss Maddie and her new stepfather.

Lulu,

I don't just wish you were here—I'm pretending you are. Every street I walk down with Mama or Pierre, I'm imagining you beside me, seeing it through your eyes. I wanted to send a postcard so you could see it at least a little, but a long, fat letter filled with all the descriptions will be coming soon! And perhaps a package with one of the fancy dresses you don't want. Hear me laughing maniacally? It's only fair—Pierre dragged me and imaginary you through the Louvre yesterday.

Celeste

P.S. Tell old Beanpole I say hello when he comes home again.

The Louvre! Louisa touched a finger to that word, too, hoping a bit of the magic of it would seep through her fingertip and into her mind. She and Celeste spent one whole summer trying to train themselves to read each other's mind. They'd fill their thoughts with words and images and then the other would try to *feel* them.

It had been a complete failure, of course, but had resulted in lots of laughter. And really, they didn't need clairvoyance. They finished each other's thoughts most of the time anyway. Still, Louisa knew that Celeste would have pressed her own finger to that word and tried to pack her impressions into it. She couldn't help but try to tease a few into her own mind. What all would she have seen? Oh, the *Mona Lisa*! She'd read all about how it had been first stolen in 1911 and then just recovered and returned to the museum last year. And her favorite sculpture, the *Venus de Milo*. Louisa had only ever studied them in books, but she could imagine them on walls or in galleries. And she could imagine Celeste saying, *Someday. Someday you'll see them in person too.*

Nothing but a dream at this point. She'd be lucky if she could ever make it to the mainland for anything but a stock-up trip for the inn.

"Another postcard from that Scarborough girl?"

Louisa straightened at the snapping voice. She couldn't help it. Marge Williams had been her schoolteacher for half her life—and she was *not* part of what had inspired Louisa to want to be one herself . . . unless one counted "so no one else has to suffer under her" as inspiration. Not that the woman was mean to anyone *else*.

But no one else on the island looked like Louisa.

Louisa pasted a docile smile onto her lips and held up the picture of the Eiffel Tower. "Yes, ma'am. Celeste and Miss Maddie and Mr. Pierre are in Paris."

Mrs. Williams shook her head and clucked her tongue like the news was a tragedy instead of a dream come true. "If Jack Scarborough could see his wife and daughter, putting on airs like that . . ."

Louisa bristled on behalf of Celeste. Jack Scarborough had been a drunk—a mean one—and no one had missed him since his boat capsized five years ago and he'd drowned. It had been guilty relief that had fueled Celeste's tears at the news, and Louisa had held her and wondered if it was a sin to thank God for the mercy of his death.

No more bruises that Celeste would have to cover up. No more slipping out of her house in the dead of night and running to the inn, terrified at the screams and begging of her mother, not knowing what she could do to stop it, and unable to do anything but obey that instruction her mama had given her so many years before: *"You hear him coming, and you run, baby girl. You run to Lulu and spend the night with her, okay?"*

Louisa couldn't begin to count the number of times she'd fallen asleep in her attic bed praying for Celeste's safety and had woken up to find her snuggled in, she and her favorite doll, the next morning. Like the sister she was at heart.

It took every ounce of good manners Louisa possessed to keep from telling Mrs. Williams that if Jack Scarborough would be displeased, then *good*. He deserved it.

Even thinking that made her conscience wriggle, though. Uncle Linc—who'd been her pastor all her life—would say that Christ, who ought to be shining through her, would never wish ill on anyone else. And Grann—as Catholic as Linc was Methodist—would chide her in French and tell her to pray for his soul.

Grann had said that about a hundred times since his death. Never once had Louisa obeyed, even though she usually did whatever her mammy said, no questions asked. Not because she feared her—like why she'd always obeyed Marge Williams—but because she loved her so very much.

Just now, she decided the best possible response she could give her old teacher was none at all.

Mrs. Williams sniffed and nodded toward the shore. "Hadn't you better see to your mother's guests, girl?"

Louisa's smile nearly flitted off her face, but she nailed it down and even polished it up a little. The way that woman said *girl* . . . She glanced down at her own hand, at the skin that wasn't quite light enough to pass Mrs. Williams's muster, even though her own got just as dark in the summertime. That didn't matter, it seemed. What mattered was that Louisa's stayed brown in the winter and wasn't quite the same tone. As if that gave anyone a right to dismiss her. As if the question of who her daddy had been was so important that her existence didn't deserve the least regard until that question was answered.

As if she even had those answers. No, she'd learned long ago that there were things she didn't ask Mama. And anything about Daddy rated. The most she ever got on the subject was the occasional *"He would have liked that"* or *"Oh, you're your daddy's girl. How he would have loved to see you now."*

Louisa cleared her throat and glanced toward the mail boat. "I was simply giving them time to get their luggage."

And while the menfolk all wrestled the suitcases and trunks to shore, Louisa had followed that siren song of "Mail's here!" to the other end of the boat and had accepted the inn's stack with a smile.

Who could blame her for then stealing a moment to read her postcard?

Marge Williams, apparently. But she'd take the excuse to escape her now. She moved back over to her pony cart and tucked the mail under the bench in front—everything but the precious postcard, which she kept ahold of for a moment more. *Ocracoke Inn* was stenciled on the side of the cart, the paint fresh and bright for the new season. She smiled a bit at the details she'd added this year—the outlines and pinstripes—even as she stroked Jingle's nose. Her pony pressed his face into her hand and snuffled at the postcard in her fingers. Greedy for a sugar cube, no doubt. She chuckled and dug one out of her pocket for him, holding it in her empty hand before he decided to taste the postcard instead. "There you go, sweet thing."

He tossed his head when he was finished, as if to remind everyone that he still had his pride, hadn't always been a sweet thing. He'd been born a wild banker pony after all, galloping over the island with the rest of the herd. And he'd been a troublemaker, too, before Louisa caught him and convinced him that sugar and ready buckets of water beat pawing his way down to fresh water at the base of the seagrass any day. All the villagers had sighed in relief when she'd finally gotten a halter over his head and had stopped him from tearing up their gardens and kicking at their cisterns.

"Well now. You must be talking to me."

The voice sounded like the North—the part of the North that called itself cultured. Young, rich, and full of itself. She couldn't help but stiffen as she turned her head to view one of the two cousins who would be at the inn throughout the summer. She could hear Mama in her head.

"You smile, Louisa, but not too bright. Make it clear you're there to serve, but only so far. Those men may only see your pretty face at first glance. It's up to you to show them your spine."

If her mother had given her that speech once since she started turning from girl to woman, she'd given it a hundred times. Especially every time she sent her to fetch the new guests from the boat.

Louisa lifted her gaze to the young man standing a few feet away, who was sporting a cocksure grin and a pale linen suit that was about as practical here as Mr. Wahab's fancy Hudson had proven to be on their sand roads last month. He was probably midtwenties. From Maryland, wasn't it? Near Washington, DC. Probably thought himself handsome, though that arrogance coating him like molasses made her want to wrinkle her nose in distaste.

She smiled, but not too bright, and kept Jingle between

them. His flirtation was best left summarily ignored. "Afternoon, sir. You must be either Mr. Culbreth or Mr. Grenshaw."

He swept his straw boater from his head and executed a bow. "Edgar Grenshaw at your service, Miss . . . ?"

"Adair." She'd rather not have told him even that much, but that was foolishness. He obviously knew their family name. It would have been on all the reservation correspondence. "You've been in communication with my mother."

"Ah yes. Mrs. Adair has painted the most alluring image of your charming little island for us too." He let his gaze trail down her, which made her spine snap all the straighter. He was about to find it was made of steel if he kept that up. "Though she failed to mention some of the most astounding natural beauty."

She suddenly wished she'd come decked out in the old, stained trousers and overlarge shirt she wore for her handywork around the inn instead of a-fluting around in her guest-fetching white dress Mama always made her don for the occasion. She stroked Jingle's nose again. "Our wild ponies, you mean? Most mainlanders are struck by how small they are—at least until you see them running wild over the dunes, then it's hard to ignore their majesty." She made a point of looking past him, to where old Doxee hovered, ready to load the cart with the gents' trunks. And watching the exchange like a hawk, of course.

She could always count on Doxee to step in if a guest got too fresh. She sent him a smile considerably warmer than the one she'd given Mr. Grenshaw. "Jing and I are ready for you, Dox."

Her neighbor nodded, repositioned his newsboy, and motioned his sons forward with the trunks.

She held Jingle steady while they loaded so he didn't get

any ideas about returning to the wild and taking her cart with him. And she made it a point not to look at Mr. Grenshaw again, nor to give in to the curiosity about where his cousin was and whether he was just as obnoxious. She'd have ample time to get to know them both over the summer, whether she wanted to or not.

Be grateful they're here, Louisa. She stroked Jingle's nose again, calling to mind Mama's gratitude when the reservation had come through—three whole months of two rooms guaranteed to be filled! Grann had crossed herself and said a prayer in Latin so quickly that Louisa couldn't follow. Much as she personally didn't care for rich tourists who came here only to flirt and hunt the ducks she much preferred to see flying freely overhead or paddling peacefully in the pools, she could be practical. Rich gents meant steady income. They not only paid for the rooms, but they also paid for meals, they paid for transportation, they paid for errands and favors.

As long as they didn't get any ideas about what kind of favors she'd give, they'd get along fine.

She glanced again at the postcard in her hand and that graceful tower touching the heavens. Their summer guests wouldn't get her any closer to Paris, but they and the other tourists who would be filling the inn throughout the summer meant one more year of bills paid and food on the table—and quite possibly a few dollars put back for college. She didn't need Europe. Just an education. That's all her heart was longing for.

Doxee gave Jingle a pat on the rump and smiled at Louisa. "All set, Weeza. And you tell your mama thank you for that cake she sent 'round the other day, you hear? It was good some."

Louisa grinned and let go of Jingle's bridle. The only per-

son on Ocracoke who could rival Mama in the kitchen was
Elsie Neal, Celeste's grandmother. "Yes, sir. She'll be glad
to hear it hit the spot."

"Hear from Gar lately? He coming home for the summer?"

She nodded an answer to both questions at once. "Couple more weeks. I don't envy him his final exams either." It
would be so nice to have him home, though. Garret—the
"old Beanpole" who Celeste always told her to say hello
to but to whom she never seemed to write herself for some
reason—had always been her only other real friend. And now
that Celeste was gone and Gar off at college . . . well, it got
mighty lonely around here in the winters. But he'd be home
soon for a couple months, and she at least had regular mail
from Celeste to spice up life.

And it was time to face her guests again and break the
news to them that the pony cart was only for their things, and
they'd have to hoof it to the inn on foot unless they wanted
to hire another cart or wait for her to come back after their
trunks had been unloaded. She turned, ready to seek them
out with her gaze, only to find that she nearly collided with
Mr. Grenshaw, who was for some reason mere inches away.

"Oh!" At least she didn't squeal like a ninny. But she did
make the mistake of shifting backward, away from him,
which meant she bumped into Jingle.

Jingle never took too kindly to random bumps. He shifted,
too, and snorted and pranced like he was going to either
buck or rear—not that he'd really do either, what with the
cart hitched to him, but it always took him a moment to
remember that such responses had been trained out of him.

Grenshaw wouldn't know Jingle's training, though. Maybe
that was why his eyes went wide with panic and he grabbed
Louisa by the elbow and jerked her away from her horse.

She wasn't exactly sure how it happened. It must have been at least partially her fault. Sure, it was Grenshaw who tugged at her, and who tugged so hard she was stumbling toward his chest. But it was her own instincts that had her lifting her hands to brace against the collision with him rather than falling on him like some fainting damsel. And her own stupid fingers that splayed out and hence let go of the postcard.

Then it was all the wind. Ever-present this close to the water and as capricious as Jingle on a bad day, it snatched the words from Celeste and flipped them up and away.

"No!" She shoved at Grenshaw and made a leap for the runaway postcard, knowing Doxee would keep Jingle in line for her.

The paper evaded her fingers and sailed away on the next gust. She was set to run after it, praying it didn't fly into the water, but someone else beat her to it. Another linen-clad figure. He dropped the bag he'd still been holding to run after the card, made a leap worthy of an Olympic athlete, and miraculously plucked the postcard from the fingers of the wind.

This one was blond where his cousin was brunette, and he didn't even pay any attention to the hat that had fallen off in his feat. He simply turned back and held out the postcard with a smile so warm, so unassuming that she found herself genuinely smiling back. "Here you are. Are you all right?"

This one wasn't from Maryland. Or at least, he didn't talk like it. English, maybe? She hadn't heard the accent enough to be sure. But when he swept *his* gaze over her, she knew well he was making sure she wasn't injured, not cataloging her curves. His gaze returned promptly to her eyes and looked relieved when she nodded.

"I'm fine. And thank you." She took the postcard from him, knowing she'd treasure it all the more for nearly losing it.

He—Mr. Culbreth, surely—smiled again. "You're very welcome. If that came all the way from France, it's precious indeed."

He said *France* like the *A* was a short *O*. Pretty much the opposite of the way Ocracokers drew the vowel out, which made her smile turn to a grin. "It is. My best friend is traveling through Europe right now."

His eyes lit up. They were a bluish-green, the selfsame color as the Atlantic in September when sunshine shot through the shallows. "Really? Where all has she been?"

And he said *been* like those double *Es* actually got pronounced like double *Es*, instead of like a short *I*. Which, granted, made much more sense. She tucked the postcard into her pocket. "They spent six months in Geneva for her stepfather's business, toured Sweden, Austria, and Germany, and will soon be settling at his home in the Ardennes department."

Grenshaw appeared at his cousin's side, effectively stomping all over the conversation by slinging an arm around Mr. Culbreth's neck and pulling him down. "Don't get this one started on the charms of Europe, Miss Adair, or you'll never shut him up again."

Mr. Culbreth ducked out of the headlock with an ease that bespoke long practice. "I apologize for my cousin, miss, since he hasn't the good grace to have already done so. I imagine he intended only to help."

Mr. Grenshaw held his arms wide to match his eyes. "I was about to offer my apologies!"

"And no doubt some flattery." Mr. Culbreth held a hand to his mouth, blocking it from his cousin's view, and stage-whispered, "Just ignore him."

Oh, she liked this one. Her grin probably went a little impish. "Already my plan."

His cousin splayed a hand over his chest as if he'd been struck to the core. "Such ice. As if anything I could say about either your beauty or natural grace could be termed *flattery*. It would have to be untrue to be that, and—"

Doxee shoved a small piece of luggage into Grenshaw's stomach, effectively cutting him off. "She's heard it all already, Yank. Do yourself a favor and save your breath." Dox winked at her when he turned her way again. "And welcome to O'coke. When you're ready for the guide for your hunting or if you want to charter a fishing boat, you come on back to town, now. Otherwise, the Adair ladies will take right good care of you."

Mr. Grenshaw stared down at the bag for a moment as if he'd never seen it before and then moved to put it atop the already overflowing load in the cart. At which time he finally seemed to notice that there were no fancy, cushioned seats for *him*. "And where do we ride?"

Perhaps she took a bit too much pleasure in saying, "You don't, unless you'd like to wait for me to come back for you. I'm afraid Jingle isn't quite up to a full-sized cart that can haul you *and* your luggage. But don't worry—it isn't far." Nothing in the village was, hence why most of them walked pretty much everywhere. Uncle Linc had bought a bicycle once, thinking it would make his calls on parishioners easier, but the thing had rusted through within a year.

Not everything was built for life on Ocracoke. Not every-*one* was either, and Mr. Grenshaw didn't look particularly suited as he blinked at her.

His cousin, on the other hand, smiled and lifted the other remaining bag from where Doxee had set it on the ground. He made no attempt to add it to Mount Luggage, merely angled his body to the road. "Oh good. I could use a proper promenade after the journey. Eddie, do take that bag back off, won't you? There's a reason our good fellow there didn't stack it in the wagon to begin with, undoubtedly because it'll come tumbling off again at the first good rut in the road." He grinned. "I did warn you to pack lighter, didn't I?"

Mr. Grenshaw grumbled something Louisa didn't catch. But he took his bag back off the wagon.

That seemed like as good a cue as any. Louisa unlooped the lead from around Jingle's neck and clucked her tongue. With a shake of his head, they were off. The pony needed no guidance in returning to the inn and his water trough and straw, but sometimes he tried to sneak in a visit to another pony he used to run with, so Louisa kept a firm hand.

Mr. Culbreth whistled some tune she didn't know as they walked, craning his head this way and that as they made their way through the village. He asked about the types of trees—cedar, wild olive, live oak, wax myrtle, fig—smiled at the turtle sunning itself on an old pylon by the water's edge, and exclaimed over the "brilliance" of the houses raised a foot or two off the ground to allow for flooding.

"Utterly charming," he declared as the lane wound its way back toward the sound and the inn came into view. He spun around to send his smile to his cousin, who was lagging quite a few paces behind at this point. "You were right, Ed. This will be the perfect place to pass the summer before I . . . return home."

The hitch in his words may not have been noticeable had his conversation up until now not been so smooth, so easy. But that single, second-long pause held a whole story. A whole history. A whole future.

Louisa loved a good story. And this one—he had one, for sure. "And where is home, Mr. Culbreth?"

Something flickered over his face, like gulls in front of the sun, there and gone. "Well now, that's the question, I suppose. My mother's people are from Maryland, but I've spent most of my life in Herefordshire, at Springbourne Hall—my father's estate. And London, of course."

London. Herefordshire, wherever that even was. She'd have to dig out a map of England and see if she could find it. Like Celeste's stepfather, his father must have multiple homes, and no doubt all of them were larger than the inn. She couldn't even imagine. "And which of those places do you consider home?"

He drew in a long breath. Was he tasting the salt on the air? Smelling the cedar they'd passed? Or perhaps contemplating how that water lapping against the shore was the same water that stretched all the way across the ocean, to that other world to which he belonged. "I don't honestly know anymore, Miss Adair."

"Louisa." She never invited guests to call her by her first name—*never*. Not since she was a child. But this one . . . this one was different.

And she couldn't regret it, not when he glanced over at her and gave her that soft, undemanding smile. It seemed to say thank you. As if he knew exactly why she'd done it—that if it was a friend he needed to help him sort through it all, to discover his place, she'd offer that. She'd listen to his melodic accent all day long if it would help him.

"Then you had better call me Rem—or Remington, if you prefer the full first name."

"Remington." She couldn't help but chuckle. "Quite a proper name to put on a helpless baby."

He laughed, or maybe snorted. "My mother's maiden name—and she was always determined I'd be *hers*, more part of her family than my father's."

Grenshaw chose that moment to pick up his pace, and she had a feeling the thundercloud on his face, masked behind

40

a tight smile, wasn't over having been left behind. "Airing all the family secrets, old boy?" He shot his cousin a warning grin. "I daresay our lovely Miss Adair isn't interested in such things."

Well, she wouldn't have been quite so interested if it wasn't clear he didn't want her to know whatever those secrets were. But one couldn't grow up an innkeeper's daughter without learning when to pry and when to button one's lips. She offered a polite smile and nodded toward the inn, where Grann paused in her sweeping of the porch to lift a hand in greeting.

"Welcome to the Ocracoke Inn, gentlemen," Louisa said. "That's Grann. She'll show you to your rooms."

Grann set her broom aside and came down the steps, a wide smile showcasing her perfect white teeth. Maybe she was biased, but Louisa had never found anyone else in the world who smiled quite like Grann.

And it was telling to watch the guests react to her. Some dismissed her with no more than a nod. Some treated her like they did Jingle, there to do the work. Some saw the unbreakable heart and took right to her like another little duckling. And there'd always been the men, too—older ones at this point—who saw the handsome bone structure and impeccable carriage and flirted. Not that she expected *that* from these two gents young enough to be her grandchildren.

Grenshaw lifted a brow. "Grann? Yours?"

A question she'd received countless times over the years when people noticed the shade of her skin—lighter than Grann's but so much darker than Mama's. It was a question she'd been brave enough to ask them exactly once when she was seven. She hadn't gotten an answer—and was that an answer in itself? Something she'd wrestled with time and again over the years.

It wasn't fair that she had no idea if the woman she loved

like a grandmother, whom she and everyone else on the island *called* grandmother, really was that to her or not. She had no idea who her father had been, beyond his name—Michael Adair—and the assurance that he was the best of men and had died when she was an infant. She had no idea at all who she was, aside from Serena Marshall Adair's daughter.

But at this point she also knew that some questions were left unanswered for a reason. She knew the answer to give people like Edgar Grenshaw, who had judgment waiting to leap out of his eyes.

She smiled—a degree warmer than any she'd given him thus far—and blinked. "She's my mammy and was my daddy's— came home with my mama when she returned from several years spent in Louisiana, widowed. Everyone on the island calls her Grann."

Most of their guests were satisfied with that. After all, a father from Louisiana who had a mammy meant a family with a heritage. And it was the only story she'd ever been told, so it surely sounded like the truth when she said it.

Still, she wondered. She'd always wondered. She supposed she always *would* wonder. Was Grann family by blood or by love?

Grenshaw looked appeased. Enough, anyway, to nod and paste on a smile of his own as Grann approached them. And since Louisa didn't much care what his reaction was, so long as he didn't cause any trouble, she let that be enough of an examination of him and sneaked a glance at Remington Culbreth.

His smile had no clouds scuttling through it at all, and his eyes were clear as a tidepool. And when Grann gave her usual French greeting—to "add a bit of flavor to the inn," she always said—he replied in flawless French himself, making Grann's eyes twinkle in delight.

Louisa let her breath ease out and led Jingle around to the back door so they could unload the luggage. But she glanced one more time at Rem. This one wasn't like their usual guests, which meant she was going to have to be careful.

This one could break her heart.

4

For a moment, as Remington Culbreth stepped out into the soft spring dawn, he forgot about everything that was falling to pieces. He wasn't thinking about his father in England or his mother in Maryland or the looming dread of his own future. He wasn't thinking about the weight of politics or legacies or decisions.

He could think only of the colors painted across the sky, the most brilliant shades of pink and orange and yellow splashed on the layers of clouds. He sank to a seat on an old wooden rocker that would have made his mother wrinkle her nose in horror and breathed in something he'd begun to think he'd never know again this side of heaven.

Peace.

"Bon matin, cher." The words came as a whisper so quiet he barely heard them, and they accompanied the press of a warm mug into his hands.

The scent of strong tea tickled his nose even as he looked up with a smile for the woman everyone on the island called Grann. He'd watched his cousin go a bit stiff when Louisa introduced her yesterday, but Rem didn't know why. He'd taken one look into her eyes, silver as the London fog, and known that here was a woman with wisdom and grace.

She also knew how to brew a perfect cup, which she'd proven yesterday when she brought him a tea tray at precisely two o'clock in the afternoon. Just like at home. And she'd given him a wink that said she knew it, knew how much it meant to him to have a steaming cup of tea instead of coffee.

"*Merci beaucoup.*" He breathed his response with a smile that no doubt looked far sleepier than hers and wrapped his fingers around the mug—no dainty cup this morning, and he could appreciate that too. This utilitarian version held twice the amount of yesterday's china. He motioned to the matching rocker beside him. "Join me?"

The mother in his mind sent him a wide-eyed scowl. *One does not*, he could hear her say in his head, *invite the help to take tea.*

But he'd had about enough of Mother's biting commentary on everything. It was why he'd pounced on Edgar's invitation to join him in Ocracoke for the summer, even though Rem enjoyed duck hunting about as much as he enjoyed cataloging the latest points of disagreement between his parents. He'd needed the escape.

And this—this was a gorgeous place to find it. Warm and sunny, with tall seagrasses shushing in the wind. They'd seen wild ponies racing along the beach as they ferried over yesterday, and dolphins frolicking beside the boat. An enormous turtle had even given them one slow, disdainful look before vanishing into the depths. It was a very different sort of shore than the ones he'd visited all his life in England or steamed into once a year in Baltimore.

Grann looked as though she could hear Mother in his head too—and took great delight in defying her. She sat with the same fluid elegance that he was used to seeing in a London drawing room, and somehow it didn't look out of place on a weather-worn Carolinian porch. Though she wore a serviceable calico dress with a crisp white apron over it, she smoothed it down like it was watered silk. "How did you sleep, cher?"

"Quite well, thank you." Remington blew a cooling breath across the surface of his tea and hazarded a sip. "Once I convinced my cousin that I didn't intend to keep London Season hours, that is, and that he ought to let me retire."

Grann chuckled and looked out over the island and the fiery sky too. This westward direction was crowded with those painted clouds, and he found himself wondering if she preferred it that way, or clear, or with rain pounding down. Everyone had a preference—and you could tell a lot about a person by what parts of nature they favored.

Father loved nothing so much as a warm summer's day that he could spend hunting in the woods on their estate. Sebastian—Rem's older brother and hence the heir to both the barony and Springbourne Hall—had always enjoyed a rousing thunderstorm that he could first take a ride in before settling to dry by a crackling fire, with a snifter of brandy and a good book. Rem was a fan of the book part of the equation, but he preferred to do his reading out of doors, so fine weather was his preference.

And Mother . . . Mother preferred not to interact with the weather at all. She stayed indoors whenever possible and always scowled when nature had the audacity to interfere with any of her plans. As if the Lord ought to be subject to her whims.

Or perhaps he was still feeling a bit uncharitable toward her after the fortnight she'd put him through.

"You don't seem much like your cousin, Mr. Culbreth."

"Rem. Please." The sky was shifting colors as he watched. The orange stretching higher, the pink going fiercer. Were they on the eastern, ocean-facing side of the island, he suspected they would see the first sliver of blinding yellow peeking its head above the horizon at any moment. "And I suppose not, though we've always got along well enough. Edgar is—well, no. He's what you'd expect. I suppose I'm the odd duck."

Or so Father always said, blaming it on the influence of his old nursemaid. As the second son, it was Rem's duty to join the military, to carry on the family name in a way that would win them glory and honor. He'd bargained instead for an education—couldn't he join the church? Or academia?—but Father had granted the education only as a stepping-stone. He was to follow the example of every other second son in the history of the Culbreth family and join the Royal Navy. The end. Rem's preferences were not cause for a change of such long tradition, and if he wanted something else from life, then it was a flaw he ought to work on.

Blast it all. Even a sunrise of fire and hope wasn't enough to keep the dreaded thoughts from his ridiculous head. He drew in a long breath and took another sip of tea.

"Well. It's always the oddest ducks that make the biggest splash in the world and are worthiest of our attention." Grann winked at him, sending a web of fine wrinkles out from her eye that smoothed again in the next second. She was probably . . . what? Fifty-five? Sixty? But she wore the age well, as if she welcomed it. Mother fought each advancing year tooth and nail, with bottles and tonics of this and that, creams and lotions and who knew what. He had a feeling Grann didn't waste time or money on any such nonsense. "That's what I always tell my Louisa. She's a bit of an odd duck around these parts too."

Rem tried to keep his face clear at the mention of their youngest hostess—and he had a feeling that Grann saw right through him anyway. Not that he could be blamed for noticing how beautiful she was. As the fellow from the dock—Doxee, was it?—had pointed out, everyone noticed, everyone flirted.

It could have been her perfect figure, with curves in all the right places. Or that headful of sleek dark-chocolate curls. The delicate features, the perfect turn of her lips. But no . . . for him, at least, it was her eyes. Such a bright, striking blue against that dark hair and her sun-kissed skin. Eyes that didn't look at you, but right through you.

A trick she must have learned at her Grann's knee. The older woman was laughing even as he hoped—in vain, apparently—that another sip would cover any reaction he made.

"It's okay, cher. You're allowed to notice she's pretty. Hard to ignore." She raised her own mug and took a sip, though he couldn't tell from here if she had coffee or tea. "It's what you do about it that'll either land you in trouble or make you a friend. You remember that." She lifted her brows. "That cousin of yours, he only sees the pretty. You I peg as the type to see more, to see deeper. But I suppose time will tell."

"I . . ." Good heavens, what was he supposed to say to that? That of course he saw more? He'd seen intelligence in those eyes, and a thirst for knowledge, a desire to see the far-off places her friend was experiencing now. He saw breadth and depth and a whole world of things he couldn't begin to name but wanted to.

But he also knew very well that he shouldn't be wanting to. And Grann had to know that just as clearly as he did. An innkeeper's daughter knew better than to look for romance with every visitor to come along, and *he* knew better than to seek it with someone who would never be approved by *either* of his parents. One thing they still agreed on was that both he and Sebastian had better soon be choosing brides from the set of preapproved society ladies they knew in either Maryland, New York, or London.

And yet, he was here for the summer. It wouldn't be horrible to become friends, would it? It didn't require romance, even if Louisa Adair *was* one of the prettiest girls he'd ever seen. She was off-limits. Nothing but friendship could possibly be allowed. And so . . . he wouldn't allow it. He'd focus on the worlds within those eyes and not on how striking they looked in her face.

Grann was still chuckling. "Knew I was right."

Before he could try to conjure up a more coherent answer, the screen door squeaked open and was smacking shut again by the time he craned his neck around to see who'd joined them. Certainly not Edgar—not at sunrise. But it could well be Louisa's mother, who was as blond and fair as her daughter was brunette and tanned. He'd been instructed to call her "Miss Serena" and had been a bit confused by that until Louisa had explained that all married women went by "Miss" and their first name. For some reason.

But it wasn't the innkeeper. It was Louisa.

Though he had to blink a few times to make sure of it. She wore men's trousers with a loose blouse tucked into them that obscured her figure, and all her curls were hidden under a flat newsboy cap.

There was no hiding her smile, though, or those blue eyes as she strode toward them. "Morning, Grann. Rem." Not waiting for their reply, she hitched a thumb toward the outbuilding that housed her pony and cart. "I'll be working on the cistern repairs this morning if you need me."

Rem nearly choked on his sip of tea.

Grann, however, nodded. "And then the phonograph?"

"Once the weather rolls in. Figured I'd get to the outside tasks before it rains." She sent Rem a grin that made his heart stutter. "Hope you boys like to hunt in the rain. That's quite a storm front moving in."

Rem cleared his throat, fairly confident that he could answer for Edgar as well as himself on this score. "Not especially. But we have all summer—the hunting can wait on finer weather."

Louisa nodded and sauntered off the porch, the swing of her hips betraying the figure hidden beneath the boys' clothes. "Well, if you get bored and want to learn how to use a tool or two, I'll be out here."

It was a challenge. Maybe even a taunt, given that cheeky grin.

Rem found himself wondering what his parents would say if they saw him with a spanner in his hand. Their imagined horror was enough to make him decide that once his tea was gone, he would take great joy in acquainting himself with a few tools. "Don't think I won't take you up on that."

She laughed, walking backward through the sand-and-grass lawn. "As if Master Remington has ever held a hammer or a wrench in his life!"

"I'm a quick study." At least when it involved a book. Tools . . . well, they'd see, wouldn't they?

Grann was chuckling again and pushing back to her feet. "I'd better get myself back to the kitchen. Miss Elsie's coming by any minute to share her cinnamon roll recipe with me. Only took me a decade of begging for it. Breakfast will be set out within the hour, cher."

"Thank you. I'll be looking forward to it." He'd already learned at supper the evening before that while the food served at the Ocracoke Inn was of a different variety than what he usually enjoyed, the ladies could cook. The fig cake had been nothing short of divine.

The screen door was soon slapping shut behind Grann, but the morning wasn't long silent. From the direction in which Louisa had vanished, there soon came the sound of hammering. Strangely, it didn't seem to shatter the peace of the morning. Somehow it added to it instead—a reminder that a new day was dawning, and with it came new creation. New work.

He took another sip of tea and prayed that God would show him what *his* work was supposed to be. Show him a way to pursue a future that would be fulfilling for him without disappointing his family.

He had no answers by the time he set his empty mug down and strode across the scraggly lawn, but he didn't need any today. That was the true gift of this summer holiday. He had weeks—months, even—when he could contemplate and pray about it without either Mother or Father staring him down and demanding answers.

He ought to write to Sebastian, though. His last note had been hurried and harried and ringing with failure. *She's not coming home, she says. I've tried everything to convince her. I don't know what else to do.*

His brother wouldn't blame Rem for their mother's decision, he knew that. Still, it felt like yet another way he'd let the family down. With each visit his mother had made to the States the last few years, this very fear had grown that she would decide to stay, decide the benefits of being a baroness in England were no longer worth the frigid waters of her marriage. It had been five years ago, when he was little more than a lad of sixteen and Sebastian only eighteen, that his brother had charged him to make certain Mother came home with him again at the end of the summer.

They both knew that eventually he'd fail. How could they

not? The ice had grown colder and colder between his parents with each turn of the calendar's pages. It wasn't his fault. It wasn't his failing.

It *wasn't*. He couldn't be blamed for that any more than he could be blamed for the rising tensions in Europe. To both conflicts, he was an observer.

So why did he taste guilt on his tongue every time he wondered what other words he could have said to Mother? Why did his spine feel so bent with the weight of it?

His feet had carried him toward the sound of the hammering, around the corner of the inn. Not toward the outbuilding after all, but to where the cistern was nestled into the ground at the side of the main building, an unlikely repairman doing . . . something with a hammer.

Not that he spent longer than he should have admiring the way those trousers fit her as she worked. Not at all.

He cleared his throat and gave himself a mental shaking. "All right. I'm ready for my apprenticeship. I expect to be a master craftsman by the end of my holiday."

Louisa shot a smile at him over her shoulder that hit his stomach with all the force of one of the Atlantic's famed hurricanes. "Will that inspire your parents to come and hunt me down?"

He made a show of considering. "Possibly. But only if they find out."

She laughed—a full-bodied, bright sound that rivaled any birdsong he'd ever heard for beauty—and turned back to her work. "I've never understood why certain sectors of society consider it demeaning to work with their hands. The guest over Christmas who tuned our piano for us admitted that his mother had threatened to disown him when he said he wanted to *create* instruments, not only play them. Tell me, how does creating a thing bring shame?"

Rem crouched down beside where she was kneeling and tried to discern what it was she was doing. Something to the hinged cover. Beyond that, he hadn't a clue. Trying to imitate Father's sternest tone, he said, "Such mysteries of the aristocracy cannot be plumbed by mere reason."

She snorted and exchanged her hammer for a screwdriver, straightening so she could reach into her pocket and pull out a few screws. "Hand."

"Pardon?" But his arm must have understood what his brain didn't, because it was already stretching out to meet the one she held out.

She turned his hand so his palm was up and dropped in a handful of screws. "There. I knew you'd prove useful."

"Oh yes. Four years at Cambridge prepared me excellently for being a bowl."

The wistful look she sent him very nearly knocked him over. "Cambridge! Wow. My big dream is to make it to a teacher's college in Raleigh." She sighed and cast her gaze toward Pamlico Sound. Beyond it, no doubt, to whatever institution housed that dream.

A teacher, was it? He could imagine that, even after having only shared a few short conversations with her thus far. The intelligence in her eyes, the spark of joy that had entered them whenever he mentioned Plato last night at dinner—yes, she was a lover of learning, so it was no stretch to realize she would love imparting that knowledge too. "Have you applied?"

"Not yet. Even if I could get a scholarship, that wouldn't pay for books or board. Not to mention," she added, flourishing her screwdriver with all the panache of a maestro and his baton, "who would do this if I'm gone?"

She couldn't seriously be letting handywork stand in the way of her dreams, could she? "There must be some local chap who could be hired for repairs. Or have you no male relatives?"

This time her laugh was a low rumble of a chuckle. "Uncle Linc—Mama's older brother, and part owner of the inn. Technically. He's also our pastor. And about as good with a tool as your cousin Edgar is likely to be."

"Ah. So how did you learn, then? From your father?" He knew that Miss Serena was widowed, but he had no idea how recent it was.

Louisa's face didn't tell him much either. Other than being so clear of grief that perhaps it did, in fact, say something. "My father died when I was a baby. No, I learned by sheer necessity, and by begging Doxee to teach me what I couldn't just pick up. I have a bit of a knack with mechanical things, actually, so he didn't mind showing me what he knows. Now I can strip a boat engine and rebuild it twice as fast as he can."

Strip a . . . well, that went a bit beyond screwing in new hinges, didn't it? Rem blinked at her.

Louisa laughed. "You'll want to close that mouth before flies fly in."

He took the advice. Held his hand closer when she reached for a screw. And knew beyond a shadow of a doubt that Louisa Adair was unlike any young woman he'd ever met or likely would ever meet again.

He was very much looking forward to becoming her friend.

5

TODAY

MAY 11, 1942
OCRACOKE ISLAND, NORTH CAROLINA

Evie drew in another gasping breath and braced her hands against the table's edge to stretch out her screaming back. She'd always considered herself in excellent condition—but then, she'd never had to carry most of the weight of an unconscious man from the sound to the kitchen before, nor heave him up onto the table.

She looked over to Grandma See, who was falling even then into a chair, waving a hand in front of her red face. Evie quickly signed, *You okay?*

Grandma nodded, motioned toward the telephone mounted to the wall, and replied, *Call Garret.*

Good advice, at least as soon as she had breath enough. She let her gaze move again over her unexpected guest, wincing at what she saw as she tried to convince her lungs to behave normally. He was badly burned on his left side, his clothes eaten away by flame and stained by smoke. Passing out had no doubt been a mercy.

But who *was* he? And where had he come from?

She heard again the explosion out at sea that morning. But he couldn't be from whatever navy ship had been targeted by the U-boats, could he? Yes, he'd claimed to be an officer in the Royal Navy, but how could that possibly be the truth? He wasn't in uniform.

She could do with a few answers, but this man before her was in no condition to offer any. Even so, he needed help and prayers. Knowing Grandma See would be on her feet in another moment and working to make him as comfortable as possible on their long kitchen table until Uncle Garret could arrive, Evie slipped a hand into her pocket and hurried to the phone. Positioning the handset between her shoulder and ear, she dialed with her right hand while her left fingered the chunk of blue-green sea glass she'd found that morning.

She'd been praying for whomever the victims of the U-boat had been when she found this bit of glass, along with the other shells there in her pocket with it. She'd pray for the victims more when she turned her finds into jewelry later in her studio. The question was, did she have one of the survivors even now on her table? Should she report it? To whom?

The question was as much to God as to her own mind, and she took the shiver that coursed through her as a warning. For now, she'd do what came naturally—protect and be as mum as possible.

She spun the rotary to the final number in Uncle Garret's office exchange, and on the fifth ring, it was finally picked up. Nancy Lee's chipper voice sang out, "Dr. Wynnwood's office, Nurse Kilroy speaking."

Evie made herself smile so that it would come through in her voice. "Hey, Nance Lee, it's Evie. Is Uncle Gar available?"

"For you, sweetie? You know he is. Well, if he isn't with a patient. I think . . . yep, he's in his office. One sec." There came a muffling noise, and then Nancy Lee calling out, "Doc? Evie's on the line!"

She heard Uncle Garret picking up his extension in his office, but the click of the first receiver being returned to its cradle never came. Evie sent her eyes to the ceiling. Nancy Lee was a good nurse, but she was also one of the busiest bodies on the island.

"Morning, baby girl. To what do I owe the pleasure?"

Even given the moan from the table behind her, her lips still quirked up into a bit of a smile. Just hearing his voice helped her believe everything would be okay. "Well, to be honest, I could use your help whenever you have a minute." She turned around to face the table, her stomach going tight at the way the man on it thrashed his head from side to side. "Having a black moment over here." It was their code for him to bring his black bag—this wouldn't be the first time there was a man in the inn's kitchen who required medical help. But usually it was a Coastie who'd done something stupid and didn't want to have to report it.

She could hear the squeak of his chair in the background, the sound it always made when he went from leaning back to sitting up straight. "I can be there in a few minutes."

She'd known he would drop everything that wasn't an emergency—that was Garret. And if her situation weren't urgent, this would be where she told him to take his time. Instead, she said, "See you soon," and hung up.

As expected, Grandma See was back on her feet and heading to the aloe plant that sprawled to the patch of sunlight from the window. They had several of them in pots around the inn—a welcome perk for tourists who spent too many hours in the sun. Evie had a feeling they may end up using quite a lot of their supply on this chap on her table, though.

She'd helped Uncle Garret with enough triage over the years not to feel at total loose ends while she waited for him. With Grandma See's help, she cut away the ruined fabric, exposing angry, blistered skin that begged for the aloe. Uncle Garret certainly wouldn't begrudge their applying some, so she left that to Grandma's careful ministrations.

Once a liberal coating of goo was applied and Evie had discarded the burnt clothing in the rubbish bin, Grandma See, her brows knit, pointed to the man and signed, *Who?*

Evie shook her head. *Name none. English Navy, he said.*

Grandma's frown only deepened, her gaze going to the charred remains of his clothing. She'd be thinking exactly what Evie had—that no sailor was permitted to be out of uniform on board his vessel. His explanation didn't quite jibe. They couldn't exactly ask for more information with him in his current state, though.

But when he was coherent again—*if* he was, Lord have mercy—then they'd see what he said. And if he tried to lie about anything, Grandma See would see straight through him. She always did, despite—or perhaps because of—her inability to hear a word he said. She could read body language and, they all swore, a person's very thoughts like none other. Probably one of the reasons Evie had kept on calling her *Grandma See* long after she'd learned to say her whole name.

His thrashings had gone still by the time the sound of Garret's car cut through the morning. Evie hurried to the door to hold it open for him before he'd even started up the walk. He ducked through the doorway, pulled her in for a hug while he was stooped, and then came fully inside. "Who is it? What happened?"

Evie let the door swing shut and followed Garret's towering form back into the room. He was six foot six—a perfect height for smacking his forehead on lintels all over the island—and he still wore his hair in a tail at the back of his neck in a fashion all his own, despite his mahogany hair now having streaks of silver. Aunt L liked it that way, which meant he'd never change it, not unless nature took over and he ended up as bald as his own father.

Which was neither here nor there, despite its being a distraction from the man on the table. "I don't know. He came ashore in a dinghy, largely unconscious. Came around enough to say he was a British sailor, then was out again." She didn't need to say he looked badly burned—that would be clear to the doctor in a glance.

A wincing glance. Uncle Garret set his black bag on a chair and leaned over their prone guest to get a better view of the flesh they'd exposed. "Poor fella. Did he say what ship he was on? Had it been struck by a torpedo?"

"He didn't. But I don't know what else it could have been." *If he's telling the truth.* She had no reason to doubt him . . . yet no reason to believe him either.

She reached into her pocket, pulled out the piece of sea glass, and held it tight as she folded her arms over her middle. Maybe she didn't have the actual words of a prayer in her mouth right now, but they filled her heart. Holding on to something helped remind her that they were real things, those prayers—things with substance, just like faith. As sturdy as the glass or a shell or the island onto which they'd washed up. She could hold those words, or even the intent of them, in her heart as surely as she could that blue-green bauble in her hand.

Garret took his time with his examination, ignoring her and Grandma See while he did so. Eventually he slung his stethoscope back around his neck and turned to meet Evie's gaze. "That's a lot of trauma he's been through. Shock is as big a threat right now as the burns themselves. If we had a proper hospital, I'd say to take him to it, but there's only the bed at the clinic, and I don't think he'd survive a ferry to the mainland. Honestly, I'm not sure he'd survive the five-minute drive in my car. He may not make it to tomorrow regardless."

He would. She gripped the sea glass tighter and lifted her chin. "We'll take care of him here."

"Evie—"

"We only have two other guests, and they're checking out this morning anyway. If you can help us get him to a bed, we'll see to the rest." She gave him her best imitation of Grandma Ree's stern look—the one that had always kept them all in line, him included. Med school or no med school, he'd never dared argue with Grandma Ree any more than the rest of them did. "Leave it to us."

He sighed and rested a long-fingered hand on the man's shoulder. "It shouldn't be your responsibility."

"We're at war, Uncle Gar. If he really is an Allied sailor, then I'm doing my bit, right?" She stepped to the side so she could look down at the man's face. It had somehow escaped the worst of the burns. There were only a few small patches on his chin, and they weren't nearly as angry as his arm and side. Even in unconsciousness, lines of pain etched their portrait on his features.

She eased closer, closer still, until she could reach out and touch those lines with gentle fingertips. Such pain. All physical? Maybe . . . but she didn't think so. There was torment of the soul in them too.

Whoever he was, wherever he came from, something terrible had happened for him to end up here. Something that had robbed him of friends, no doubt. Something that could shatter him like broken bottles and tumble him about like shards of glass.

She drew in a long breath. "God washed him up here for a reason. Let me try and help him."

"Evie." Uncle Garret's hand moved to *her* shoulder and squeezed it tight. "We've been through this—it's why I wouldn't let you train to be my nurse. You're too tenderhearted. You empathize too deeply. He could—probably *will*—be dead by morning. Don't let that take another piece of you."

Her shoulders went stiff. All her life, people had been chiding her for caring too much. But how could that ever be true? "I'll be fine." She wanted to add that she wasn't missing any pieces, thank you very much.

But that was a lie, and he'd know it. She was missing nearly *all* her pieces right now. Davie, Mama and Daddy, Job, Grandma Ree and Grann. So much of her family gone where she couldn't follow. Leaving her with borrowed blood—but genuine love, all the same. She smiled up at Grandma See. "Right?"

Even though they hadn't been signing, Grandma See had had no trouble reading their lips—or knowing what they'd say. With a decisive nod, she pointed to their patient and signed, *Stays. Lives.*

Garret held his hands up in surrender, adding a gusty sigh. "All right, all right. I won't argue. I'll mix you up some poultices and give you a vial of good stuff for him too. For now, let's get him out of your kitchen. Which room do you want him in? I'd advise a downstairs one, if possible."

"Sure." There was only the one bedroom down here, and she never put guests there—how could she, when it was still her parents' room in her mind? She herself slept in the same one she'd always slept in. Old habits. Comfort. Familiarity.

But this was a fine reason for letting someone into the sanctity of her parents' haven. They wouldn't mind. She led the way, opening the door and moving to turn down the bed. The sheets weren't exactly *fresh*, but they didn't feel too sand-covered, anyway. That stuff had a way of working into every crack and crevice, but the windows in here had been sealed up all winter.

Garret followed her in a minute later, their patient in his arms—and he had a much easier time of it than she and Grandma had, even though the chap had to be nearly six foot himself, perhaps an inch or so shy of it. She forced a grin. "Handy to have a giant around for this portion of the moving."

He chuckled and set his burden softly down. "That's how I advertise, you know—doctor and ambulance, all in one."

She snorted a laugh at the idea of his needing to advertise at all. As if there were any choice in medical care on Ocracoke, and as if everyone didn't know and love him anyway. "And why we keep you around."

His smile faded once they had their guest situated. "I don't know how we'll figure out who he is. Guess we see if he wakes up again enough to tell you."

There was no word in the English language she both loved and hated so much as *if*. "He will."

"Evie—"

"He will." Never mind that he was so still now that she found herself wishing for that thrashing of half an hour ago. She ran her fingertips down the unburned side of his face one more time and then tucked those fingers back in her pocket. Back into prayer. "You do your part for him, Uncle Gar. And I'll do mine." And they'd see whose determination won out, theirs or the enemy's.

The commotion at the shore drew Evie's feet like magnets, the basket on her arm and the errands it demanded temporarily shoved aside. Not that she could detour long from her task. It had been a long day, an even longer night, and she needed to get back to the inn as soon as possible to take over the vigil again from Grandma. But the same something that had put her on her guard yesterday pulled her toward the small crowd of villagers today.

She slid up beside Job's youngest cousin, Ernest John, and rested a hand on his back. "What's going on, EJ?"

Ernest John—who should have been on his way to school right about now, not hanging out at the shore—looked up at her with wide eyes that said he'd forgotten all about his own mission, too, in the excitement of whatever this was. "Evie! There are *bodies*. Washed ashore. I heard the Coasties saying they musta been from that ship torpedoed yesterday. There are *two* of 'em!"

Evie's throat went tight, and her gaze went up, toward the two uniformed guardsmen doing something down by the water. Bending, dragging, straightening. Arranging bodies in the sand, out of the reach of the water.

Her throat went tighter still, and she rubbed her hand in a circle on Ernest John's back. "You shouldn't be here watching this. Get on to school, now." He may be twelve, old enough to understand death and war and its price, but that didn't mean he needed to invite it in.

"Aw, come on, Evie! I just want—"

"No back talk. What would your mama say if she knew you were here?" She sent him a quick look, the kind that reminded him that she was one of the grown-ups, even though she was like as not to be the one playing tag with him at a family gathering instead of listening to the gossip of the adults.

He let out a breath as blustery as the wind over the sound and scowled. "She would say I'd better come home with all there was to know about it, that's what."

Evie arched her brows.

Ernest John rolled his eyes. "Okay, okay. Geez. She'd say if I'm late to school again, I deserve a whupping. I'm going, I'm going."

"And no mischief on the way. The neighbors have been complaining about things going missing when they're left outside." She doubted it was Ernest John himself doing the lifting—not alone, anyway—but it was without question kids who were nicking the clothes from lines and cooling baked goods from windowsills, and he'd know who it was.

He held up his hands, all innocence. "Wasn't me, I swear it! Wasn't Mickey Ron or George Michael neither."

"So warn whoever it *was* to cut it out before they get in trouble." She offered him a tight-lipped smile to send him on his way, and then, once he was dragging his feet back to the road, she moved closer to the narrow strip of beach and the busy Coasties. It only took a shift on her part to catch the eye of Herbert O'Neal. She'd seen him an hour ago when she dropped off the day's baked goods, joked with him about how tired she looked, and tried to evade too many questions about why.

Now *he* was the one who looked exhausted. Even though his shift had just started, this wasn't the kind of job he would have anticipated doing. He bypassed the three fishermen standing in a cluster between them and stepped to her side.

"The U-boat victims from yesterday?" she asked in a whisper.

"Has to be." His larynx bobbed as he swallowed, his gaze going back to the two dark-clad figures stretched out on the sand. "Must have been the *Bedfordshire*. That one there," he said, motioning to the body nearest them, "Mr. Howard recognizes." He nodded toward Wahab, who was standing grim-faced a few feet away. "He met him in Norfolk a few nights ago. Lieutenant Thomas Cunningham—he was the captain of the *Bedfordshire*. Converted trawler."

Evie let a long breath ease its way out, praying it would steady the shaking that wanted to start somewhere deep inside. She committed the names to memory. *Bedfordshire*. Thomas Cunningham. "Who found them?"

He motioned to the fishermen. "We'll be patrolling the beaches the rest of the day, looking for more."

More. More bodies. Not *others*, indicating people, survivors. Because there shouldn't have been any, clearly.

Yet that quivering in her core insisted that the unnamed man still barely holding onto life in her parents' room must have been from that same incident, just like he'd alluded to. "I'll keep my eyes peeled on my stretch of sand." She'd already had Uncle Garret help her haul the beat-up Zodiac into the barn. He hadn't understood her insistence that they hide all the evidence of the sailor's arrival—frankly, she didn't understand it either—but he'd helped anyway.

Maybe she was way off base . . . but someone claiming to be a sailor but who was out of uniform screamed "secrets" to her. And her family, both sides of it, had long been in the business of protecting secrets. She couldn't help but try to do it here, too, at least until her guest told her to do otherwise.

Her heart whispered another prayer. She angled away from Herb. "If I can do anything, let me know."

"You know we will. Get on with your day, Evie. My next stop is to talk to some of the neighbors. We'll have to bury them somewhere."

And all the cemeteries were family plots. Someone would have to donate land. She nodded, mentally going over her own family plot in her mind. There might be room, if these two were the only ones found. But not if there were more.

What a sad thing to start a beautiful May morning contemplating.

She hated war. Sometimes she thought she hated it all the more because she'd been born in the middle of one. Wondered if that was part of what had marked her spirit, her heart, for peace.

Didn't seem to have marked the rest of her generation for it, though. Too many friends were in training even now, or already deployed either to the European Theatre or the Pacific.

The whole world had gone mad—again. Hadn't they learned the last time?

She said her farewells to Herb and turned back to the path and then the road into the village. She needed more honey for the man's burns, and a few other things too.

Somehow word had already reached the village about the bodies washing ashore, which meant everyone was distracted and not interested in the more normal variety of chitchat, which suited her fine today. Five minutes was enough in the store to see her business finished and her feet aimed back for the inn. A quick stop to make sure Miss Marge was doing all right, and she was swinging back through the screen door.

Evie stowed her newly purchased supplies in the pantry and then moved to her parents' room, where Grandma See was dozing in the chair they'd pulled up beside the bed. Poor thing. They'd taken shifts during the night, but even so, she knew the older woman had to be even more exhausted than she was. She roused her with a gentle touch and made a quick sign to send her to bed. The fact that she didn't argue was clear proof of that exhaustion.

Evie settled into the chair she'd vacated with a sigh. Leaned forward. Touched the man's uninjured hand.

It flexed under her touch, and his breathing hitched. He even moved his head a little in her direction.

Evie wrapped her fingers around his hand and squeezed. "Still with us, then. I knew you'd pull through. Listen, mister, I need you to come to enough to tell me what you want me to do. Were you on the *Bedfordshire*?"

His hand jerked under hers. An uncontrollable spasm? A response to the pressure of her fingers? Or was it a reaction to her words?

She chose to believe it was the latter. "Bodies have begun washing ashore. My friend recognized one of them, said it was the captain."

The man's lips parted, even moved. They'd done their best to keep trickling water into his mouth, but even so she barely caught his parched whisper. Barely, but she did. "Tommie."

Her throat felt every bit as parched. "That's right. Thomas Cunningham." He had to have known him pretty well to call him Tommie, right? But that in itself was odd. Cunningham was the captain, and it was a small ship. There wouldn't have been many others on board who would dare to call him by his first name. She leaned down a little more. "Do I need to get in touch with the navy? Let them know you survived?"

His eyes fluttered open, though they didn't fasten on her. His head moved back and forth in a slow-motion shake. "No. Not supposed . . . no one knew . . . mission."

Mission. She nodded, even though he didn't look at her to see it. A mission. A sailor not in uniform. One no one knew had been on board and who didn't want his whereabouts reported. It sounded for all the world like he was an intelligence agent.

But what were the chances of that? That he'd wash up *here*?

Low . . . but they did serve a God who had orchestrated the seemingly impossible countless times. She lifted his hand off the bed. "I need to know your name, sir. I can't keep calling you 'the supposed Englishman' in my thoughts."

Now he actually rolled his head her way and looked at her. One moment, two, their gazes held. Then his eyes slid shut again. "Sterling . . . Bertram."

"Sterling Bertram." She'd bet against it being his real name, but it beat calling him "her guest" all the time. "Well, Sterling Bertram, you're in good hands. We're going to see you get well again."

His fingers curled around hers. Thanks? Or . . . no. "Tommie," he whispered again.

She sighed. "He was a friend." It wasn't a question—she could tell it from the way he breathed the word, the agony screaming from the flare of his nostrils. "I'm sorry. He'll be given a proper burial, I can promise you that. As soon as it's been worked out and a funeral date set, I'll let you know. I'll go on your behalf."

He swallowed, the movement so laborious that she released his hand so she could reach for the glass of water on the side table. "Here. Let me help you drink."

He managed several good sips before he pulled his mouth away. They'd call that a victory. She smiled, so that he'd hear it in her next words. "There you go. I consider that a corner turned. You're going to pull through this, Sterling."

The way he opened his eyes again when she said his name, looked over at her . . . maybe it *was* his name. "Who . . . are you?"

She kept that smile on her face. "Evie Farrow. You're at my inn on Ocracoke Island, North Carolina."

His lips mouthed the island's name, but no breath backed it to make the word emerge.

She patted his hand. "Rest. I'm going to make some broth and mix up your next poultice and then be right back."

She'd call Uncle Garret, too, and let him know—in their Nancy Lee–proof code—that their patient was hanging in there and had even woken up.

Then . . . then she'd plan out the telegram she'd send as soon as she could get away.

As she mixed honey and herbs in the kitchen, she thought over each and every word she meant to send over the Atlantic. The only telegraph machine on the island was at the Coast Guard station, and civilians weren't supposed to use it, not for anything less than an emergency.

But they had an understanding. Once it was dark, she'd steal over to the station, slip inside, and the men would make a show of looking the other way while she slid to a seat in front of that familiar machine. She'd tap out the message dot by dash and trust it would make its way over the ocean. All the way to England. To that ancestral estate that had been converted into one of the Allies' most critical operations— the intelligence hub at Bletchley Park.

She'd include, of course, the code at the beginning that would tell whoever received it that it was for David Culbreth. And then her message.

She'd better keep it short and sweet. *Sterling Bertram. Friend? Just washed up.*

Yes, that would do. She licked a stray drop of honey off her finger and turned back to the bedroom with her shoulders rolled back. It might be a few days before she had a response, but whoever Sterling was, he was no great threat now. She could wait.

Especially because she knew well she wouldn't have to wait a moment longer than necessary.

David Culbreth had never once let her down.

6

YESTERDAY

JUNE 2, 1914
OCRACOKE ISLAND, NORTH CAROLINA

Louisa told herself, like she did every morning, that she was going to *go*. She wasn't going to wait around, she wasn't going to dawdle. In fact, she was going to get out earlier than usual. Feed the hens, gather the eggs, bring them back in to Mama and Grann, and then scat. No helping to set out breakfast for the four guests currently under their roof, no being lured into a conversation about whatever book Remington Culbreth had borrowed from Uncle Linc this time, no dodging the scowls of Mr. Grenshaw, who apparently didn't take too kindly to the help being able to carry on an intelligent conversation about said books.

And certainly no allowing Rem to bow out of the day's hunting—again—and tag along with her instead. Absolutely not. No more. Not today.

She recited it to herself as she stomped her way to the chicken coop, but she knew even as she did so that all her words were bluster, no more serious than the summer breeze toying with her curls. Because while that would be the smart thing, she wasn't that strong.

Talking to Rem was the closest thing to college she was likely to get anytime soon. And he looked at her, listened to her, like she mattered—like her thoughts mattered. They could laugh together over old Greek plays that no one else she knew even wanted to read, much less dissect. He was without question one of the most interesting, intelligent young men she'd ever met . . . and she was going to miss him like the dickens when he left at the end of summer, which was why she really ought to pull away now, when her heart still had a chance of staying in one piece.

"You're not collecting eggs without your basket-holder, are you?"

Or perhaps it was too late for that. She made a show of sighing as she held up and turned, even though his voice sent a happy shiver all over her. Just like his easy smile lit up the morning every bit as much as the sun. He was jogging toward her, his hand outstretched for her egg basket. What was a girl to do but hand it over? "I told you to sleep in this morning. Your cousin wants you to go to the duck blinds with him today."

He screwed up his face and nodded toward the coop. "The ladies will be fowl enough for me, thank you. I don't understand how he can go out there day after day. Utterly boring."

"You could bring a book." He'd done that the three days he'd let his cousin bully him into hunting, she knew.

"But in the duck blind there's no one bringing me lemonade and cake while I read." He offered her a grin that combined teasing and innocence.

She couldn't resist a chuckle, but she turned back to the chickens, who were squawking their hello, no doubt eager to be let loose. "You want to scatter the feed today?" All last week he'd watched her do it like it was some great mystery to be unraveled.

"I don't know. That rooster of yours is vicious."

She'd only had to kick him away from her twice last week—rather tame, by Chanticleer standards. And she'd done her best to make it look more like a nudge, so her audience wouldn't think her rooster unmannerly. Though he *was*. But she could hardly let Rem get away with insulting him. She tugged open the rough wooden door to the coop and sent Rem an arch look. "Are you saying you're too chicken to feed chickens?"

Oh, when he grinned like that . . . Those blue-green eyes sparkled behind the cheeks that rose, turning them to half-moons, and her heart did the strangest thing in her chest, seeming to both squeeze tight and take on wings.

"Think to taunt me into doing your chores, do you?"

"Will it work?"

He handed her the basket again by way of answer and reached for the metal scoop. "Only for you, Lu."

She made a show of wincing at the nickname, which she'd never let anyone else in the world apply to her. "Must you call me that?"

He lifted the lid off the feed bin and dug the scoop into it. "Sorry. But you said Celeste calls you Lulu—"

"That's different."

His lips twitched. "Quite right. It's doubled. All the difference in the world."

"Well, it *is*." Rather than argue, she stepped into the coop, bypassing the hens that were fluttering and clucking their way out as they heard the seed and corn scatter. The involuntary wrinkling of her nose told her it was time to clean out the coop again, but she'd do that sometime when Rem wasn't at her side. She couldn't bring herself to grab the hose and spray out all the muck with a baron's son right there.

For now, the eggs. She gathered the dozen that awaited her, shaking her head at the empty boxes. A couple of their girls were getting too old to be good layers. Then she stepped back outside into the warm morning, just in time to see Rem backpedaling away from Chanticleer. With a laugh, she stomped between them, making a shooing motion—okay, a *kicking* motion—with her foot to send the rooster about his business.

Rem tugged his vest back into place, which made her laugh anew. There he stood, decked out in his fine aristocratic clothes but holding a metal scoop still dropping corn. She needed to get her hands on one of those new Kodaks so she could take a few snapshots of these times, to prove it had happened. Wouldn't Celeste get a kick out of it?

Rem tossed her a halfhearted scowl. "Don't you ever tire of laughing at me?"

"Nope. And if you could see yourself, you'd know why. I was thinking I need a camera." She held her hands up as if to frame him, letting the basket slip to her elbow.

"Careful now." As if he'd been tending eggs his whole life and she'd never juggled a basket of them until that moment, he leapt forward to steady the basket. And smiled at her from a foot away. "Miss Serena and Grann need those eggs for whatever confection they're baking up for us today."

"True enough. But I'll have you know I haven't dropped a basket of eggs in at least ten years." She traded him basket for scoop so she'd have the excuse to step away and return said scoop to its bin. A little space between them was a good thing.

"So, what's on the repair list today? Roof? Drains? Porch steps? I think I'm ready to try my hand at a saw if we want to build something truly magnificent."

Louisa turned back to him with a laugh. "I'm afraid we're not building anything today, Master Remington—or at least, I don't think we are. Today we go visit Celeste's grandmother, Elsie, and see what chores she needs help with."

"Elsie." Rem's brows drew together. "Have I met her yet?"

She had to give that a moment's thought as they made their way back to the porch. Grandma Elsie had been in church each of the weeks since Rem's arrival, but she wasn't the type to elbow her way forward for an introduction to each and every guest of the inn. "I guess not. You'd remember it if you had."

She didn't even need to look at him to know his brows had arched up. "Why is that? Has she two heads?"

"Five. And dragon scales besides." Even saying that made her laugh again and shake her head. "Celeste would slap me upside the head if she heard me say that. No, Grandma Elsie is the sweetest woman you're likely ever to meet. She's pretty young as grandmothers go too—only just turned fifty. She didn't move to Ocracoke until her husband was stationed here with the Life Saving Station back in the eighties, when Miss Maddie—that's Celeste's mama—was a little girl."

Rem nodded along, smiling all the while. "I look forward to meeting her." And then came the twinkle in his eye. "Is she going to be charmed by my supposed accent like the rest of your friends and their mums?"

She barely kept the bark of laughter from slipping out. "I can promise you she won't be. She's far above such things." And poor Rem, he was no doubt tired of people running up to him just to make him say *something* so they could hear him talk.

Not that she blamed the neighbors. She could listen to him all day too. And often did, really. When they weren't talking about everything as he worked alongside her each day, he was often reading aloud to her and Mama and Grann in the evenings.

But for once, her thoughts actually shifted away from Rem as she helped get breakfast on the table for him, his cousin, and the two other hunters who had arrived last week and who, thankfully, had been keeping Grenshaw occupied.

It had been too long since she'd dropped in to see Miss Elsie. Granted, she'd set up this date with her for the first Tuesday of each month to make certain none of the chores got too out of hand—and Elsie wasn't exactly a slouch herself. She had as much energy as anyone on Ocracoke, but she hadn't ever learned to handle the tools that Louisa had picked up by necessity. Still, she felt bad that so long had gone by without any kind of visit.

Elsie didn't have anyone else left on Ocracoke, not anymore. Her husband had died way back when Louisa and Celeste were in their first year of school, which was when Jack Scarborough had really started getting mean. She'd stayed here, though, because it was where Miss Maddie and Celeste were.

But now? There was nothing tying Elsie here. Her parents were still living, so far as Louisa knew, up in the North somewhere. Louisa had asked her last Christmas, when that wistful look had been so heavy in her eyes, why she didn't go visit. She'd said it was too complicated for them when she showed up, not that they'd ever admit it.

Louisa hadn't had to ask why. Not when Grandma Elsie had pulled out the old photo of her parents and showed it to her. They were of mixed blood, both of them. A handsome couple, with kindness shining from their eyes, but no

76

one would look at them and have to wonder if they had any African in them. It was obvious.

Yet there was Elsie with her blond hair and hazel eyes. She didn't look the part of their daughter. And though her parents and darker-skinned siblings surely loved her beyond all reasoning, there would be questions any time she showed up. Questions and more questions, and not only for them. For Elsie too.

She was living the life of a white woman. And though maybe—*maybe*—people in the North wouldn't kick up a fuss over it all, people down here likely would if they knew.

No doubt that was why Elsie had never gotten that photo out before. And the fact that she'd shown it to Louisa, trusted her with that . . . well, that was when she'd sworn that she would take care of Miss Elsie as if she were her very own grandmother. Celeste and Maddie weren't here to do it, and it seemed Elsie didn't have anywhere else to go. Though she had decades' worth of friends here besides, she had no other family. No one but Louisa.

So she'd be the best adopted granddaughter anyone could ever want, that was all. For Celeste, and for Maddie.

And because Elsie may be the only other person on Ocracoke who knew what it was to wonder about your own blood.

<hr>

Rem knew something was off the moment Louisa raised the latch on the gate and let herself into Miss Elsie's fenced lawn. Unlike every other time he'd tagged along when she visited a neighbor, she didn't call out a greeting. And when she went to the door, she didn't knock. Perhaps he would have written it off as familiarity, except that she knocked even on her uncle's door—before opening it and letting herself in, granted.

They'd gone in the back entrance, straight into a kitchen that smelled every bit as divine as the inn's always did, and he was still breathing in a long, yeast-scented draft of ambrosia when he spotted the woman smiling at them from in front of the sink.

His first thought was that she reminded him of Mother. Same height, same fair hair, though with hazel eyes instead of blue. Same aura of beauty emanating from her—but in the way of the islanders, not of a socialite. Comfortably worn, faded calico made up her dress rather than silk. Her hair was swept back in a simple chignon at the base of her neck, and freckles dusted her nose that would have horrified Mother had they had the audacity to touch *her* skin.

Then she greeted Louisa, not with words but with gestures. Gestures that clearly *were* words. They were precise and quick and meant something to Louisa, who responded with a few gestures of her own. Louisa motioned to him and used her fingers to do something, rather than her whole arms, like she'd been using before.

He probably looked like a lad in a sweet shop. "Is that sign language?" He'd read of it but never encountered it. In their set, if a child had the misfortune to be born deaf, he or she was shipped off to an institution. No doubt they learned this language there, but the families never did. And if one lost one's hearing later in life, one made do with ear trumpets and writing tablets and more crude gestures to get one's point across.

"American Sign Language, yes. Grandma Elsie was born deaf, but her parents taught her." Louisa waved him forward. "Here, this is how you say 'good morning.'" She touched her right-hand fingertips to her mouth and then lowered her whole arm in a ninety-degree arc to rest those right fingers against her left palm, next moving the back of that right hand against the inside of her left elbow and lifting the left arm around it to her chest.

He did his best to imitate the movement, though he had a feeling he didn't look nearly so graceful as Louisa did.

But then, Louisa managed to look graceful while swinging a hammer or torquing a screwdriver. And when she ran along the beach, it was like watching leaves dance on the wind—spontaneous, unpredictable, but so beautiful he couldn't ever convince himself to look away.

And whether he bumbled his attempt or not didn't seem to matter to Miss Elsie, who gave him a sunshine-filled laugh and made a motion that he knew must mean something along the lines of *Welcome*, even though he had no clue what exactly the gesture meant. Then she made a show of studying him, tapping a fingertip to her lips.

Louisa grinned. "She's coming up with a symbol for your name."

"Really?" Did she do that for every guest she met? He would have asked, but it seemed presumptuous. So instead he watched, waited. "What's the one for yours?"

For some reason, that made Louisa laugh. She formed an *L* with her thumb and forefinger, touched it to her left shoulder, and then lowered it to the opposite side of her waist, making a dancing loop in the middle. "When Celeste and I became friends, we were both obsessed with princess stories. That motion—only without the loop—is the one for royalty. An *L* from shoulder to waist—like a sash, see?—is 'lord.' A *K* with the motion is for 'king,' a *P* for prince, and so on. She gave me the symbol because of how much I loved princess stories, but with the loop in the middle because I was always spinning around, dancing, when I was a girl."

She still did, when it was just them and the sand and the

ocean singing its serenade. He couldn't have held back a smile had he tried. "It's perfect."

Her gaze was still on Elsie, and she laughed again when the older woman twisted her first and second fingers together and then tapped them to her head. "As is yours—an *R* for Rem, of course, and then the sign for 'think.' I knew she'd be able to tell at a glance that you're a thinker."

She could? Rem didn't know whether to feel complimented or insulted, though either way he was impressed. "How do I say 'thank you'?"

Louisa touched her hand to her mouth again and then moved it away from her. Rem mirrored the motion but aimed it at Miss Elsie with a smile.

She grinned back and stepped forward, taking his hand and tugging him toward the table. Louisa followed, chuckling again. "You have been accepted. She will now ply you with food while I look over whatever chore list she has for me this month."

Sounded like a lovely arrangement to him. He let himself be plied, having learned in his weeks on the island that to refuse the offer of food was a grave insult to a Southern hostess. Not that it took but a single bite of the sweet berry-studded scone she slid in front of him for it to go from obligation to sheer delight. He didn't know any signs to tell her how good it was, but he must have worn a look of ecstasy on his face, because she grinned at him and patted his cheek and motioned toward the kettle. He nodded and said *thank you* again.

She held up both tea and coffee, and he indicated the hand holding the tea with a grateful smile. While she clattered about the stove, Louisa came back into the kitchen from wherever she'd been for the last few minutes and opened the cupboard under the sink. He watched as she emptied it of its contents, apparently to make room to all but climb in herself. "What are you doing, Princess Lulu?"

She sent him an eyeroll over her shoulder, but a smile had possession of her mouth. "Drain's slow. Need to clean it out."

He hadn't the foggiest notion how one actually accomplished such a feat, but he knew he was about to learn. And since Elsie soon vanished with a basket of wet laundry for the line strung across her lawn, he didn't feel terribly rude to be talking to Louisa when she couldn't hear. "So, this American Sign Language—you learned it as a child, when you became Celeste's friend?"

"Mm-hmm. Picked up a bit naturally by being around them, but then I made a study of it. The women in the family had a lot of silent conversation, so Celeste's daddy couldn't understand them. I wanted to know what they were saying."

Poor Celeste—and even poorer Maddie. He'd already heard enough of their woeful tale to be so glad on their behalf that they were leading such a happy life now. They deserved it after the misery that blighter had put them through. "I can understand that. You'll have to teach me some this summer so I can tell Miss Elsie how delicious her scones are."

Louisa's laughter echoed in the cupboard. "Sure. Though I daresay your face says it all. No one can read expressions and body language like Elsie."

No doubt. She'd have to, to get along with so many people who didn't know her language. He'd wager she was good at lip-reading too. "You said she didn't move here until her daughter was small?"

"That's right. She was born in Baltimore, then her family moved north after the war—War Between the States, I mean. She grew up somewhere in New England, mostly, and met and fell in love with a Coast Guardsman. They married when she was just sixteen. He ended up stationed here. Would you hand me that wrench—or spanner, as you call it?"

Rem cast his gaze around until he saw the tool with a mouth big enough to fit around a pipe. He handed it to her but then settled back onto his chair to watch the master at work. "It must have broken her heart to see her daughter mistreated so. And now to have her so far away."

Louisa's hands stilled for a second, then moved again with renewed energy. "Yeah. And when I think about it, what really hurts is realizing she'd have been the first to see it. I wouldn't be surprised if she'd even seen something in Jack before he and Miss Maddie got married and tried to warn her—but Maddie was always headstrong. You know the really funny thing?" She angled her head and caught his gaze for a moment. "Uncle Linc carried a torch for her back in the day. Or maybe he still does, I don't know. She could have married him instead, and look at what a different life she'd have had. Celeste would have had a father who adored her—I mean, I realize she wouldn't have been *her*. But if we squint at that part. She'd have been my cousin, and she'd have been happy, and . . ."

And she'd still be here, not touring Europe with her new stepfather. Rem sighed. "Those decisions affect not only an individual's life, but a family. A generation, every generation." He took a sip of the tea steaming at his side. "No doubt Miss Maddie thought she was making a choice for love. With my parents, it was for the social connections and financial gain." He heard the catch in his own throat and knew Louisa would hear it too.

Indeed, she not only paused but scooted out to better look at him. "You don't talk much about them."

No. He'd mentioned them that first day, yes, and then had to listen to Eddie hissing at him about not airing family business. So, he'd stayed mum on the subject weighing most heavily on his heart and focused instead on learning about island life and drawing Louisa out in academic matters— which had proven endlessly entertaining.

But she was fast becoming more a friend than any other he could claim, certainly on this continent. And maybe she could offer a new perspective. He trailed a finger along the rim of his cup. "My family has always done what was expected—made a good society match and hoped that some fondness would follow. My paternal grandparents, I believe, claimed a love match—but then she died in childbirth when delivering my youngest aunt, so I certainly never saw it. My parents . . . well. Father is a baron, as you know, and that's all that matters to him. The estate, the title, the responsibilities. Poor Sebastian has had it all drilled into him since we were lads. To each our duties. Family honor. Responsibility. Expectation."

Louisa reached back under the sink to unscrew something from the pipe. "And your mother?"

"Her family wanted to reclaim a bit of the old-world pedigree, I suppose. She was one of the Dollar Princesses of that generation—she brought an influx of wealth to the estate in exchange for a title. And I suppose that was all the exchange ever was. More often than not, they wouldn't even stay under the same roof, much less be in the same room. And since Sebastian is Father's heir, that meant that Mother claimed me. Always taking me to Maryland once a year, to make certain I know her family there. Grooming me to take over her father's estates, since she has no siblings. Edgar is actually her cousin's son, so he's not a direct heir to my grandfather."

Louisa granted him the mercy of turning her gaze back to the pipe. It allowed him to put words to the ache inside.

"Mother left England. This spring. We've known it was coming, Sebastian and I, but we've always been able to lure her home again. Not this time. She informed me as soon as we docked that she'd not be crossing the Atlantic again. She was, in her words, home to stay. As if England has never been anything but a stopover for her, as if the rest of us aren't there. As if *I* can abandon that entire side of my family because she's made yet another decision about what she deems to be best for the both of us."

He had to squeeze his eyes shut, because he'd never understood that about Mother. How she could at once love Sebastian but dismiss him as being *Father's*. How she could cling to Rem as if he were hers and hers alone—as if he had no bonds to either Father or Sebastian, as if he could drop everything and stay at her side.

Meanwhile, of course, Father demanded he join the navy. Both of them, only ever demanding. Never asking. Never considering who he was or what he wanted to do. Never considering that making decisions like that was what led to such a disaster of a family to begin with.

Something clanked under the sink, and Louisa reached for the old metal pail sitting by her knees. "Sometimes I wonder how different it would all be if we could be who we are. If freedom really meant we were free—to choose, to discover, to explore. If we weren't always bound by assumptions and prejudice and bias." She paused. "But that's never been the human story, has it? No one's ever really had that perfect life. Instead, it's all about what we do with the hand we're dealt. How we overcome. Who we choose to be despite who the world tries to make us."

His lips turned up a bit at that. He knew—had always known—that he'd been born with what the world called privilege. He never had to wonder if there would be food enough or clothing enough or shelter or the funds to pay for more. The same couldn't be said for Louisa's family. They worked because they had to, put their hands to soil or wood or mop or flour. They built a home, a family, from determination rather than social dictates.

But still, here they both were, fighting against their respective molds. Trying to spread their wings and discover who *they* wanted to be. And maybe . . . just maybe it was part of the Lord's plan that they discover it together. Maybe it was His will, rather than Edgar's, that led Rem here this summer, to ask these questions with this particular young woman.

"I think you may be on to something," Rem finally said. "Very rarely is history written by people doing what's expected of them. If we want to make a difference—well, we do it by defying the norms, don't we?"

She slid the bucket back out again—Rem didn't care to investigate what was in it now—and flashed him a smile half shadowed by the sink but still bright as noonday. "Is that what we are? History-makers?"

"Who's to say? We could be. We could write books that change a generation or help man travel to outer space as we've done to the ocean's depths or—"

"Improve upon Mama's fig cake recipe?"

He pasted an exaggerated look of patronization on his face. "Now, Lu, I said make history, not perform miracles. Some things are simply impossible."

She laughed and reached for the section of pipe she'd set down two minutes before. "So, which of those dreams is yours? Writing books? Delving into science? Are you going to build a spaceship like in *A Journey in Other Worlds*?"

They'd spent an entertaining few evenings reading that together, wondering what the world really would look like in the year 2000. He'd met the late Mr. Astor, the author of the novel, before his unfortunate death on the *Titanic* two years ago, and Rem had wondered the whole time what he was imagining behind that staid and somber exterior. Whole worlds of life on Jupiter and Saturn, a universe at their fingertips . . . There was a man who knew how to dream.

Rem could learn a few things from him. "Maybe I shall. Who's to say? There's a whole world out there. Certainly I can find *some* way to leave my mark on it. And not by running a company here in America or vying for rank on a Dreadnought. There has to be more than that. Something exciting and mysterious and clever."

Wiping her hands on the men's handkerchief she always kept in her pocket, Louisa scooted back out and flashed that grin of hers. "It's excitement and mystery and mental games you want, is it? Come on, then." She jumped to her feet, nudged the cupboard door shut, and wiggled her fingers at him.

He put his in hers without a qualm, even though each and every time she'd done that over the last three weeks, she'd led him straight into mischief. Though as she tugged him to his feet and pulled him out of the kitchen, he did feel the need to state a few ground rules. "We're not terrifying any other hogs, are we? Or switching out fruit pies on two neighbors' windowsills?"

She pulled him along a short, bright corridor whose walls were adorned with faded photographs he'd have liked to examine more closely. He was guessing the trio of blondes in one of them were Elsie, Maddie, and Celeste, all with matching smiles, but he didn't get a good enough look at it to know for certain. It would be nice to have a face to put to all the stories Louisa told, though.

"Nothing like that. I'm going to show you how Celeste and I entertained ourselves on rainy days."

"Paper dolls? Draughts? Whist?"

"How plebeian." She lifted her nose and pulled him around the landing and toward a narrow staircase that led to attic space.

When Edgar had asked him what he would do that day since he refused the invitation for hunting, he never would have guessed that the answer would be "going through a stranger's attic." But since he'd always had a fascination with the old, dusty things that generations past had seen fit to close up but not get rid of entirely, Rem made no objection.

Louisa was clearly at home in the space. She opened the door, ducked her way inside, and went straight for an old trunk under the garret window, which had two rickety-looking chairs set up by it already.

It wasn't even dusty up here, which either spoke to Miss Elsie's fastidiousness or . . . well, he couldn't think of an "or." But he knew for a fact the attics of Springbourne Hall weren't nearly so tidy. He'd spent many a rainy afternoon of his own childhood going through them.

"Here we go." Rather than take one of the chairs, Louisa crouched down in front of the trunk, unhooked the latch, and raised the lid on its hinges. "Have a seat, Master Remington. Let's see how clever you really are."

He sat, thoroughly intrigued as she pulled out reams of yellowed paper. Some were folded, some bound with twine, all with ink that had rusted with time. Then she pulled out a considerably newer-looking stack, the handwriting on those looking young and bold and in pencil instead of ink.

Accepting the stack she handed him, Rem knew his brows were knitting together the more he looked at it. "What's all this, then?" Letters, from the look of them. A few telegrams that made no sense at all, being a jumble of numbers. Pages with burnt edges. Pages with lines in that normal brown-black ink and then lighter words between those lines.

"Secrets." Louisa reached into the trunk again and pulled out a leather-bound journal. "Those you're holding now, they were from the War Between the States, as you can see from the dates. Secret messages from spies."

She was trying to pull one over on him. He sent her a dry look. "Right."

"They are! Look." She came up on her knees and moved to his side, pointing at the letter on top of his stack. "See how there are two different inks? This lighter one was invisible. They called it the 'sympathetic stain' and wrote sensitive information in it. You needed a specific formula of a counter-agent to develop it, nothing else would work. Foolproof."

"You're quite serious?" A little trill ran through him. There was no shortage of espionage throughout history, he supposed, and no shortage either of chemists willing to put their trade to the task. Still, he'd never come across anything so interesting in *his* attic.

"And look at this. This is what we played with." She flipped through his stack and drew out another page to put on top. This one was filled with nothing but gibberish—numbers, periods, spaces. Lines and lines of it.

That trill began to hum. "Codes." He'd played at those a bit over the years, too, in school. But they'd been for fun—never actually used for a purpose.

Louisa nodded vigorously, sending a stray curl into her eyes that she was far too quick to push back behind her ear. "That leather book is the codebook. Look." She lifted it, opened it with care to the first page. "There are numbers assigned to all these different words. Celeste and I memorized the whole thing and used it to send each other notes, so her father couldn't read them."

Signs for when they were in person, secret codes for when they were apart. Rem lifted his eyes from the stack of papers to the beautiful young woman with dancing eyes who said such things as if they were no more noteworthy than switching pies. "Sophisticated games."

Her smile was cheeky. But a bit of sobriety filtered into her eyes. "We're sophisticated girls. In case you couldn't tell through my overalls and dungarees."

"I could tell." Maybe it came out more serious in tone than she'd expected—or wanted. Maybe that was why she knee-walked over to the other chair and hoisted herself up.

"Looking back, I guess it's sad that we had to resort to this. But at the time, it felt like God himself had led us up here, showed us this stuff. That He'd given us a way to communicate, to make sure she stayed safe. It felt like . . . like if we were smart enough and brave enough, we could do anything."

"Mm. The story of humanity, as you said before." He tried to brighten his tone, but he wasn't certain he'd pulled it off. Because in his hands was proof that humanity had always needed to protect itself from itself. That there were always wars and rumors of wars. Tyrannies and oppressions. People willing to kill for their own way, who considered their secrets worthy of such levels of protection.

They weren't wrong either. That was the thing. Secrets *were* worthy of protection.

"So, do you still remember the code? You could teach it to me on rainy days this summer."

Louisa grinned and flipped through one of those newer sheets. "Of course I do. Celeste still writes to me in it sometimes. Not always, but sometimes, just for fun. And we made copies of the codebook, one for each of us. I still have mine back at the inn."

What a remarkable person she was—she and her friend both, apparently. Two girls, teaching themselves a secret code apparently used by American intelligencers in ages past. With, it seemed, no instruction beyond their own digging. She had a mind that any of his fellows at Cambridge would envy.

And yet she couldn't scrape together the funds for a teaching college. It was a shame, that. More than a shame. It was a tragedy. A tragedy so easily remedied, if he could sort out how to arrange for a scholarship without her realizing it was from him. She'd feel honor bound to refuse it if she knew. He'd become familiar enough with her pride and the do-it-yourself attitude of all these Americans to know that. But she deserved the aid. And it would cost him virtually nothing.

He'd send a letter off to his Baltimore-based lawyer at once and ask him to see to it. Rem would turn twenty-one next month, which meant he'd have full access to his trust fund. They could then make some clever arrangement with the school to let her in this autumn and offer her a scholarship. Then all he'd have to do in the meantime was make certain she applied.

She angled her gaze up at him, a teasing blue arrow that struck him right in the heart. "I could teach you. Though sign language *and* the code—are you sure you're up to it?"

He was up to anything if it meant more time at her side.

7

JUNE 29, 1914

Louisa had never considered herself sullen by any stretch of the imagination, but she'd never laughed as much as she'd done so far this summer. Not at all what she would have expected at its start, when all she could see was that her friends were gone and she was still here.

She splashed her bare toes through the wavelet caressing their narrow strip of beach and kept her gaze on the task at hand—counting sea snails visible in the clear water—but her whole body was aware of where Rem did his own splashing a few feet away. He had his trousers rolled up to his knees and was belting out an Italian opera in a surprisingly good baritone. His attempts to sign along with the lyrics were what had resulted in her newest case of giggles.

When she'd suggested pairing signs with a song, she'd been thinking of "Jesus Loves Me," not an aria from *The Marriage of Figaro*—in Italian, no less.

But though she laughed, she didn't interrupt him. No, she

waited until he'd sung the last note before shaking her head and asking, "And how am I to judge your accuracy on that? I have no idea what that song was supposed to say."

He widened his eyes, all feigned innocence. "What's this? The lady doesn't speak Italian? I don't believe it."

Still chuckling, she leaned down to send a lazy splash his way. The water was still cool. It wouldn't really warm up good until August. "She doesn't. Not that she couldn't if you want to add it to the list of things to learn before you go."

She made herself say it regularly—*before you go*, *when you go*—keeping that eventuality always before both of them.

But it pierced. Oh did it pierce, each and every time. He'd been here seven weeks, and it felt as though her life would be empty when he left, even though it would have all the same things it had before he came. Mama and Grann and the inn. Uncle Linc. Grandma Elsie, letters from Celeste, and eventually Garret would come home.

She'd still have Marge Williams scowling at her. Doxee warning guests not to flirt. All the questions, all the wonders, all the scrimping and saving for a someday dream that might never get out of her head and onto the page of life, even though Rem had badgered her into admitting her dream to her family, filling out the application for the fall term, and sending it in just that morning.

And if that door didn't swing open, then she'd know it was the Lord's way of telling her to stay where He'd put her. To focus on her family and on the inn, at least for now.

Rem splashed her back with about as much force, landing all of two drops on her shins. "All right, you've called my bluff. I know no more Italian than is in the few songs I've learned in school."

She opened her mouth, ready to make another joke, but

she caught sight of a towering figure silhouetted against the fire of the evening sun, and her tease turned to a shout of joy. "Garret!" There was no one else it could possibly be, not given the height of him.

Rem spun, already smiling. He'd heard plenty about Garret in the last seven weeks, though not as much as Celeste by half. Louisa laughed, gave his arm a squeeze on her way by, and ran toward her long-lost friend. "Garret Wynnwood! Finally decided to grace us with your presence?"

Garret laughed, too, and opened his arms. "Couldn't stay away another minute, no matter how desperately they needed me at the hospital."

She slammed into him as hard as she could—a game they'd been playing since they were kids and he started shooting up in height. She managed to knock him back a whole step this time, which was quite an accomplishment, before he closed his arms around her, lifted her from her feet, and twirled her in a circle.

When he put her down, she punched him in the arm, solely because he expected it. "Desperately need you to carry the patients and reach things on high shelves, you mean?"

"It is a particular talent of mine. And hey, orderly today, doctor tomorrow—if we don't take 'tomorrow' too literally." He grinned at her, flashing his straight white teeth, though his smile dimmed a notch when he looked past her.

Rem had meandered a few feet closer, but not so close as to be eavesdropping or awaiting an introduction—always mannerly. Garret would know at a glance that he was a guest, given his fancy clothes. But he'd be wondering if he was an annoying, clinging guest who he needed to save her from.

Best to put that thought to rest straightaway. "Let me introduce you to Rem."

"Rem." He said the name suspiciously, like it belonged

to the villain in a fairy tale. But then, she didn't usually call guests by their first names—certainly not guests who were young men. He'd know it meant something, which was no doubt why he went stiff and straightened his spine.

As if he needed to look any taller. Louisa huffed out a breath and did her best to slip her voice to his ear under the breeze. "Don't get all protective on me, Gar. I don't need you playing big brother here."

Or worse, potential beau. They'd had that talk before he went off to school, and she'd thought . . . hoped . . . *prayed* he'd forgotten all about it while he was away. Known he would, as a matter of fact, just like he'd managed to forget that he'd once favored Celeste over *her*. What chance, then, was there that he'd really continue to prefer Louisa after he met all those mainland girls with their fashionable hair and pretty clothes and polished manners?

Girls who knew their own blood. Girls who could pledge their lives to his without wondering if it was legal here in North Carolina, where a white man couldn't marry anyone with more than a sixteenth of African blood.

Questions. Always the questions. Questions that tainted every single potential future she tried to envision. Questions she'd never dared to put voice to, not to anyone. Not to Garret, not to Rem. Not even to Celeste.

Questions Garret sure didn't look like he was thinking about when he turned those deep brown eyes of his on her. Gracious, but he could look straight through a body. "I have no desire to play *brother*, Louisa." He didn't even crack a joke about the *big* part, which told her he was definitely thinking about *it* again. The evening that would not be named.

She rolled her eyes to lighten the mood and did an about-face. "Well, don't play ogre either. Come on, you'll like him. He's English, second son of a baron, but not nearly as stuffy as you'd think." This part she said loud enough for Rem to hear, if the wind didn't snatch it away.

Must not have. He donned half a grin and shook his head.

Never one to stand by when there was intimidation to be done, Garret strode forward with more gusto than was really called for, so he could tower over Rem all the sooner. If he didn't have the kindest, most caring heart of anyone she'd ever known, she'd have gotten mighty tired of that habit of his ages ago.

But he only ever put his height to use to try to protect or help someone. Misplaced as it was right now . . . and what in the world was *that*? Her eyes went wide as he passed her by, giving her her first view of the back of his head and the tail of hair bound there at the nape. "Garret Wynnwood! Your hair!"

He'd always worn it too long, brushing his collar, but it had never been long enough to tie back before. And if nothing else, the exclamation drew him up short, made him turn back to grin at her and lift a self-conscious hand to the short tail. "Haven't had time to find a barber in Raleigh."

"Ha! Right. More like your mama wasn't there to badger you, so you finally grew it like you always wanted." She hooked a thumb at him and looked to Rem. "Told you he always wanted to be a pirate. Stand aside, Blackbeard. Brownhair is on the loose."

Garret snorted his opinion of that. Turned back to glaring at Rem. And stuck out a hand that would swallow Rem's whole if he dared to shake it, which, of course, he did. "Garret Wynnwood. Sounds as though Lulu has told you all about me."

Rem deserved some credit. He didn't wince at what was probably a too-tight grip on the handshake, and he somehow managed not to look uncomfortable as he tilted his head back to take in Garret's height. All that good breeding, she supposed. "How do you do? I'm Remington Culbreth."

"Remington Culbreth. Remington Culbreth . . ." Garret made a show of considering the name, squinted up at the sky, then shook his head. "I don't believe Louisa's mentioned you in any of her letters. Though she writes every week."

Accusation, aimed at her. And doubts, planted in Rem.

Louisa sighed. No, she hadn't mentioned Rem in any of her letters. Because . . . how could she? How could she explain to her overprotective friend who had told her he wanted to be *more* than a friend, that she was losing her heart to an English aristocrat piece by piece? That her heart and soul were trickling his way hour by hour like sand through an hourglass? That even though she knew it was the worst idea ever to be had and that nothing could ever come of it, she couldn't help but dream of him?

But hang it all, Garret's words hit their mark in Rem. His eyes dimmed. "Well. I suppose she doesn't bore you with talk of the guests. She has certainly told me much about you, though."

Louisa's chest went tight. After Gar left, she'd find a way to make Rem understand. To realize it was a compliment, not an insult. That she'd wanted to keep him as *hers*, not share him with Garret. To assure him that she *had* written about him—all about him—to Celeste, who would be more likely to sigh at the romance of it all and less likely to turn into a surly porcupine with jealousy poisoning the tip of every quill.

Not that there was romance between them, exactly. And not that there should be. But there *could* be, so easily, if he gave her the slightest indication that he wanted there to be.

Fool. She knew it—knew she could never fit into his world, knew that he was too kind a man to try to force her to when it would only make her miserable. She had no business in fancy dresses and high company. She wouldn't know the first thing about how to behave. She'd disgrace him—his whole family. They'd never accept her. Give her a fortnight in his circles, and he'd be looking for excuses to get rid of her. She knew that.

Her head did, anyway. Her heart seemed to be as deaf to logic as Grandma Elsie was to sound. If only it had her way of adapting and would learn to compensate.

For now, she had to settle for trying to mitigate the damage Garret was quite purposefully doing to her friendship with Rem. She linked her arm through Rem's and grinned up at him. "Some things don't go into letters. I knew I wouldn't be able to do you justice with a description, and since I *thought* you'd be home a month ago, Gar, and could *meet* him . . ."

Neither of the men looked convinced. Rem's smile was still strained and too polite, and Garret didn't even bother refreshing his. He slung his hands into his pockets and focused on her instead of Rem. "I don't suppose the news from Europe has reached you yet? Everyone on the mainland was abuzz with it, but yesterday's newspapers were on the boat with me, so I didn't figure you'd seen."

She felt Rem's whole body go tense beside her, including the arm she'd looped hers around. "What news?" he asked, voice as taut as a sail in a hurricane.

A bit of the antagonism in Garret's gaze softened as he looked back at Rem, maybe realizing that any news from Europe would likely mean more to an Englishman than it would to her. "The Austrian archduke and his wife were assassinated. No one seems to know yet if it was a political move or not, but with tensions as high as they've been . . ."

Rem let out a long, slow breath. From her current position at his side, she couldn't see into his eyes, but she had a feeling storm clouds had marred their ocean blue. "Could be the spark to a powder keg."

"So say the journalists. Speculation is abounding, but we'll pray it was a rogue assassin operating alone and not some kind of act of war."

Rem nodded. But he also stepped away, gently removing his arm from Louisa's as he did so. "You say there were newspapers on the boat with you?"

"I brought the inn's with me. They're in the main room."

"Thank you. If you'll both excuse me . . ." He nodded to Garret but barely even glanced down at Louisa in his haste to leave the beach and make for the inn. But the true sign of his distraction was that he didn't pause the moment his feet hit the walk to unroll his trouser legs.

Louisa waited until he was out of sight and then gave Garret her best imitation of Mama's glare. "Shame on you."

"What?" His eyes went wide, but she couldn't tell if the innocence was feigned or real. "Shouldn't I have told him about the news? He was going to find out anyway, as soon as he went inside."

"That's not what I mean, and you know it." She shook her head, motioning toward where he'd gone. "What business do you have coming out here and belittling someone? Making him feel unwelcome and unappreciated? You know *nothing* about him. You certainly don't know whether he deserves that sort of attitude from you. Why—*why* could you not assume that he's a potential friend instead of a potential enemy?"

She watched each arrow hit its mark, watched them sink in, measured how deep they went by the ticking of his clenched jaw.

One thing she'd always loved about Garret—he may get overprotective, but he wasn't a thoughtless guy, once you got him thinking. He didn't fly off the handle or get so defensive that he'd argue against all reason if emotion said he should.

He thought it through. His chin lowered from that spoiling-for-a-fight angle. And he sighed. "I'm sorry. I just—the way you were looking at him."

She folded her arms across her chest. "You and Celeste have always been my two best friends. Have I demonstrated bad taste or poor judgment in those decisions?"

He pulled one hand out of his pocket to rub at the back of his neck. "Obviously not. And so you'll say I should trust your judgment here too. Try to determine *why* you like him instead of getting upset that you clearly do."

"No surprise you're at the top of your class."

He pursed his lips and looked out to the water instead of at her. "You were supposed to change your mind while I was gone. Realize how much you missed me."

"Garret . . ." She heard a world of things in those two little syllables—how many did he hear? The acknowledgment? The frustration? The agony? The disappointment? The fear? The last thing in the world she wanted was to lose him as a friend. She needed him—needed him like the wild horses needed the fresh water that sifted up through the filtering sand.

But there was a difference between the water you drank for survival and the ocean that swelled around you, that carried you and crashed over you, brought you life and brought you death.

She squeezed her eyes shut. "Please don't do this again."

"You can't make me not love you, Louisa."

Her eyes flew back open. "You *don't*! Not like that. It's only that I'm the best option for you on the island after Celeste left, but she was always the one—"

He scoffed a laugh. "She was *never* the one. And she's gone and she's never coming back here."

The look on her face must have been stricken, given the way he winced. Backpedaled. "Sorry. Maybe for you she will, but—well, not for me. She's gone for me."

Louisa shook her head. "You're proving my point. Celeste left, and you moved on. Well, now *you've* left. You're out in the world now. You're going to meet someone else, and it would be mighty awkward if you were committed to me when that happens." The same words she'd given him last year, more or less.

And he was shaking his head now just as he had then. "There's no one in the world like you."

Another woman forced to do a man's work? Who dreamed for things that could never be? Who didn't even know who she was, what blood flowed in her veins? Oh, she had a feeling he'd find plenty of women just like her, if he looked in the gutters and the slums instead of the university halls.

With another shake of her head, she strode past him, aiming her feet for the inn. "I did miss you. I'll always miss you when you're gone. But that doesn't mean I changed my mind about anything."

Garret shadowed her steps, though he had the good sense to stay quiet this time. At least for a minute. "All right."

That brought her up short, and she turned to look back at him.

He lifted his brows. "You can't tell me my own heart, but I can't tell you yours either. That's only fair. So, I'll get to know this English bloke. But I promise you this, Lulu—I'm not going to stand back and let him hurt you."

The tension in her shoulders eased, and the relief of it brought a bit of a smile to her lips. "Once you get to know him even a little, you'll see that he'd do anything to avoid hurting anyone." Or make himself miserable trying, when it came to his family.

She prayed he didn't have to make the same sort of decision about *her*.

———

Rem sat at the water's edge long after midnight. A new day, but there was no evidence of it in the star-studded sky overhead or the endless horizon, so dark that he couldn't tell water from sky. There was no comfort in knowing that in Europe, in England, it was already a new dawn.

Because he didn't know what would come with that dawning. War? Political alliances? Ultimatums? Would it be relegated to the Continent, or would it infiltrate his own homeland? And if the unthinkable happened and England entered a war, what did that mean for him?

That was one question he had an answer to: It meant a summons from Father. It meant all choice being taken from him. It meant doing his duty and living up to the family legacy and all that rot. It meant the Royal Navy and a commission and a future of strategy and battles and war and men under his command and . . .

And leaving Louisa. Leaving this idyllic place that had somehow started to feel more like home than anywhere else ever had, even though he'd known with every sunrise that he was one day closer to leaving.

He dug his bare toes into the cool sand and breathed in the scent of salt and sea.

Maybe that was for the best. It had only taken one look at Louisa in Garret Wynnwood's arms for the truth to come crashing down. She wasn't meant for Rem. She was too beautiful, too vibrant, too much a part of this place. She was racing wind and rising tide and rollicking waves. She was not staid and somber drawing rooms, tight laces, and proper address.

He must have begun to dream at some point that he could vanish from the world that had once known him, claim this one instead. Become the island's resident English expatriate, living off his trust fund until he could learn some skill to make him a real part of island life. Maybe he could teach alongside Louisa. Or study under her uncle Linc. Or even learn how to make the best fig preserves on the island, perfect the age-old drying of yaupon leaves for tea. He'd even take up fishing if it meant making a place for himself.

Impossible, all of it. As impossible as bridling that wind or netting that tide or taming those waves. Louisa deserved more than a stuffy Englishman who could never truly belong here. She deserved someone like Garret—tall and strapping and handsome, of whom everyone on the islands was so ridiculously proud that they bragged on him as their future doctor even when he had years of schooling ahead of him. *He* was everything Rem could never be for her. He wouldn't ask her to give up anything of herself. And he was in love with her—that had been evident in a glance and was no doubt why he'd greeted Rem with such hostility.

Well, Rem wasn't the competition. Clearly. He was just a guest. One here for a summer and then gone. One who quite possibly would get swept up in whatever unrest was going on in Europe. One who would never step foot on Ocracoke again once he left.

Down to his very bones he knew that there could be no coming back. No seeing her again. No checking in on her life. She would marry Garret, they'd have a horde of beautiful children, and Rem would eventually, after a few years of career in the navy, obey his parents' promptings toward whatever socialite they'd decided would make a good addition to the family.

"Since when are you the night owl, cher?"

He craned around—not that he needed to move to see who'd joined him. But tonight he couldn't even summon a smile for Grann. All that would come out was a sigh. "Since the world is tottering on the brink—or so it seems."

She settled beside him in the sand, her face pointed to the horizon as his had been, and as he let it be again now. "Just the newspaper troubling you? Or maybe one Garret Wynnwood coming home?"

Blast, but she was too astute for her own good—or for his, anyway. "Just the news."

"Didn't you hear Linc's message on lying last week?"

His breath was half-sigh, half-laugh. He let it apologize for him. "He's a nice young man. I can see why he and Louisa have always been friends."

"Mm. And I admit there was a time her mama and I hoped they'd be more. No better choice for her in these parts, we imagined. But it never quite settled, that thought. Maybe because we always knew she'd want to go off to school, even if she hadn't said it. Or maybe . . . maybe we always knew you'd show up."

A snort slipped out before he could stop it. "Maybe it would have been better if I hadn't." If he'd never come here, never met Louisa or this clan that saw too much and knew too much and made him wish he could stay. Show Elsie what signs he'd learned that week. Talk to Grann in French about her early life in Louisiana. Listen to Serena sing in the kitchen. Muse with Linc long into the evening about theology and philosophy.

Take Louisa into his arms and hold her, not until he tamed the waves, but until they consumed him. Made him part of them.

Grann leaned closer until their shoulders touched. She'd told him about growing up on a plantation, about how her mama was a pretty house slave, and how everyone had known the master was Grann's father, but no one ever said it. How the other children, his legitimate children, hated her and made her life miserable. How the other slaves, the ones toiling in the fields, saw the privileges her father granted her and hated her as much as her half-siblings.

She'd told him about how, when she was fifteen, she'd been sold off. How she'd watched all the white boys go off to fight for the right to own her, all the Black boys go off to dig the trenches for those white boys. She'd told him about how she'd seen freedom come, but not really. How she couldn't marry the man she loved because he was white and she wasn't white *enough*. She'd told him how they'd found a minister to marry them anyway, even though the law said they couldn't, and she had asked Rem if they had any laws like that in England.

They didn't. But he'd had to admit that it wasn't because his countrymen were so enlightened—it was because it hadn't come up enough to require one. Though plenty of the nobility had once made a tidy profit on the slave trade and colonial plantations, they hadn't brought many slaves to England's shores, certainly not in the last hundred years. He'd honestly never even met anyone with skin the color of hers before he came here.

He couldn't know, not really, what she'd gone through. He couldn't know her beyond those glimpses she showed him. So why, sitting here beside her in the sand, with their arms touching, did he want to rest his head on her shoulder like he'd once done with his nurse and pretend he was a lad again, one who could pour out his woes and trust her to fix everything?

"You heard yet about the big storms that divided Hatteras from Bodie and Ocracoke both, nearly seventy years ago?"

It sounded like a non sequitur. But because he'd already heard many stories of hers, he knew she would have a point in telling it. "I don't believe so. A hurricane?"

"That's right. Blew in one day out of nowhere, as they sometimes do. And the waters didn't rise like they do—they *cut*. Cut that land right in two. Dug a trench where before there'd been solid land, or as solid as any land is down here. Too wide to walk across, currents too strong to swim across. Two islands made where there'd only been one. Neighbors suddenly separated, communities forced apart."

Rem tilted his face up to the sliver of the moon's. "That had to have been difficult."

"I imagine it was—that was well before even my day, mind. But they were still talking about it, folks still remembered when I came here. The older ones, they still mourned what they'd lost and wished that storm had never hit. Funny thing, though. Most people now forget it had ever been any other way. They focus on what's here, what's been made, what new communities were forged, what new paths opened between the Atlantic and the Pamlico Sound, and the new shipping that came because of it. That's the best way, I think, to handle what life throws at us. Grab hold of it. Make whatever we can with whatever pieces we have."

"What if we haven't pieces enough left?"

She leaned into him, and he caught the scent of floral soap and yeast and yaupon tea. "Can't say as I've ever seen that. Certainly not now, here, with you. It's all there before you, Remington. All you've got to do is grab hold."

He saw the stars, countless suns of untold planets burning for worlds so far beyond his own. He heard the water singing and dancing its way up this beach but also on England's shores, and Europe's, and every other continent's. He felt the grit of sand between his toes and knew that it had once been rock until time and water wore it away.

What is man, that thou art mindful of him? and the son of man, that thou visitest him? The words from the psalm came unbidden to his mind, a perfect summation. It was so easy when faced with the vast expanse above and before him to think himself nothing. Unworthy. A speck to soon be forgotten by everyone he wanted to remember him.

But God had fashioned him. He couldn't know why the Lord had placed him in the Culbreth family, or the Remington one. He couldn't know why he'd been born after Sebastian or before Edgar. But maybe he *could* know why God had led him here, to this tiny little island in the Atlantic, at this particular time in his life.

To meet these people. To be changed by them. Elsie and Grann and Serena and Linc and even the intimidating Garret Wynnwood, who'd shown him so clearly what he had to lose if he didn't risk it all.

Louisa. The young woman who everyone he knew would say couldn't be his. The young woman who would always be able to claim, whether she wanted to or not, that he was hers.

The question was what he would do about it. What history they would choose to make.

He leaned back until the sand cradled him, until only sky was before him. Until the eternity of it serenaded him. Even if they made the wrong choices, then life—the world, the universe—would still go on. But that didn't mean they shouldn't make their choices with care. He didn't want to wreak the kind of havoc on anyone that Jack Scarborough had. He didn't want to live with ice and stone like his parents. He didn't want to hurt the one person who had come so quickly to mean so much. "She would be smart to choose Mr. Wynnwood."

Grann chuckled. "She's a smart girl—but her heart's even bigger than her mind, and that's the part that will make that decision for her, I think. You've brought sunshine back into her life, Remington. Sunshine that's been missing since Celeste left. Garret hasn't done that. Never could. Which means his part is to bring it to someone else, someday. Heaven knows he has plenty of light to shine too. Hers just isn't the heart ready to receive it from him."

But it was for him? Was she certain of that? He knew she wouldn't be saying this if she weren't . . . but even so. He didn't have as much faith in himself, it seemed, as she did.

Then again, it only took one of those faraway suns to pierce the darkness and make it beautiful. He could surely gather enough courage to punch a single hole through the night before him. Just enough to let in the light. Just enough for Louisa.

8

TODAY

MAY 14, 1942
OCRACOKE ISLAND, NORTH CAROLINA

Seven. Seven bodies had been recovered from the beaches over the last couple days. Seven from a crew of thirty-seven on the HMT *Bedfordshire*.

Evie stood shoulder-to-shoulder with pretty much everyone in the village who could get away from normal tasks on a Thursday morning, her dress a somber gray, her hat a veiled black, her mind a swirl of torment. Seven bodies, but only two had names they knew—the one Mr. Howard had recognized, and another whose name had been written on his uniform. The other five were listed on that makeshift marker as *sailors*.

Five unidentified people would soon be buried in the O'Neal family plot. Two whose families would soon get the news that would change them forever.

One named but would-be-anonymous spook alternated between wakeful agony and fevered thrashing in her inn. She hadn't heard back from Davie yet, but she knew she would soon. And in her gut, she knew he would say that Sterling Bertram was an intelligence agent. It was the only thing that made sense of all his rambling and muttering.

Thank God that He'd sent him floating up to *her* stretch of beach and not someone else's, someone who wouldn't have known what to do with him. Who would have reported him. Who may have even thought him an enemy, given his constant mumbling of German names.

She didn't know how those fit into his puzzle yet. But she'd find out.

Wondering about that did nothing to soften this, though. On the contrary—she was determined to commit each detail to memory for him. The way the sun filtered through the trees. The snap of the Union Jack from its pole, where they'd raised it out of respect for these sailors who had given their lives to protect *them*. Not their own, just allies on a far-distant shore. The harsh call of the doves, the melody of the pipes that old Sean Avery was playing, the smell of fresh-turned sandy soil.

He'd want to know. He'd want to have been here. He'd want to have buried his friend, to be able to tell Thomas Cunningham's widow that he'd done so. She'd seen that need deep in his eyes that morning as pain burned through him. He'd been awake, which was good. Coherent, which was better. But she'd almost wished oblivion for him instead, given how deep it had lanced him when she told him they'd be burying the dead today.

Someone shifted, moved closer to her side, leaned down. Calvin Johnson. "You okay, Eve? You look . . . I know this is the first funeral you've been to since Job's."

Was it? She jumped a little at his words, pressed a hand to the slim black belt that encircled her waist. Surely someone else had died since Job—and yes, a few had, but she'd made her excuses. Brought meals and flowers to the family and apologized for not being at the funeral. No one had, in her hearing at least, judged her for her absence at the gravesides.

But she hadn't even thought of that this time. Hadn't considered how it might hurt to stand over another open grave. She'd come because she knew she had to, in Sterling's stead. And until this moment, that other funeral on that other sunny day hadn't even entered her mind.

Guilt pummeled her.

Calvin cupped her elbow, squeezed it. "You need anything? Water? A cookie?"

She was in no danger of fainting, but she offered him a tight-lipped smile. He'd been Job's closest friend in the Guards, after all. If anyone else was thinking of that day on this one, it would be him. And because it was in his thoughts, he'd graciously assumed it was in hers. He offered comfort because he needed it.

"Some water would be wonderful. Thanks, Cal," Evie said, just to give him something to do until Reverend Fulcher arrived.

He nodded and slipped away again, leaving her there with the rising May heat and the smothering guilt. Her hand slid up to touch the necklace she wore, covered by the somber gray of her dress. Sea glass, worn by time into a shape that had no name. A pale blue-green that she'd encircled with silver and put on a chain for herself—the only piece of her jewelry she'd ever kept and worn.

She'd walked for hours, days after they buried Job. She'd felt so hollow, so empty that she couldn't remember much from that time. Everything to come in had flowed right back out, into the water, through the sands. Her first real memory again was opening her eyes to her old room at the inn, Mama asleep beside her, her own cheeks wet with tears. And this piece of worn, smooth glass clasped tight in a fist. She must have found it while she wandered. Must have, but didn't remember doing so.

She'd slid out of her narrow bed, tiptoed out to the little corner of the old barn that her parents had converted into her studio, and gotten to work. It hadn't taken long to turn the glass into a pendant. She'd fastened it around her neck, tucked it under her shirt, and sworn to God and Job that she'd never take it off. Never forget.

She hadn't taken it off. But how long had it been since she thought about Job—really thought about him? Days, at least. Maybe more than a week.

Healing, Uncle Garret would say. But that's not what it felt like. It felt like betrayal.

More neighbors crowded around. Cal returned at some point and slipped a glass of cool water into her hands. The pastor showed up.

It couldn't be easy, giving a funeral for total strangers who had washed up on your shore, but it was something island ministers had done for ages, and Reverend Fulcher did a fine job. He reminded them all of the sacrifice these brave young men had made for them to protect America's vulnerabilities even though they weren't Americans. He commended them for that selflessness before the Father. Prayed that their souls find rest in Him. Charged every villager with remembering them, even if they knew not their names. God knew who they were, how many hairs were on their heads, and He knew those who would be missing them so keenly.

There could well be families and friends in England even now getting news that the *Bedfordshire* was gone, their lads lost, taken by torpedo to a watery, fiery grave. Perhaps they would take some comfort from it if they knew that an ocean away, a whole town had gathered to honor their boys.

Perhaps. Or perhaps they'd wander for hours, for days, in a hollow cloud of pain.

Fanny Pearl Fulcher, the pastor's daughter, somehow ended up by Evie's side at the close of the service. She was a few years Evie's elder, but they'd always gotten along fine. Now Fanny Pearl took her hand and gave it a squeeze. "I saw you with a whole tin of shells and glass last night. More than your normal collecting."

Evie lifted her hand to take a drink but found the water glass gone. Cal must have taken it from her at some point during the service, though she couldn't say when. She nodded. "I want to make something to send to each of the sailors' families. The whole crew. We don't know which of them we buried here, but we know they all died to protect us. I thought a memento from us to those grieving families would be nice."

Fanny Pearl's smile was soft and sad. She lifted her free hand to touch the shell earrings Evie had made for her when her daddy was sick five years ago, when they'd all been praying so fiercely for him. "I'd hoped that's what you were about. I managed to get an address for the one whose name we know—Thomas Cunningham. The navy fellas slipped it to me when I said I wanted to send a note to his widow, telling her about the funeral. You can send your tokens and jewelry along with my letter, if you'd like. I'm sure Mrs. Cunningham will know better than we could what to do with them."

"That sounds perfect, Fanny Pearl. Give me a week or two?"

"Sure, take your time. No telling how long it'll take to get to her, anyway. I can't think a few more days'll make much difference."

She ought to be able to find the time, now that it looked like Sterling was through the worst of it—she prayed he was, anyway. And Grandma See was in favor of the memento idea, so she would be happy to sit with him whenever necessary to give Evie time in her studio.

Neighbors were still milling about, chatting and enjoying the beautiful day, but Evie turned away. And then stopped. It took her a long moment to place what was off about the people now in her line of vision, but finally her eyes narrowed on the man slouching against a live oak at the edge of the cemetery. He wasn't standing quite right, and his gaze was fixed firmly on the graves. Oddest of all, he looked decidedly like the man who shouldn't have been out of her parents' bed.

How in the world had he given Grandma the slip? Evie shook her head and moved his way, her lips ready to form a rebuke. He looked awful, his face white as the sea-foam. He really shouldn't have come.

But the look on his face stilled her words. Tears had left a damp trail down his cheeks, she saw as she drew closer, and the agony in his eyes was far deeper than the physical. She eased close to him and turned her face back to the graves too. Sometimes all someone could do was *be* with you when the pain was so deep.

After a minute, he dragged in a breath. "I should have done something. I don't know what, but—I should have been in it with them. Maybe if I'd been fighting the fire—or perhaps if I'd been closer in my Zodiac, I could have saved someone. Saved Tommie." His every word screamed England, making her realize how long it had been since she'd left the island.

But his words also were so very wrong. "You would have

gone down with them." That was the most likely "perhaps," which he had to know, logically. If only logic meant anything in such a situation.

"It would have been right. Just. I was the reason—at least then I wouldn't have to face his family and know I'd failed him. Failed them."

He was the reason? For what? Probably nothing. It was probably the guilt of a survivor talking. She reached over and rested a hand on his unburned arm, which was when she thought to wonder where he'd unearthed the too-big white shirt he was wearing. Perhaps in the bin of clothes guests had left behind? It was huge on him—no doubt necessary for his burns and bandages. "There's a reason the Lord spared you, Sterling. Your job is to live each day determined to live that reason out."

"I know my reason." He finally moved his gaze off the graves, down to her.

When their eyes met, the breath she'd been drawing in got all tangled in her throat, and she found herself wishing for that missing glass of water again. He was handsome—had she realized that before?—with his auburn hair and eyes so dark a brown they looked black. But it wasn't only that. It was the fact that she knew the moment he looked at her that, yes, he *did* know his purpose, his reason. He knew what so many people spent a lifetime looking for. And not only did he know his reason, but he was also so loyal to his friend that he'd stand here in obvious agony because he couldn't bear to miss this chance to say a final farewell.

She'd met a lot of people in her life, on three different continents and a half-dozen countries. But not many who had that kind of certainty, much less that kind of strength. Maybe that was what made her throat close up, what made her stomach go tight. Maybe that was what made the weight of her pendant hang heavy over her fickle heart. She'd always had a soft spot for determined people.

She made herself nod, swallowed to open her throat back up. "Good. Knowing your purpose will make it easier to keep going."

"You say that like someone who knows."

A sigh leaked out. "I've stood over my share of graves, Mr. Bertram, and seen my share of services with no graves. Too many of our men are lost at sea and never even make it home for burial. At least your friend's family will know where he is."

Unlike all the other men aboard the *Bedfordshire*. It made her fingers itch for her silver wire, her jeweler's tools. Whether buried here or at the bottom of the sea off their coast, all those men were now a part of their islands. As she turned the shells and glass and stones she'd collected into small keepsakes, she would pray that God would grant their families a bit of comfort in holding a small piece of it in their hands.

Sterling nodded slowly and carefully, clearly aware of what each movement cost him. "He was Catholic. I realize no one knew, but . . ."

But his family, when they learned of his death, would want those final rites given, those prayers said. "I imagine the navy will send someone to take care of that when they realize. There's no priest on Ocracoke. The closest Catholic parish is on Hatteras Island."

Another nod, even shorter, and punctuated with a wince. "I think perhaps I've overdone it."

Not surprising. "Did you walk here?" She didn't know what else he could have done, but the O'Neal family cemetery was about as far from the inn as anything in the village could claim. How had he even found it?

115

A careful shake of his head. "Your . . . grandmother? C—whatever that stands for. She drove me."

Evie's mouth gaped open. Grandma See rarely dared to get behind the wheel of the inn's old car. And even more surprising was that she'd aid their guest in leaving his sickbed. She must have seen his desperation as surely as Evie had. "Elsie. Though if you mean to talk to her, I'll have to teach you the sign for her name, not its sound. She's deaf."

"I gathered." His wince stuck there on his face, and he motioned to something behind her. "The auto is parked over there."

"Well, let's get you back over to it, shall we? Do you need to lean on me?"

He shook his head, though she had a feeling it was more because he didn't want everyone asking questions about who the injured Brit was than because he really felt up to the trek. Respect for him deepened another notch as he straightened and started back toward their old Ford.

Within a few steps, she'd intercepted quite a few curious glances. There weren't many strangers on Ocracoke, and those who were usually had reservations either at her own inn or at the new hotel Stanley Wahab had built six years ago. Either way, the guests could only arrive by ferry, which meant someone had seen them. Talked to them. Learned their names.

She smiled at her neighbors and murmured to her guest, "You've been seen now, which means people will want to know who you are. Do I tell them the name you told me?"

He didn't answer for the space of several shuffling steps. "Perhaps we could leave the 'Bertram' off and offer them 'Sterling'? Put a 'mister' in front if you like?"

"All right. And if you care for a cover story, I've already thought one through."

She hadn't thought his gaze could go any sharper, but she was wrong. It turned to a razor. "Have you?"

Evie waved to the pastor and his wife. She didn't like the thought of lying to her neighbors, it was true, but she knew better than most how important secrecy was if one was in the intelligence game. If it meant helping the war effort and keeping those neighbors safe, she'd tell whatever tales she must.

"You didn't seem keen on anyone knowing you'd been on the *Bedfordshire*. So, we'll say you were on a sailing yacht with friends. There was a small fire on board, and they came ashore with you to seek medical help, Ocracoke being closer than elsewhere. Uncle Garret—the doctor—asked me to board you while you recovered. Meanwhile, your friends continued up the coast to seek repairs for their ship. They'll call for you again when they can."

Similar situations had happened before. And while everyone would find it odd that they hadn't seen this sailboat, there was a lot of unpatrolled coastline on the island, especially on the north end. And Uncle Garret would back her up. It would be odd, but not so very odd that anyone would think to question it, only to gossip about how a handsome Brit had appeared out of nowhere.

"It seems you have thought it through. All right, then. Your story works for me."

She saw Grandma See standing with a few friends and managed to catch her eye. In a few gestures, Evie had conveyed that Sterling needed to return to the inn. Grandma nodded and signed, *Go ahead. I'll walk.* Then she motioned to the cars parked in a neat row.

Evie spotted the gleaming red paint of their eleven-year-old Model T behind an even-older truck. Miss Marge and Miss Ulie were between them and it, and there wouldn't be any bypassing them without saying hello. "Brace yourself," she murmured. "You're about to meet your first of the old guard of O'cokers."

"Hmm?"

But there was no time for more of an explanation. The two old ladies were coming toward them, hands waving and smiles stretching webs of friendly wrinkles over their faces. "Afternoon, ladies," she said before they could get out a word. "Have you met my most recent guest yet? This is Mr. Sterling. He's here to recover for a few weeks." She offered them the short explanation when they asked for it, tucking a smile away in the corners of her mouth when they fussed over his visible burns and made a big to-do over his fine features and lovely accent.

Miss Marge turned back to her. "I sure am glad you and Miss Elsie aren't alone in that big old inn right now, Evie. It isn't safe for two ladies, isn't that right, Ulie May?"

Ulie May Brown—who was even older than Miss Marge—gave a decisive nod that sent the silk flower on her hat bobbing. "Not with Germans in the woods, stealing from us the moment our backs are turned."

Evie barely stifled a sigh. Apparently the talking-to that she'd given Ernest John had not made it back to the trouble-makers. Or even if they'd repented and turned from their ways, it was too late. "Now, ladies, I can't think we really have anything to fear." She could try logic, but that never seemed to get her far with these two. So instead she put on her cheekiest grin. "Another couple weeks and the mosquitoes will be so thick in those woods that any German trying to hide in them will be eaten right up."

The ladies didn't laugh, they cackled. "You're right about that!" Miss Marge said. She aimed her smile at Sterling. "You be careful, too, young man, when you go outside. The skeeters favor the visitors, you know. They get tired of us islanders and look for the new blood."

"That's right. You'll want to brush off your clothes before you go inside. They hide in the folds, you know."

There. Wisdom dispensed, Germans hopefully forgotten, the ladies moved on, leaving them free to continue toward the car. Evie chuckled.

Sterling did not. "Germans in the woods?"

Her smile faded away. It was more of a threat in England, where Europe was a short channel away. Where bombs fell like lightning from the sky. But here? "Miss Marge has gotten a bit paranoid lately, thinking every noise in the night is a threat. And then a few boys started nicking clothes from the line and food, so—"

"Food and clothing?" He came to a halt, pivoted to face her. His gaze cut her to ribbons. "What else? Water? Medical supplies? Things, perhaps, that an operative would need to survive in these woods?"

She shifted from one foot to the other. That glint in his eyes looked nearly feverish, but she knew better than to test his forehead as she'd done so many times over the last two days. "Is that what you're doing here? Looking for . . . But that makes no sense. This is *Ocracoke*. A tiny little island. One little village. A couple hundred citizens and visitors, no more. Strangers don't exactly blend in around here, especially if they're speaking German. And our woods aren't so thick that you can vanish in them for weeks at a time."

But then, no one really went into them. There was a trail or two to the beach through the woods, but it wasn't a hospitable place to while away the hours. Mosquitoes, snakes, poison everywhere. Most of the villagers stuck to the village and the water. She shook her head. "Ridiculous notion."

"It isn't." He leaned down, pitching his voice low. "There

are similar stories from Hatteras and Bodie Islands. It's what brought me here—well, to the Outer Banks. I wasn't exactly aiming for Ocracoke. I didn't realize he'd made it this far south."

"He. *He?*" That made it sound like he knew exactly who this German was. Which meant he was tracking someone in particular. Which meant that this someone needed to be tracked. A shiver wracked her, and her chest went tight, just like it had done on Monday morning, only magnified about a million times. "Into the car, Mr. Sterling. You can explain who *he* is when we can't be overheard."

They didn't need the whole island going into a panic if this was all a bunch of spooks and shadows and rumors. On the other hand, if the threat was real . . . well, then she'd do anything in her power to help Sterling Bertram neutralize it.

9

Sterling had been very carefully trained in distrust. He'd been schooled on what names to give for himself, what secrets never to share. He'd had to prove himself capable of bowing under pressure without breaking.

There was no reason to assume a false name in America, one of their allies. Even so, he didn't recall telling his real one to the very pretty innkeeper he'd seen hovering over his bed nearly every time he opened his eyes over the last three days. He didn't know what else he may have babbled in his delirium either.

But what he did know was that, as astute and trustworthy as she appeared, and as much as she'd already helped him, he couldn't go spilling all the secrets of his mission to her. So, as he tried to hold his injured side off the Model T's seat while it bounced over every blighted rut and pothole in the known world, he gritted out a semblance of truth rather than the pure, unadulterated variety. Enough, he hoped, to secure her help, since he'd obviously need it.

"His name is Karl Meyer." Partial truth—it was one of

the pseudonyms the man had used. "Hitler Youth, SS officer. Do you know much about the German ranks?"

She shot him a look he couldn't quite interpret. Patronizing but patient. "Let's say I don't. What would you want me to know about them in relation to this Karl Meyer?"

He couldn't quite place her accent. It was a far cry from the deep drawl of the two older women they'd been speaking to, nearly transatlantic. She must have been well educated, which surely meant educated somewhere other than this minuscule island. Which also meant she may have learned more about European politics than the average person. "The SS are Hitler's elite officers."

She gave no indication of this being news to her. She still drove with perfect confidence, making the old Ford look more elegant than it had a right to be.

He probably shouldn't have been so touched that she'd donned a dark gray dress for the funeral and wore a black hat with a stylish little black veil. But he was. It meant a great deal that she would mourn Tommie and his crew. "They're also the ones most frequently selected for intelligence work, and Meyer was apparently selected for that years ago because of his ability to blend in with other societies."

"Such as?"

He debated for a long moment. Would it do any harm to share a few bits of information? He didn't see how it could . . . so long as they were isolated bits. "France. England. And now he's suspected to be here."

"Here." Now she shot him an incredulous look through her ice-blue eyes. "On Ocracoke, of all places."

To that he had to shrug. He hadn't imagined for a moment when he was in Norfolk that Mansfeld would have turned up here. It made far more sense that he'd be on the upper islands, with their larger populations and more frequent visitors. How would he have a hope of blending in *here*? She wasn't wrong to find that absurd.

But rumors were all too often indicators of the realities that civilians weren't supposed to know about. "I know it sounds far-fetched, but he could be scouting all the islands in the Outer Banks for his base of operations."

"Operations." Blimey, she had a way of repeating one word so that it drew a giant question mark all over his assumptions.

They bounced over a particularly cruel rut as she made a right-hand turn, and he had to avert his face to keep her from seeing his newest wince. "It's no secret, I assume, that the shipping channels are lousy with U-boats?"

Even her snort sounded lovely and elegant. "It hasn't been dubbed 'Torpedo Junction' for no reason. And of course we know it. We hear the explosions regularly."

They did? He winced again—this time for them. Perhaps it wasn't quite as bad as the Blitz, where those explosions could land on you at any given moment, but still it shook you down to your soul. Knowing that war, that destruction was so very close. And that you were powerless to stop it.

"The theory is that someone is—or will be—signaling the U-boats from the shore, alerting them to prime targets."

This time she didn't echo him. This time she sat in silence, silence that stretched all the way through the last minute of the trip until she'd turned her car onto the sandy drive that led to the inn and parked it in front of the white house. Then she looked over at him, eyes so steady in the face of his words that he had a feeling she'd heard many more shocking things before.

Who in the world was she? Evie Farrow, he knew—but the name didn't tell him why she spoke with a different accent, or why she'd put the pieces of his story together far too quickly. It didn't tell him why she measured him now as if *he* was the one who had to pass some sort of test. "Let's say you're right, and this Meyer chap is here. What do you intend to do about it?"

The walk to the inn's porch looked like it stretched for miles. Which made his next words all the more ridiculous. "Well, first things first. I need to scout out the island and see if he's actually here, or if there are signs that he has been."

The impossibility of the task didn't escape his hostess. "Assuming he is here now—you think he still will be by the time you can do that? That he's looking to set up a permanent or semi-permanent base of operations here?"

"It's possible." Unlike the prospect of getting out of the car and making his way inside without embarrassing himself with his own weakness. "And it won't take me all that long to get back on my feet. I'm made of pretty stern stuff."

"Don't push yourself too hard. *I* can scout the woods if you're seriously concerned about this. I know them better than you would anyway." She pulled the keys from the ignition but sat there for a moment, gloved hands resting on the wheel, slight figure belying the efficiency with which she seemed to run her world.

Not so unlike Mum, in that regard. She may only weigh seven or eight stone, but when she put her strength to something, there was no stopping her.

Sterling forced what he hoped was more smile than grimace. "You seem to run yourself ragged as it is. You don't need to do this." Because how would she know what to look for? What meant Mansfeld and not some local spending time out of doors?

He'd spent the last two years tracking this man down. He knew him better than anyone else outside of Germany, he reckoned. He'd studied his habits, his preferences, his strengths and weaknesses. He knew what he ordered in restaurants in Paris and what brand of cigarette he'd favored when he was in London.

If he was here now, Sterling would know. He'd find him. He'd do it for Tommie, for the rest of the *Bedfordshire* crew. They'd died for it, after all. He'd better make sure it wasn't in vain.

Evie's fingers dropped from the wheel to her lap. "And then what? After you find him?"

Could she read his mind? Her grandmother had certainly seemed to that morning when he was grunting and groaning his way to his feet. Perhaps it was a family trait. "I apprehend him."

"Apprehend—not take out?" She said it so calmly, evenly, like she discussed the killing of spies over dinner every evening.

Sterling reached for the door handle as he shook his head. Might as well get the torture started so it could be finished. "He would be more valuable for the Allies as a live asset. We need to know what information he's gathered, what he's passed on." And, if ever it became useful, use him against the Axis. His father was a high-ranking general. One never knew when that might provide exactly the leverage one needed to turn the tide at a crucial moment.

Details this woman did *not* need to know.

"All right, then. Consider my family your allies. We'll do whatever we can to help—on the condition that you take the time necessary to heal."

He wanted to argue, but he hadn't breath enough. He'd pushed himself to his feet, and the world was spinning around him, sucking all the air from his lungs. He had to brace himself between the door and the car's frame until his vision stopped rocking.

When it cleared, Evie was before him, concern making lines in her forehead. "Let's get you back inside. Perhaps once you're settled, you'll feel up to eating something? Or at least having some broth. That could be part of why you're so weak."

She had a point. And though the idea of food held no allure right now, he might change his mind once he was resting again. And regardless, he needed to try to take in whatever nutrients he could handle. That was a key part of healing. One that he'd praise God was doable, that he hadn't washed up on some uninhabited stretch of beach somewhere with no one to help him, nurse him, or feed him.

His teeth clenched tight against a moan, and all he could manage in reply to her was a nod. She slid an arm around his good side, anchoring him with that arm straight up his back rather than wrapping around to his burned skin. He knew his wounds weren't as bad as they could have been, knew he'd heal . . . but far too many of his dreams over the last few days had been of fire eating away at him, and he could still feel its teeth now.

The journey from car to inn was easily three times as long as the reverse trip had been an hour earlier. At least. Maybe five—if one were measuring distance by his speed. A snail could have passed him without any effort, but at long last the wood of the porch was under his feet and that of the banister in his hand.

"Evie!"

Oh good. He could pretend he was pausing because of the male voice calling her name and not because that tiny shift in altitude up the two steps had felt like climbing the Matterhorn.

Evie made certain he was steady against the railing before she turned. "Afternoon, Herb."

126

Sterling shifted a bit so he could glance backward at the newcomer, who also didn't sound quite like the other locals he'd heard. This one made sense, though. He was wearing a Coast Guard uniform, which meant he'd been stationed here from who-knew-where. He was probably in his forties, this Herb chap, and jogged up the walkway of shell and stones at a mockingly quick pace, face all ease and smiles.

"This came for you. I knew you'd want it right away."

This. It wasn't that Sterling *meant* to be curious about the paper the chap held out. It was that he'd been so well trained in it that he couldn't help himself. He saw the type and heading that indicated a telegram, but it certainly wasn't from Western Union. No yellow paper, no logogram.

A telegram hand-delivered by the Coast Guard? Curious.

Very curious, actually. He'd done what research he could on all the towns and villages in the Outer Banks while he was still on the mainland, trying to identify which would be the most likely base of operations for Gustav Mansfeld. Another reason he'd ruled Ocracoke out was that they were completely cut off. No telegraph, not for the public. Only twice-weekly mail boats. It would be a long and clumsy way to try to get intelligence back to Germany.

There were always the old naval signals. He could literally flash messages to the U-boats with lanterns and electric torches at prearranged times in prearranged places. One couldn't discount the possibility.

But that didn't help civilians receive telegrams. No, so far as he'd been able to glean, they had them delivered with the mail from the nearest office. He could imagine that in emergency situations, someone may send something care of the Coast Guard . . . but Herb didn't have the look of an emergency situation about him.

What, then, made Evie Farrow so special that she could rely on them to play courier?

He watched her fold the paper once, again, and then tuck it into her pocket without so much as glancing at it. Proof that it wasn't important? If so, that made it all the more curious. Or was it, on the contrary, proof that it *was*, but was private?

Under normal circumstances, he would have felt no need to find out what messages his innkeeper was receiving. He didn't make a habit of snooping through other people's post or telegrams unless it was necessary.

But Evie Farrow wasn't an average innkeeper, clearly. She saw too much. Perhaps knew too much. Had perhaps heard him mumbling who-knows-what while he was feverish. For all he knew, she had already reported him to someone or another on the mainland and had made a show to him of protecting his secrecy to keep him here until someone could come and arrest him.

And out-of-uniform intelligence operatives, even when allies, weren't generally well received by the higher-ups. No one liked to think that spies were needed in *their* country. He'd be able to sort it out if he were arrested, of course, but it could lose him weeks of time, during which Mansfeld could vanish again.

Unacceptable. He needed to know if he could really trust his pretty innkeeper with any part of his business, which meant he first had to determine who and what she really was. Which meant he had better get a glimpse of that telegram. Maybe it was as simple as having a relative—or even a husband?—in the Coast Guard or navy who'd received special permission to send her updates. If so, then he'd know it soon enough.

She and Herb exchanged a few more pleasantries that

Sterling barely even heard. It didn't take any great skill on his part to project an air of total exhaustion that gave him a fine excuse for going straight to bed once they said their farewells and Evie returned to his side and led him through the door. He didn't have to exaggerate the groan that had her declaring she'd fetch supplies for a new poultice as well as some broth.

The only thing he had to work at was slipping his fingertips into her pocket, slipping that paper out without her noticing, and tucking it under the blanket until she was gone. That required more effort than it should have, but he managed it. Just as he would manage to slip it back in within another minute, when she returned with more of the honey, aloe, and herb spread she'd been slathering on his burns.

He granted himself a moment to draw in a deep, steadying breath once she'd bustled out to the kitchen. Then he eased the paper out and unfolded it.

His brows knotted. This wasn't a message from a relative. It was gibberish. Random-looking letters and numbers and—no. Not random. Encrypted. He recognized that much, having a code of his own assigned to him that he was to use on any communications between him and his superiors.

But what in the world was a North Carolinian innkeeper doing with encoded telegrams?

Even were the lines not blurring before his tired eyes, he knew he wouldn't have a prayer of cracking it, not without some sort of key to guide him. He was no cryptographer. He could decipher his own communications only because he had the instructions on how to do so, and even that took him half of forever each time.

"I'd ask if you were in the habit of stealing things from your allies' pockets, but the answer seems obvious."

He started, silently cursing himself for not hearing her approach. Though now he had to wonder if it was because he was so tired or because she was trained in sneaking up on people herself. He looked up, half-expecting to find that wicked little pistol she'd first greeted him with aimed at his face again.

But no, she didn't need the weapon. Her eyes were doing a fine enough job of piercing him through. Sterling held the paper back out to her, not certain whether he ought to apologize or try to convince her that it had simply fallen from her pocket.

She'd know the lie, though. Of that he had no doubt. So, as she took the page back—not snatching it, just taking it as easily as one would a promised recipe—he offered only the truth. "Merely trying to puzzle you out."

Her smile was somehow teasing and challenging all at once. "I daresay you need a few more pieces yet to do that with any success, Mr. Bertram."

"Sterling, you'll recall. And I should call you . . . ?"

That question seemed to give her more pause than finding him with her private correspondence in hand. She held completely still for the space of three heartbeats and then slid the tray she'd been balancing on one palm onto the bedside table. "Let's stick with Evie. Keep it simple, shall we?"

Simple? Laughable. But he wasn't going to argue with the name. "Evie." He leaned back against the pillows and gave in to the pull of weight against his eyelids. "I wager I can find those missing pieces in no time. I'm quite good at such things, really."

"Think so?" She chuckled, even as her fingers moved with their usual gentleness over his bandaged arm. Rolling up his sleeve, unpinning the bandage, rolling it away from his mottled flesh with more care than he'd proven himself deserving of.

"I do." It wasn't just his training. It was what had made him a prime candidate for it. "Do you not? Perhaps you want to spill your life story to me."

"And deprive you of the joy of discovery?" She shot him a grin that was enigmatic in its very openness. "But let's strike a bargain, shall we? I promise to answer your direct questions with honesty. So all you have to do is land on which questions will give you the answers you really want."

Fair enough, if she meant it. And it was hard to be suspicious of someone whose touch was so careful and whose voice was so bright and who had promised not only to help but to keep *his* secrets.

Besides, his recovery would no doubt be long and boring. Playing sleuth would be more of a joy than counting the knots in the wood panels of the floor, once he was up to it.

He nodded. Stole one last glance at her. And then let the sweet waters of darkness lull him away.

Evie slid into the warmth of her studio, letting the scent of salt and the hay from the main part of the barn ease the knots from her shoulders. As she always did when she came out here, she let her gaze drift along the walls, where countless baubles and sculptures dangled or rested on shelves. Sea glass in every color of the rainbow. Shells of every shape and size. Some married to silver, others to gold, still more to wood. Boxes and necklaces and earrings.

Prayers, all of them. Each piece found while she was praying for a particular friend or relative or need of her own heart. Each piece a reminder of God's faithfulness.

Many she'd given away over the years. Others she kept. A

few, now and then, she sold to a visitor who offered her way too much for them, when she felt that whisper in her spirit that said she needed to give this piece of herself, and they needed to give of their bounty.

On her desk sat the bucket of shells and glass that she'd mentioned to Fanny Pearl, but she wasn't quite ready to start on those.

Not as long as that telegram from Davie rested unread in her pocket.

She heaved a sigh as she slid onto the bare wooden chair she kept out here, shaking her head against the image of Sterling Bertram with her letter in his hands, total confusion on his face. It had been amusing enough to defuse the quick snap of anger she'd felt.

But then, what had she expected? She'd already decided he was an intelligence agent. She oughtn't to be surprised, then, when he acted like one.

But he was a field agent, not a cryptographer. She'd seen none of the excitement at the recognition of a puzzle that Davie always had in his eyes.

She'd never loved the mathematics of it quite as much as he had, but it still only took her a few minutes with a pencil and a fresh sheet of paper to turn the short message Herb had delivered into something legible.

He is legit. One of ours. Did not dig much deeper to learn why there but will. Thanks for helping him. Miss you. Love from all.

As she had suspected. It brought a measure of relief to know her instincts had been right. But not enough to long counteract the penetrating sorrow when she spotted that new collection of shells and glass.

She could help Sterling Bertram do his duty to king and country, and she could create something of the Ocracokers with which to memorialize those sailors who had died for them . . . but in neither case could she actually *fix* anything that had gone wrong. She was one small grain of sand squaring off against a hurricane.

But each grain of sand played its part. She drew her tools to her, turned her heart to prayer, and prepared to do hers.

10

YESTERDAY

AUGUST 5, 1914
OCRACOKE ISLAND, NORTH CAROLINA

It was over. Finished. Done. Rem had known for two months that this day was coming, yes—or feared it, anyway—but now he held the proof in his hands. A telegram, its paper yellow and uncompromising, Father's words upon it. It had arrived with the other mail, and he'd taken it from Miss Serena without any sense of foreboding, without any shake of his hand, without any shadow of doubt passing before the sun.

He'd been laughing with Louisa. He didn't even remember why, now, as he stared down at those stark words. Something about . . . Grann? Elsie? Garret? Or about his own clumsiness with whatever tool she'd tried to teach him to use that morning?

He couldn't remember. It had been only twenty minutes

ago—but yet another lifetime. Because now, on this side of the telegram, everything was different. The idyllic had been proven a lie.

Had he said anything or just stumbled out of the kitchen, off the porch, to the sand? He didn't know that either. Only that now he stood on a beach far from the inn, facing east. England. His future.

England had declared war on Germany. It wasn't a surprise, but he'd hoped the day wouldn't come. He'd prayed it. And he'd deliberately kept the blinders in place beyond those hopes and prayers. He'd avoided the newspapers and walked away when talk turned to war. He'd focused on Louisa. Learning her and Celeste's code. Learning sign language. Reading, teaching, chatting.

Two days ago, he'd been all smiles when the letter from the teaching college arrived for Louisa, saying not only that she'd been admitted, but that her tuition had been paid in full by a scholarship. He'd taken his turn when she embraced everyone there but hadn't let himself hold her too long. Hadn't let himself even *think* about his own part in it, lest she see it on his face.

Just as he hadn't given in, in these months since Garret Wynnwood had come home and Archduke Ferdinand had been assassinated and Grann had sat with him in the sand and told him to take the risk of loving Louisa, to the urge to draw her into his arms and kiss her.

He still wasn't certain that Grann was right. Especially the more he saw Louisa with her longtime friend. Perhaps Garret wasn't the second son of a baron, nor the heir to a business magnate in Maryland, but he was everything Rem wasn't—confident, strapping, and completely at home in Louisa's world. He knew her in ways Rem couldn't. They had a history together. Rem ought to leave them to each other and be grateful for all he'd learned about himself this summer.

"Hey. I was beginning to think you'd started swimming for England when I couldn't find you." Louisa's words slid like the tides up the shore of his soul, soothing and yet obliterating all the sandcastle arguments he'd been building. His eyes slid shut as he felt her slip up beside him.

Her fingers slid into his. She'd made the move before, when she meant to tug him somewhere. But never like now, to let her fingers rest in his, around them, between them. Taking their two separate worlds and declaring they could be, at least for a moment, one.

He tightened his fingers around hers, not caring if she could tell from the way he clung to her how desperate he was. "England declared war on Germany." Five simple words. Five simple, earth-shattering words.

She squeezed his hand right back. "I saw in the newspaper. It was on the front page. The telegram was from your father?"

He nodded. He'd told her all about his father's plans for him. Family honor and duty on that side, Mother pulling him from the other. He'd told her everything, these last few months. Everything but the most important thing. *I love you.*

"He called you home?"

I love you. He nodded again and kept his eyes on the choppy waves of the Atlantic. If he looked at her, saw the light in those sky-blue eyes, he'd forget himself. Forget all his reasons for leaving her to her island life. Forget that she'd be better off without him. "It wasn't as bad as it could have been. He says the Admiralty is creating a new division that I'll be perfect for—something at a desk. He said I don't even need to officially join the navy."

That one had taken him by surprise. A job with the Admiralty that didn't require a commission? Father's exact words had been *It's perfect for you and you for it. You can do your country good and enjoy every day of the work.*

He would have been thoroughly intrigued, had the reality of leaving Louisa not cast a pall over everything. What could Father possibly have found for him that he'd actually enjoy doing?

And more unbelievable still—did Father really know what would make him happy? Or would he get home to find a prospect even worse than a naval command?

"Well, that's good, then, isn't it?" The words of a friend—except that they cracked and broke on the word *good*, making them sound anything but.

"Louisa." He didn't mean to turn to her, to look into her perfect face. But never had he imagined hearing her cry. Laughing, teasing, yelling—yes. But crying? He could scarcely believe he was hearing it now, and what could he possibly do but wrap his arms around her and hug her close? *I love you.* "It'll be all right. The war won't last long, Father said." Which was why he had to get home now, to catch it before it was over. As if war was something he ought to want to be a part of.

But she shook her head against his shoulder and held onto him like she'd be sucked out to sea if she didn't. "I'm sorry," she gasped out through a sob. "I told myself I wouldn't—I can't ask you to stay. I know that. But . . ."

But she wanted him to? How could that even be? His hands, without any command from his thinking mind, slid up her back, into the hair pinned at the nape of her neck. He tilted her head back, needing now to look into those eyes he knew would brand him. Had already branded him. He saw there what he could scarcely believe. An echo of the pulse beating through his own veins. A reflection of the words beating their way to his lips. "I love you."

He shouldn't have said those words—had spent two months talking himself daily *out* of saying them. But there they were, bald and bold and spoken, and he couldn't have wished them back even had he tried. They sounded too true to his ears. Tasted too right to his tongue. Felt too necessary to his heart.

Her nostrils flared, and her fingers knotted in his shirt-front. "I love you too, Rem. I—I didn't mean to. I know it can't end well. But I do."

They were just one in a long history of ill-fated romances—he knew that. He knew neither of them would be well served by surrendering to it. Yet he felt completely helpless to resist its pull. To back away again.

Or perhaps that was an excuse he tried to make for doing what he'd been wanting to do for so long. For leaning down an inch, another. For letting her see his intent in his eyes. For giving her a long moment to pull away, to run, to insist on reason and list all the ones that said this was a bad idea.

But she pulled him closer instead, and she strained up on her toes, and in the next moment, his lips were on hers.

She tasted of the sea—her tears, or from the salt breeze?—and of a million impossible tomorrows and of every hope he hadn't dared to dream. He kissed her until he couldn't even hear the birds drifting overhead or feel the rush of warm seawater over his feet, until there was no differentiating any-more between her and him, possible and impossible, dream and reality. And when at last he pulled away, he said the only words that would come to his lips.

"Will you marry me?"

Her eyes, hazy blue skies, cleared with a snap, and she eased back an inch. "What?"

Her incredulity should have made him stumble, fumble his way backward. But it didn't. He tucked one of her escaped curls behind her ear and held her familiar electric gaze. "Marry me. I know all the reasons we shouldn't, but I don't care. You can come with me now—I'll see you're enrolled in a college at home while I'm doing whatever it is Father's arranged for me. And then, when the war's over, we'll split our time however we need to. Here, there, Maryland—I don't care where we end up, so long as we're together."

"Rem." Her tone sounded like it always did when she was chiding him for something he'd forgotten, some task he hadn't known to perform. But her eyes were blazing hope. "Your family would never accept me. You know that."

"They'll come round. And really, what choice would they have if we presented it as a *fait accompli*? We could marry here, have your uncle perform the ceremony. Now, today, tomorrow—whenever he would agree." He needed to ease off, give her space. Let her think about it. He knew that, but even so he had to bite his lip to keep from demanding an answer quickly, now, before whatever mad courage had seized him vanished again at the thought of parents and wars and a tall, handsome doctor.

She looked first in one of his eyes, then shifted her focus to the other. If it was doubt she was searching for, she'd see a multitude—each and every doubt about whether he was really the best thing for her. But if it was assurance of his love that she sought, then she would see that too. The certainty that he'd spend a lifetime trying to be the best thing for her, if she granted him the chance.

Her smile started slow, small, just a seed, then a rosebud. It unfurled like petals in a warm spring sun, opening fully with beauty enough to knock his breath from his lungs. She came up on her toes again and pressed her lips to his. "I'll marry you, Remington Culbreth. Today or tomorrow or yesterday, if you could have arranged it."

Either the sun exploded or that was the purest joy he'd ever known. Laughter bubbled up, and he pulled her tight to his chest again.

Yes, there were still a million reasons this was a bad idea, but they could provide a million and one to make it work.

⁂

"You are a stark, raving lunatic. I'm going to have you committed to an institution."

Rem had never much cared that his cousin was an inch taller than him—until today, when he would have loved to outpace him. He didn't slow his stride or change his course at Edgar's buzzing about like a mosquito at his ears, but Rem's ignoring him didn't slow his whine any either.

"And your mother! What in blazes do you think *she's* going to say when you tell her you've up and married some innkeeper's daughter who—"

"Edgar, do shut up." If only he could bat him away like one of those mosquitoes—or slap him. That would have a certain satisfaction. "There is nothing in the world you could possibly say that I haven't already considered."

"There has to be—because if you had considered everything, then we wouldn't be walking to the church right now to ask Linc Marshall to *marry* you to his niece!" Edgar leapt in front of Rem to block his path, swiping his hat off his head and slapping Rem on the arm with it.

He halted to keep from running into his cousin. And he snatched the offending hat from Edgar's hand, too, and tossed it to the ground. The walk from inn to church was a short one, which his cousin had apparently taken to mean he had to interrupt if he meant to have his full say.

Rem hadn't often taken a stand against anyone in his family, not for anything more substantial than whether or not he'd join the day's hunt. But this—this was important. This was crucial. This was *everything*, and his cousin wasn't going to get in his way. Rem only knew one way to stand firm, though. He drew in a long breath, blew all the frustration out with it, and looked deep into his cousin's eyes. "Eddie, I appreciate your concern. Truly. I know you want the best for me. I know this isn't a logical decision, and it's a match society won't accept. I know all that. I know that I'm likely consigning myself to a life lived here with her and her family, because mine won't accept her. I know that too. But even knowing all that . . . this is what I want. It's the only thing, I think, that I've ever really wanted. I love her in a way I've never imagined loving anyone. Can't you understand that?"

Edgar looked physically pained. "Of course I can—but that doesn't mean you should *marry* her."

And that was why he hadn't sought his cousin's advice *before* he went to find Louisa's uncle. With a pointed look that made it clear he wasn't interested in any less-moral options, Rem sidestepped Edgar and continued his march toward the church and the small living quarters Linc occupied beside it.

The mosquito followed. "This is absurd! If you marry her now, so quickly, you're going to regret it for the rest of your life!"

"Quickly! What do you think I've been wrestling with all summer?" He'd spent two entire months trying to talk himself out of the possibility of declaring himself to Louisa.

Edgar blinked at him, eyes blank. Apparently his dear cousin hadn't even noticed his internal conflict—yet he thought himself worthy of offering advice now? Hilarious. "Well, wrestle some more. If you love her now, you'll love her still after the war, won't you? The papers say it'll be over by Christmas. Come back then, and if you still feel as strongly—"

"No." He knew how it sounded, like he was certain it wouldn't be the same in another four or six months. And he *was* certain of that. Not that his heart would change, or that hers would, but that the sand could wash out from under them by then. A hurricane would cut a gulf between them, like it had done to Hatteras seventy years ago. Circumstances would change. They'd get caught up in their careers. Logic and fear would gnaw away at him until he'd convinced himself it had all been his imagination.

They had one chance—this chance, today. If they were bold enough and brave enough to take it, then they could forge a path forward together. But if they turned away, if they hesitated . . . then the rest of their lives, they'd wonder what could have been.

He didn't want to wonder. He wanted to *know*.

"Rem!"

But he was at the parsonage now and jogging up the stairs, raising his hand to knock on the door. He'd done this very action scores of times since his arrival in May. Linc Marshall had the best library on the island, and Rem had taken him up on his offer to borrow anything he liked from it.

Edgar, however, had never joined him here and didn't seem inclined to mount the steps now. As if putting foot to a pastor's home might somehow effect a change that attending church never had, unfortunately. Hesitating at the bottom of the steps, he called up, "Ask him who her father is!"

Rem didn't even spare his cousin a glare at that one. He didn't care who her father was. This wasn't about social standing or family ties, which he'd seen firsthand did not create a solid foundation for marriage.

Linc pulled open the door, his usual smile looking half-doused in confusion. "Rem?"

ROSEANNA M. WHITE

Before Rem could so much as open his mouth, Edgar called up, "Tell him, Reverend! Tell him he *can't* marry her!"

Being an intelligent man, Linc apparently didn't need any help figuring out who the "her" was. He stepped aside, clearing the path for Rem to come in, and let out a heavy breath. "Are you going to join us, Mr. Grenshaw, or simply shout from my step for the whole village to hear? Yes, hello, Miss Marge! I see you there listening."

Rem turned just in time to catch the nosy neighbor—the one who'd never seemed to like Louisa for some reason—slam her door closed across the lane. But Edgar spun away, too, so that was good, at least. Rem let loose a sigh of his own and slipped through the door, to the familiar room lined with books.

He'd perused these shelves almost daily since he'd arrived and more often than not had taken a seat in one of the buttery leather chairs after he'd done so. He and Linc had talked about everything—theology, mythology, the theory of evolution, scientific advancements, automobiles, aircraft, mathematics. Everything, that is, but Louisa. Rem had no idea what her uncle might have to say about this, and the not-knowing made it impossible to sit. Instead, he paced to the shelves, hoping they could provide calm.

Behind him, Linc clicked the door closed. Rem heard it catch, heard soft footfalls, the squeak of the leather sofa giving way to Linc's weight. Then the gentle clearing of Linc's throat. "Well. Took you long enough. I was beginning to wonder if you weren't the type to seek the permission of a young lady's closest male relative after all."

So then he *had* known. Rem spun around, glad he didn't have to explain his heart again. "We're hoping you'll marry us. Before I have to leave in a few days' time." Despite his relief, he very nearly launched into a heartfelt assurance that

143

he loved Louisa more than life itself and would do anything for her . . . but the look on Linc's face stopped him cold.

It wasn't disapproval. It wasn't quite wariness. But it definitely showed concern. Linc glanced toward the door. "Your cousin seems to object."

Rem moved to his usual chair and sank into its welcoming embrace. "My cousin has been too well indoctrinated with the family biases."

Linc didn't laugh it off—that was one thing that had made Rem take to him so quickly. No matter how absurd, the man always gave each thought due consideration. He treated everyone and every opinion with respect. And now he held Rem's gaze steadily, something odd in his. "If you *were* to ask me the question Mr. Grenshaw said you should . . ."

Rem shook his head. "I won't. I don't care who her father was."

Linc tilted his head to the side. He was in his midforties, his hair more silver than the sandy brown it must have once been, but he had the same piercing blue eyes as Louisa. "If you were to ask . . . I wouldn't be able to answer."

"You—what?" Rem felt his own face mirror the confusion that had been on Linc's when he opened the door and saw Edgar. "Wouldn't be *able* to?"

Linc shook his head. He didn't look bothered by this inconceivable fact. He looked, rather, as though he were testing Rem with it. "When my sister moved back here, bringing baby Louisa and Grann with her, I'd just been appointed to the island parish. I'd known that she'd married a man named Michael Adair, but I hadn't been able to make it to the wedding. I'd never met Michael. I knew he'd died, knew it had broken my sister's heart. But I never saw him, other than in Louisa."

Not knowing what else to do, Rem nodded. He couldn't

144

imagine having that between two siblings as close as he and Serena were . . . but then, he was doing something similar to Sebastian, wasn't he? Marrying a woman he'd never met, not waiting for him to come, even if he could. Was that why Linc was cautioning him about it?

Linc leaned forward, resting his forearms on his legs. "I took one look at that beautiful little girl, looked at my sister, and she said, 'Don't ask me, Linc. Don't ask me any questions whose answers will hurt the life you've chosen. If you don't know, then you don't have to answer for my decisions.'" He shook his head, broke eye contact, dropped his gaze to the rug at his feet. "Perhaps I should have pushed. Perhaps it was cowardly of me not to. But I never did. And that's what I've therefore been able to tell my parishioners for the last eighteen years—that I don't know who her father was, who my sister married, other than that he was a fine man. We'd exchanged a few letters, and I respected him. I knew he loved Serena. That was all I knew. All I know to this day."

Michael Adair must have been something more—or less?—than a regular laborer, then, to warrant that sort of response. Ocracoke Village, after all, wasn't exactly the high society of the capital area. They wouldn't have judged him for humble origins.

But there were plenty of things they *would* judge. Perhaps he'd been an illegitimate child. Or something far worse in the eyes of a Southerner—from a family who had sided with the Union during the War Between the States.

He didn't quite comprehend all the nuances of the relations between North and South, but he knew enough not to try to insert himself into the middle of it with anything so futile as logic. It would have to be enough that he didn't care about Michael Adair's history in relation to Louisa. "I

145

don't think it's cowardly to protect your family or the peace. And I don't intend to ask those questions either."

"And you've made that clear to Louisa? That you don't intend to pursue that line of questioning?"

He couldn't imagine she'd ever think he *would*, given the many serious conversations they'd had about the worlds they came from. His very proposal was an assurance of how little that mattered to him, wasn't it? He nodded. "Crystal clear."

Linc still held him in that serious gaze of his. "Because it matters to *her*. It matters that she has no more answers than I do about such things."

Rem's nod was somber, understanding. Now that he thought back on their many conversations, he could see that quite clearly through the empty places, the questions she didn't ask, the subjects she veered away from. "I can't give her those answers, obviously. But I can promise her that we'll make something new together. That I will help her discover what I can, if she wants to learn it, but will never push her." He didn't know what else to offer, what other assurances to make.

Linc nodded and pushed to his feet, paced to the window. Was Edgar still out there? Was that what kept the frown creasing his brow? "It'll do her good to get away from Ocracoke for a while. But she'll want to come back. She'll want to see some of the world but then come back here, like her mother and I both did."

"And that's my plan too," Rem put in quickly. "I said as much to her right away. That we can split our time between the island and England and even Maryland—wherever she wants to be. And I'm not asking her to give up on her schooling either. I would never ask her to give up her dream."

At last, Linc's lips turned up in a soft smile. "I'd never

think you were. I suspect you had something to do with her receiving that scholarship, actually."

Yesterday he may have denied it, when his plan had still been to simply leave her to her life. But what was the point of such a denial today, when their lives would be one? He shrugged. "She deserves a chance at an education."

"She does." Linc turned away from the window. "You're a good man, Remington. One I know we're all proud to welcome into the family. As long as you're both fully aware of the challenges that await you—"

"We are, sir." He stood, too, unable to stay seated now, when the thought of all that lay before him shimmered there just beyond his vision. "But we'll weather them together."

Linc nodded. "Then you have my hearty approval, my blessing, and my willingness to perform the ceremony."

Rem may never stop grinning. "I'm truly honored by your approval. I'll do everything in my power to make her happy, sir, I promise you that."

Linc nodded again, and his smile didn't fade. But he glanced again to the window—a reminder of all those mosquitoes waiting to bite.

Well, they could wait awhile longer. He knew that trials would come, and in droves, most likely. But today, tomorrow, however long he could, he'd cling to the good. To the sunshine. To the blue skies. To the dream.

Louisa Adair was going to be his wife. How could even war in Europe dim the joy of that?

11

The train chugged and churned and hurtled Louisa ever farther away from everything familiar, ever nearer to whatever a future as Mrs. Remington Culbreth would hold. She was two parts excitement and one part pure fear as she sat in her first-class seat, nose practically pressed to the window, as the mechanical beast took her from familiar lowlands to rolling hills.

Rem slid closer to her, and his fingers found hers. Untangled her clenched hands, then re-tangled her fingers with his. Funny how much safer, more certain she felt when she was touching him. Hoping her sigh captured only that happy two-thirds and none of the abject terror, she leaned back against him. "I wish this trip would go on forever."

His chuckle sounded like the ocean to her ears, deep and strong and beautiful beyond words. "That fond of train travel, are you?"

More than she suspected she would have been had she taken her first train ride by herself—in third class, on her way to the teaching college in Raleigh. But her desire for time to stand still had nothing to do with the plush seats or the sumptuous meals they'd been served and everything to do with not wanting to arrive another step closer to the war that was pulling them to England.

But this was their honeymoon, short and stressful as it may be. She wasn't going to sully it with too many questions about what lay ahead. Better to enjoy the feel of the arm he slid around her, the citrusy scent of his cologne, the way he trailed his nose down the side of her face. "Maybe the war will be over before we can even get there."

"Perhaps so. In which case, after I show you all my favorite places in England, we'll simply hop over to Paris and look up Celeste, shall we?"

"That sounds perfect." She smiled, not just at the thought of the reunion with her best friend that her soul certainly craved, but because of how amazing it was that she'd found a man who dreamed of it along with her. Whenever she'd mused with Garret about finding Celeste, he'd always shaken his head in that too-practical way of his and said, "Neither of us will ever make it to France, Lulu."

She squeezed her eyes shut, not wanting to think about Garret, but thoughts of him were already pummeling her. The way he'd been so tight-lipped when she told him she was marrying Rem. The hurt in his eyes. He hadn't said anything against it. The two men had gotten to know each other over the summer, and even Garret with his biases couldn't argue that Rem wasn't a fine man.

But she'd never meant to hurt Garret. And much as she was certain that there was someone out there to love him like she loved Rem, someone he would love far more fiercely than he did her, her certainty didn't soften the blow any for him.

She'd had to pretend she hadn't seen the sheen in his eyes when she stepped out on the inn's porch in her wedding dress—Mama's wedding dress, frantically remade. She'd never even seen it before Mama pulled it out the evening Rem proposed. But then, as she'd fingered the lace and the silk, she'd wondered. Wondered at the wedding it had been made for, the quiet affair with none of her family present. Wondered at the man who had inspired frugal, selfless Mama to spend so much on such a fine gown.

Wondered if that wedding had been legal. Wondered if her own would be. Tried a dozen times to work up the courage to ask, and a dozen times she had taken the easy way out and stayed silent. She told herself that if it was a problem, Mama would have said something. She hadn't, which surely meant it wasn't.

Right?

Her silence had been cowardly, yes, but she'd needed it. Needed to let herself get swept up in the joy and not worry about those shadows. She'd focused on the meal and the cake and that too-beautiful dress.

It had seemed a crime to alter it, but Mama had insisted, and before Louisa had been able to wrap her tongue around an argument, Grann was there with scissors and a seam ripper, laying out the plan for how to make it more modern, and the two had set to work. All Louisa had been able to do, then, was try the dress on when they told her to.

It had been gorgeous. Perfect. Fit her like a glove, looked just like a dress from one of the magazines Mama subscribed to. And somehow it didn't feel too strange on her, even though she'd never had a life that gave itself to silk and lace dresses.

She was wearing another one now, though. The first order of business when they reached the mainland had been to take a day to do some shopping. It had been Edgar's idea, and though he'd said it with the same patronizing tone she'd loathed all summer, she'd decided to assume he was being kind. He could have let her arrive at Rem's mother's home in her old dungarees and humiliate both herself and him. Rem hadn't seemed to have given her clothing a moment's thought.

But they'd had fun, going into stores whose doors she never would have dared to darken. They hadn't gone too crazy or anything. A couple of nice but understated day dresses, one nicer dress for church, and—at Rem's insistence—two evening gowns for dinner.

Because apparently his family dressed—as in, dressed *up*—for dinner each night. Obviously they weren't first the ones making and then serving the meal. At least thanks to all that serving, she knew proper etiquette. He'd be proud of her, she'd make sure of that. She'd learn quickly, and she'd make it her goal never to embarrass him. It shouldn't be too hard in Baltimore, but the thought of learning to keep titles and aristocratic address straight was enough to make her stomach flip.

Though, to be fair, so did the thought of meeting his mother. He certainly hadn't made her sound like the warm and accepting sort, and if Edgar's mumbled warnings were a good indication, she was about to enter a battle zone long before they reached Europe.

Well. She came from a family of strong women well used to carving out the life they wanted. She would simply live up to that legacy and do them proud in the face of however many scowls Edith Culbreth directed her way.

A knock sounded on their compartment's door, and when Rem called out a "Come in," Edgar Grenshaw slid inside. Over the last few days, he'd gone from vocally opposed to resigned to even wishing them well . . . with his lips, at least. She knew he thought she was the biggest mistake his cousin had ever made, but when Rem had threatened to have him barred from the ceremony if he didn't promise not to object, he'd done a pretty quick about-face. Whether he'd meant his well-wishes remained to be seen.

He didn't even look her way now, though. He had a newspaper in hand and tossed it to their table, his expression what she could only term worried. "Have you seen this? What the Huns have done?"

Louisa looked to the front page along with Rem and sucked in a breath. GERMANY TAKES THE WAR BENEATH THE WAVES WITH U-BOATS. "U-boats?"

"Underwater boats equipped with torpedoes. Our surface ships have no way of spotting them. No warning until they strike." Edgar slid onto the bench across from them, his gaze locked on his cousin's face. "They're patrolling the waters around England, Rem. Between these new menaces and the mines we already know are being laid in the water—it's too dangerous. You can't go back. Tell your father you'll do your duty from here somehow or another."

U-boats . . . and mines? Louisa made sure her breathing stayed calm and even, even though every nerve in her body turned to ice.

Rem went so still beside her that she suspected he was taking every bit as much care. "And you think my father would be convinced by the argument that I cannot join a war because it's dangerous? It's *war*. Of *course* it's dangerous."

Edgar slapped his palm to the newsprint. "But to take such risk to get home to a desk job? Rem—"

"You know that won't budge him."

It was more than that. She could hear it in his voice. He might chafe against the yoke of expectations draped over him at birth, just like Jingle did from time to time, but much like her pony, he didn't *really* want to rebel, not in any lasting way. A toss of the head, maybe a dash here or there to somewhere he shouldn't be. But when it came down to it, he would do exactly what was expected of him because he wanted to. Wanted to make his family proud. And the fact that Lord Culbreth had made an effort to find him a position he would enjoy, that meant the world to Rem.

She squeezed his fingers, hoping the silent encouragement would tell him that she understood. That she loved him for it, even as she wished there were another way.

He squeezed her fingers back, but the gaze he turned on her was troubled. "He does have a point about the dangers, though, darling. I'm not certain I'm comfortable bringing *you* into such waters."

For a long moment, the words didn't compute. And even when they did, she wished they hadn't. "I'm not afraid." She made sure to keep the words soft, gentle, as sweet as she could make them, keenly aware of Edgar watching them like a hawk.

Rem shook his head. So why did she know in her bones that it wasn't a refutation of the claim? "Of course you're not. But *I* am, for you. I can't bear the thought of you being in harm's way. It's something we'll have to think about. Pray about. Perhaps it would be wisest for you to still attend school here this autumn after all. If the war is over by Christmas, we could reunite in the new year, either here or there, whichever you prefer. A spring trip to Paris, perhaps?"

She loved his eyes. The way that hope and fear and sorrow and joy all mixed in their depths, just as blue mixed with green mixed with gold, just as water mixed with minerals mixed with sand. If they didn't have an audience, she'd lean over and kiss him—something still so new even as it was becoming deliciously familiar. She'd assure him with a touch that any risk was worth being with him. That if he found that danger, she wanted to be right beside him.

For now, words would have to do. Careful words. She didn't want to argue with him in front of Edgar. "Springtime in Paris sounds like just the thing, regardless. We'll sort out the best way to arrange the meantime."

"Could be for the best," Edgar said, as if they'd asked for his opinion. "Or even, rather than school, some training time with Aunt Edith. No offense intended, Louisa, but you'll need some instruction on how to run an estate, you know."

She knew how to run an inn, didn't she? How different could it be? But rather than speak that thought, she simply sent her new cousin a smile that didn't feel nearly as warm as the one she'd given her new husband. Maybe that was her pride talking. Maybe it *was* different. She'd never had to manage servants or anything like that, after all. And, frankly, she didn't want to imagine doing it now. Not with all of Grann's stories always floating around the back of her head. Granted, servants weren't slaves these days, but she'd seen the way visitors sometimes treated their hired help, and it wasn't a whole lot better.

Maybe she could teach *them*—this whole world of society—a thing or two.

She turned her smile back to Rem before it could turn amused while directed at Edgar. Listen to her, thinking she could remake the world. She never used to be such an idealist. Blame Rem's love for that, she supposed.

She couldn't tell whether Rem was seriously considering Edgar's words or not. "We shall sort it out soon enough."

They'd have to. His father expected him back in England.

Louisa settled back against the cushion, keeping her shoulder touching Rem's arm as Edgar launched into a list of all the many reasons why "training" in Baltimore would be bet-

154

ter for her than a semester of school, not the least of which was that she was never going to be a teacher if the two of them intended to travel.

Details they hadn't fully sorted yet—details that it would be a joy to sort with Rem. But Edgar didn't get a vote in how they chose to map out their future. She let her eyes drift back to the window and the ever-changing scenery. It looked different now. Less like the gleaming new world that they'd walk through together. More like a bare-toothed monster ready to leap between them.

She'd known when she accepted his proposal that it would require revising her old dreams, exchanging them. She'd been eager to make that trade—still was. But something went tight and hot in her chest as she looked down to their joined hands. His, the hands of a gentleman—fair and smooth and elegant. Hers, the hands of a workman—callused and chapped and several shades darker than his. That heat in her chest was sparked by the flint in Edgar's eyes and fanned by the notable contrast between their fingers.

For the first time since he kissed her four days ago, doubts crept in. What if she *couldn't* fit into his world, even with training at his mother's hand? What if she embarrassed him? Shamed him? What if he regretted marrying her?

She couldn't let that happen. Wouldn't. If that meant studying titles and proper address and how to dress rather than how to teach children, so be it.

She was Mrs. Remington Culbreth now. Whatever that meant, she'd take it.

◆━━━◆

Remington House wasn't a *house*, not like Louisa was used to seeing on the islands. Even the grandest of the homes on Ocracoke were no more than six or seven bedrooms, the inn included. It, after all, had been designed as a wealthy ancestor's home. But her ship-captain great-great-grandfather who'd made enough of a fortune to build a nice house for his family clearly had nothing on the Remingtons.

The place was a palace, a mansion like the ones she'd seen only in sketches and photographs. Maybe not quite Versailles, like she and Celeste had once drooled over together, but as she caught her first glimpse of it, it took all her self-control to keep her jaw from dropping. It was huge and white and had manicured lawns that looked as big as all of Ocracoke. They were a few miles outside of Baltimore now, this beautiful car having met them at the train station, and in a whole other world.

One where a chauffeur in livery had greeted them with a stiff bow and held open the door for them. She'd tried to smile at him, but the man hadn't even met her eye.

Maybe he'd noted, as she had, that their faces were the same color, even though the shape of his nose and mouth said that he had African ancestry. Maybe he saw it and hated her for being the one climbing into the car instead of driving it. Maybe he'd labeled her an interloper in that first second of seeing her. Maybe he knew she'd be more at home poking under the hood of this car and figuring out how its engine worked than sitting here on the plush seat beside the heir of its owner.

The engine coughed as they made the final approach, and she saw the driver wince and glance at them over his shoulder, like he expected a rebuke.

Edgar, it seemed, was never one to disappoint. "I say, Adam, aren't you supposed to give this thing a fine-tuning before you take it out? What if it died alongside the road and left us at the mercy of the undesirables 'round about?"

Undesirables? Who exactly were *they*? Louisa arched a

brow at Rem, but he only gave her an embarrassed little smile—one she'd seen from him countless times over the summer, whenever he wanted to apologize for his cousin but didn't dare to do so out loud.

"Yes, sir. Sorry, sir. I did, sir, but I'll go over it again as soon as we get in, sir."

Four *sirs* in that little line, which she suspected said more about the kind of family the Remingtons and Grenshaws were than how decorous this Adam fellow would have been by nature.

She tried to bite her tongue—she did. But she'd had enough of Edgar over the summer when *she* didn't dare say anything to offend him. She couldn't when he was a guest at their inn, when his money was what would keep them fed and warm that winter.

Now, though, she wasn't at his mercy. She was Rem's wife, not just an innkeeper's daughter. Which must have made her bold enough to overcome that long-trained silence. "Edgar, don't be a tyrant. This car is in excellent condition. A hiccup now and then is to be expected of any mechanical device. Or are you the kind who will berate your doctor for not prescribing you a syrup *before* you begin coughing?"

Edgar shot her an unamused look, an arrow of ice. Rem, however, chuckled and reached for her hand, gave it a squeeze. "He is, at that."

His cousin rolled his eyes, but his face brightened again. "It's good to be home, isn't it? I didn't realize how much I missed it until now."

He must be referring to the area in general. Rem had already told her that Edgar and his family lived a couple miles away, closer to the city. But maybe not. Edgar was looking toward the imposing facade of Remington House the same way she always looked to the Ocracoke Inn—like it was where everything in the world that mattered could be found.

Rem barely glanced at it. Nor did he make any reply beyond a noncommittal hum. Because it *wasn't* home for him. Yet he was the one who stood to inherit it all.

Edgar couldn't appreciate that. Perhaps Mr. Remington was only his great-uncle, but they must be close for him to feel so welcome here. Did he resent Rem for being the grandchild instead of the great-nephew? For being in line to inherit based on nothing but expectation?

She was careful to keep the sigh that leaked out quiet. And winced along with Adam when the car coughed again as he slowed before the massive front entrance. Edgar wasn't the only one to glare at him this time—so, too, did the quartet of well-dressed people waiting on the front steps.

The eldest of them was clearly Rem's grandfather. He had a full head of snow-white hair and Rem's eyes and nose, but a mouth that seemed permanently set in a grim line. He held a cane in one hand but didn't seem to be putting much weight on it.

Beside him was a woman who looked to be in her mid-forties, dressed to the nines even in the afternoon. Rem's mother? She must be, given the way her gaze went straight to him through the window, and a smile broke out on her mouth. She had familiar coloring—hair the same shade as Mama's. Funny how the same words that could be used to describe them both—blond-haired and blue-eyed—totally failed to capture their differences, though. Mama had Southern stubbornness and grit to underscore her grace and beauty. Edith Culbreth looked like something chiseled out of granite and then draped with gold and silk. Her smile was beautiful but not, to Louisa's eye, warm.

The other two must be Edgar's parents, Henrietta and

John Grenshaw. They came forward, too, hands raised in greeting and a great deal more cheer in their faces.

Maybe Edith Culbreth wasn't as demonstrative a person. Or maybe her joy at her son's homecoming was overshadowed by the knowledge that he'd soon leave her to go and fight in England's war. Or maybe it was because she didn't appreciate the fact that her son had gone and gotten married while he was away.

That final option seemed far too likely and made Louisa's pulse skitter like Jingle in a thunderstorm.

All too soon, Adam was opening their door and helping her out. She stepped aside to make room for Rem and Edgar, willing them to emerge quickly so she wasn't out here alone.

Because none of those four people so much as looked at her. Their eyes were only for the young men, and they converged upon them in such a way that Louisa found herself stumbling back a step, out of the way, nearly tripping over her new pumps' heels. She might have fallen and made a true spectacle of herself if not for Adam, who steadied her with a gloved hand to her elbow and a low "Whoa there, ma'am. You all right?"

Ma'am. She'd been called that a couple times in the last few days, and each one of them was a bit of a zap. She smiled and nodded. "Thank you."

Maybe she would have said more, but Adam moved off, and she felt Rem searching for her, even as his mother took his arm. She turned them both toward Louisa, beamed a smile at her, and said, "Now introduce me to your bride, Remington."

Edith had to have been hurt over not being invited to the wedding, but her countenance showed nothing but welcome. Not exactly *warm* welcome, but Louisa had no trouble returning the smile. Rem, though, looked a little odd as he glanced past his mother, toward his grandfather. Mr. Remington didn't say so much as a word of greeting, nor did he even glance at Louisa.

It seemed to have the effect of turning Rem into a granite statue himself. For the first time in their three-month acquaintance, she had the feeling she was looking at a baron's son. Master Remington Culbreth, not just Rem.

He lifted his chin, sidestepped his mother, and held out a hand for Louisa. She slid her fingers into his as he said, "This is my wife, Louisa. Lu, my mother, Edith. Grandfather Remington. And Aunt and Uncle Grenshaw."

Louisa curtsied, just as Grann had taught her and Celeste to do in a giggle-filled lesson when they were ten and Grann said it was "high time you learn to comport yourself like young ladies instead of wild beasts." Louisa said, "How do you do?" just like Rem had told her she should, because apparently society in England never said "nice to meet you" for some reason he hadn't been able to adequately explain.

So why did Edith Culbreth break into laugher and press a hand to her mouth? "Oh, Remington—her accent! No doubt you've put it on, my dear, to shock me. It can't *possibly* be so thick!"

It wasn't the insult that got to her. It wasn't the flash of cruel amusement in the eyes of the Grenshaws or even the way Grandfather Remington spun for the door without any word of greeting at all. It was the way Rem's muscles jerked as if he'd been hit by a dart, the way his nostrils flared in an anger she'd never seen in him before.

It was because she'd been there all of a minute and already she was causing more strife between her husband and his mother, adding to the burden on his shoulders instead of shouldering it with him.

His words came out tight and low. "There is nothing wrong with how Louisa speaks."

Edith's face froze, then horror flashed across it. "Forgive me! I thought you'd planned a silly joke. Of *course* her accent is perfectly charming—and we can certainly polish it before we introduce her around. A few diction classes, and all will be well."

Diction classes? Louisa had to bite her tongue then and there. But Lady Culbreth was reaching out a hand in greeting, thinking her offer was one of graciousness, so what was Louisa to do but take her fingers and dredge up a smile? "Whatever you deem necessary, my lady."

Edith smiled again. At least until her gaze fluttered down to their joined fingers, and then a little gasp chased the smile away. "It seems my son didn't think to buy you gloves, my dear."

Louisa reclaimed her scolded fingers and curled them into her palm. The shopkeeper had in fact tucked in a couple pairs, but Louisa hadn't thought to wear them. And Rem hadn't told her she should. "I beg your pardon, Lady Culbreth. I'm not in the habit, but for when we go to church." Gloves had, in fact, always been for Sundays only in her mind. Why wear them otherwise, when they'd interfere with her work and get soiled in a matter of minutes?

Edith renewed her smile. "No matter, it's all family here. And we'll make certain you learn all those small details before anyone else meets you."

Louisa tried to keep her smile on her lips, but it was spluttering far more than the car's engine had done. Only here for minutes, and already she was failing to live up to her mother-in-law's expectations. "I'm ready and eager to learn whatever you have to teach me."

Edith nodded, smiled at Rem, and patted his arm. "Well, darling, we have your rooms ready for you. Why don't you show Louisa inside? I imagine she's eager to tidy up after your journey."

They were kind words, gracious words. But still Louisa barely saw the entryway, the sweeping staircase as wide as their whole front room, nor the endless corridor he led her down. All she saw was the wall of things she didn't know, the things she hadn't learned, the certainty that a few days or even weeks wouldn't be enough to teach her how to keep from disgracing her husband in his world.

She wasn't sure all the time in the world could accomplish that.

12

Rem strode into his mother's drawing room with frustration pumping through his veins. He slammed the door instead of clicking it shut, in a way he hadn't dared to do since he was a child.

Mother looked up from her book, though Grandfather didn't stir from his newspaper. Rem marched over to where she sat on the sofa and glared down at her. "Why? Why did you have to greet her like that, to make her feel immediately lacking? Gloves—who really cares about gloves? And you, of all people, ought to have had the grace not to comment on her accent! How many years did it take for society to stop mocking your American intonations?"

Mother sighed and looked up at him like he was a dunce. "Remington, do calm down. *You* are the one who has done that girl a disservice. What were you thinking, bringing her into this world unprepared? How could you be so cruel to her?"

"What?" He backed up a step, brows knitting. "You will make this *my* fault?"

Her lips turned up a bit into an indulgent smile. "Who said anything about fault? And I *am* sorry if I offended her or hurt her feelings, and I'll be happy to apologize. But truly, darling, I only want the best for you both—and you have to see what a hard spot you've put her in. Now, sit down and we'll decide how best to undo the damage you've done."

Damage? He sank to the sofa, obedience too long ingrained for him to flout it. "I love her. And I—"

"Good, I should hope so. I can't think why else you'd do this to the poor girl, if you weren't blinded by affection." Mother reached over and rested her gloved fingers on his wrist. "Remington, you *know* what a challenge it proved for me to enter your father's world, and I was only an American, not from a completely different social set. This girl, lovely as she is, is completely unprepared. Why would you ask this of her if you love her? Why would you force her to walk this gauntlet?"

At this rate, he'd spend the rest of the day frowning. "What gauntlet? Mother, you make it sound like I've turned her over to an executioner by asking her to marry me."

"Is it really so different?" She straightened, angled away from him, toward her father. "Perhaps it would be different if you meant to stay here. We could look out for her, teach her. But if you mean to take her to England with you . . . Well, I certainly hope she loves you as much as you clearly love her. And that it's strong enough to withstand the cruelties of the London *ton*. I assure you, comments about gloves and accents will be the least of it."

He darted a look at his grandfather, too, though he didn't quite know why. Rem had visited Remington House every year of his life, but his patriarch felt as much a stranger to him as the portraits on the wall. He was all things austere and stoic, a man who had traded his daughter and a sizable portion of his wealth across the Atlantic just for the prestige of a noble alliance. He had never been the sort of grandfather to bounce a lad on his knee or play tag with him, to teach him how to shoot or how to ride a horse. No, he was the type that expected a recitation of one's accomplishments since the previous year, laid out in a neat queue that would never, ever get full approval from him.

But he looked up from his newspaper now. Even folded it and put it aside. "Perhaps that is the answer, then. Remington, I have already made arrangements for you to take up leadership of the business upon your return from your duties in England. From all I hear, that shan't be but a few months. Why not wait until your return to present your wife to *our* society and save her the trial of London's? In the meantime, we can tutor her. See her properly outfitted. Make a few private introductions, even, to other young ladies whose husbands you'll enjoy getting to know upon your return."

His return . . . to the family businesses. They'd written out everything for him while he was gone, it seemed. Never consulting him.

But they were suddenly granting the need for him to do his duty to England. That was new, and surely a good sign. And perhaps they had a point about London being too big a leap for Louisa just now. Still, he had to sigh. "We were discussing the possibility of her staying here for a while, anyway. It seems the waters around England are a bit dangerous. But I don't think she'll agree to it." And much as he wanted her safe, he also wanted her with him.

Grandfather's face darkened. "I was reading about that myself, and I admit to great uneasiness. I know there will be no talking *you* out of traversing them. Your sense of duty is strong, and that is to your credit. But one cannot be too careful in such times. The Germans, too, will be determined

165

to end this war by Christmas, and that could well mean un-precedented attacks on even civilian ships."

Unthinkable. And yet he'd read the words himself in black and white in the newspaper. U-boats and minelayers were in English waters, and the mines didn't know which ships were going to sail across them. They may be intended for the Dreadnoughts and battleships, but that wouldn't stop a cruise liner or merchant ship from crossing one and paying the price.

A risk he would have to take—but not one he wanted Louisa to take. Especially if life would be as bad for her in England as Mother seemed to think.

But how was he to convince his wife of the wisdom of that without making it seem like he was changing his mind about wanting her to be a part of his world? Especially now, with all those Mother-inspired doubts swirling through her head?

No. No, they would simply entrust themselves to the will of the Lord and proceed with their plans. "I can appreciate that concern, but even so. It would hurt Louisa too much to leave her behind, even for only a few months. I'll be booking two tickets at the first opportunity."

Mother's brows drew together. "Can't you see, though? What will hurt her far more is to subject her to English society. They will destroy her, Remington. She will be mis-erable there."

She was surely exaggerating—wasn't she? And besides, he didn't really intend to pick up with high society in London. That was Sebastian's lot, not his. He'd prefer to carve out a circle for himself somewhere in the academic crowd, and Louisa would get on fine in that society.

Still, it would be wise to prepare her. To let Mother take her shopping and go over any finer points of etiquette that Louisa would need. Give his bride a couple weeks to acquaint herself with his world before she was expected to perform in it. "Perhaps a short delay, then. A fortnight here, so you can train her."

He pinched the bridge of his nose at the headache those words brought on. Maybe he *had* been cruel to expect this of her. Maybe it had been purely selfish of him—he loved her, wanted her beside him. But what if she hated life away from Ocracoke, like Mother had hated life away from Baltimore?

Mother's blink was too long. "A fortnight. You think a *fortnight* will be enough to teach an island miss how to be a lady of society?"

"It's all I can spare."

Some of the testiness he knew so well filtered into her gaze. "You're being obstinate. The best thing for her would be to let her spend the autumn here with us. I know you don't want to be separated, but that's what happens in war. A thousand quick marriages, a thousand quick partings. Perhaps it will be difficult, but you'll have the certainty of knowing she's waiting for you."

He met his mother's gaze, trying to see her as a woman, as Edith, instead of as *Mother*. Tried to understand what it had been like for her, moving an ocean away from everyone she knew to marry a stranger she'd only met a handful of times at a few summer balls. "I appreciate your concern, I do. I know how difficult coming to England was for you. But it'll be different for Lu. I'll make certain of it. We simply won't move in those circles, we'll—"

"Remington." Mother patted his wrist, annoying condescension on her face now. "Whether you like it or not, you *are* in those circles, and she will have to be as well. And while I'm certain it *will* be different for Louisa than it was for me, I can only think it will be *worse*. Had I thought for a moment that I ought to take all those warnings your cousin was sending home seriously, I would have come down there weeks ago to meet her for myself."

Rem had been poised to argue about that "worse," but frowned now at that new information instead. "Edgar? What has he been saying?"

Mother waved a hand. "He was simply concerned with your growing attachment to a girl he said would be unsuitable to be your wife. I hadn't thought it worth our intervention, but—"

"Intervention?" He stood, knowing his face was every bit as stony as Grandfather's. "Let's establish this here and now. I do not need you to intervene in my life and certainly not in my marriage. Louisa and I will make our own choices. When we need your advice, we will ask for it. Otherwise, please respect our decisions and trust that you have raised me to make sound ones. Am I understood?"

Mother regarded him steadily for a long moment, not so much as blinking. Then she glanced over at Grandfather, some silent communication filling the air between them. At last, she shifted her shoulders and nodded. She didn't go so far as to smile, but he dared to think a measure of respect had entered her eyes. "You are understood. And you have my word that I will apologize to Louisa at once, and that I will do all in my power to see you happy."

Rem released the breath that he hadn't even realized he'd pent up. "Good. Thank you." That was all he could possibly hope for. More. Because he knew better than anyone that when Edith Culbreth put her force behind something, she was as unstoppable as nature.

A few minutes later, he climbed the stairs again to their suite of rooms. And smiled when he let himself into their private sitting room and saw Louisa at the window, looking out over the expanse of gardens and lawns. "A far cry from the view you're used to, I know. But hopefully one you can appreciate for a short while now and then."

He'd half feared that he'd come in here and find her with tear tracks on her beautiful face, that she'd have cracked at the sudden burden thrust upon her. But he should have known better. She turned to him with a smile, her blue-as-the-sky eyes boldly unclouded. "As often as you like. And I won't embarrass you either. I know there's plenty I have to learn, but I will. I'll change my accent if I have to and wear stupid white gloves and dress up like it's Sunday every day of the week if that's what it takes."

He laughed because she said it like . . . like *Louisa*. Like she knew it was ridiculous but would do it anyway and find joy in it. Like she'd focus on the challenge, but not without poking a bit of fun at it.

How could it be that she was his? All summer he'd felt that pull to her, like one end of a magnet to its opposite. But all summer, he'd made himself stop just short of touching her, just short of moving *friend* into more. Now he could walk right up to her, slide his arms around her. Now she came up on her toes and pressed her lips to his.

She still tasted of sunshine and ocean waves. He hoped she always would, even after months in Baltimore or years in England. That she would always look at a new car not for its beauty but for the engineering that went into it. That she'd admire a suite's plumbing above its decorations. He rested his forehead on hers. "I love you. And I have no doubt you'll not only learn but soon be an expert—it's your way, after all."

Her fingers brushed through his hair, trailed down his neck, and came to rest on his chest. "Well. I don't know that this will be as easy as fixing a boat motor for Doxee, but I'll give it my best go."

He smiled again, kissed her again. Then sighed. "My mother means to apologize later, and she promised to do all she can to help you. She and Grandfather think it would be wise for you to spend the autumn here, but . . ."

Louisa narrowed her eyes. "You're not going to England without me. If the Germans mean to take you out, they'll have to take me too."

He had to smile at her ferocity. That, also, was pure Louisa. "I told them we weren't going to be separated. And we'll show the Germans, won't we? We'll win this war ourselves. Single-handedly. With our tactical genius and unparalleled strategy."

Her eyes slid closed. "And then Paris in the springtime."

"We'll find Celeste. Impress her with your new fashions, which Mother will insist on before we go anywhere. Drag her to a few museums."

That earned him a real smile, one even his mother couldn't cast a shadow on. "I think I'll write to her before we go back downstairs. Tell her all about the glove fiasco."

"As long as you exaggerate how I heroically defended you." He swept her up into his arms, smiling into her laughter, and carried her toward their bedroom's door. "You really do look tired, Mrs. Culbreth. I think it would be wise to rest before dinner."

"You know, Mr. Culbreth, I was thinking the very same thing."

THREE WEEKS LATER

"There. Give it a try now, Adam." Louisa straightened from where she'd been bent over the engine bay, wiping her hands on the already-oily rag she had sitting there. When the engine turned over without the cough and sputter that had been

170

plaguing it, she let out a whoop of victory and brandished her wrench in the air like a sword.

Adam slid out from behind the wheel, a grin all but splitting his face. "Cain't believe it. This thing's never started up so smooth, not from the day they bought it."

Louisa laughed and slid the wrench back into its spot in the toolbox. "That's because it's never come up against Louisa Adair—Culbreth." Blast. She still wasn't used to answering to her new name. Rem's mother always called her Louisa, his grandfather never even acknowledged her, and they hadn't really ventured out in public too often to make introductions to anyone. Instead, their free hours—when they weren't trying to secure tickets across the Atlantic, which had proven a challenge, what with everyone afraid of the new U-boats—were spent in etiquette and diction lessons.

She tried to tell herself it was schooling, that it would help not only her but Rem, and so she ought to be grateful for each moment of her mother-in-law's time. But mostly she left each encounter all the more certain that Edith Culbreth would dismiss her from Remington House in a heartbeat if she could.

No matter. They were leaving for New York on this afternoon's train, and from there, England.

Adam came around the hood to look at the engine with her, everything purring and rotating and spinning like it should. "Never imagined saying this to a Mrs. Culbreth, but you have a real gift with mechanical things. Ma'am."

She snorted and slapped the rag to his arm. She wouldn't exactly call Adam a friend—not like Celeste or Garret were, not like Rem had so quickly become. But he was the closest thing she had at Remington House other than her husband.

"Lu?" Speaking of whom.

A smile sprang to her lips and had her darting out of the

carriage house with a wave of farewell for Adam, barely remembering to swipe the dratted gloves off the roof of the car where she'd left them. Her good mood froze when she saw the look on Rem's face as he approached, a telegram in hand.

Telegrams, it seemed, only ever carried bad news these days. Her stomach dropped. "What? What is it?"

He sighed and looked up, his blue-green eyes clouded. "There's been a mix-up with our booking on the *Ignatius*."

"A mix-up?" She stepped to his side, slipping her arm through his, so she could look at the note from the shipping company.

The words were short and blunt. There had been an error, and they had overbooked the ship. One of their tickets had been moved to their sister ship, which would be departing from Baltimore Harbor in three days' time, rather than from New York tomorrow.

Louisa huffed. "That's absurd. Why would they split our tickets instead of moving someone else who was traveling alone?"

"I have no idea. I rang them up and tried to argue the point, but they insisted they had no way of rebooking a pair of tickets unless we wanted to wait another three weeks."

Louisa wrinkled her nose. Three more weeks here, with etiquette lessons and diction classes, with Mr. Remington ignoring her and Edith trying to hide the fact that she thought her a dunce?

Rem sighed. "I can't wait that long. Another wire came from Father, too, telling me in no uncertain terms that if I didn't get home soon then that peach position may not be there for me."

"So then . . ." It didn't sit right, the idea of separating. But was she being childish? Selfish? "It's only a week. Ten days at the most, right? You go on the one from New York, I go

172

on the one from Baltimore. You'll probably arrive a day or two ahead of me, but I'll be right behind you."

Not ideal . . . but not horrible. A week apart. Yes, she'd have to brave the steamer on her own, and it wouldn't be nearly as much fun as traversing the Atlantic by her husband's side. But she would bring reading material to keep her company and spend the time writing long letters to Celeste and Mama and Grann.

Rem heaved a sigh and pulled her tight to his side. "I don't like it. But I don't know what else to do."

"It'll be fine." And surely it was her job to encourage him. She conjured up a smile and nestled close. "We'll be back together in no time."

Which was why, a few hours later, she was waving farewell to her husband as Adam drove him away and left her behind. When she finally lowered her arm after the car was out of sight and turned back to the front door, she turned to find her mother-in-law behind her, her face cold and hard.

Disappointment that her son had gone back to England? Or was that ice aimed at Louisa?

The question seemed answered when she said, "Perhaps you should take your dinner in your room tonight. I don't believe my father is feeling up to a formal meal, and I feel a headache coming on."

Right. More like she didn't want to suffer Louisa's company without Rem there to make it necessary. Well, that was fine. A quiet evening sounded far better than subjecting herself to a maid's fussing over her hair and gown. Even if it *was* strange to go back to her room and see all Rem's things gone. Her trunk looked lonely there without his, and the room felt absolutely cavernous.

But it was only for a few days. She sat at her desk and wrote a love-filled letter for him, running it down for the mail with a grin. It would likely arrive right around the time he did, only days before she rejoined him. Still, it would be fun for him to get a note from her. Maybe she'd write one for each day they were separated.

Which could be longer than expected. The next morning, another telegram came, saying her ship was delayed. Instead of leaving in a couple days, it would be another week.

A *week*. It shouldn't matter, but it made her shoulders go tight and tense. She didn't want to spend another week here. She didn't want to be away from Rem for a fortnight or more. But what was she to do?

She tried to find Edith to ask her advice, but her mother-in-law had gone out, apparently. Calling on friends—friends to whom Louisa wasn't ready to be introduced, it seemed.

Not certain why that made her mood tumble even further down, when she didn't even *want* to meet the lady's friends, Louisa sighed her way back to her room again.

Her trunk still sat, lonely and solitary, in the middle of the floor. She'd told the maids not to bother unpacking it. It seemed too much of a hassle for two days. But a week was different. Everything would be a wrinkled mess if she left it all in there that long.

She wasn't about to pull the bell for a maid, though. Not when she was perfectly capable of unpacking a trunk herself. It wasn't as though it took her more than a few minutes to hang the lighter garments back in the wardrobe and fold the heavier ones into drawers. The few books she'd brought with her went onto the little desk, along with the paper and pens Rem had restocked for her the other day.

That was all. Which made her frown. It *shouldn't* have been all. Where was the little box of jewelry that had gone into the very bottom of the trunk? She hadn't all that much— a topaz necklace Rem had bought for her last week, claiming it complemented her eyes, and two pieces he'd selected from the family vault for her.

Pieces she didn't dare to lose. What would Edith say if she knew? They weren't Louisa's, not like the topaz. They belonged to the Remington family.

But it wasn't as though Louisa had lost them. She'd tucked them into the bottom of her trunk herself, and then the maids had packed her clothes. If the jewelry case was gone, *she* wasn't the one who'd done it.

Did that mean one of the maids had stolen it? Louisa frowned at the thought. The last thing in the world she wanted was to get any of the hired help into trouble. She'd tried to befriend them all, in fact, but had been ignored. Rem had finally convinced her to leave them to their distance, saying it was the way of things and provided them with a comfortable invisibility.

She had her doubts but had relented. On this, though, she couldn't exactly remain silent. So, she waited at the window until she saw the car coming back up the driveway, then hurried down to meet Edith before she could disappear.

Her mother-in-law didn't look exactly thrilled to see her, so Louisa got right to the point. "So sorry to bother you, Lady Culbreth." Never, even with Rem here, had Edith invited her to call her anything but Lady Culbreth. Calling her by her first name in her thoughts was all the rebellion Louisa allowed herself. "I was unpacking my trunk just now, and the jewelry case is missing. I hate to implicate anyone in taking it, but—"

"There are no implications necessary." Edith unpinned her hat and lifted it from the pouf of her hair. "I instructed it to be removed."

She—what? Louisa blinked at her.

Edith sailed past. "Did you really think I'd let you take my mother's jewels to England? Never."

175

Louisa spun after her. Was this about Remington pieces going to England, or was it about *her*? "You could have simply said as much when Rem gave them to me! You didn't need to order them stolen!"

Perhaps that wasn't the right way to approach it. Edith halted, pivoted, her eyes flashing fire. "It is hardly *stealing* when it is one's own things being reclaimed."

Louisa didn't mean to lift her chin in defiance. She just couldn't stop it. "The topaz was not *yours*. Rem bought it for me, and it's the only thing I really care about."

Edith released a delicate, derisive snort. "That thing? It's worthless. Which is, I suppose, why you like it so well."

Louisa's mouth fell open. "I beg your pardon?"

"You haven't the taste to match your scheming. But know this." Though she only took a single step nearer, it somehow felt like she'd reached out and slapped her. "I see right through you. You lured my son in with your wiles, you convinced him to marry you all because you wanted him to take you from that miserable little island and spend his money on you. Well, it won't work. I have investigators working even now to determine the best grounds on which to have your ridiculous marriage annulled. That 'booking error' was a well-placed bribe, so I could get the two of you apart long enough to sort it all out. You will *not* be joining my son in England, and you will *not* be so much as touching anything of my family's with those filthy brown hands of yours!"

Filthy? Louisa sucked in a breath as if she'd been punched. Her hands had been dirty plenty of times in life and would never be the shade this woman wanted them to be. But to accuse her of low motives, of money-grubbing and conniving? "You think you can stop me from rejoining him?"

Edith's smirk may have been another slap, if she weren't still reeling from the first. "There was never any second ticket from Baltimore, girl. And the only one I will be purchasing for you is back to North Carolina, I promise you."

Girl. She said it like Marge Williams always had. Not like she was a child, but like she was a servant. A slave. Without the dignity of a full person. "You think you can bribe and pay off every steamer in America? I'll go to each and every port myself and find my *own* ticket back to my husband."

"And pay for it how? Without my family jewels, you don't have anything worth enough to hawk for a ticket. That topaz is barely worth more than glass."

As if Louisa would sell the one piece of jewelry Rem had actually bought her. For that matter, as if she'd have even thought to sell his family heirlooms. "Why would I need to do that?"

Edith paused, thoughts flashing through her eyes. "He didn't leave you with cash. He was carrying it, and I assured him he didn't need to get it back out, that I would supply you with pocket money."

"No, but I have the accounts." Even as she said it, she wondered if it was an ace she should have kept up her sleeve. If perhaps Edith had forgotten that Rem had turned twenty-one while he was in Ocracoke, which meant that he came into full possession of the accounts held in trust for him. She certainly hadn't considered that he'd have added Louisa's name to them all last week.

But she realized it now, and a dark, angry victory flashed through her eyes. "And there we have it, all laid bare. You have his money—all you wanted. And what are you going to do with it, hmm?"

Louisa's nostrils flared as she backed up a step. "What will I do? Buy a ticket to England! *Rem* is all I want, you horrible woman, not his money!"

She flew for the stairs before Edith could impart another

barb, though it didn't stop her from imagining a dozen more insults hurtling toward her.

She should have known that the woman's apology, her seemingly cordial reception, was too good to be true. She should have known that there was no way she'd accept Louisa so easily, that the woman Rem had always said had tried to dictate his life wouldn't let him make such a big decision for himself without trying to ruin it all.

Annulment! The very notion made Louisa slam her door closed in a way that would have had Mama scolding her had she dared treat a door at the inn that way. But she didn't care if it brought all of Remington House down around her. She flew to the wardrobe, grabbed out all the clothes she'd just hung up, and tossed them toward the trunk.

Her eyes were burning. Her chest was heaving. Her stomach was churning.

She gave the trunk a halfhearted kick and collapsed onto the chair at the desk. She just wanted Rem. Not his horrid mother or his dismissive grandfather or this stupid world to which he belonged. Just *him*.

She pulled forward a piece of the paper, uncapped the pen, and scrawled *Rem* at the top. She wouldn't send this to him, whatever she poured out on the page—it would be too ugly and full of recriminations. But she needed to get it out.

Why did you bring me here? They hate me. Your mother has told the staff to steal from me, has accused me of all manner of vile motives. Your grandfather simply pretends I don't exist. I know I promised you that I'd learn, that I'd become a part of your world, but how, Rem? How, when they so clearly want to believe the worst of me?

I don't know how to fight this battle. I don't know how to win this war. Give me a hurricane, give me a flood—there are actions I can take there to keep things safe. I can board up windows and move valuables to higher ground.

But there is no higher ground here. I've been nothing but kind since I came here, I've done everything I could to convince them you didn't make a mistake in marrying me. But they don't want to see. They don't want to give me a chance. And if they won't, when they have a reason to love whoever you love . . . how will anyone else in your world?

What have we done, Rem? Have I managed to ruin your life, like your mother thinks I have? All I wanted was to fill it. To be a part of it. But if instead I've ruined everything, then what am I to do?

She squeezed her eyes shut, not even sure where that fear came from. She ought to scratch it out, not let those words stand, even if no eyes but hers ever saw it.

She'd burn them later. For now, she might as well finish.

I wish . . . I wish we'd never come here. I wish I'd never stepped foot in this accursed house. Then, at least, I wouldn't know. I wouldn't know how much they hated me simply for being me. For not being good enough or sophisticated enough or . . . or whatever it is that's wrong with me. I wouldn't know, and then I wouldn't have to wonder how many doubts they've managed to plant in your mind. I wouldn't have to wonder if, when we're together again, you'll take one look at me and wonder why you married me, what you'd been thinking, how you ever could have thought that I'd be able to be Mrs. Culbreth.

I wouldn't have to wonder if you'll soon hate me too.

She tossed the pen to the paper, staring at the words. Hating them, those deepest fears of hers, now spelled out in black and white.

Her vision blurred again. And she jumped an inch off her chair when someone knocked on her door. She'd barely spun around to croak out a "Come in" before it flew open.

Edith swept in—an Edith she'd never seen before. An Edith with hair a-shambles and cosmetics smeared and cheeks paler than the moon. An Edith clutching a yellow piece of paper like it was the dagger that had pierced her heart.

Dread hit harder than a freight train, propelling Louisa to her feet. "Edith?"

Edith pressed a quivering hand to her throat. "There was a fire. On the ship, just a day out. He . . . he . . . he's *gone.*"

Gone? No! Louisa wasn't aware of moving, but in the next second she was at Edith's side, taking that telegram from her fingers. That ugly yellow paper with its horribly official letterhead and its impossible, impossible words.

Fire aboard the vessel Ignatius. *All souls lost.*

There were more words, condolences, empty letters and spaces that had no meaning.

Nothing had meaning. Not anymore.

She wrapped her arms around Edith. And they wept.

13

TODAY

JUNE 13, 1942
OCRACOKE ISLAND, NORTH CAROLINA

Evie took the last of the towels off the line, humming as she dropped the wooden pins into the bag with their sisters. A few quick folds with the help of a raised knee, and into the basket went the towel. She took a moment to turn her face up to the warm sunshine, to breathe in the scent of clean laundry and salt air and the bread that Grandma had baking in the kitchen.

There'd been another explosion somewhere out at sea that morning. The Coasties had been manning their boats as she arrived. She could only pray no other sailors were about to wash ashore, absent their souls.

Better to focus on the world that kept turning, the small mercies God poured out day by day. Clean towels, good food, a home she loved. Work to keep her hands busy.

She glanced at her studio but felt no pull to go there right now. She'd finally finished the last of the pieces for the families of the crew of the *Bedfordshire* and walked them over to Fanny Pearl that morning after she'd dropped the men's sweets off to them. Her fingers, truth be told, were still a bit cramped from the many hours with her tools in hand in that final push, and she was ready for a break from silver wire and needle-nose pliers.

She always felt that way—until she found another piece of glass while she was walking and praying, until she needed to turn that prayer into something solid. But for today, it was enough to carry her basket back into the kitchen.

Grandma See stood at the stove, stirring a pot that would be soup for lunch. They exchanged a smile as Evie slipped through, then out toward the linen closet. She peeked into the main room on her way back, where Sterling was supposed to be propped up on the couch with a pillow and a book.

Sterling was *not* propped up on the couch with a pillow and a book.

She'd already passed the bathroom, which had stood empty—where was the man now? Back in his room, maybe? He was supposed to ring a bell when he needed something. She could have heard it, even out in the yard, with the windows being open.

Stubborn man. How did he ever expect to get well enough to go galivanting through the woods in search of German agents if he wouldn't rest? He'd already set himself back two different times by trying too much too soon. She stepped into the room, hoping he was perusing the bookshelves for something more interesting than the history he'd chosen an hour ago.

He was in there, at least, not traipsing through the trees or trying to catch minnows in a net like last week. But he was not at the bookshelves. He was at the wall, like he'd been three different times in the last two days, staring at the family portraits. Again.

She slid over to his side, trying—again—to see the old familiar things like he must be seeing them. Though today he wasn't looking at the old snapshots from her first trip to London. He was studying the more recent ones. "Are you going to ask? Or wait for answers to materialize in the background?"

His lips quirked up in that way they always did when she all but offered to lay her life's story out for him. "I'm puzzling it out. I'll have you all sorted in another day or two, Evie Farrow."

He'd been saying that for a fortnight already.

He tapped the frame of the photo they called "all the womenfolk." Grann, Grandma See, Aunt L with baby Vi in her arms, Mama, Grandma Ree, Evie when she was no more than six. Women with skin of every shade, hair of every color—though the black-and-white photograph hadn't captured that—but their smiles were all matching. Family, even where they weren't. Family, even when they shouldn't have been.

"I recognize Elsie, of course." He moved his finger from the younger Grandma See to Grandma Ree. "Her daughter? And . . ." The finger moved to Aunt L. "Granddaughter? Is that your mother? Or—no, that was a direct question. Don't answer yet. I'm not finished stitching it."

Evie laughed, even as she drank in the images for the umpteenth time. Not everyone in that photo was still alive to smile at her, and she missed the ones who were gone something fierce. "Keep stitching, then."

"Shall I confess something?"

There was a twinkle in his eyes as he asked it, which made

her think the confession couldn't be too heavy. She tilted her head. "I hear it's good for the soul."

He nodded toward the photo to the far left, the one of her and Davie, their arms around each other's waists, a manor house behind them. "I peeked behind the frame on that one. So I know that this fellow's name is David. And that your full first name is Evelyn."

He'd have had to take the whole frame apart to see where those words had been written on the back of the photo. *David and Evelyn.* "Then you also know it was taken at Spring-bourne Hall on June 12, 1935."

He nodded, looking mighty proud of himself as he rocked back on his heels. "I thought that looked like familiar terrain, and I was quite right. You've been to England."

And she loved it there. It wasn't quite Ocracoke, but it had its own charm. Peacocks strutting around the grounds, a house you could get lost in, and a cook who slipped you biscuits and called you *luv* and shooed you away if you offered to help with the baking. Evie loved baking—but she also, it had to be said, loved not having to now and then. "I've also been to . . ." She paused a moment to see if he'd interrupt her, but apparently he decided this was information he could be handed. "France, Spain, Belgium, Austria. I spent a very memorable two terms at a finishing school in Switzerland."

"Finishing school." He'd been reaching for another photo but paused, turned, and looked at her with wide eyes. "I didn't know innkeepers were so well educated."

She flashed him her thoroughly finished smile. "I wasn't always an innkeeper."

"Clearly." He made a show of looking her over, as if seeing her for the first time, and shook his head. "Finishing school. A *Swiss* finishing school, no less. And here you are slumming it with the likes of me."

"Oh now, don't be so hard on yourself. Davie assures me you're a fine, upstanding chap."

Just as she'd hoped, that brought confusion back to his face, and his eyes flew to the photo of them again. "And how would Davie know a blamed thing about me?"

"He didn't, until I asked." She reached up, tapped the manor house behind them. "He's still there. Or, rather, again. You didn't think I'd let a mystery like you stay here with me and Grandma See without verifying you were on the up-and-up, did you? Davie has connections."

He narrowed his eyes at the picture, perhaps noting again the size of the house in the background. Perhaps wondering who, exactly, *David* was. "Is he some sort of lord?"

"Not yet, thank God. But he will be someday." She'd looked at that photo a million times, and at others with his familiar, smiling face. But it never stopped hurting when she was only looking at a photo and not at *him*. She missed the quick flash of his dimple. The way their hands had always fit perfectly together—and they'd done a lot of holding tight to each other over the years. She missed the way his dark hair was always falling into his eyes, and the look in those eyes as he concentrated on a puzzle he was trying to solve, be it mechanical or mathematical. She missed, most of all, the way they knew each other's every thought.

Everybody needed somebody who could read their mind. She still had Grandma See for that, it was true . . . but it didn't make the ache of missing Davie any less.

After the war. After the war, they'd be together again. They'd laugh and hug, he'd swing her around, they'd stay up all night talking.

"What sort?"

"Hmm?" She started, turned back to face Sterling.

"What sort of lord? Are we talking a duke there with his arm around you, or . . . ?"

"Ah. Baron. He will be someday, though hopefully not for many years to come. The current one may be seventy, but he's still strong as an ox and determined to 'see the Boche taught a lesson once again, hang it all.'" She did her best imitation of his lordship on that last part, which earned her a grin.

"You have *clearly* spent time in England. You've nailed the Eton intonations."

She leaned over, since she was on his good side, and bumped their arms together. "You should know, having gone there yourself." On scholarship, but she wouldn't let him know she knew that. Some chaps were sensitive about such things.

"On scholarship. But yes." Apparently not this chap. Good to know. He turned back to the photographs and nodded toward the one on the end, of her and Job. "That one was going to be my next sneaky investigation, but you came in too soon. So you might as well tell me what, if anything, would be on the back of it."

She sighed. Job, looking so handsome in his uniform. And she, looking so proud as she stood at his side in her matching white dress. Understated but elegant, that was what she'd wanted that day, so that she fit in nicely with him and his fellow Coasties. "You wouldn't find much there, I'm afraid. Just 'Evie and Job, September 14, 1936.'"

He tapped a finger to his lips. "A year and three months, then, from the one of you and David. I have to say, Evie Farrow, that you look quite comfortable in both sets of arms."

Because he sounded teasing—and was obviously fishing—she planted her hands on her hips and gave him her best impression of Mama's stern look. "Are you implying something, Mr. Bertram?"

He held his hands up, palms out. "Not I. Mere observation."

He was good at observation, clearly. It would be part of his job. And it was proving entertaining to see what he sorted through on his own and what he got so hilariously wrong that she could only laugh when he presented a theory. Moreover, she was glad he was feeling well enough this week to actually be presenting theories every day, to be up and looking behind photographs, to be ignoring the bell. Glad there hadn't been a hint of fever for the last eight days, and that finally, finally, most of the burns were beginning to look less angry and new skin, pink and fresh, was growing. It had taken a month, but he was finally out of the woods.

Which meant he'd be ready to go into the literal woods.

A puttering engine interrupted their smiles, drawing Evie over to the wide front windows. Not that she needed to look to see what her ears already told her—Uncle Garret, coming by for his routine check on their patient. And by the bounce in his step when he got out of the car, he was having a good day. She smiled anew at that. When Garret was in low spirits, it usually meant someone on the island was in a bad way.

"Ah, good." Sterling had moved with her and nodded his approval of the approaching form, flexing his burned hand. "He's going to officially sign off on my release from hospital today, so that you can start treating me as a normal guest rather than an invalid." He shook his head, mock consternation on his face. "Bells and bandages."

At least, she assumed it was just mock. It had to be infuriating to be trapped in an injured body and at the mercy of two female jailors when one had an operative to find . . . but it had been for his own good, which he had to know. "Certain of that, are you? You thought the same last week."

"Last week the doctor came in with frowns and a heavy

step, so of *course* he wasn't inclined to be generous with my prognosis. But today, look at him. That right there is a man inclined to grant me freedom."

She chuckled because she suspected he was right—and because he was well enough to actually deserve that freedom now. The same had not been true last week.

He was also right about Garret's mood when Sterling asked for "release" last time. He'd had a letter from Aunt L saying she couldn't leave her cousin quite yet, which naturally soured his disposition. Much as he knew his wife needed to be tending her ailing relative, he wasn't, as he had been proclaiming for the last two months, ever since Aunt L headed inland, cut out for the bachelor life anymore. Not to mention that he missed the woman he loved like Evie missed all of *her* missing family.

A moment later, the door swung open, and soon Garret was ducking into the room, his face bright with a grin. "Well, isn't this good to see. Not only up and about, but with healthy color in your cheeks."

Sterling nodded, straightening his spine. "I've been following your directions to a *T*, Doc."

Evie shot him an arched brow.

Sterling cleared his throat. "Well, I mean, over the last week. No more setbacks, as I haven't the time for them. So I thought I'd better behave myself."

"Wisdom that had you observed from the start . . ." But Uncle Garret smiled and waved the patient to a chair. "Sit. Let me take a look under the bandages. Any fever?" This he directed to Evie, given that Sterling always said no, even when the answer was most definitely yes.

But today she could smile. "No fever. I think he's actually as well as he'd been pretending to be."

"That's what we like to hear." He unwrapped the bandage with all the speed and care of one accustomed to such actions, nodding at each inch revealed. "Very good indeed. A good day all around." He turned to grin at Evie. "Had a letter from your Aunt L. She'll be home next week."

"Ah!" She clasped her hands together, though even that couldn't contain her joy, both for him and for her. "Finally! Her cousin is well?"

"Well enough."

Sterling looked from one of them to the other, that look in his eyes again. The one that said there was information he didn't have, and he'd like to remedy the lack. But never in an easy way, this man. He had to turn it into a puzzle to solve. "Grandma See—the See short for Elsie. Is this Aunt L, as in the letter, or is her name Elle? Or something else altogether?" Leaning close to Garret, he stage-whispered, "She has the strangest nicknames for people."

Garret laughed. "They all date from when she was a little thing. Babbling constantly, but not always with the best diction yet." He sent her a wink. "For the longest time, I was 'Uncle Gert.' I finally broke her of that, but the others rather liked their silly names and let them stick."

Evie folded her arms over her stomach as she smiled at all the memories. "Aunt L is another of my abbreviations. Short for—"

"Lester," Garret said on a grin.

Sterling snorted a laugh. "Aunt Lester. *Right.*"

Garret sent her exaggerated wide eyes and a full-arm shrug, which he turned into a smirk and the signs for *everything* and *doubt*, and Evie caught his question. *Does he always doubt everything?*

She knocked a *yes* even as she chuckled.

Sterling's scowl looked more amused than irritated. "Not *everything.*"

Evie's lips parted, and Garret stared at him.

Sterling grinned. "My next confession. I found a book on American Sign Language my first week here and have been studying it daily. It's an ancient thing, but I've been careful with it—and I'm a quick study with languages."

No doubt she looked every bit as impressed as she felt. No, not just impressed. Warmed. They'd had many a guest who stayed with them for a whole season, but no one ever took the time to learn more than a few basic signs—*yes, no, thank you, good morning*. No one ever looked for or studied the book on the language. It said something that he would. That he cared to. Even more than it said about his intellect, that he'd learned so much so quickly and without any live lessons.

Garret turned back to the bandage. "That was the book Elsie learned from when she was a girl."

Evie nodded. "I believe her parents found it when the language was only just created officially. They and her god-mother taught her, and of course they gave her the book. One of the few things she brings with her wherever she goes." Seeing the concern in his eyes, she added, "For the sake of those she's with more than for herself. She's learned it all long ago, but it's a handy thing to share with those who care to learn."

"I've been practicing when I can't sleep at night. I thought to surprise her with a full conversation one of these days, but there are a few signs whose descriptions I'm a bit unclear on. Perhaps we could practice when she's not in view, now and then?"

He wanted to surprise Grandma? Evie hadn't seen that thread of sweetness beneath all his stubbornness and dedi-cation to his mission and strength, but it clicked into place beautifully. A complementary undertone to the picture that was Sterling Bertram. She smiled. "Sure."

Garret lifted Sterling's arm and turned it toward the light from the window. "This is looking much better. I think we can forgo the bandages during the day. I'd say to apply a fresh one with honey and aloe at night until these last areas heal over. How's the side?"

Evie decided it was a testament to how much better he was feeling that he glanced at her rather pointedly before lifting the untucked hem of his shirt. If he had the wherewithal for modesty after she'd been nursing him for over a month, then he *must* be nearly back to normal. She tucked her smile away into the corners of her mouth and turned to the window. If he wanted to pretend that she hadn't seen his bare chest and back daily, she'd grant him the illusion.

Motion outside caught her eye. Just a dove flying from the live oak to a cedar, but she watched its path against the blue of the sky and tried not to notice the shiver that tickled its way up her spine. Tried to tell her eyes not to search the trees for other movement. Tried not to feel the creep of shadows over her spirit at what this "release" of Sterling meant.

Time to keep her promise. To take him into the woods. To look for a German agent.

Part of her still thought his theory was too far-fetched to be real. Another part of her wanted desperately to believe that but didn't. Not really. Because a third part had been cataloging everything her neighbors said, keeping an ear finely tuned to the gossip.

Food was still going missing. Not in large quantities, and never from the same person twice, which was what was slowly convincing her that it *wasn't* kids. She knew the youngsters around here, knew they were most likely to pick their favorite marks—those neighbors or relatives most likely to tease or shake a fist at them, or against whom they had some petty grudge. This, though. This had the marks of care and planning. A fishing pole had vanished, too, and a net from someone else. All the things a man would need if he was to survive on an island for an indeterminate amount of time.

From this window, all she could see were a few trees, that final curve of the drive, and the sound, its waters urged up by the wind today into a million sparkling diamonds. Nothing out of the ordinary. Nothing to suggest that trouble could be hiding somewhere nearby. Nothing but the tickling chill and the whisper in the back of her mind, the memory of explosions out at sea, and the fact that an intelligence officer was even now sitting five feet away, champing at the bit to get out into the field—or forest, as it were—and get back to his business.

She drew in a long breath, noting absently that the bread smelled done, seconds before she heard Grandma See open the old oven with its happy squeak of metal hinges. Maybe all that didn't add up to *nothing*. Maybe, instead, it was foolish to think that the idyllic could ever really last, that because a place looked sweet and calm and peaceful meant it was.

Every Ocracoker knew how deceptive a calm surface could be. The water's appearance didn't always tell the tale of the currents underneath. Rip tides were capricious things, appearing and disappearing—like all the hard things in life. Death and betrayal, lies and secrets. No community was immune to those on the personal level. It was just that this was on a national level that made it hard to wrap one's head around.

"All right, then. I'm happy with how you're healing up. Consider yourself free of prison—as long as you promise me you'll pay attention to what your body is telling you. When you're tired, rest. If the pain increases again, rest and call me. Agreed?"

She turned in time to see Sterling's nod. "Agreed. Thank you, Doctor."

Garret smiled, moving his gaze from Sterling to Evie. "Once your aunt's settled home again, we'll have you and Grandma over for dinner. And this one, too, if he behaves himself."

Sterling settled his right hand over his heart. "I solemnly swear."

Evie tried to let her grin chase away those shadows, but all it really did was banish them to the background for a few heartbeats. It wouldn't last, she knew. Because she could see in Sterling's eyes that the moment Garret left, he would pounce on that promise she'd made him. Might as well start planning what clothes she'd wear for what was sure to be a longer traipse through the woods than she should really let him cajole her into. "Tell her to name the day."

"Will do, baby girl." He picked his black bag up from where he'd left it, moved to her side, and leaned down to drop a kiss onto the top of her head. "I'd love to linger, but I have a few more stops to make today."

"Go out through the kitchen. One of those loaves of bread Grandma took out is for you."

His grin was all eager little boy, despite the silver in his hair. "You ladies sure are good to me. See you later, sweetie. Take care of yourself, Sterling."

They both replied, then fell into silence while Garret ducked his way out of the room, strode down the hallway, and stepped into the kitchen. They held that silence for the next minute, while Grandma was no doubt wrapping a loaf in a clean tea towel and handing it to him with a few signs, which he'd answer in kind. Then came the sound of the screen door squeaking open, slapping shut.

She slid her gaze over to Sterling. He was watching her,

but still he said nothing, so she didn't either. Not while Garret's whistle came piping along on the breeze through the window, not while his engine roared to life. Not until it traveled down the lane and faded into the hush of birdsong and water on shore.

Then Sterling lifted his brows and his lips both. "Ready?"

She made a show of looking down at herself. She always made it a point to look nice for the day's work, never knowing when a guest might show up out of the blue. Which meant she was in a well-tailored dress, pearl necklace around her neck, comfortable but far from hike-worthy pumps, her hair pinned on the sides but otherwise falling in curls to her shoulders. "I'm going to need a few minutes to change my clothes. And a few more to pack us a picnic."

"Picnic?" She couldn't quite tell if the expression on his face was appreciation, surprise, or outrage. "We're not going on a *picnic*. We're scouting."

Outrage. But it would melt into appreciation soon enough. "It's eleven o'clock. By the time we get to the woods on the north end of the island, it'll be nearly noon. If you don't want me to pack a lunch, then our choices are to either wait until afterward to head out, or to turn right back around. Which would you prefer?"

He pursed his lips. Sighed. And said, "You know, it *is* a fine day for a picnic."

"That's what I thought." Chuckling, she strode for the door, the stairs, her room. It only took her a few minutes to change into a pair of jeans and a serviceable blouse, to tie her hair back into a tail, and to slip her feet into her boots, then she was back downstairs.

She found Sterling in the kitchen, making sandwiches alongside Grandma. "We'll drive as far as we can to the north, though the road up that way is more a path, and it'll be rough going—there's a footbridge across to the main section of forest. Did you want to cover everything in a grid?"

He shot her an impressed look. "You are an efficient lady, Evie Farrow. A grid, she says, like she searches the woods all the time."

There had, in fact, been a few times in her life when a tot had wandered off and the whole village had turned out to find him. Not that she'd spoil his impression by pointing out that every villager knew to search in a grid. "I have a map we can use to divide it up and mark what we've covered."

"The one that was in the desk drawer in the main room?" His grin was every bit as boyish as Uncle Garret's, now that it wasn't underscored by constant pain. It was a good grin, bringing light to eyes that were otherwise far too serious, even when he was teasing her. "I may have found that already."

She breathed a laugh and pulled out a couple of canteens to fill with cool water. "Of course you have. And divided it into a grid already, I presume?"

"I had to do *something* to occupy myself while I was under house arrest."

Apparently learning ASL and reading half her library while he should have been resting hadn't been enough. She shook her head and concentrated on putting enough food together for both lunch and dinner, packed it all into a rucksack along with the canteens, and hitched it onto her own back, despite his outstretched hand.

She shook her head. "You may be able to walk now without pain, but these straps would not be kind to your side."

It affronted him to admit she was right on that, she knew. A dozen silent arguments sparked in his eyes before he finally admitted defeat with a huff of breath and turned for the door. "May I at least drive? Just to feel like I'm contributing *something* to the outing?"

It was on the tip of her tongue to refuse. Driving on sand roads was a learned skill, after all, and she didn't much fancy digging the Model T out of a rut today. But she happened to glance over at Grandma, who must have been following the conversation with her eyes. She gave Evie a pointed look and signed, *Allow.*

She released her own huff of breath. But she nodded, reached for the keys where they dangled on a hook by the door, then handed them to him. "Let the adventure begin."

14

Sterling had hiked through many a wood in his day. He'd explored every forest and glen and dale near his home or where they holidayed when he was a lad, each one within a day's travel of Eton while he was at school. In more recent years, he had done a fair bit of tramping through the French variety in pursuit of the elusive Mansfeld.

None of them were quite like the maritime forest Evie was leading him through. Here there was sand instead of soil under his feet. Here there was the strangest hush, as if the trees gathered all external sounds into their branches and held them captive. Here, then, came new sounds he had to search for the source of.

The wind, dancing over the tops of the trees without slipping through them to cool his brow, had a new song. And its percussion came in strange knockings and creakings. He could have asked Evie what they were—she certainly didn't look bothered by them—but instead he took the chance to tune his senses back into what they should be.

There, the source of the creaking—branches rubbing together high above him. And the knocking, too, was branches and thick grapevines clattering their hello to one another as they met and then retreated again. The birds sounded abnormally loud here.

As did the mosquitoes buzzing incessantly around his head. He waved them away, glad Evie had cautioned him to keep his sleeves rolled down and his trouser legs tucked into his boots. She'd found him a hat that fit so well he was already plotting how to let her make a gift of it to him, but just now he could have done with a net over it.

He smacked a hand to his neck. It silenced that particular hum, but the smear of blood on his palm told him he hadn't saved himself from the bite. "Are you not getting eaten alive up there?"

Evie had taken the lead solely because she knew the paths, and he wasn't fool enough to insist on it for the sake of his pride when it would hinder their purpose. She paused and turned back to him, those golden brows of hers arched as they often were, and her always-ready smile hovering just out of sight, ready to spill onto her lips at the slightest provocation. "Don't you remember what the ladies said? The mosquitoes favor the visitors."

"That makes no sense at all." And was blighted unfair, to boot. Maybe he oughtn't to have turned down her offer of citronella oil. He'd thought it useless—the stuff only lasted a short while, anyway, and he didn't want to have to be reapplying the oil all afternoon. But now he wished he had the bottle of it in his pocket.

Her smile winked onto her lips, joined with a short laugh as bright as the sunshine had been before the trees caught it, muted it, and cast it onto them as humid shade. "Sensical or not, it's the truth. Ask anyone who moves here from the mainland. First couple summers they're swarmed, but then they start leaving them alone for whatever reason. We like to say that that's when you know you've really become an Ocracoker. When the skeeters leave you be."

She delivered that last sentence with the drawl of the villagers, just as easily as she'd imitated the English lord's accent earlier. He'd always had an ear for languages and accents himself—another reason he'd been selected for intelligence work, and why picking up ASL had seemed a fun endeavor, even from his sickbed. But he didn't know too many others who shared that particular bent. "How many languages do you speak?"

Though she turned back to the path, her laughter drifted back to him. "A direct question!"

"Some things are best asked." And just weren't as sporting to try to discover on his own. He'd noted books in a variety of languages at the inn, but that didn't mean she spoke or read them. It could instead mean that they had guests who did and wanted to make them feel welcome.

"English and French fluently, and I read Latin and ancient Greek—with lexicons at hand, I admit. I had passable German while I was in Switzerland, though it's grown a bit rusty. You?"

"We're a matched pair, it seems. Well, I'm rubbish at Greek—and my German has been rather well polished since we declared war. I have a smattering of a few Germanic dialects too." He made himself move his gaze from her to their surroundings again. This, after all, was neither a hike nor an excursion for fun. They must keep their eyes peeled for evidence of Mansfeld. It wasn't about speed, but thoroughness. "Hold up."

He took a few steps off the path, careful to reach around and not through the patch of poison ivy between him and what had caught his eye—a tin can. Its paper label was gone, but the can itself wasn't rusty. Not old, but not new either. "When was the last rain?"

"Wednesday evening." She came up at his side, holding out a thin bag. "We might as well collect anything we find. Both to look over later and because I hate to see garbage in the woods."

They could agree on that. He slid the can into the bag and looped the sack around his good hand. "Is the poison this thick everywhere?"

"Mm. Ivy and oak, all through the woods. Another reason you want to make sure your trousers stay tucked into your boots." Hands resting on her pack's straps, she looked out at the trees. "Snakes too. This really isn't a hospitable place to stay. There's a reason all the locals live in the village and haven't claimed plots out here for their homes."

Snakes. Poison. Mosquitoes. All marks against this as a good base of operations, to be sure—but the woods on Hatteras and Bodie Islands wouldn't be any different, most likely. And he knew for a fact that Mansfeld had had wilderness training in the Hitler Youth. Perhaps he'd come prepared with his own arsenal of citronella oil and calamine lotion. "Are the other locals as fastidious as you about cleaning up out here?"

She had a way of pursing a single corner of her mouth in thoughtful disapproval. "Sadly, no. But I suspect your spy would be, don't you think? He wouldn't want to leave a trail of tin cans leading us straight to him."

"You have a point. We'll have to have a far keener eye than that." Still, everyone slipped up now and then. He could have dropped something without realizing it.

They picked their way slowly through a few sections of their grid, looking for bent twigs, disturbed sand, anything to indicate that human feet had come through here before them. Precious little presented itself, it was true. A few indications of someone having come through, but nothing to shout it was a German and not a local fisherman.

Eventually the path ended, as all paths here did, at water. And since the mosquitoes vanished when he left the woods and moved out into the wind and the sun and the sand, Sterling indulged in the respite with a happy sigh. "This looks like a fine picnic spot, I should think."

"I was thinking the same."

He helped her spread out the small blanket she'd packed, anchored the corners down with their various bags and canteens, and sank to a seat beside her, a sandwich in each of their hands. As he ate, he alternated between watching the line of dolphins frolicking in the waves to watching Evie watch them.

Those two photos of her at the inn kept nagging at him. He had not, in fact, been trying to insinuate anything when he observed how happy she looked in both masculine sets of arms. But he *had* been hoping for a reaction from her that would tell him something about one or either of those men.

One, a lord-to-be. One, a Coast Guard officer. Neither around now, so far as he'd seen. David and Job. Who were they? Brother? Boyfriend? Husband? Friend? Cousin? Those were the options that would account for the familiarity the camera had captured, the joy on their faces—and the presence of the photographs on the wall. But he had no way of knowing which designation belonged to whom. Not yet.

What he'd seen in a glance, though, was that Evie had looked perfectly at home in front of that enormous manor house in the background of the first photo. She'd been wearing clothes a good deal finer than the skirts and dresses she wore around the inn, though with equal confidence. That was telling—his mum would be far from comfortable in silk and satin. She'd be tugging at it, smoothing it constantly, afraid of doing it harm. And the times he'd seen aristocrats in common clothes, they either looked like it was a great joke, a costume, or as if they were undergoing some sort of torment by wearing them.

He hadn't been able to see much of her clothing in the photo of her and Job, only an elegant neckline in white or some other light color that the camera rendered as such. But it had been the ocean behind them. And they'd been smiling at the camera with pure happiness, just as she and David had been in the other.

His gaze drifted to her left hand. She wasn't wearing a wedding band or even an engagement ring, and most women did. But that didn't mean she wasn't taken by one of those handsome, smiling men hanging on the wall. And though he was rather enjoying his game of puzzle-her-out, he was also enjoying her company . . . and would greatly like to know if that was inappropriate.

At this point, though, it felt a bit like defeat to ask her anything point-blank. He'd have to settle for roundabout. "Tell me the story of one of those photographs on the wall. When it was taken, what was happening that day."

Did she know he was fishing? Probably, given the grin she flipped his way. "Which one?"

"Your choice."

"All right." She made a show of considering, trailing her free hand through the sand at her side. Building little mountains in one second, sweeping them into plains the next. "The one in the center—we call it 'all the womenfolk.'"

He very nearly objected. That was the one photo he *didn't* want an explanation of right now.

Perhaps she knew it, and that was why mischief twinkled

in her eyes. "It was no special day, really. Just a Sunday dinner here at the inn. One of many. But Aunt L had gotten a new camera, and Uncle Garret wanted to try it out. He and Daddy spent so long fussing with it that Davie and Job both ran off to play in the water."

She leaned back onto her elbows, tilted her face up to the sun, and Sterling's breath caught. Maybe it was the way the sunshine tangled in her hair and made it shimmer like fire. Maybe it was the look on her face as she let her mind drift back to that golden day. Maybe it was that she was without question one of the most beautiful women he'd spent any amount of time with—and kind and gentle and caring and quick-witted and intelligent. Maybe that was why his heart stuttered in his chest and he found himself wishing he'd been there that day. Any day. A part of her memories, living them with her. Seeing firsthand what brought her such joy.

Of course, he filed the facts away, too—David and Job, together here as children. Her father too. And, of course, all the womenfolk. "You didn't run off with them?"

Her smile was the sort that would have inspired a master to put her to canvas with oils and brush. "Not that day. I was too busy trying to convince baby Vi that I was her favorite person in the whole world."

Didn't seem like much of a chore. "Did you?"

She chuckled. "Sure, until she got hungry. I wanted her in my lap for the photo, but she started fussing, and only her mama would do then." She fell silent for a moment, then shook her head. "That was the last photo we took before Grann died, though."

"Grann." A grandmother? But there'd been several ladies in the picture old enough to fit that bill for her.

"The one in the center." She peeked an eye open and turned it to him, testing him to see if he recalled the image that well.

Clearly she'd never been through his training, or she wouldn't have to wonder. The figure in the center had been the oldest and also the most curious to his English eyes, though perhaps not so curious here in the American South. A woman of color, perhaps of mixed race—beautiful even in her advanced years. It would have been easy enough to look at her and assume her to be a servant, but why would she be in the photo, then? And in the center? Moreover, she'd been wearing a dress every bit as nice as anyone else's, perhaps even nicer. And the hands on her shoulders bespoke not only love but respect.

He'd thought he'd noticed a bit of a resemblance between her and one of the younger women, but he wasn't entirely certain. It could have been that they were the two brunettes in a group of blondes.

Grann. He nodded at the name. "How did she die?"

"Cancer." She said the word like it was a curse—rightly so. A dreaded word to anyone. He'd lost an uncle to it himself.

"I'm sorry. You loved her very much."

As evidenced not only by the warmth with which she spoke, but the sorrow that painted itself over her face as she remembered her, though it must have been twenty years ago that she died. "So many of my favorite childhood memories revolve around Grann. She was the first one to teach me French—she was from Louisiana. The one who taught me how to pray. How sometimes, when it feels like the wind and the water are stealing those prayers, we can anchor them to something in our thoughts, as a reminder that no one and nothing can really snatch them away."

She reached down, plucked up a bit of seashell, purple and white, and held it up to the sun. "She was Catholic, like your friend. That was a hard thing to be here, where no one else was. She never made a fuss about it, never complained about the community she sacrificed to live here. But she always had her rosary in her pocket. Always. And that's what she called it—her anchor. A physical reminder of how real our prayers are."

He suddenly wondered if Tommie had carried one. If it had been in his pocket or stolen by the waves. If, perhaps, when he saw that torpedo tunneling through the water, he let his fingers tangle with familiar beads and knew God was there.

Sterling hoped so. Prayed so. "That's beautiful."

"*She* was beautiful, and so full of wisdom. I'll never forget the way she'd cup my cheeks in her hands and call me *ma cherie*." She sighed, and sorrow claimed her expression. "It was a week later that she was diagnosed. Uncle Garret suspected and sent her to a hospital on the mainland. She didn't tell anyone but Grandma Ree—they said they were going shopping. But they didn't come home with presents. They came home with a death sentence."

He wanted to reach over and cover her fingers with his. He wanted to take that shell from her and press it to his palm until he could feel the certainty, the solidity of all God made, the assurance that it couldn't stop when a human drew her last breath. He wanted to travel back in time and meet the woman who'd had so profound an impact on this woman when she was just a girl. "How long did she have?"

"The doctors said six months, but she only made it four. And they were a painful four." She sat up straighter again and brushed the sand from her fingers. "I spent hours each day at her side, trying to ease her pain however I could. Mama had to drag me away every evening. That's when everyone started saying I was too sensitive, too tenderhearted. That it wasn't good for me to be around such suffering. They threatened to limit me to an hour a day with her, but Grandma

Ree put her foot down. Said God had given me a gift, and He'd given me the strength to share it. I didn't really know what that meant at the time. But it's something I've never forgotten."

And something she still lived too. He ought to know, having been the recipient of it himself. His angel of mercy, tending him tirelessly, always seeming to sense what he needed before he could moan out a request. "I think Grandma Ree was right."

Her smile returned. "I didn't fade away when she died like they feared I would, so I suppose so. But that photo has never been changed out. The others have. Countless pictures have hung in those other frames, and countless others will. But not that one. That one is always there, a reminder of who we are. The family we built from love and blood and stubbornness."

And maybe that *was* the story he most needed to hear. He finished the last bite of his sandwich and watched the waves lap the shore. "I'm glad you spent that time with her. You were a comfort to her. You *did* relieve the pain."

He could say it with certainty because that's what she'd done for him. Not just the medicine she brought him or the compresses and poultices either. No, the true relief had been opening his eyes through a haze of agony and seeing her there. Hearing her singing. Feeling her gentle touch on his brow when he was in the throes of delirium and knowing that whatever happened, someone was there who cared, even if she had no reason to. Perhaps now that he was well he could joke and call her his jailer—but what she'd really been was his rescuer.

He didn't know how to repay her but by keeping her and this island she loved safe. He had to find Mansfeld. No other option was acceptable.

She didn't say anything in response to his assurances. But she looked over at him with a smile that said they were friends, and that was far better than an empty thank-you anyway. She searched his face for a moment, nodded, and started packing up. "Let's keep looking." He didn't know how she knew that was what he needed to do as his own thank-you—but she did. Which meant he owed it to her all the more.

They had everything stowed away within a few minutes, and he lifted the pack onto her back again, though it chafed him to do so. Then off they went along the beach until another path opened up into the wood for them to follow.

Another hour of searching crept by before a spot of color caught his eye. A corner of red, half-buried in the sand directly off the path. But his pulse kicked up when he picked it up and saw that it was a matchbook.

Not just *a* matchbook, though. One with distinctive artwork and a logo he'd know anywhere—the double star of the Astor Club, one of London's premier nightclubs. For a long moment he held it, felt it. Dry, no wear or curling on the edges to say it had spent much time in the sand or been out in Wednesday's rain. It looked brand-new. Crisp. Its colors bright and glossy.

He could hear each beat of his heart as it crashed against his ribs like the sea. "He was here. Right here. Recently." He spun to face Evie. "Unless you know someone else around who frequents a London club? Your David—is he a member there? Did he bring matchbooks and hand them out to all his island friends?"

When she shook her head, golden curls bounced. "Davie doesn't belong to any clubs. He's a bit of a recluse." He'd never seen that particular look in Evie's eyes. A touch of panic, a pinch of excitement, a boatload of uncertainty. "I don't know anyone who's been to the Astor Club. I've heard of it, though. In Mayfair, right?"

He nodded and turned his attention to the matchbook again, flipping it open. Three of the paper matches had been torn free, the rest remained. Losing this, then, would have been a blow. Mansfeld could well come back looking for it. "It's his favorite club in London—Karl Meyer's. I nearly caught him there six months ago. He was rubbing shoulders with the aristocrats."

And doing a better job of blending in with them than Sterling had done, hence why his quarry escaped him. When he'd questioned the men with whom he'd been dining, claiming that their companion reminded him of an old school chum from Eton, they'd thought Mansfeld was the wealthy son of a businessman from Johannesburg, recently arrived from South Africa. A clever ruse, to be sure. It would account for any oddities in his speech, any German accent that slipped in, thanks to the influence of the Afrikaans.

"Which aristocrats?"

"Hmm?" He turned back to Evie, and the wariness in her eyes sparked new questions. Good questions. "You may know them, is that what you're thinking?" It was possible, if she had connections to a barony in Herefordshire. His brows pulled down. "Lord Somers and his cousin. Isn't the earl's estate in Herefordshire?"

Her cheeks washed pale. "Eastnor Castle, yes. About half an hour's drive from Springbourne Hall. The earl has a daughter my age. I dined with them when I was last there. You don't think the earl is caught up in this?"

"No, nothing like that." They'd looked into it. They'd looked closely at *all* the people Mansfeld had been befriending in London. Because there had to be a reason he'd chosen them, didn't there? They'd yet to determine what it was, but he wasn't a chap who did things by happenstance. He plotted, he researched, he carried out detailed plans after months of preparation, after he'd woven a story so layered and believable that no one thought to question him—and if they did, they found only the truths he'd carefully planted to back him up.

The earl had nothing linking him to the Nazis . . . but it was strange, wasn't it? That of all the rich blokes in London he could have befriended, he chose a neighbor of the Culbreths, whom Evie Farrow seemed to know quite well. And then, six months later, he came *here*. Where she was. With her fluent French and rusty German.

He crouched down and put the matchbook back in the sand where he'd found it. "Did you say you'd been to France?"

"Mm-hmm." She was reading his mind again, moving off the path, motioning toward a little grapevine-enclosed grove that would render them invisible once night fell. "Here, do you think? We'll be close enough to pounce when he comes back for it, but he won't be able to see us. We could have a long wait, though. Good thing I brought enough for dinner."

He smoothed out their footprints from the path and then picked his way through the underbrush to where she was setting up camp. "Where in France?"

He did his best to sound casual, just looking for a distraction. He must have managed it because she didn't send him any probing looks. "Mostly Paris, several times. A week in Charleville once, in the Ardennes department."

Paris. Charleville.

His blood ran cold even as the map he'd studied for hours on end appeared before his mind's eye. Mansfeld's journey, as much as he'd been able to track it. From Rüdesheim am Rhein, where he grew up, to Berlin. From Berlin to

Charleville, France, as soon as it was under German control. From Charleville to Paris. From Paris to London. From London to Herefordshire. From Herefordshire to, of all places, the Outer Banks of North Carolina.

To a pretty, sophisticated innkeeper whose life had traced a far-too-similar route.

He'd thought it a game, puzzling out who Evie Farrow was, with her encrypted telegrams. He'd thought it a distraction, something fun to take his mind off the hunt his body hadn't been well enough to complete. He'd thought it the hand of Providence that had landed him on her doorstep—the one person on the island who somehow knew not to report him immediately to Norfolk or the civilian authorities.

And maybe God *had* led him here. But maybe it hadn't been to make a friend and then find his enemy.

Maybe all along it had been to find the enemy posing as a friend.

Evie wasn't sure what had come over Sterling. For all she knew, it was the way he acted when he was hot on the trail of his prey. But his jokes had a strain to them that afternoon, and they'd fallen completely silent once dusk fell—by agreement, but even so. It wasn't their usual silence. There was no comfort in it, no understanding.

But again, perhaps the tension was because of the situation.

And perhaps his clear irritation now, as the car bounced over the rutted lane to the inn, its headlights cutting a weak swath through heavy darkness, was because the sudden, steady rain had called a halt to their stakeout after midnight. There'd been no point in staying out there in it. Wherever he was, Meyer would have hunkered down in an attempt to stay dry, not gone groping in the inky darkness for a pack of matches already doused in water.

Perhaps it was only that, all of that. But it didn't feel like it. It felt like the sand had shifted under their feet, and she wasn't sure why.

But she knew beyond any doubt that it was about to get worse when the headlights caught on a white uniform on her porch. She parked, killed the lights and the engine, and wondered if she dared to pray that Herb was waiting for her because he and the boys had been goofing around and someone had gotten a gash and needed her to fetch Uncle Garret here, quietly and off the record.

The manila folder in his hands told a different tale, one that made her heart sink into her stomach when she glanced over at Sterling. His jaw was clenched so tightly that a muscle ticked there, and she didn't think it was because he was in any physical pain this time.

Which was all sorts of unfair. Packets like this had always made her come to attention, made her smile, made her feel *alive*. She'd never dreaded one before, and why should she now, just because Sterling Bertram was here watching?

Because if he asked, she couldn't tell him. Not this. This was the one thing she couldn't be honest about. And that secret could well ruin the friendship that had blossomed between them.

A thought that shouldn't pierce so deeply, should it? She'd only known him for a month, and he'd been unconscious for much of the first week. But once he'd awakened . . .

Well, there was nothing for it. She pasted a waterlogged smile onto her face and marched to the steps.

Herb took in her rain-soaked form, her backpack, and her companion with a mute glance. He wouldn't ask what she'd been doing out there with a male stranger, but she could see the questions in his eyes.

He put on a good show, though. Easy smile, quiet words. "Hey, Evie. Sorry to come by so late—just got off my shift. I thought I'd slip this under the door for you, but your car was gone, and I was worried. 'Fraid you were stuck somewhere, what with the rain."

"I was, at that." By choice more than the fault of the rutted, sandy roads, but it was a handy excuse. She reached for the folder. It was hefty, thick with papers. It would have taken forever for this to come across the telegraph, dot by dash. That meant it was serious. "Thanks, Herb. I'd invite you in, but—"

"Oh gracious, too late for that! You go on in to bed, and I'll get home to Clara. Have a good night now, Evie. Mr. Sterling." Without another word, Herb hurried back into the rain, pulling his slicker's hood up as he went.

She ought to offer to drive him.

She ought to offer Sterling some plausible reason why the Coast Guard was yet again hand-delivering messages to her at odd hours.

She ought to offer prayers to the Lord that whatever had come unraveled, whatever had shifted, whatever was wrong, would be restored.

She reached for the knob, but Sterling's hand covered hers and kept her from turning it. "Direct question, Evie Farrow."

She squeezed her eyes shut.

"Why does the Coast Guard hand-deliver messages to you at midnight when the telegraph at the station is not for civilian use?"

She sighed. Tilted her face up and around until she could look at him in the porchlight. "That's the one question I can't answer."

He twisted the knob, pushed open the door. But another swung shut, there in his eyes. In his heart. In his soul. The door to their friendship, slammed closed. He didn't say a word, just strode inside, straight for his room, and left her there in the night.

She stood in silence for a moment. Alone. Again. Always, it seemed. Alone and wet and cold and so, so tired of that too-familiar feeling that she only realized had been absent since he came. It was all the colder, all the darker upon returning.

Eventually, she slipped inside, closed the door, made her way upstairs. She changed out of her wet clothes and into her warm pajamas. And then she sat at the little desk in the corner and opened the folder and took in the lines upon pages upon stacks of gibberish. Topped with a short note from Davie.

My math is failing me. Could really use your intuition. All my love, D

Her fingers reached for her pencil, and she shoved all the night's disappointments aside. She couldn't change much about this life she'd been given, the yesterdays that dictated today and tomorrow. But she could do *this*. She could look at things in that way God had given her. She could look and she could see and she could pray and she could write notes that Davie would make sense of, even if she didn't, exactly.

She could help. An ocean away from them all, yes. But she could help.

15

YESTERDAY

OCTOBER 21, 1914
LONDON, ENGLAND

B usy tonight, Culbreth?"

"Hmm?" Rem looked up from the page before him, having to blink to clear the numbers and letters from his vision and let the image of his colleague take shape. Though he didn't need to offer any apology to Dilly Knox for his distraction. Dilly understood as well as anyone else how consuming the work could be. But eventually the words penetrated, and Rem offered a smile. "I am, at that. I have a pressing engagement with a bathtub, a steaming mug of tea, and the stack of correspondence that was delivered as I left home this morning."

Knox chuckled and slapped a hand to Rem's shoulder. "Sounds riveting. De Grey and I are going to the pub. You ought to join us."

He liked Knox and De Grey. He liked all the members of the codebreaking team that had been dubbed Room 40, after the tiny office they'd all been shoved into until bigger accommodations could be found. But what he liked even more was the handwriting he'd spotted on some of that post as he hurried out the door that morning, already late. *Louisa.*

Perhaps whatever letter had come from her would explain her continued absence from his side. He understood that initial delay. When he'd arrived in London aboard the *Wilmington* and seen the report about the *Ignatius*, he'd known that it would have caused all manner of horrors with Mother and Lu. But he'd sent a wire home to Remington House right away to let them know he'd missed that ship when his train was late arriving in New York, and Mother's return wire had been full of relief.

But there'd been nothing directly from Louisa. He'd assumed at first that she'd send a separate telegram, but she hadn't. And the only letter ever to arrive was one she must have penned and posted the very hour he left, full of sweet nothings and promises of a quick reunion—which he'd read every day since he received it.

Yet here they were, six weeks later. Father was probably beginning to think he'd fabricated the tales of his beautiful bride. What could be keeping her? Had something gone wrong? Mother had simply said there'd been delays.

Finally, though, word. It would have some reasonable explanation, and no doubt had been too long in reaching him, thanks to the U-boat–infested waters that were slowing everything down so dreadfully.

He offered his friend a warm smile. "Any other night, old boy."

"Tomorrow, then. Tell your teacup to wait up for you."

Rem chuckled and fished his watch out of his pocket, eyes

bulging when he saw how late it had grown while he was fussing with a bothersome code. Well, it would have to wait until tomorrow. He pushed to his feet, expecting to find that everyone else had left for the day already.

He ought to have known better. Two ladies were still in attendance—their secretary, and her daughter, who everyone *thought* was a secretary, but who most assuredly was not. Margot De Wilde was by nature, it seemed, what the rest of them were being trained to be: a cryptographer. They claimed she was sixteen, but she looked younger to his eyes. Until one looked into her eyes, anyway. Then she looked positively ancient.

She reminded him just a bit of Louisa. It wasn't the dark hair that they had in common, and they certainly shared no mannerisms. But the intelligence. The way their eyes lit with challenge when a new puzzle was put before them.

He couldn't wait to see how they got along once Louisa joined him here. Perhaps he'd even secure her a position. She could sit alongside De Wilde and pretend to be a secretary if anyone from the navy came in to visit their director. She'd love this work every bit as much as he did.

Intercepting German codes. Using stolen codebooks to decipher them. Cracking the variants day by day, logging the ones they didn't yet know, sending the information to those who could use it to help the Allies.

For once, his father had proven that he *did* know Rem, throwing all his previous grumblings into question. Perhaps Rem hadn't given him enough credit after all. This was exactly the work he would have created for himself, had he known to dream of it. But he hadn't even realized, until Father had introduced him in hushed tones to Alfred Ewing, that technology had been developed that could snatch wireless signals right from the air. Whoever would have thought such a thing possible?

More, who would dare to send telegrams with anything private if they knew their words could be stolen so easily? Each and every one, he now knew, was intercepted by British Naval Intelligence and examined. Every. Single. One. England was the relay point for all of Europe to the rest of the world, which meant all messages came through them before going on.

All of them were read now. All of them.

It was enough to give a chap chills if he thought too hard on it.

He slipped into his overcoat and aimed a smile at Margot De Wilde, which she didn't look up to see, so then at her mother. "Have a lovely evening, Mrs. De Wilde."

Mrs. De Wilde smiled back, warm and serene. "Good evening, Mr. Culbreth. See you tomorrow."

As he strode down the corridor, he heard her repeating her daughter's name over and again, trying to break her from the trance of numbers that held her enthralled, and he chuckled to himself. It took more than a few soft words to pull Margot De Wilde out of the world of mathematics—and they were all grateful for it.

Darkness was already falling as he made his way through the park and toward Culbreth House, and the new blackout orders meant no streetlamps lit the way. But his feet knew the path, and soon he was jogging up the front steps and through the door that a servant opened for him. He smiled his thanks, handed off his hat and coat, and prayed for a negative answer as he asked, "Is my father in?"

It wasn't that he didn't want to see Father. It was just the *letters*.

Maybe Babcock understood their allure because he smiled

as he said, "No, sir. We were told he'd be dining at the club tonight. Will you take your meal in the dining room, or would you prefer a tray be prepared?"

If Father was at the club, there was no need to sit alone downstairs. "A tray is perfect, thank you." He took three steps and then halted. "Any word from my brother?" Sebastian had been due in Town two days ago but thus far hadn't seen fit to show up at the house. Not exactly unusual, but it put Father in an increasingly sour mood.

Babcock's face remained blank, and Rem could all but imagine the butler's long-ingrained training marching through his head. *Offer no judgment. Only the facts.* "No, sir. Shall I let you know when he arrives?"

Rem's lips quirked up. "Oh, I'll know. Thank you, Babcock."

"My pleasure, sir."

He found himself whistling as he hurried up the stairs and to his room, unknotting his tie as he went. The whistle turned to a grin when he spotted the encouragingly thick stack of post, bound with twine, sitting on his desk. He cast a quick glance at his windows to make certain his curtains were drawn and then turned the knob for the lights, closed the door, and settled himself in his chair.

A snip of the twine and he was flipping through the stack, smiling at Louisa's familiar script. A fat one from Mother, too, and two from Edgar. Lovely—enough to keep him company all evening.

Not that there was any question about which he'd read first. He set the others aside and the one from Louisa in front of him.

He pulled out his wallet and extracted the small photograph of her on their wedding day, smiling at the perfect lines of her face. Tracing it with a light fingertip and wishing the photo was larger, life-size, so he could see her more clearly. Wishing it were in color, so he could see the startling blue of her eyes. Wishing it weren't a photo at all, but was her, there with him, so he could press his lips to hers and laugh with her and hold her close to his chest as the cares of the day eased away.

Setting the photo in its place of honor against his Bible, he opened the letter. His smile faded fast.

Her script was shaky. And were those tearstains? Not good. Definitely not good. There was no date at the top, no signature at the bottom, but the first words scorched his eyes.

Why did you bring me here?

His breath was all a-tangle in his chest as he read on, each word burning a new brand into his heart.

Your mother has told the staff to steal from me, has accused me of all manner of vile motives. Your grandfather simply pretends I don't exist. I know I promised you that I'd learn, that I'd become a part of your world, but how, Rem? How, when they so clearly want to believe the worst of me?

"Mother, what have you done?" He had to pause, look to Louisa's image instead of her words. He should have known. He should have *known* Mother wouldn't accept Louisa as easily as it had seemed. When had that ever been Edith Culbreth's way? No, she simply said whatever she thought would be expedient. Whatever would get her her own way. She'd never intended to teach Louisa to be Mrs. Culbreth, only to bide her time until she could scare her off.

I don't know how to fight this battle. I don't know how to win this war.

Poor Louisa. He rested his hand on the page, swearing he could feel her anguish in the ink. She had to have been beset indeed to actually put these words to paper and send them, to admit that she felt defeated—something his warrior beloved would never want to grant. He moved his hand aside to read the next line and nearly wished he hadn't.

What have we done, Rem?

He squeezed his eyes shut. But forced them open again a moment later. He owed her this, to read each word in the same amount of pain she'd been in when she wrote them. No respite, no turning away.

I wish . . . I wish we'd never come here. I wish I'd never stepped foot in this accursed house. Then, at least, I wouldn't know. I wouldn't know how much they hated me simply for being me. For not being good enough or sophisticated enough or . . . or whatever it is that's wrong with me. I wouldn't know, and then I wouldn't have to wonder how many doubts they'd managed to plant in your mind. I wouldn't have to wonder if, when next you see me, you'll take one look at me and wonder why you married me, what you'd been thinking, how you ever could have thought that I'd be able to be Mrs. Culbreth.

I wouldn't have to wonder if you'll soon hate me too.

Mother had been right about one thing anyway—he'd done this to her. Brought this terrible pain upon her. Used his love selfishly as an excuse to bring her to a place she never wanted to be. He rested his head against his hand and stared at the words, willing them to change. For more to appear. For another letter to manifest itself somewhere in this stack in her precious hand, telling him all was well, forgiven, made new. That somehow she'd fixed it—wasn't she the one who could fix anything, repair any damage?

But he'd known from the start that fixing an engine or a cistern or a roof was far simpler than fixing a family—*his* family, anyway. There was no sanding down the cruel streak of Edith Culbreth or thawing out decades of ice with a butane torch. She couldn't fish out a spanner and give the situation a quarter turn.

And here he was, on another continent, one it seemed she had no intention of joining him on. What was he to do? *God, what am I to do?* Not that he was any better at fixing his family than she was, but why, why had he left her to deal with it on her own even for a minute?

When had she even sent this? Had any of his letters reached her, his telegrams? He'd sent them all to Remington House, but if she and Mother had a falling out, she very well could have left. Weeks ago.

Why did no one tell him? Louisa herself or Mother?

The inn—that was surely where she'd go if she'd run from his mother. He would try to reach her there. Perhaps he'd even say privacy be hanged and send a telegram to the nearest station to be sent to her by boat.

He pulled open his drawer, pulled out his fresh stock . . . and then paused. His eyes went to the three remaining letters. Two from Edgar, one from Mother.

It wasn't as though his words would reach her any sooner if he wrote them this minute versus in an hour. The telegraph stations and post offices were all closed for the night. He couldn't send anything until morning anyway. Better to see what, if anything, they had to say about it all.

He hesitated, hand hovering between the Edgar stack and the Mother stack, and finally settled on the one from her. She had been at the root of Louisa's problems, not his cousin. She, then, was the one who had better have a good explanation and preferably assurances that she'd set it all to rights sometime after Louisa penned that note and when she wrote this one.

It was dated a month ago, two weeks after the telegram exchange about the *Ignatius* disaster.

Remington,

I must begin by offering my deepest apologies. I am so sorry, my son. I never dreamed it would come to this, but things escalated beyond my control. I cannot know when any of our letters will reach you but I pray they arrive before you take any action that will only make the situation worse.

I treated your wife badly—this will come as no surprise to you. I was angry with both of you for making this decision, one that will affect the rest of all of our lives, without even speaking with me first. I was angry that you chose someone so inappropriate. I was angry that you expected me to clean up your mess by trying to turn that country bumpkin into a lady.

I maintain that my anger was justified. But still, I was wrong in how I acted toward her after we received that word of the fire. I should have been kinder, but I thought that she would simply return to her mother's inn. I never dreamed it would come to this. But your cousin's actions made everything worse.

I am getting ahead of myself. Allow me to backtrack.

As I mentioned when you were here, your cousin sent us regular updates while you were on Ocracoke, and when you wired about getting married, Edgar sent a message, too, saying he suspected that your bride may have a bit of colored blood. I know you do not understand the implications of this, having spent so many years in England, but let me assure you it is a very serious matter in both North Carolina and Maryland. According to our laws, no one with one-sixteenth or more African ancestry is legally permitted to marry a white man. Do you see what this means, Remington? Edgar wrote to me to say that if the woman called Grann is truly her grandmother, no marriage that took place between you would be legal. Of course, this was but a suspicion.

Until now. Your cousin spent the weeks since your marriage hiring investigators and tracking the actions some twenty years ago of Serena Marshall when she left Ocracoke and spent time in Louisiana to help a cousin with her young children. He knew that she married Michael Adair, that Mr. Adair was killed in a tragic accident, that Serena returned to Ocracoke with an infant Louisa and this woman called Grann, supposedly Michael's childhood mammy.

What they failed to tell anyone was that Michael Adair was Grann's son. That he was killed in a fire set to their house by outraged neighbors who could not bear the abomination of this man married to a white woman, and rightly so. It was well known that Michael Adair was one-eighth Black.

You can do the math, my son. That means that your Louisa is one-sixteenth. Nearly legal for you to marry, but not. I am sorry. So sorry. I wish you had followed your cousin's advice and investigated this matter before

*you let things go so far. Though the blame is not fully
yours. Her family, who surely knew of the illegality of
the marriage, ought to have spoken up, and for their
failure to do so I cannot forgive them.*

Rem could scarcely breathe. Couldn't actually read the
next words, not until he'd taken in the ones that had already
come. Not until he'd untangled what they meant.

Not until he'd plucked from his memory all the things
Edgar had said. That Linc had. That Grann herself had.

She, asking him if England had any rules about races
intermarrying—not because she was interested hypotheti-
cally, but because she knew how his and Louisa's hearts were
inclining. She was probably intending to tell them to marry
in England, had they had the leisure to choose a date and
location at will.

Edgar, saying they needed to know who her father was—
not because he may have been on the wrong side of a war or
of humble origins, but because he could be of mixed blood.
Something that mattered nothing to Rem, but which clearly
mattered to the law.

Linc, staring him dead in the eye and asking if Rem intended to pursue "those questions." If he'd made it clear to
Louisa that he didn't.

Because Louisa—precious, contemplative, ever-busy Louisa. *She* would have asked the questions all her life. She would
have known that there was a reason her mama and Grann
refused to answer them. For her good, they'd say. That then
she, like Linc, couldn't be held accountable for Serena's decisions. But it had to have torn her up inside not to know.
To always wonder. To feel as though her own father, whom
Serena had loved deeply if she was willing to take such a risk,
was a stranger to her.

Why had she never said anything to him? Never shared those questions, that agony? Had she . . . surely she hadn't. She couldn't have *meant* to deceive him.

His gaze drifted back to his mother's words.

When Edgar reported all of this, he did not simply present the facts, of course. He said, Remington, that you asked him to initiate the investigation and that he had explained the implications to you. Knowing you as I do, I must doubt this part of your cousin's story. I cannot think you so base that you would live as a husband to the poor girl for weeks simply because you knew that if she were in fact of inferior blood, then your marriage would simply be null and you'd be free to move on with your life. I do not believe it of you.

And perhaps Louisa would not have either, had she not already been so upset by the mistaken report of your death, had she not already resigned herself to your loss. Had I not already upset her with accusations of foul motives on her part. But I am afraid, my dear boy, that we created a terrible storm for her, your cousin and I and Fate itself.

I cannot think it anything but the hand of Providence, though. Perhaps you ought to consider that; consider that God himself spared you by delaying that train but had already set in motion the terrible accident that would lead to Louisa cutting all ties with us.

She left here mere hours after Edgar presented his findings. I did not mention it to you earlier because I thought to tell her in person about your not being on the Ignatius *and see what her response would be. But your wire came on the very heels of this report from the investigator.*

Perhaps we should not have confronted her with that, but I was beside myself and your cousin was insistent. Perhaps it was because she could so easily believe the worst of me that she extended no grace to you when Edgar presented her with the unfortunate fact that your marriage was never legal, never binding, and that you were the one to commission the investigation that proved it so.

From here, I shall be brief. She had her name removed from the accounts onto which you'd added her and has disappeared.

Here is where I confess my greatest failure: I do not know where she is, nor does her family. I thought perhaps she went to the teaching college at which she'd been enrolled, but they have heard nothing from her. We did indeed track her to Raleigh, North Carolina, but not to the school, and thus far we have not been able to find her in the city. I am certain we will, and we will endeavor to make amends. I will tell her, in full confidence and faith in you, that you were not the one to ask those questions, that it was all Edgar. I will simply assure her that the two of you can be married legally in either a northern state or in England once you're reunited, and all will be well.

Before you act rashly and start sending messages to everyone you can think of, please allow me the grace of setting this to rights. Please, Remington, let me ask for her forgiveness as I am asking now for yours. I know you love her, and I know she loves you. This will be but a bump in the road of your lives.

Raleigh. Rem's eyes returned to that word and stared at it. Because though he'd never been there, he knew the city.

Knew it by reputation, having heard far more about it than he really cared to do. Because Raleigh was where Garret Wynnwood was attending university.

He pushed his chair out a few inches, feeling as though he couldn't breathe, didn't have space enough. Of *course* she would go to Garret—where else would she turn? She'd need a friend above even the family who had lied to her about her own blood, and what other friend did she have? She couldn't turn to Celeste. Rem was, so far as she knew, the cause of it all and just as out of reach, and she would be too angry to confront her mother and . . . and *grandmother*, apparently.

So, she would turn to the one person who had never let her down, who would champion her, who would take her side no matter what. She would turn to the man who was also in love with her, who had let her go because she said it would make her happy, but who had already threatened Rem bodily harm if he hurt her. She would turn to the man who would be all too eager to persuade her to move on and forget about him, unworthy cad that he was.

"God, please . . ." He didn't know, though, what to pray. That He would somehow preserve their marriage, yes. That she would know that he'd never meant for any of this to happen. That she would trust in his love for her and see through his family's deceit. That she wouldn't fall into Garret Wynnwood's arms.

But it had already been weeks. Weeks in which she hadn't come. Which meant weeks that she'd been there. With him.

That thought made him push away from his desk entirely and pace the length of his bedchamber. She'd told him she didn't care for Wynnwood like that, never had. That he was a brother to her. But what if—what if this was the blow that turned her heart in his direction? What if she took one look at that towering giant with his kind heart and realized she'd made a mistake, that she should have chosen him from the start? Or if she was so blinded by pain that she *wanted* to believe her heart had moved toward him?

He rubbed a hand over his face, not wanting to doubt her fidelity, but—but it wouldn't be infidelity to her mind, would it? First she'd thought him dead, and then she'd been informed that they weren't legally married. Never had been in the eyes of the law, which meant that *theirs* was the illicit affair.

"No." He stopped in the middle of his room, not looking at the mahogany bed frame with its elegant hangings, nor at the matching desk where her photo was still propped up, smiling at him. Not looking at the curtained window meant to hide his light from any enemies abroad, nor at the mantel with its mocking clock, shouting that too much time had already slipped away. It had already been so long since this all happened. While he'd sat blissfully in the little cupboard of an office called Room 40, decoding German messages, telling himself she'd been delayed.

But one thing settled in his heart with the weight of truth—a truth even Mother had known. Louisa *was* his wife. Legal or not, he'd stood with her in a church before Almighty God and taken his vows before a clergyman and her neighbors. They were married morally, just like Grann and her husband had been. Ethically. *Rightly.* Who cared what some convoluted, outdated, bigoted law said on the matter? How could any law tell her what her blood even *was*? For all they knew, one of Grann's forebears had also been of mixed blood, making that fraction a little smaller in her own veins.

She was his wife. His heart. His everything. And the minute this blasted war was over, he'd be on the first steamer back to America for her. He'd find her, wherever she was, and he'd promise her he'd never cared about any of that, that it had been Edgar, not him, to ask such questions.

228

Edgar. New fury washed over him, making his hands shake as he strode back to his desk and snatched up that traitor's two letters. He had half a mind to toss them into the fire rather than read them—but no. Information was key. Information was how he would set all this to rights. He needed to know what he'd done.

Edgar's explanation offered no insight, though. The first was simply an *I told you so*, and the second was a copy of the investigator's report. As if that mattered a bit.

He tossed the nonsense back to his desk and picked up the photo, staring into Louisa's colorless eyes, tracing the curve of her smile. He couldn't let her go, let his mother sort it out. He would sit and write letters to send to the inn, to the college. He would even write to Garret Wynnwood in Raleigh if he knew how to reach him, which he didn't. He would write to anyone and everyone he could think of, his mother's begging be hanged.

But from below came the crash of a door and the cheerful bellow of the bull known as Sebastian, his words indistinguishable through floors and ceilings, but their message clear as a church bell: His brother was home.

Rem turned from desk to door, fingers curling into his palm and indecision rendering him into stone. Words pounded at his heart, his mind, begging to be put to paper. But *Sebastian.* He hadn't seen his older brother since he left for Maryland last spring, six long months ago. He'd been waiting rather impatiently for him to return from whatever friend's country house he'd been visiting this time so he could tell him . . .

His shoulders sagged. There was too much to tell him, and all those words were tangled up with these new ones, knotted with anger and frustration and betrayal so that he didn't even know if anyone else could make sense of them.

There was first the confession about Mother—that she

was never coming home. Then the news of his marriage. And now . . . now the news of how Edgar and Mother and a tragic fire on the ship he should have been on had made a mess of absolutely everything, and he didn't know how to set it to rights.

But maybe Sebastian would. Knowing him, he'd do as he always did and rush into the thunderstorm, ready to dance with the lightning. Charge across the torpedo-and-mine-dotted sea and promise to sort it all out for him in half a wink.

A bit of the weight slipped off his sloped shoulders. Sebastian would come up with a plan within seconds. He would help him put it all in perspective, sort it out.

Decision made, Rem tucked the photo back into his wallet and then pulled open his door and hurried down the stairs to intercept his brother before he could either vanish again or come up to find him.

Or, he realized with a wince when raised voices reached him as his feet hit the landing, find Father, who must have returned while Rem was reading.

He sighed as he hurried down the final stretch of stairs. The problem was that those two were too much alike. They were constantly butting heads, and they both seemed to enjoy it too much to ever put a halt to it, no matter how often Mother had begged them. And it only took them seconds to lock horns and start trying to shove each other about.

Once in a while, Rem could bring a peace to their meetings, though now he was more in need of it himself than ready to interject it into *their* relationship. But maybe if he charged in and demanded assistance, it would shock them into settling down.

Except that when he strode into the library, mouth open and ready to call a halt to their ridiculous argument of the hour, whatever it might be, his words died on his lips. Because though Father's face was flushed with rage, yes, this time Rem could see why in a single glance.

Sebastian stood in the center of the room, honey-brown hair gleaming nearly as much as his polished black boots and the brass buttons on what was, without question, an army officer's uniform.

"Sebastian?" It wasn't a greeting so much as a demand for this hallucination to clear from his eyes. Because what else could it be? Sebastian couldn't have joined the army. Sebastian was the heir. *Rem* was the one who was supposed to be in the military, but who had sidestepped it for now by working within the Admiralty as a civilian. And for that matter, their family was a naval family, not an army one. There was no way—absolutely none—that Sebastian could really have signed up to fight in this blighted war.

Yet his brother spun to face him, a stubbornly bright smile upon his lips, arms outstretched as if to say *Look!* Handsome as ever, bold as those brass buttons, and with Father's stubborn cut to his jaw. In olive green. "Remmy! There you are. Tell him, won't you? That I *had* to sign up. Someone has to fight for Brave Little Belgium. See the Boche are taught a lesson."

Rem's lips moved, but he couldn't make any other words come out. He could only stare at Sebastian, dart a look to their father, and feel the earth shudder beneath him.

Father rounded the table from which he'd no doubt been about to pour a cognac and strode their way, face still red. "You have pushed too far this time, Sebastian. It will be undone. Now. Immediately. My heir cannot go gallivanting off to Europe. Take off that ridiculous uniform this instant. I'm going to go and make a few calls." He strode from the library, no doubt on a direct course for his study and their telephone.

The moment he was gone, Sebastian relaxed. His smile turned to a grin, and he ran a hand down the front of that "ridiculous uniform" with what could only be called pride. "I think it looks rather smashing. Matches my eyes."

"Sebastian." Rem let his eyes slide closed for a heartbeat while he drew in a fortifying breath, then he opened them again. "This is a stunt, right? A joke. Your newest plan for riling Father."

"*Au contraire*, brother dearest." Sebastian swaggered over to the table Father had abandoned, unstopped the decanter of cognac, and poured two fingers into one of the crystal tumblers always ready for such a libation. "It's very real." He held up the decanter over a second glass and shot Rem a raised brow.

Rem shook his head. "But—why?"

Sebastian set the decanter down again with a happy thunk and lifted the glass. "Because there's glory to be had. I can't let all the other chaps find it while I sit about twiddling my thumbs and going to the club, can I?"

Rem stumbled his way to a chair and sank into it. "Well, *yes*. You could."

His brother shook his head and took a sip from his glass before settling into the armchair across from Rem. "No, actually. I couldn't. I'd never be able to look at myself in the mirror if I did that."

"But . . ." He groped around his overtaxed mind, searching for all the many reasons that this was impossible. One that didn't ring of fear or cowardice or the selfish insistence that he needed Sebastian to solve *his* problems, not Belgium's. All he could find were Father's words. "But you're the heir."

"Please." Sebastian snorted and looked deep into the amber liquid, as if some moving picture were playing out in the inch of liquor. "I'm a lousy heir anyway—how often has Father said as much? He'll probably be relieved to know I'm out of the way for a while, once he calms down enough to think of it and gets over the affront to his pride. He still has you. You'll do a bang-up job of helping with things while I'm gone, and if the unthinkable happens, you'll carry on the family line. Marry some fine, boring gentlewoman and produce the next generation of fine, boring Culbreths." He tossed back enough of the cognac to make him wince.

Rem winced along with him. He'd told Father about Louisa, of course, given that he'd expected word of her impending arrival each and every day. But he hadn't seen Sebastian yet and hadn't even known where to send a letter. "Actually . . . I've already married. While I was in America. And she isn't exactly a 'fine, boring gentlewoman.'"

Sebastian choked on his next swig, coughing and sputtering and smacking the tumbler down onto the side table with wide eyes. It was a long moment before he managed to gasp out, "You *what*? Who? When, how, *what*?"

It would have been amusing, had he not come home to that stack of disastrous letters. Propping his elbow on the arm of the chair, Rem leaned into his hand, exhausted by it all. By the whole blighted world. "Her name's Louisa. She's the daughter of the innkeeper where Edgar and I spent the summer." In as few words as possible, he explained falling in love with her, marrying her when he received Father's summons home. How Mother had received her—and the plan to teach her all she needed to know.

He leaned forward, ready to say the rest, what those letters had told him. But something stopped him. Maybe it was the way Sebastian was fiddling with his buttons. Maybe it was the light of pride in his eyes. Maybe it was the knowledge that his brother couldn't fix this for him any more than Louisa had been able to. Sebastian's boldness and bluster would be applied to another cause, not his. And it would be terribly unfair to send him off to war with that burden on his shoulders. So, he stopped the explanation at his departure.

Sebastian let out a low whistle. "Fire and brimstone, little brother. I didn't realize you had it in you. Good show, I say. Nothing will teach Mother a lesson about humility like choosing your own bride on your own terms." He chuckled, shook his head, and his eyes positively sparkled. "I wish I'd been there to see the look on her face. But why didn't you bring Louisa home with you? I wish I'd been able to meet her before I go off to rout the Huns!"

Rem sighed. "I meant to."

"But the U-boats, I suppose. And the mines." Sebastian nodded. "Well. I suppose I shall have to secure victory for His Majesty quickly so that we can all rally back here and get to know each other. I ship out in two days, you know." Grinning, Sebastian shoved to his feet. "Do you at least have a photograph of this new sister of mine?"

He fished it out of his wallet, caressing her face with his own gaze before handing the photo to his brother.

Any other day, Sebastian's bulging eyes would have made him laugh. "Remmy! She's . . . she's *gorgeous*."

Today he could barely manage a lift of his brows. "You say that as if you're surprised that I managed to convince a pretty girl to marry me."

"*Pretty* wouldn't have been surprising at all. But she's well above *pretty*." Laughing, shaking his head, the old familiar teasing in his eyes, he held the photo back out. "What's she doing with a dog like you, old boy?"

Just a jest. A joke. A tease. Like a million others they'd given each other over the years. He couldn't know how it would pierce, dig in, go straight to his heart. He couldn't know how it shattered him.

It was all too much. He wanted to pretend he was a lad again and curl up in a ball and cry over it. He wanted to slap at his brother for his careless words, pick a fight he could never win just because a sock in the nose would take his mind off the deeper pain. He wanted to take a page from Sebastian's playbook and shout and bellow and defy expectations.

But he didn't know how to do any of that. He only knew how to paste a small smile onto his lips, false cheer onto his face, and send his brother off to the trenches with hope. "I suppose you'll have to ask her that question after you've secured the victory for His Majesty."

16

TODAY

JUNE 30, 1942
OCRACOKE ISLAND, NORTH CAROLINA

For the first time since he first washed ashore seven weeks ago, Sterling was alone at the Ocracoke Inn. He waved Elsie off from the front porch with a smile, holding the book in his hands casually, praying she'd be convinced by the pages he'd turned steadily all morning as the rain pattered down and kept him inside. Praying she wouldn't know, as she too often seemed to, what he intended instead of what he'd claimed.

Maybe she believed him. Maybe she'd given up on him. Or maybe she was so eager to go see Mrs. Wynnwood, who'd been delayed again but had finally made it to Ocracoke on the mail boat yesterday afternoon, that she deemed it worth the risk of leaving him unattended in her home. Maybe— and this he doubted—she didn't care if he went snooping because she thought they had nothing to hide.

She could have thought it. But she was wrong. He knew that to his very bones. What he didn't know was how, even if he uncovered the worst about Evie Farrow, he could ever explain it to Grandma Elsie. How did anyone ever tell a sweet old lady that her granddaughter was quite possibly in league with the enemy?

He waited until she'd disappeared around the bend on foot, a basket on her arm bursting with baked goods that she'd been preparing all morning. The minute the rain let up, out the door she went, slipping him a note on her way by. *Going to see my girl now that she's home. Back by dinner.*

He didn't know where Evie had gone and had made a point of not asking. Probably running errands. Shopping. Dropping something off to a friend.

Or going, as she did every morning, to the Coast Guard station with her bribe of sugar-laden pastries. Ensuring that no one looked twice when those messages came in for her. Sending off her replies, no doubt, to whomever her contact was.

He turned another page, then flipped to the next chapter, not trusting either her or Elsie not to be keeping account of where his marker was. Then he slid the book onto the little wicker table beside his rocking chair and stood.

There was no telling how long he had before Evie returned, so he'd better not waste a moment's time. When would he have this chance again? Keeping an eye on every window he passed to make sure she wasn't even now strolling up the lane, he mounted the steps two at a time and moved to the room he knew was hers.

The door was shut, as always, but he didn't see any hairs or small seals that would tell her if someone entered. Not surprising, really, given that Elsie frequently came in here to deposit clean laundry and linens when she was the one to fold them. The knob turned under his hand without any protestation, and no one was around to hear the soft squeak of the door's old hinges.

He slipped inside, gave the small room a once-over, and frowned as he moved to the window and cracked it open. Not enough to be obvious from the outside, but enough that he'd hopefully be able to hear her coming, especially if she was humming as she so often did. As if she hadn't a care in the world. Hadn't secrets abounding.

He turned back to face the room, that frown only deepening. The space was all but empty. No photographs on these walls, no paintings, no drawings. No doilies on the dressing table. No vases with wildflowers. None of the many homey touches that made the rest of the inn so welcoming. The bed was neatly made with a quilt of pink sprigged cotton, a pair of soft house shoes sat on the floor at its foot, a short dressing gown of white hung on a hook.

Nothing that said *Evie*. No books but for the worn Bible on the bedside table. No personal touches, no sentimentality.

Strange, for a woman who put on such a front of being sentimental. Was that, too, a lie? All the stories about how deeply she cared? Was each smile, each touch she gave a neighbor part of her cover story? Had she even really grown up here, or had it been a place she visited now and then? For all he knew, her family had come to the inn as guests, and *that* was when that photo downstairs had been taken. Who was to say?

And why, why did it hurt? He'd been asking himself that question every day for the last two and a half weeks, as they tromped together through another square or two of his forest grid. He'd been tempted to tell her he'd do the search alone, but that would tip his hand. So he'd let her drive him to the end of the road, walked over the footbridge with her to the uninhabited part of the island, and he'd put on a show just like she did. He smiled, he teased, he laughed in all the right places.

He showed her the obvious items they came across—other rubbish, discarded knots of fishing nets, remains of campfires—and did his best to keep her from seeing the subtler ones—a tiny, bloodied piece of cloth stuck on a thorn, and the true linchpin to his theory about Mansfeld: a crumpled, half-buried Gitane cigarette box.

It was Mansfeld's preferred brand, and who outside of France smoked them? Even the box was French blue, proclaiming its national pride.

Thank the Lord he'd seen that corner poking up out of the sand while she was in the next grid-square over. Thank the Lord that she hadn't seemed suspicious when he suggested they split up to cover more ground. And pray to God *she* hadn't found anything even more telling and failed to show him just as he'd failed to show her that.

He shook himself back to the present. Her room. Shoved aside that naïve, too-hopeful voice inside that said she must have an explanation, and maybe *that* was what he'd find when he searched. Answers that would say he could trust her like he desperately wanted to. Assurances that he wasn't either an idiot or a cad admiring the trim curves and the generous smiles and the quick wit of his hostess.

Idiot. And he certainly felt the cad as he slipped open each drawer of her dresser and went through them. Touching her things, making certain he returned each to exactly the place it had been.

But all his squirming conscience was for nothing. She had absolutely nothing in there but clothes, and the expected ones, at that.

After another check of the window, he moved to the desk. The drawers were locked, but barely. It only took him a second to pick them, slide each one open, and draw in a breath at the neat manila envelopes inside. Just like the one that Herb fellow had dropped off at midnight after their first day searching.

He peeked inside each long enough to tell him that they were all encoded. That would have to be enough, since he certainly had neither the time nor the skill to decipher them now. Instead, he settled for tallying up how many of them there were and making a mental note. *Fourteen.* Fourteen manila envelopes. Some thin, some thick. A few single-page telegrams, including the one he'd seen on the day of Tommie's funeral.

The other drawers held blank paper, pencils, pens, rubber bands. Nothing alarming. No codebooks or keys he could use to make sense of those blighted envelopes.

He closed the drawers, relocked them with his makeshift pick, and moved on. Testing the floorboards and molding didn't reveal any hiding places, and the mattress gave up no hidden items, so he shut the window again and let himself out.

There was only one other place in the inn he could think to look, but it was a risk. If he was up in the attic, he definitely wouldn't know when she came home. But again, when else could he look there?

It was a risk he'd have to take. And what was the worst that could happen if she caught him?

A memory of that wicked little pistol she'd first greeted him with crashed into his skull. He paused with his hand on the string to the attic's drop-down stairs, nostrils flaring. He hadn't seen *that* in her room either. Where did she keep it?

And why, if she knew he doubted her allegiances, which she was too clever not to realize, had she not pointed it at him again?

The only answer that made any sense was that she really

was as tenderhearted as she seemed. That most of what he'd learned of her was true. She couldn't hurt him—she couldn't hurt *anyone*.

He pulled down the stairs and made quick work of them, even as that hope he'd been trying to keep banked sparked to life again.

She may well have a connection to Mansfeld, she may be helping the enemy—but did she know it? Was it of her own free will? What if she was being coerced? What if she needed him to help her but was afraid to say so, lest it draw him into more trouble?

Or maybe he was too eager to play her hero. Too eager to excuse her. Too eager to have a reason to take her in his arms and promise her that everyone would be all right.

The attic was hot and dim and dusty, the smell of mold and damp taking him immediately back to Jolly Old England and his own family's damp, musty, but considerably cooler attic.

No surprise, then, that this one was filled with the usual detritus. Boxes of this and that that meant nothing to anyone but the person who'd shoved it up here—not important enough to display, too dear to toss out. Faded old photographs of strangers, broken vases, books whose bindings were falling apart and whose pages were spotted and yellowed.

His torch beam flashed from one tattered box to the next until finally, under the small garret window that didn't open to relieve the stuffiness, he saw something that looked more promising. A trunk, old but not covered with the same layer of dust as most of these things. He settled on the floor in front of it, flipped its latches, lifted the lid.

On top were newspaper clippings dating from the Great War. He flipped through them, looking first at the dates—

ranging from 1914 to 1918—then went back and read the headlines. They were all general war pieces, nothing that mentioned any names other than the brass in charge.

There had to be a reason they'd been kept though, so he read through them more carefully. The first, the second, the third. That was when he realized that they were general stories with a particular angle—they all detailed the German advance into France, the territory they'd claimed.

His eyes fell on that word that sent a shiver, now, up his spine. *Charleville.*

He read through them all, looking for any other clue, but that seemed to be the only thing they had in common. Careful to keep them in their proper, chronological order, he set them aside and reached into the trunk for whatever was next.

A postcard with the Eiffel Tower on the front. On the back, words written in a looping, feminine hand.

Lulu,

I don't just wish you were here—I'm pretending you are. Every street I walk down with Mama or Pierre, I'm imagining you beside me, seeing it through your eyes. I wanted to send a postcard so you could see it at least a little, but a long, fat letter filled with all the descriptions will be coming soon! And perhaps a package with one of the fancy dresses you don't want. Hear me laughing maniacally? It's only fair—Pierre dragged me and imaginary you through the Louvre yesterday.

Celeste

P.S. Tell old Beanpole I say hello when he comes home again.

Lulu? Celeste? The names meant nothing to him—but they became increasingly familiar as he pulled out a stack of letters, all from Celeste to this Lulu. All dated from 1911 until . . . 1914, it looked like. He opened the last one and read it.

Pierre says he's not worried, that this war won't last long. That we'll be fine. So don't fret about me, okay? We'll hunker down in Pierre's big old mansion like we did in the lighthouse during that hurricane when we were kids, and we'll be just fine. Pierre says that with Charleville being on the Belgium border, it's the safest place in all of France, since Belgium is neutral territory. I'll write as always, but don't be alarmed if they're late getting to you. Pierre says there may be some interruptions to the post.

I hope you're well and enjoying your summer and that those rich gents aren't proving too much a pain. Sounds like Master R has become a good friend! And maybe more? (Imagine me wiggling my brows at you.) I can't wait to hear more about how everything has developed, but I haven't gotten any letters from you in weeks—which I think is evidence that Pierre is right about the mail, because I know you'd have written two or three times since that one. Well, a chance to exercise my patience, as Grandma would say.

Give her a hug for me and tell her I love her. I've written to her, too, and told her to give you the same.

Yours always,
Celeste

His gaze skittered back to the articles. Lulu must have been the one who kept both the clippings and the correspondence and tucked them away up here. And it was no wonder why, if Celeste had been in Charleville. Pierre, whoever he was, had been very wrong. Germany hadn't respected Belgium's neutrality. Marching through the small country, taking it over, and from there, launching into France had been their first moves.

As for what happened to Celeste . . . Sterling flipped through the other papers in the trunk, but they only got older from there. Nothing to tell him what became of the girl who must have ended up behind the German lines for the entirety of the Great War.

His stomach went tight as he recalled his history, though—history he'd already been refreshed on as he tracked Mansfeld. The Ardennes department had been hit hard and early as the German army advanced into France, and Charleville had become their base of operations throughout the conflict. All the once-prosperous town's mansions and municipal buildings had been requisitioned by the army—and all their food and resources as well. According to the 1919 account he'd read in preparation for his own clandestine journey into the region, the German officers had dined and enjoyed themselves while the French citizens starved and froze to death, ousted from their homes.

He set the papers down, more reverently than he'd really anticipated doing as he searched through Evie's family's things.

Maybe this was her connection to it all. Maybe she had some relation to Lulu or Celeste and had visited Charleville in search of the truth about what happened to her. Lulu could even be Aunt L, Garret's just-returned wife, couldn't she?

More pieces. More puzzles.

More questions that rose up as he sifted through those older documents. Yellowed and fragile enough that they weren't from the lifetime of anyone of relevance today, but telling nonetheless. Codebooks. Encryption keys. Intelligence materials.

Who in blazes *were* these people?

He packed the trunk back up carefully, did his best to obliterate the evidence of where he'd sat on the dusty floor, and climbed back down the rickety ladder, half-expecting to find either Evie or Elsie waiting for him at the bottom, stern-faced and pistol-toting. But the house still echoed his footfalls back at him, empty and, it seemed now, haunted by all the tears that must have been shed in its halls and rooms. All the worried conversations it must have soaked in. All the pacing feet that must have worn paths over its floorboards.

The sun had peeked its head through the clouds while he was lost in history, so he followed it out onto the porch and into the lane. He had no goal in mind, just the need to get away from the inn for a little while and see if he could make any sense of all that he'd learned.

The village was small enough that he'd already explored it several times in its entirety. He'd gotten in the habit of walking at least every other day to the O'Neal family cemetery and its donated graves, and that was where his feet pointed him this time too. It meant he would see more neighbors than he really cared to, given that he had to cut through the main part of town, but it was a risk he was willing to take. No one ever asked him anything beyond the mundane anyway—he was, in their eyes, a guest. And guests were never trusted with more than exchanges about the weather, old ghost stories, and commentary on the news. No one ever asked him about Evie or Elsie or why he was making daily excursions into the woods. They simply recommended a few of the local favorite paths and wished him happy exploring.

He still had five minutes left in his walk when motion

caught his attention. A flash of purple, somehow familiar. He stopped, drew back, hid himself behind the twisted trunk of a live oak before he even realized that it was familiar because it was Evie's favorite dress, the one she wore more than any other. And it was Evie standing at the faded door of a little bungalow, turning a key in the lock on the door.

His brows knit. Unlike every other house on the lane, that small one at the end had a neglected air about it. The shutters had peeling paint, the siding was faded and splintering, and the lawn was overgrown, though not gone to seed. No bright flowers curled up the fence posts, no pigs or chickens darted about. It was a sad little place. Not exactly derelict, but . . . neglected. Waiting, it seemed, for someone to remember it.

A neighbor who was ill? Had gone inland? It would make sense—someone could have asked her to check on things, and of course she would. But why in the world was she locking the door? No one on Ocracoke locked their doors, not that he'd ever seen. Maybe they would, though, if they were gone for longer than a few hours.

She didn't turn his way, which surprised him, given that the lane ended at the house. Instead, she chose a path that cut through the trees. It would take her home faster, no doubt. In fact, had he known it existed, he may have been taking it every time he walked to the cemetery. He looked again to the forgotten house. Debated.

Well, in for a penny, as they said. He'd already broken into her room, her desk, her attic. Why not whatever this place was?

His conscience gave him any number of perfectly good reasons not to slink along the empty lane toward the house, but he shushed it and reached into his pocket for the same metal file and slender rod he'd used to pick her desk's lock. A glance over his shoulder assured him that no one stirred at the other houses in sight. No doubt everyone was about their normal days, unaware that anything unusual was going on with the young woman they all loved and thought they knew.

Still, he moved around to the back instead of testing his skills on the front door's lock. He found a second door without any trouble, and this one offered him the shelter of nothing but trees to watch him. It took him a bit longer to convince this lock to give than it had her desk, but soon enough it clicked, turned, and he stepped inside.

The inside was nothing like the outside. Everything was neat, dust-free, well ordered. More. *Pretty.* Well decorated, he saw as he meandered from the kitchen into the dining room, and not with the cheap bric-a-brac he'd expected to see. Well-kept antique furniture, much of it screaming *England* to his eyes. Quality upholstery. Silver gleaming from the Chippendale cupboard.

It was *her* house. He didn't know how he knew it, but he did, the moment he looked around. He knew it even before he spotted the photo hanging on the wall—the same one as was hanging at the inn, only larger.

Evie and Job.

He moved toward it, his eyes falling to another frame, propped up on the sideboard. But this one didn't hold a photo, not exactly. It was a newspaper clipping. With a photo of that same smiling young man—Job—decked out in his Coast Guard uniform, cap on his head. His official photo, from the looks of it. Somber, proud, handsome.

But it was the headline that made his breath catch. LOCAL HERO DIES IN MARITIME RESCUE. Sterling checked the date—July three years ago—and then read the article. The one that told of the storm that had come up unexpectedly. Of the Coast Guard cutter that responded to an SOS that came in over the wireless, manned by Herbert O'Neal, Job Farrow, and Calvin Johnson.

Job Farrow. His gaze jerked back up to the photo, the one whose back he hadn't looked at, but whose words he'd committed to memory nevertheless. *Evie and Job, September 14, 1936.* Back down to the newspaper.

The storm had been fierce. They'd done everything by the book. But something had gone wrong. Job Farrow managed to save the injured owner of the storm-tossed sailboat, but he'd lost his life in the process. *Leaving behind a young widow, Evelyn, his parents, William and Yolanda, many aunts and uncles and cousins, and countless neighbors who will grieve the loss of so fine a man and so worthy an officer . . .*

"Evie Farrow." He whispered the words even as he looked at her portrait again—wedding portrait, he suspected. Married in 1936, when she would have been, what, twenty-one? Twenty-two? Widowed three years later. Three years ago.

It didn't explain everything, not even close. But it explained a little. It told him who Job was, and why she looked so happy in his arms. It no doubt explained a few of the shadows in her eyes too. It even explained why she went every day to the Coast Guard station, why those men greeted her like she was one of their own.

She was. She was theirs, they were hers. Bound together not only by marrying one of them, but by losing him.

He didn't bother looking at anything else in the house, even though this may well be where he'd find more answers. He'd intruded enough for one day. Learned enough. Trod, he knew, on something precious.

He let himself out, locked the door, and took the long way back to the inn, by way of the cemetery. He had a lot of praying to do.

17

YESTERDAY

DECEMBER 1914
OCRACOKE ISLAND, NORTH CAROLINA

Jingle sauntered along, the bells on his harness matching his name but making a mockery of Louisa's plodding steps. The inn's wagon was loaded with the supplies they'd ordered for the winter, but empty of what she'd hoped for—news. News from Celeste, news from Garret, news from the Remingtons in Maryland.

The whole world, it seemed, was conspiring against her when it came to correspondence. Yet another boat with no mail for her. For the third week in a row. It was going to be a bleak Christmas, that was certain.

She ran a hand over her stomach and whispered a silent apology to the little one inside, making her dresses strain against her abdomen. It wasn't the baby's fault that she couldn't raise her spirits beyond half-mast. It was, in fact,

249

the baby who deserved the credit for even that much height. Without that hope growing inside her, that promise that she had a bit of Rem still to hold and cherish, she didn't know what she'd have done.

But Edith still hadn't so much as acknowledged the letter she'd sent last month, when she was absolutely sure it wasn't wishful thinking, that she really did carry Rem's child. She'd thought . . .

What had she really thought? That this would be the thing to build a bridge between her and her mother-in-law, when nothing else had done it? *Stupid.* Maybe Edith had let her cry with her that first night, when the news had been so fresh and bleeding, but the very next morning she'd told Louisa it was best if she packed her bags and returned to her mother.

She'd thought maybe they would grieve together, at least for a few days. But if Edith instead needed to grieve alone, she could respect that. She'd packed her bags. And to prove to her husband's family that she hadn't married him out of anything but love, she'd even had her name taken off his accounts before she left Baltimore, keeping out only enough to pay for her trip home.

There'd been a time or two since then when she'd wished she'd kept a bit more. Enough to pay for baby supplies. But she hadn't known she'd need that. And they'd get by, just like they always did.

The wind blew off Silver Lake, cold and cruel and cutting right through the wool jacket she'd slipped on. Still, she couldn't quite bring herself to pick up her pace. It was all so . . . *heavy.* The hurting. The worry.

She hadn't heard from Celeste since the war started, not but for that one letter that she'd penned before the German advance through Belgium, but which hadn't arrived until September. The one telling her she'd be fine, just fine. That

Pierre said so. They'd hunker down in his big old mansion like it was the lighthouse in a storm.

But Louisa had read every newspaper to come to the island. She knew that Charleville had been one of the first places seized by the German army. She knew that its fine mansions were now the headquarters of military officials.

And what of the families they'd displaced? Where were *they*?

Maybe they'd fled before the Germans arrived. They could be even now in Pierre's favorite hotel in Paris, eating baguettes and shaking their heads over the home that was lost to them for now, laughing over how wrong he'd been to assume the Germans would respect Belgium's neutrality.

She wanted to believe it. But she didn't. Because if Celeste was in Paris, she'd have sent letters and postcards and telegrams by now, just to assure her and Grandma Elsie that she and her mother were alive and well.

Grandma Elsie. She'd nearly forgotten, and that proved how not herself she was feeling. A sting of shame heating her cheeks, she altered Jingle's course and headed for Elsie's house, checking to make sure Doxee had left enough room in the wagon for the three trunks she said she'd bring with her.

The moment she stopped the wagon, the front door opened and Elsie stepped out, looking every bit as tired as Louisa felt. She, too, had been waiting every day for assurances that Madeline and Celeste—the two people she had left in the world—were okay.

But they didn't know it. They didn't know, and the wondering was killing them both, and that was why Mama had finally convinced Elsie to come to the inn with them for the winter. No one needed to spend Christmas alone with their questions, she'd said. They'd be one another's family while their true family was gone.

Gone forever, some of them. But maybe only for a while, for others. *Please, God. Please. You took Rem. Don't take Celeste. Be with her, wherever she is. Be her comfort and her strength. Be her salvation.*

Between the two of them, Louisa and Grandma Elsie loaded the three trunks into the wagon—two with her needful things, no doubt, and one that made Louisa's eyes flood with tears. *Their* trunk. The one full of wonder and history and hours of fun. The one with a heritage that she'd made her own even though she had no right to it. The one she'd shared with Rem on that beautiful summer's day.

It took some mighty rapid blinking to convince her eyes to stop with the waterworks—she *did* blame the baby for how often she lost that struggle these days. But she'd more or less gotten them under control when she looked to Elsie. *Sure?* she asked, brows raised.

Grandma gave her a small, sad smile. She pointed to the trunk, then to herself, and signed, *Together.* She tilted her head, reached out to touch warm fingers to Louisa's cold cheek, and added, *Yours also. Two of us need.*

Maybe they did, at that. Maybe those memories would help somehow. She nodded, fastened the tailgate of the wagon again, and clicked Jingle back into a walk.

The bustle as they arrived distracted her for a while, at least. Getting everything unloaded, put away, Elsie settled, and then it was time to help Grann make supper. Hours and hours of enough busywork to keep her mind occupied with the mundane so that she didn't have to think. Hours and hours to wear her body out until it was just as tired as her spirit, so maybe she'd actually sleep tonight.

Hours and hours when she didn't have to face that empty desk with its lack of letters.

In days gone by, she may have slipped up to her room after

252

the meal to read or write a reply to Celeste or Garret. These days, she headed for the main room instead, and she picked up the cloth and needle and thread that had felt so awkward in her hands when she first got them out two months ago. Give her a wrench or a hammer any day.

But wrenches and hammers wouldn't clothe her baby, so she sat close to the lamp and focused on tiny, even stitches while the older women laughed together in the kitchen as they tidied up after the meal. They'd shooed her out, and she hadn't protested. Her stomach tended to rebel a bit in the evenings, and it was better when she was sitting.

One stitch, two, three, ten. *Don't think. Don't think. Don't think.*

She must have succeeded in drowning out her senses as well as her thoughts, because she started when the cushion beside her sank under someone's weight. Mama smiled, smoothed back a curl that had slipped from Louisa's chignon, and looked deep into her eyes.

"I don't like to see that sorrow in your eyes, Louisa my girl."

Then best to avert them. Though Mama would have none of that. She put a finger under Louisa's chin as she'd been doing all her life and turned her face back again.

Their eyes were the same blue, she knew. But that was where their resemblance ended. Maybe if she'd looked more like Mama—had her fair hair, fairer skin—Rem's family wouldn't have dismissed her at first glance. Maybe they'd have given her a chance. Maybe then, somehow, it would all be different. She didn't know how, but surely it could have been.

Maybe they'd have been so busy with introductions and celebrations that they'd have planned their departure for another time. Maybe then they'd have left together. Maybe

Rem would still be alive, proud of her. She'd never have thought those horrible things in the minutes before it all came crashing down. She wouldn't have to live each day with so much regret.

She should have spent his last days of life differently. She should have tried harder to show Edith and her father how much she loved their Rem, her Rem. Why he'd loved her.

Mama sighed and shook her head, cupping Louisa's cheek. "You remind me so much of your daddy when you look like that. So set on carrying the weight of the world on your shoulders, even when it's not yours to bear. Even when your shoulders can't be that strong."

The foolish tears surged again, hot and blinding. She was afraid to say anything—afraid not to. Afraid anything she did would stop her mother's words.

But Mama plucked the tiny little white gown from her fingers, set it aside, and then wove their hands together. "It's time you know, honey. I wanted to spare you the truth and all it means for you. But maybe it'll help somehow now. I don't know how, but . . ." She choked a bit on her words and looked away.

Toward Grann, who had apparently also come in and taken up her usual rocking chair in the corner. She was stitching, too, and making far quicker progress on the pieces she'd assigned herself than Louisa was.

Grann looked up now, met Mama's eye, and gave her a slow nod. "She can handle it, Serena. Always could have, I think. But definitely now."

It? Louisa didn't know what more, honestly, she could handle—but *it* sounded like the story she'd always wanted most. She gripped Mama's fingers and held her gaze.

"You know I went to Louisiana when I was your age. I had a cousin who'd settled there after the war, and she was in a delicate condition with three young children already to take care of. So I went to lend a hand."

It was the part of the story she'd been granted before, so Louisa nodded. "Cousin Maxie." She'd never met her, nor anyone else from that part of the family, but they got a card every Christmas—already had one this year, as a matter of fact.

Mama nodded and turned her face toward Grann again. "The Adairs were Maxie's neighbors. Not next door, mind—but their properties abutted in the back, and I'd only been there a couple weeks when I was outside running from a gator and Michael came to my rescue." Mama smiled a smile Louisa had never seen before. "Handsomest man I'd ever seen. And kind, too, even as he laughed at me."

Grann laughed now. "Tiniest gator anyone ever did run from. Scarcely more than a lizard."

"Well, this Carolina girl wasn't used to gators, small or otherwise, sunning themselves under her clothesline." Mama chuckled and leaned back against the couch. "Once he'd finished laughing, he introduced himself and helped me take the rest of the laundry down. I learned he and his mama owned that whole tract of land behind Maxie's and the pretty little house I'd admired when I drove around to town. I couldn't figure why Maxie hadn't told me about him yet or made introductions."

Grann sighed. "Then she learned. That cousin didn't waste any time telling you, did she?"

Mama shook her head and looked Louisa straight in the eye. "He and his mama owned more land than anybody but the old families—because they were part of it, the part no one wanted to talk about. His daddy had been one of the sons from the big plantation, but his mama . . ." She looked to Grann again. "His mama had been one of their slaves, until Emancipation came."

His mama. Her daddy's mama. Louisa reclaimed the fingers of one hand so that she could press them to her lips to hold in all the questions that wanted to spill out. Best to hold them in, she knew. Let Mama and Grann finish the telling. But she didn't even try to keep her eyes from blurring with tears this time.

Grann—Grann *was* her grann. Her grandmother. Blood as well as love. It changed nothing and everything all at once.

And it explained things, that simple knowledge, as surely as Mama's continuing words did. How the neighborhood treated that mixed-race family who "lorded over them all." How Mama had enough of a rebellious streak in her to keep seeking out Michael Adair's company, even when her cousin and Maxie's husband warned her against it. How they fell in love. Decided to get married, though they had to go far north to be able to, legally.

"But we did. Went all the way to Pennsylvania—farthest I've ever been from home. We found a preacher who would do it, which took some convincing. Married, had a honeymoon in Philadelphia, and then went back in time for spring planting."

"Folks didn't like it." Grann rocked forward and back, her needle flashing in and out of the soft white cloth with the speed of lightning. "But they were used to it. They'd been seeing me and James and Michael so long already. But my Michael." She halted, rocker and needle both, closed her eyes, and smiled another smile Louisa had never seen.

One she knew, though. A smile of sorrow as deep as pride, one of pain as wide as love.

"My Michael never could leave things be. When he saw an injustice, he had to fix it. When he saw a hurt, he had to try to heal it. When he saw someone in need, he had to try to help."

Mama's fingers squeezed Louisa's tight. "He was the best man in the world, Louisa. The kindest. Had the biggest heart. When you were born, the way he looked at you—like you were the very sunshine sent by God to warm his face and bring life to the earth."

Louisa moved her free hands to her own rounded stomach. She hadn't felt the quickening yet, but it should be coming soon. She was waiting for it. Wondering at every flutter, whether it was her own stomach or that life within, making itself known. Big as she was already, she'd been hoping she'd feel that first kick sooner than Mama said she would. Was it a little girl in there? A little boy? Would she look like Rem? Would he have his wit and heart?

Did she have any of *her* daddy in her, to live up to that love he poured out on her like anointing oil? She kept her eyes on Mama's beautiful face. She'd gone silent, remembering. But Louisa needed more. "What happened?"

Mama's sky-blue eyes fell to the ground. "There was tension between the sharecroppers and the white folks—nothing new there. But your daddy started urging all the colored men to register to vote, so they could change things. Some had before, after the war, had even held office—but then new laws started coming down. Laws that did their best to limit what a Black man could do. Michael was trying to help them meet those impossible standards, and . . . well. No one took too kindly to that."

Grann's needle flashed again. "What they *said* was that our family was an abomination, a sin against God, with our mixed blood. That we ought to be wiped off the face of the earth to atone for it. But we were hardly the only ones around those parts, so it wasn't our blood that offended them. It was the fact that we wouldn't keep to the colored sections. Wouldn't bow our heads and go quietly wherever they pointed. That we didn't know our *place*." Her needle jabbed, the thread pulling so taut it was a wonder it didn't snap.

But something had.

Mama shook her head. "You were five months old when they came one night. Came under cover of darkness, like the cowards they were. They came with rocks and with torches and they wanted to kill us all, even you. But your daddy had known it could happen, and he had an escape plan ready for us."

She looked up again into Louisa's eyes. Reached again to cup her cheek. "I didn't want to leave him. I'd rather have died that night in our blazing house than walk a day without him. But there was you to consider. He'd made me swear I'd get you to safety if anything happened. He made me swear it again as he shoved us and Grann out that hidden back door, as I begged him to come with us. Made us swear we'd protect you, keep you safe, bring you home here where no one had to know. He made us swear, and then he went to face the monsters."

Even if she hadn't been prone to too many tears thanks to the pregnancy, Louisa knew her eyes would have flooded at that. All these years she'd wondered about her daddy. Wondered who he was. Wondered what blood flowed through her veins.

Now she knew. The blood of a hero.

Mama was crying too. Mama, who *never* cried. Mama, who had faced all the questions in her hometown for twenty years without a flinch, without a sag of her shoulders, with her chin held high. Mama let out a sob and pulled Louisa to her and held on tight. "I'm so sorry, baby. Sorry I couldn't convince him to come with us. Sorry I didn't find a way to turn back and save him, so that you could know that wonderful man. Sorry I never told you. It was the only—the only way I knew to protect you. To keep you safe. To keep it all from following us. Happening again."

Louisa squeezed her eyes shut, buried her face in Mama's shoulder, and breathed in her familiar scent of lavender and chamomile. "You have *nothing* to be sorry for. Nothing. You think I'd have done any differently? You did the best you could with the blow you were dealt. The very best, always."

Grann came over, too, on Mama's other side, and wrapped her arms around them both. "He'd be so proud of you— both of you."

For half of forever they sat there like that, a tangle of limbs and tears and sniffles and the occasional assurance. There came the sound of the wind gusting through the porch, the occasional creak of a floorboard overhead as Elsie settled into her new room. But mostly there was the solace of answers long withheld, the certainty of love never withheld, and the realization that this time, at least, in this new chapter of their family story, things could be different.

Would be different. She would tell her baby every day about his or her father. About how ridiculous he'd looked with a tool in his hands, but how he wanted to learn anyway. About how smart he was, but how he viewed each person with the dignity they deserved as a child of God, never caring about the shade of their skin. About how he'd been the kind, too, to face all the injustices in his quieter way and demand something better.

She'd make sure this baby knew how much Rem loved them. The future they wanted to build together. They'd kiss his photo together every night. Pray for his family, even though that family wanted nothing to do with them. They'd make him proud, just as Mama had made Daddy proud.

Eventually, Mama pulled her embroidered handkerchief

from her pocket and dabbed at her face. Drew in a long breath. Dabbed at Louisa's face too. And said what she must have been wanting to say the whole time, to bring this all up. "It can be different for you, honey. I know you'll mourn Rem—but it can be different. You don't have to hide anything. There are no secrets handcuffing you to the past. You can . . . you can move on, when you're ready, like I never could."

From the next cushion over, Grann nodded, though her eyes weren't bright with hope for it so much as somber. Sad. "We all know Garret will marry you in a heartbeat whenever you're ready. He could be a daddy to your little one, if you give him half a chance."

"Or *ones*, the way you're growing." Mama tucked a dimpled grin into the corner of her mouth. "You do know that twins run in our family, right? Skipped a generation, but that's what they do. Sue and Sam, though," she said of the siblings who were ten years older than she and lived on the mainland, so that Louisa scarcely knew them. Linc was the only one of her uncles she really knew. "And my grandma had a twin sister too."

Twins. The word lit a hope inside her. Was it possible? Possible that she'd have two of Rem's babies to love through life? Two little Culbreths to teach? She rubbed a hand over her stomach.

"Don't focus on that 'twins' idea, Louisa." Mama bent to catch her gaze. "Think about what I said. About moving on—when you're ready. Give yourself permission, that's all I'm saying. Someday you may want that. Need that."

A someday when she was ready to stop loving the man who had completed her heart? She couldn't imagine that day. Didn't even want to. She looked from Mama to Grann. "You ever want to move on from your James, Grann?"

A knowing smile curving her own lips, Grann shook her head. "There was never anyone for me but him."

Back to Mama then. "And do you mean to tell me none of those handsome visitors who spent weeks and months flirting with you wouldn't have been willing to overlook the question of my daddy? You think none would have even applauded you for the stand you took, and that Daddy died for?"

Mama's face relaxed a bit too. "There may have been one or two. But not for me."

"It seems Adair women love once, with their whole heart. Forever." She squeezed Mama's knee, reached across her for Grann's hand. Admired, this time, the gradient of their skin tones. "Garret is a good man. But he's not mine."

"I'd never push you on it. Just wanted to say you *could*, if you wanted to. You could give yourself that second chance. You don't *have* to be like us."

That brought a tired smile to Louisa's lips. She couldn't imagine anyone else she'd rather be like than the women under this roof right now—Grann, Mama, Elsie. And if she had twins, how would there be any time for a man anyway? She looked down at that soft round of abdomen, wishing she could see within it. "Guess I need to start thinking up names."

"Mm." The question made Mama's face relax again, back into its normal ease. "Family names, do you think, or original ones?"

She'd been thinking at first that she'd choose something new, maybe something from one of the books she and Rem had read together over the summer. Something that spoke of their short history together. But now . . . what better way to honor the legacy of their families than to choose names from them? "Family, I think. But not Remington Junior—not with the way the Remingtons have acted."

261

She'd forgive them—she was trying to, every day. But the cut still stung. Rem had never liked that his name was a branding, his mother's way of claiming him for her family. He wouldn't want his son, if she carried one, to bear that mark as well. "Maybe after our fathers, if it's a boy. Rem's daddy is David. And Michael—Michael David, or David Michael, do you think?"

It was gratifying, seeing the way their eyes both lit at speaking her daddy's name. Grann answered first, with a nod. "David Michael—only fitting that the paternal side comes first for a boy."

"So then for a girl, our side would come first. Serena Edith." She didn't even wince at that middle name. That counted for something, didn't it?

Mama did, though. Or maybe not at the *Edith* part. "Gracious, honey, not Serena. We don't need two of us running around the same house. Trust me, it gets confusing. I think . . . I think for our side, you ought to go with your grandmother." She turned her head, smiled at Grann. There was an exchange there that Louisa couldn't quite see, but she knew what it said. That they were family, mother and child, made that way through Michael's love and many years spent toiling together.

"Evelyn," Mama said. "If it's a girl, name her *Evelyn* Edith. Grann never goes by it, but someone should."

Louisa smiled, too, and placed both hands on her stomach. *Let there be two,* she prayed with more fervor than she'd felt for anything since that terrible telegram had come. *One of each, if I'm allowed to make demands.* David Michael *and* Evelyn Edith. David and Evelyn.

Davie and Evie.

18

Because it was still the start of his lunch hour, Rem gave in to the urge that had been plaguing him all morning and pulled out his wallet. Pulled out the photo. Caressed the face that smiled up at him. The edges were getting worn from the many times he took it out and put it back, all the times he'd held it. He kept telling himself he'd stop, leave it in there, put it in a tiny little frame in his room at Culbreth House so that he didn't damage it any more. And yet every morning he put it back in his wallet so he could carry Louisa with him to the work she would have loved.

He knew it was pathetic—that this was all he had left of his wife. A flat image in black and white. A flat hope that she'd forgive him. A flat future without her.

"Take a look at this, will you, De Wilde? It doesn't follow the usual patterns." The voice belonged to Dilly Knox and barely even registered in Rem's ears except to tell him that

Margot must have yet again begged off eating lunch with her mother and the other Admiralty secretaries.

That meant he wasn't alone in here, as he'd thought. Assumed. Perhaps he should have investigated it before assuming. He did so now, belatedly, and saw not only Dilly Knox bent over De Wilde's desk, the young lady still there with pen and paper before her, but also one more figure perched on the corner of her desk. Barclay Pearce wasn't a cryptographer, wasn't a navy man. Honestly, Rem wasn't sure *what* he was, aside from the one the bosses always turned to when they needed answers found or tricky errands run. And now he was watching Rem instead of his . . . whatever Margot was to him. They were some sort of family, he thought. Perhaps. Sort of—his sister was engaged to her brother, that was it.

Rem slid the photo back into his wallet, wishing Pearce didn't note absolutely *everything*. Wishing he wasn't walking Rem's way even now. Wishing that grin of his didn't say that he knew more than he should have. "You look like you could do with a bit of cheer, Culbreth. Why not join us at Pauly's Pub tonight? Margot's coming. Aren't you, Margot?" He said this last part louder, but De Wilde didn't even glance up.

She was looking at whatever Knox had put in front of her, pen flying over paper that had been blank a moment ago, lips moving in some silent litany that Rem could never follow.

It was humbling, sometimes, being in the presence of a girl who was so much his junior but who could outdo him in mathematics every single time. Every. Single. Time.

Pearce chuckled. "She's coming. You should too. It would do you good."

Rem sighed. Since Pearce had begun frequenting the halls of the Old Admiralty Building, he'd issued that same invitation to Rem no fewer than a half-dozen times.

One of these days he should probably accept. To be polite. "Perhaps I'll try. Where is it?"

"Poplar. I'll give you the direction—or maybe you should come with me the first time. Safer for you."

Poplar? Rem blinked, waiting for Pearce to say he was joking and break into laughter. Because why in the world would he frequent a pub in the city's poorest district? *Safe* was not a word ever applied to that particular neighborhood. "Em." It was all he could say to that.

Thankfully, Margot saved him the need to say any more when she leaned back with a shake of her head. "It isn't a German code. Isn't in German at all, I don't think. Where did it originate?"

"France, behind enemy lines. That's why I thought to show it to you—your French is better than mine." Knox delivered this with a grin that earned him a sardonic lift of De Wilde's brows.

She was Belgian, not French per se, but it was her first language, and you could still hear it in her vowels. Though Rem had to give her credit—her accent improved almost daily. Her mother's accent was still heavy, and she would lapse into French at the drop of a hat, but Margot seemed to be studying her new neighbors' intonations and idioms with as much dedication as she was studying the mass of intercepted telegrams that descended on them each day.

Rem had braved the unsafe airwaves and tried to send a telegram to both the college Louisa had been accepted at and the Ocracoke Inn via the nearest station, but he'd never heard back. He'd tried sending letters to Louisa at both places, but those he couldn't even be certain had made it across the Atlantic. He'd considered hunting up Garret Wynnwood's address in Raleigh to send something through him, but how would he find that? Not to mention that if Louisa had run to him, what hope was there that Garret would even deliver anything Rem sent? Especially if . . .

He squeezed his eyes shut. He couldn't imagine her in his arms. Wouldn't. It hurt too much.

He shoved away from his desk. "You know, I think I'll run home for lunch after all. See you all in an hour."

Not waiting for a reply from anyone, he gathered his hat and overcoat and made a dash for the door, out into the bracing winter chill. A brisk walk would do him good—more good than a meal at home. Father would be in his study as he always was during the day, poring over estate reports and ledgers and every newspaper to be found. Trying to guess where Sebastian was, how he fared.

The war, needless to say, had *not* been over by Christmas. It would not be over by spring. When Rem read the accounts of the trenches and the mere inches of land their men were bleeding for, he wondered if it would *ever* be over. How could it be, when they were fighting over feet instead of miles? It was nothing but a game of tug-of-war, and the no-man's-land was the mud pit between the sides, one that sucked men down whole and promised there could be no winning team.

Maybe there never was a winning team, not really. Not when war was tanks and guns and trenches instead of laughter and innocence.

It was an ugly world. Always had been, probably, but he'd never been able to see that so clearly before.

He reached home before he was really ready to, though his ears ached from the cold wind and his fingers were chilled even in their leather gloves.

What was the weather like in North Carolina right now? Warmer than this, most likely. But the wind could be nasty at the shore in the winter, Louisa had said. *"Could cut right through a body."*

266

Was she on Ocracoke? Back with Miss Serena and Grann by now? He hoped so. Prayed so. Even if that meant she'd poured out all the stories of his family's hatred, painted him with that same brush. Even if those women despised him now, still he hoped she was there. Among the people who could rub solace over the wounds for her.

And, yes, *not* then in Raleigh with Garret.

He would take a sandwich up to his room and write to her again. Maybe this letter would make it to her. He would try again and again and again and again until one of them reached her.

What if she's received them all? What if it's just that she doesn't want to respond?

The doubt was loud enough, gnawing enough to bring him to a halt, and he may have stood there like an utter imbecile, staring at his own door, had Babcock not opened it. "Master Remington. Good day. Shall I have Cook prepare you luncheon, or did you only forget something?"

Master Remington. He heard it in her voice more than the butler's. Saw that playful, mocking smile.

He shook himself and stepped inside so the cold and damp could be shut out of the house, if not from his soul. "A sandwich would be appreciated. Up in my room, if you please, though. I—"

"Remington? Good." Father appeared in the corridor, thunder in his eyes. "He'll eat in my study with me. Come. Now."

And why did he suddenly feel like a truant lad caught skipping class? Father pivoted back around, trusting he would be obeyed as always. Rem first took a moment to send Babcock a silent question.

The butler cleared his throat softly. And said even more softly, "There was a letter from your mother in this morning's post."

Heaven help them all. He turned his hat and coat over to Babcock and followed in Father's wake, wondering if it was an exaggeration to feel like he was marching toward his execution. Mother's letters never brought anything but more pain these days.

Father had taken his seat at his desk again, which was just like him. There were a pair of perfectly comfortable leather chairs before the hearth that would have made for a rather cozy luncheon, but no. The desk, always the desk, with his impressive throne of a chair behind it. Where Rem was forced to take a smaller chair across that wide expanse of wood and leather and paper and ink.

He sat and waited for Father to decide to speak.

He didn't wait long. Father sorted through a few papers, pushed a few across to him, and looked up. His gaze was heavy—but not stoic. Not cold. It was . . . apologetic. Soft, even. "It isn't good news, Rem. I'm sorry. The girl, Louisa— she's remarried."

"She's what?" He snatched at the papers, seeing that there were two letters folded together. One to him, one to Father. Both with the same news, just different slants. To him, with effusive apologies and long, drawn-out explanations of how their investigator discovered it. To Father, with only the cold hard facts, and the instruction that he should see Rem reenter society immediately and move on, so that he would forget her the sooner and put this whole "unfortunate incident" behind him, marry someone appropriate, and start a family.

"'Unfortunate incident'?" He had to read that phrase aloud, knowing incredulity saturated his tone. He looked up, ready to duke it out with the baron if he must. "This isn't Sebastian getting into a row at the club and socking the wrong chap in the nose. This is my *marriage*, my *life*. I won't be pushed beyond it!"

"Of course not." The simplicity of Father's words and the steadiness of his gaze defused a bit of Rem's temper like his usual command never would have done. "I don't expect you to do so. Here." He pushed a steaming mug of tea toward him. He must have poured the water just before Rem came in.

Never in his life had his father offered him what was *his*. Rem took it, held it in his thawing fingers, and stared into the cup. Even that hurt. "They have a tree that grows on the island—the yaupon, they call it. Its . . . its leaves. They harvest the leaves and dry them, then brew them as tea. It is, they say, the only native plant in North America that has caffeine in it, like coffee or tea. Everyone has old barrels that they use for the drying. They layer the leaves with hot stones. Let them roast and dry for weeks. I tried it. It was quite good."

It was inane. Irrelevant. But it was all he could think of to say.

"Rem. I'm sorry, my boy." Father took the letters back, folded them. "I know you've been writing to her. No doubt hoping she would see your side of things. Do you know if she's received any of them?"

He shook his head.

Father sighed. And reached his hand out, across the desk. It was too wide to really get close to Rem, but even so. David Culbreth was actually reaching out to him. Trying to offer comfort. "Then . . . I know you will not like to hear this. But it is probably best if you stop trying to reach her, knowing this. She has made her choice. It would be cruel of you to keep pursuing her. If she *hadn't* got them, if she made this decision in anger, it still wouldn't change it. If a letter were to reach her now, when she's married to another, if it were to make her second-guess herself . . . that would only be more painful for her."

Rem lifted the cup, took a sip. It tasted like gall. Because

Father was right. She'd either received his letters and not believed him, decided not to forgive him . . . or she hadn't. Either way, she'd turned to an old friend for comfort and let him give it. Either way, she'd decided to treat *their* marriage as the one that had been invalid. Illegal. Null. She and Garret had gone to Pennsylvania, Mother had said, to wed. Had a honeymoon in Philadelphia, and then returned to Raleigh.

Rem had failed her. Completely failed her. He'd proven so miserable a husband that she'd run from his family, from him, and chosen to scrape together what happiness she could find elsewhere. He couldn't blame her for that.

Father was most definitely right. If he tried to undo it now, he'd only make everything worse. It would be better for her if he accepted her decision. If he let her move on. If he . . . if he let her forget him, even if he could never forget her.

He had to set the cup down on the desk again.

"Rem—Remmy." Father never called him that, only Sebastian ever did. It brought his gaze up from the cup, the saucer, the glossy wood under them, and to the man still looking at him with something he'd never seen in his eyes before: vulnerability. "I loved your mother once, you know."

Rem could only blink at him. It shouldn't have sounded like such an admission, should it have? But his parents' hostility had only ever been covered with the thinnest veil of civility. At least in his memory. "Did you?" He didn't ask why—that was surely to his credit.

Father sighed and turned his face to the window. "When I spent that Season in New York, where I met her when she was there with a cousin—I thought her the most beautiful woman I'd ever met. Charming. So bright and lovely and clever. I did everything right, sought out her father, courted her. I didn't realize she was in love with someone else. Didn't realize that my proposal undercut her plans. I was the better match, of course. Her father informed her that she would accept."

He looked back to Rem, held his gaze. "I tried for years to make her happy. To love her, to earn her love. I thought when you lads came along that you would knit us together. Instead, she drew even further away, saying I had no need of her anymore. I argued, but she was so miserable here. . . ."

Rem shifted in his chair. Misery—the story, it seemed, of their life. And here he was, carrying on the tradition when he'd tried so hard to defy it. "I'm sorry too. That things grew so cold between you."

Father nodded. "Eventually I came to the conclusion that the kind thing would be to let her live her life however she saw fit. Spend whatever time she wanted in America with her family. Be at the Hall when I was here in Town, here at the House when I was in the country. All I ever did, it seemed, was remind her of the life she didn't have and had wanted so keenly. Perhaps it's a sad sort of kindness. But it's the only one she would accept from me."

And would be his lot, too, it seemed.

Rem nodded. Sat there for a moment more in silence. And then pushed to his feet. "I don't think I can eat just now, Father. Forgive me. I . . . I'll go back to the office."

Father made no protest, though he stood too. "Your mother seemed quite adamant about your moving on—but I am quite serious about not pushing you on that front. And I'll provide a buffer between you two, if I can."

Funny, since *he* had always tried to be the buffer between *them*. He offered what was probably a poor excuse for a smile. "Thank you."

A minute later, he was back outside, then in the park, then through the park. Climbing the familiar stairs into the

Old Admiralty Building. Moving along familiar corridors. Sliding back into that tiny little office.

De Wilde was the sole occupant now, she and her half-eaten sandwich. She'd shoved the mystery code to the side and must be working on one of their regular interceptions, given the codebook at her side.

This, at least, he could do without making a mess of anything, without hurting anyone. He could take codes, break codes, write decryptions, put them in the basket for the secretary to type up. He didn't have to make any decisions about what to do with the information. Couldn't be held responsible for what they chose.

It was a cold comfort. But it was all he had now. He slipped past De Wilde, toward his own corner desk. "Was that new one nothing of interest?"

De Wilde looked up at him, blinking to clear the numbers from her eyes before seeming to parse what he'd said. "Interesting, perhaps, but in a code we don't have. In English, though, sent to a government office here in London. I just had Barclay look into it on his lunch break. He said they'd tossed it out, saying it wasn't really for them. Very odd."

English, not French? Though originating in German-occupied France, aimed at a seemingly random office? Interesting indeed. Sounded like the sort of lunchtime distraction he could use right now. "Mind if I take a look?"

"Be my guest."

Grateful that Margot wasn't the type to ask about his emotional state, though he suspected other people would see in a glance that he was anything but all right, he scooped up the paper and took it to his own seat. He didn't honestly expect to make any sense of it if Margot De Wilde couldn't.

But it only took him a few minutes to realize these code

words looked familiar. Their arrangement, the interposed numbers . . . the very syntax. He had seen it before.

He hissed out a breath and snatched a clean sheet of paper from his stack. He'd seen it before, all right. First in Elsie Neal's attic, and then at the inn, Louisa at his side. They'd written countless letters to each other in this code, and she'd even let him decode some of the ones Celeste had sent to her over her years away.

Celeste. Who was living in France with her stepfather. Clearly not in Paris anymore. Where had Louisa said Pierre made his home? Somewhere, God help them, in the Ardennes department. Charleville, if he recalled.

Charleville—the base of German operations in France. Stomach going tight, he bent over the paper, focusing first not on the meaning, just on the words themselves. He'd memorized the base code, thank the Lord, and it came back to him now without any trouble. There were a few places where she'd spelled a word out with numbers, which meant she would have been using the dictionary they'd designated as their key, which he didn't have.

But he had enough. Enough to make sense of it, and to fill in the blanks with the only words that made any sense and were the right number of letters. And it made his already-chilled blood freeze over in dread.

I pray somebody receives this. I pray somebody knows how to make sense of it. I do not dare to write in plain speech. We need help. Please. They have taken everything. We are starving. They shot my father when he tried to defend our house. Please. We are going to die here if no one comes to help. Please. Somebody save us.

"Celeste." He'd never met her, this girl who was like a sister to Louisa. But he felt like he knew her, after hearing so many stories from Louisa's lips. He felt like she was his sister too, in some small part—sister-in-law, at the least.

"Back already, Culbreth?"

He spun around and all but leapt to his feet as Dilly Knox came back in, shrugging out of his coat even now. Rem picked up the two papers, the encrypted message and his translation, and waved them both at the senior cryptographer. "Knox! You have to see this."

Margot stood, too, brow furrowed. "You cracked it?"

No doubt she would have taken it as a personal slight, had he managed to do it so quickly without a codebook. Rem shook his head. "No cracking required—I knew the code. It was an old American one I learned last summer, actually. Used in both their war of independence and then their civil war."

"You don't say." Knox took the papers from him, intrigue in every line of his face. Intrigue that turned to consternation as he read. "Poor creature. I wonder who it is."

"Her name is Celeste Scarborough. The family I stayed with over the summer—she and the daughter were best friends." He'd yet to mention Louisa by name here. No one had really shared much about their personal lives thus far. He certainly couldn't imagine being the first. But this was different. "They communicated in this code all the time, especially after Celeste moved to Europe with her stepfather. It *must* be her." At the frowns that information earned him, he spread his hands wide. "How many people with an old American code could there possibly be in Charleville, France?"

Knox shook his head. "Funny coincidence. What are the chances that it would find its way to you?"

"Well, given that they *all* find their way to us, not so bad,

274

really." More surprising was that one of Room 40's code-breakers would have happened across Celeste's best friend. Learned their code. Fallen in love with her. *That* was the part no one would believe.

Not even, apparently, Louisa anymore.

Knox handed the papers back to him. "Sad. I wish there were something we could do."

"Well, there is—there must be. Mustn't there?" His gaze moved from Dilly to Margot, though he saw the same sad look in both their eyes, and he knew exactly why. They could never actually do anything with the information they de-crypted. Only pass it on and pray someone *else* could act on it, though they rarely did. The Admiralty didn't yet trust them nor their information. They certainly weren't going to authorize a rescue mission into the heart of German-held France just to answer the cry of one civilian. "There has to be something."

Knox shook his head and patted his shoulder on his way past. "Sorry, old boy. We'll include it with the rest, but I daresay the brass aren't going to modify their plans because some American girl is trapped behind enemy lines. They're doing all they can to reclaim that territory as it is."

Rem bit back a retort about how they were doing a lousy job of it and turned, silent, back to his chair. He set both sheets of paper on his desk, side by side, and stared at them.

Funny coincidence. Perhaps for Dilly the atheist it was no more than that. Perhaps for Margot the mathematician it was only statistical probability. But it had to be more than that, didn't it? It had to be God at work, making certain Rem was here to see this, that he knew the code, that he could decipher the message.

"You are not helpless, you know."

He looked up with a start to see Margot standing before

275

him, those ancient eyes of hers drilling into him. Drilling down to his deepest pain.

Helpless. That's exactly what he was. Helpless to change the things that most needed it. Helpless to reclaim his wife. Helpless to fix his family. Helpless to solve anything for this poor, trapped girl or any of her neighbors. "Am I not?"

Margot looked from the pages to him. "*Action* is not the only way we can help. Sometimes I think it isn't even the best way."

He let his fingers curl into his palms. Heaven knew his actions hadn't helped anything, try as he might. "Then why did God put me here to see this, if I can't do anything?"

Her smile called him foolish. Her words told him why. "He gave you knowledge—the best tool any of us are ever given. And He showed you a need. So you pray." She lifted her brows, looking suddenly like any other adolescent girl. "I'd have thought that was obvious."

He breathed a laugh as she sauntered back to her own chair. "I suppose it should have been." *Pray.* He could do that, certainly. And he knew that Louisa, wherever she was, would be praying constantly for her friend, too, even without this knowledge he'd been given.

How much more effective could those prayers be *with* the knowledge?

He'd just promised his father he wouldn't write to her again—and chances were good she'd never read anything he wrote to her anyway. She was probably burning every letter he sent, unopened.

But if it came from another source, if she saw the code for herself . . .

For a long moment he stared, pondered. He could send it in the post, but she'd recognize his hand. He could send the typed version, but if it came without a source, it would be viewed with suspicion.

There was only one thing for it, then. He'd have to wire it to the only telegraph on Ocracoke—the one at the Life Saving Station—and trust island gossip to do its work. Sooner or later, someone would mention the strange, encrypted messages that kept coming in and that no one could make sense of. Word would get around. Make its way to her. Her ears would prick up.

And she'd know. She'd know it was Celeste. She'd never dream he had any part of it, and that was all right. That was perfect, even.

Perhaps he'd failed her totally as a husband. But he loved her. And he would do anything in his power to save her best friend, even if that power had severe limits. He wasn't doing it for her thanks. Simply with hope that maybe, somehow, someday, it would make a difference.

And in the meantime, he would pray.

19

TODAY

Evie always awoke before the first breath of dawn, but that morning sleep had fled earlier than usual. Early enough that she'd had time to slip out to her studio while the freshly baked pastries cooled. Sit at her worktable. Switch on the light and stare at the two pieces of sea glass she'd set there last night.

She couldn't believe how long it had taken her to see this. A strange coincidence, nothing more. But striking nonetheless.

On the left she'd set the piece of blue-green glass that she'd found the morning Sterling washed ashore. The one that equaled prayers for him in her mind. The one she'd been carrying around in her pocket those first weeks while he healed, the need for his care being too urgent for her to ever take it out and work with it. And those other projects, the ones for the crew's families, had taken up all her time.

It wasn't until a few days ago that she'd finally felt it was time to turn this glass into art and had drawn it out, set it in the sunlight, and really *looked* at it. But she hadn't seen it then. Not until last night.

On the right she'd set an old piece. The one she did three years ago. Job's piece. The pendant she'd worn every day for the last three years.

They were the same shape. *Exactly* the same shape, which didn't happen with the shards of glass that nature tumbled. Not the same size, though. Job's glass was smaller by about an eighth inch all around.

It shouldn't shake her so. It was glass. Not prophecy. Two random bits scooped off the seashore three years apart, not any sort of testament to her own fickle heart.

"Wow. How have I not poked my head in *here* before?"

She started at the voice, turned, and would have scooped those two pieces off the wood of her workbench and into her pocket if it wouldn't have drawn Sterling's too-sharp attention. As it was, she settled for slapping a hand to her rampaging heart. "Sterling! Don't scare me like that."

He grinned, but he didn't direct it at her. He was too busy moving to the portion of wall nearest him and squinting at the pieces fastened there. "You made these? All of them?"

"Mm-hmm." Two decades of prayers. Telling her heart to stop its racing, she pushed to her feet. "That was the first one, there in front of you. I made it from all the shells and glass I collected while Grann was sick." It had taken her months after Grann's death to decide what she wanted to do with them, but when she'd gone to Grandma Ree, that box in her hands, and shared her big plans, her grandmother hadn't laughed. She'd said she'd find her the wire and the tools, and then she'd sat with her each night for a week and they'd learned together how to fasten and fashion each piece just so.

"Who was she? To you, I mean?"

The question should have been weighted, should have carried the expectation of condemnation, given that he'd seen Grann in that picture. He would know, then, the implications if she admitted the truth.

She'd never shied away from it. If someone was going to judge her for the blood she so loved, she'd just as soon know it—and there was still plenty of judgment here in the South. Less common in England, where the question simply didn't come up so often. Regardless, her chin came up. "She was my great-grandmother."

Maybe, like some of her not-so-favorite people who lived under Jim Crow, he was doing the math, calculating what that made her. White? Black? Something in between—and how *much* in between? But she didn't think so.

Sterling simply nodded, absently enough that it bespoke a lack of concern, and traced the long lines of the art with his eyes. "Looks like a rosary."

"It was meant to. We buried Grann's with her, but I wanted something to remember her by, and that was the only thing I could think of." She moved to his side, arms folded over her chest for the comfort of it.

He shifted to the next pieces, just like that, and away from the questions that had caused such pain for her mama. "Do they all have a story like that?"

Well. If he wasn't going to dwell on it, then neither was she. "Each and every one." This was her life, the island's life, there on the walls. And a fair bit of England too. "This one here—this is Grandma Ree's." She indicated one of the largest pieces she'd ever attempted, a mosaic that shifted from white to purples and pinks, arranged in the shape of a heart. "Serena was her real name. She died when I was ten. Her heart."

He didn't say he was sorry, didn't even look at her. But somehow that was the kind thing in that moment. He paid her the respect of studying the artwork instead of her face.

It was more than she'd dared to hope for after that night Herb had shown up with the packet from Davie. She didn't think Sterling would ever look at her with anything but hostility. She'd played along with his false politeness—she knew all about that veneer of English civility, after all—but it had chipped at her heart a little more each day. She hadn't realized until then how much she'd been enjoying his company. How much she'd been treasuring his smiles.

She knew he'd been poking about, trying to find answers. How could he not be? And he'd been hiding things he'd found in the woods too. She didn't know what, hadn't pressed him there. That was *her* way of showing him kindness and respect, when what she'd really wanted to do was give him a good shake and shout at him to *trust* her, give her a chance, be patient.

Patience. That's what this glass and silver and shell had taught her over the years. Patience was what wore old broken bottles into bits of color and light. Patience was what created those shells, wore them away again, tossed them onto the shore. Patience was what it took to turn those bits into something new with silver wire and a soldering iron.

And patience had rewarded her here too. She didn't know what had changed two weeks ago, other than that he'd searched her room while she was out. Had he found something to ease his mind? She couldn't think what. If anything, what he saw in her desk drawers should have convinced him more than ever that she had secrets.

She did. But they weren't hers to tell.

He'd started warming up to her a bit after that day. Little by little. A thaw here, a helping hand there, genuine smiles again. And since Monday, he'd been joining her on her morning walks to the Coast Guard station too.

At first she'd thought it was another way of looking into those secrets—and maybe it was. But she thought it was mostly because somehow or another, he'd discovered the truth about Job.

That had only been a matter of time. She looked over at his handsome profile and drew in a long breath. Those pieces of glass may be the same shape, same color, but he and Job looked nothing alike. It wasn't any false familiarity that drew her to him. It was just . . . *him.*

It shouldn't be, though. She shouldn't be feeling anything for any other man. The Adair women loved once, with their whole heart. Forever. She'd known that all her life.

Sterling slipped around her, to her other side, to more of her collection. Though he sent a soft frown her way. "Are you all right?"

She was so far from all right. And that necklace on her table shouted why. Job had been Davie's best friend, always there, the one she'd chosen over English aristocrats or capital businessmen. He'd been her rock in the storms, her lighthouse, always calling her home. He'd been the reason she stayed here on this tiny speck of sand in the Atlantic instead of living the high life in London or Paris. When he died, he should have taken her heart with him into the sea. Like Grandpa James took Grann's. Like Grandpa Michael took Grandma Ree's. Like Daddy took Mama's.

But here she was, three little years later, praying this other man would stop being angry and smile at her again. A disgrace to that family of strong women. Untrue. Shifting. Inconstant.

She sighed and looked at the wall to avoid his gaze. "You found out about Job, didn't you?"

A beat of silence, and then he sighed too. "I saw the newspaper article." Another beat, and he turned to face her instead of her multicolored art. "Explains why you're so chummy with the Coasties."

Her smile felt small and sad. "I started taking breakfast to them all after our honeymoon. Every day, until . . . until the morning after that storm. I was numb. So numb." Where had that numbness gone? The grief? How could it have ebbed away so quietly, so gently, so stealthily that she hadn't even noticed its leaving? She closed her eyes, pictured it again. Waking up that morning, stumbling into the kitchen of their little bungalow, reaching for the flour and the yeast, and then stopping. Because it hit her. He was gone.

She'd nearly jumped out of her skin when someone banged at her door. She'd turned, expecting it to be a family member. And it was, in a way. It was the men. Job's men, his brothers, his best friends. There with armloads of flowers and loaves of bread, fruit pies, and cakes made by their own wives and sweethearts and mothers, for her.

She was theirs. They were hers. Job had cemented that with his death just as he had with his life.

Opening her eyes again, she found her smile came easily. "They saw me through the rough patch afterward. Then, when I could, I took up the tradition again. To thank them, and because I knew it would have made Job proud."

His nod said he'd figured that much out.

But there were other parts he probably hadn't. And she didn't want those parts standing between them. She couldn't tell him all the secrets—but she could tell him *why*. "Davie is my brother. Twin brother, actually."

She wasn't sure what response she'd expected. Narrowed eyes, wide ones? Lifted brows? An exclamation?

All she got was a long look, a slow blink. "Your brother."

He didn't believe her, that was why he barely responded. Which was funny enough to bring laughter to her lips. How many times had they encountered that through the years? Too many to count. "I know—we look nothing alike, aside from eyes the same color, which you wouldn't have seen in that photograph. Davie takes after our mother. I take after our father. Well, and both our grandmothers, actually."

"Your brother," he said again. And now his eyes narrowed. "David . . . what? I've yet to learn your maiden name."

She hadn't exactly gone out of her way to tell him, truth be told. For good reason. "Culbreth."

And now the wide eyes. "Culbreth? As in—as in *Remington* Culbreth? But I've met him!"

Hence why she hadn't gone out of her way to toss the name around. "I imagined you had. I know he's trained most of the agents in the field in basic cryptography."

He fumbled for her chair, pulled it out, and sat in it, all without taking his eyes off her. "Culbreth. Lord Culbreth is your grandfather. Remington Culbreth—one of the founding professors at the cryptography school—is your father. And your brother . . . ?"

"Is working at Bletchley Park now." She really shouldn't have said so—to anyone else. But he could learn it himself easily enough when he went home again. This next part, though, she shouldn't say even to him.

So why did she want to? Why did the words surge to her lips even as her eyes met his? "Those telegrams that Herb brings over—they're from Davie. When they don't have a key or codebook and the math is taking too long, sometimes he'll send a snippet. It's not that I'm some genius or anything," she added when he gave her a strange look. "It's that we always worked best together. Saw different parts of things. He has the mathematics, I have the intuition."

His look didn't change any. "Evie . . . what the devil are you doing *here*? Keeping an inn on this tiny little island? Why aren't you there with him?"

"Because . . ." Why? Because of Job and that empty house at the end of the lane that she hadn't lived in since he died, even though she went back every month to dust and run the sweeper. Because of the responsibility of running the inn. Because of Grandma See and Aunt L and Uncle Garret. Because of Fanny Pearl and Ernest John and Herb and Calvin and . . .

No. That wasn't quite fair. All those people, those precious people, had one another. And they'd gotten along fine every other time she was away, for months or years at a time.

No, the truth was something far less pretty. And far more treacherous, a riptide she'd never been able to swim out of. "Because this felt safe. Steady."

Habit. That's what it was. What kept her here. Habit, trussed up with names like "duty" and "responsibility."

Somehow his hands had found hers, and now her fingers were resting against his palms, his thumbs stroking over her knuckles. "Evie. Evelyn Culbreth Farrow—I say this as a friend. You are made for more than safe and steady. They don't do you justice."

She choked on a laugh—because how many people would kill for safe and steady? And yet he was right. That had never been what she wanted, what she loved. She'd always sought out the tender spots so that she could try to heal them, the troubled currents so that she could ease them. Because she'd always known that "safety" was an illusion. And "steady" too often meant stagnant. Neither was what brought life, with all its abundant, chaotic beauty. "I know."

"Good. Admitting it is a good step. Now." The light was back in his eyes, brighter than ever. Or maybe it looked that way through the sheen of moisture in her eyes. "Direct question."

She blinked a few times to clear her vision. Sniffed. Nodded. "Ask away."

He looked at her for a long moment first. "What were you doing in Charleville?"

That was his question? She frowned. "It's where Mama's best friend, Celeste, lived during the Great War. She was trapped there, behind enemy lines, through the whole thing. Her stepfather owned a house there and had left it, left everything, to her. Eventually she wanted to go back and sell it all, but she didn't want to go alone. So we all went with her."

"Celeste." He said the name like he was testing it for familiarity.

She grinned. "Also known as Lester, to me and Davie. Or as I shortened it even more—"

"Aunt L. The doctor's wife."

Whom he would have met by now if he hadn't been in such a snit over those telegrams. She nodded.

He opened his mouth, likely to pose another direct question, but engine noise cut through the morning quiet, drawing them both up short. It was rare to hear a car out this way at this hour, when dawn was still a young, pink thing on the horizon. She jogged to the barn door, Sterling a step behind her, and then picked up her pace when she recognized the Coast Guard trucks pulling in—three of them.

Something must be wrong. Terribly wrong. She clutched at the lightweight cardigan she'd put over her summer dress and was at the lead truck as Calvin climbed out of the driver's seat. "Cal! What is it? What's wrong?"

He shut the door behind him, looking sheepish. But also

smiling, however sadly. "Sorry, Evie. Didn't mean to scare you. We just wanted to surprise you."

Surprise her? She looked from Cal to Herb to the other dozen men climbing out of the trucks. From the flowers in their arms to the loaves of bread and fruit pies to matching soft, sad smiles on all their faces.

Oh heavens. It was July 8. How could she not have realized that it was *July 8*? The anniversary of Job's death. Of that terrible, sudden summer storm. She let go of the death grip on her cardigan so she could press the fingers to her lips instead. "Oh, Cal. You didn't have to do this." They hadn't last year on the anniversary—she'd come to them instead, feeling self-conscious about the silver wedding ring she'd decided to put on her necklace that morning, so it could be closer to the sea glass that meant Job. And on the anniversary before that, the first one, Davie had been home, and he'd taken her out on the water for the day—the place Job had always been happiest.

Calvin strode to her side, slid an arm around her, and gave her a brotherly squeeze. "I know we didn't have to. But we wanted to. Just to remind you that we haven't forgotten. That we still miss him, still appreciate you taking care of us like you always did. And because . . . well, we're worried for you, Evie. I knew you must be having a hard time of it when I saw the candlelight in the bungalow's windows this last week."

"You saw . . ." Candlelight? In the windows of her house? But she hadn't been there. Not since she went to clean two weeks ago.

Calvin rubbed a hand up and down her arm. "I could tell you were trying to cover the light, but some seeped around those broken slats in your blinds. I nearly knocked a time or two, but I thought you'd resent it. So we planned this."

Herb stepped forward, too, pressing a big bouquet of his

wife's roses into her arms. "It's all right to mourn, Evie. We've mourned with you, and we always will. But it's okay to go on living too."

They thought . . . they thought she was still so wracked with grief that she was sneaking away from the inn and back to her old house to be nearer to Job. They thought this anniversary had been looming so large in her mind that it had driven her to secret grief. They'd thought to come and comfort and urge her to healing.

She suspected it *would* be comfort and healing when she could sort through it all. But something else needed sorting first.

She smiled and dispensed hugs and collected baked goods and flowers and put them all on the porch, invited the men inside to enjoy it all with her, was genuinely sorry when they declined since duty called. But then not really sorry when it meant that they were all piling back into their trucks and driving away. Because that meant she could turn to Sterling. Grab his arm.

"I haven't been at the house." She didn't even know if he knew about her house, but he didn't look surprised. "Not since I went to clean it two weeks ago. It wasn't me trying to hide candlelight."

Something sparked in Sterling's eyes. "It's conveniently situated, though—abutting the woods."

Well, apparently he knew about the house. Had he followed her? Possibly, or a neighbor could have simply pointed it out while he was walking. Regardless, she nodded. "Easy to come and go from without the neighbors hearing or seeing. And one of the only unoccupied buildings on the island. I hadn't noticed any signs of someone having been there two weeks ago, but—"

"But the weather had been good until recently. That batch

288

of storms we've had this last week, though, could have pushed him to find real shelter."

She spun for the porch. "Help me get all this inside, and I'll grab my key."

"Grab that wicked little pistol of yours too."

They didn't say much as they rushed the gifts into the house, explained it all to Grandma See with a few quick signs, and hurried back out into the early morning. Evie took the path through the woods so they were less likely to run into neighbors. And ten minutes later, she led him up to the back door, silent as two cats on the prowl.

The key sounded loud in the lock, and the door creaked like something out of a horror flick, but nothing stirred within.

Sterling stepped through first, his shoulders in that defensive position that men seemed to don as easily as they did their hats. She would have smiled about it, had her own shoulders not been knotted with tension.

Someone *had* been here, someone other than her. She could smell it—the lingering scent of fried ham, though she hadn't cooked in this kitchen in three years. She could see it—the water droplets from the sink that shouldn't have been turned on since she'd done the cleaning. And she could *feel* it—that sense that things weren't quite as she'd left them.

Sterling didn't have to press a finger to his lips, she knew to be quiet. Even so, she feared anyone still here would be able to hear her heart galloping like banker ponies on the dunes. She slid her fingers into the handbag she'd slung over her torso and wrapped them around the cool metal of her derringer. She'd never shot at a person before, and she didn't want to now, but she'd been well trained, if it came down to it.

Not as well, though, as Sterling. He led the way through

each room, holding her back with one move of his arm, gesturing her forward with a flick of the wrist, using Grandma's signs now and then to ask whether this or that was out of place.

Not much was, here on the main level of the house. But when they climbed the stairs to the low-ceilinged second story, the same couldn't be said. There was no German spy sleeping in her bed like Goldilocks—but there had been. The quilt was askew, the pillow creased. Neither by much, but enough for her to notice.

And a half-burned candle sat on the nightstand where she'd always kept her Bible instead. The candle had been on Job's side, so he could light it if they lost power, and the oil lamp too. She had a flashlight in her drawer, but the batteries had probably gone flat long ago.

"Evie. Look at this."

She jumped at Sterling's voice after so many minutes of silence and spun to see what had caught his attention.

He'd opened one of the dresser drawers—one of the few things that had changed here since Job died. She'd taken all of her own clothes to the inn and given his to his family and the Coasties so they could be put to use. The drawers should have been empty.

They weren't. They were filled. Absolutely *filled*. Newspaper clippings, yellowed photographs of people and places she'd never seen, church bulletins, even a few of the school papers they'd made when they were kids. "What in the world?" She drew out the topmost item, a folded newspaper not even a week old. An *Ocracoke Current*.

A chill went down her spine. "Guess he's keeping up on local news."

"International too." Sterling slapped a French paper to the table, dated several years ago, a German one with a photo

290

of Hitler emblazoned across the front page, along with London's *Sunday Photographic* for good measure. From 1918.

"Where did he get all of this?" Because it had to be Karl Meyer—it had to be. No local would have a collection of international newspapers dating back to the Great War. "And why does he have it here?"

Sterling shook his head and kept emptying the drawer. "Not sure we can really know until we go through them. See what the common thread is between them." He looked at her over his shoulder, flashed her a grin. "Welcome to the exciting world of intelligence field work. Get reading. I'll take the German ones, since yours is rusty. You take French and English."

She gathered them up, not even taking more than a second to feel odd about doing so on her long-abandoned bed that had recently cradled a German spy as she stood beside an English spy who she may be falling a little in love with. She didn't have time to dwell on any of that.

She spread the French and English newspapers out on the bed, side by side, as many as would fit.

Sterling made an annoyed noise. "I said *read* them, Evie, not stitch a new quilt. You could leave a bit of room for me, you know."

She tossed a pillow at his head for his impudence—and because it was in her way. "Trust me, Sterling, you don't need me reading. You need me *looking*."

"I do?"

"You do." She smoothed the last of this batch down, took a step back, and let her eyes move across the many pages.

"What exactly are you doing?" He moved to her side, facing the paper-strewn bed with her.

"Looking for patterns. Repeated words."

"A, an, the?"

"Don't be an idiot. No. Words like—there. *Château Challant.*" She pointed to one, two, three places where it appeared. "And here, *Pierre Challant.*" Four times, five. Her heart sank. Or rose into her throat. Or perhaps went paralyzed. Pierre. Pierre Challant was Celeste's stepfather. Which sent her eyes flying anew over the French articles, the English ones, and digging through the ones from her own tiny little island, still on her dresser.

The linchpin rested at the very bottom. A whole article with a faded photo, clipped long ago with the fancy patterned scissors she'd loved so fiercely as a child. The article she'd had here, stuck to her fridge with a magnet, along with all her other favorites from her childhood. She hadn't even noticed it was missing from its place downstairs.

"What's that?" He came up behind her, touched a hand to her back that shouldn't have made a wave of pleasure race up her spine, given the circumstances. But did.

He'd see in a glance what it was, but she told him anyway. "Marriage announcement. Celeste Scarborough to Garret Wynnwood. October 7, 1922." A day she hazily remembered with all the golden joy of a child. The day two of her very favorite people, Aunt L and Uncle Garret, became Aunt-L-and-Uncle-Garret.

Sterling frowned down at her. "Why would my German spy care about your aunt's marriage announcement?" But he wasn't doubting her—he was piecing it together, turning again to take it all in. "She's the one he was tracking. Starting in Charleville, where she spent the war. To Paris?"

"Her next stop after liberation. And then to London."

"London." She could practically see him tracing the path in his mind's eye. "That fits. Then—why Herefordshire?"

"Because it's where Springbourne Hall is. She recuperated there several months." She'd been in such terrible shape, they

292

said. Evie didn't remember much from those days, but it had taken years—*years*—for the haunted look to leave her eyes, and she had plenty of memories of that. Of watching Garret woo her slowly, gently, proving to her that he could be trusted. Of wondering if Aunt L would ever really be happy.

She was. She'd made a life here again, built a family.

But sometimes Evie still caught that haunted look in her eyes. She'd never asked why . . . but maybe it was time she did. She held out a hand for Sterling. "Come on. I think it's time you meet Aunt L."

20

YESTERDAY

MARCH 28, 1918
OCRACOKE ISLAND, NORTH CAROLINA

Louisa set the last of the bouquets of Easter lilies on the last of the inn's tables and blew out a long breath. She still needed to take the day's towels off the line, help Grandma Elsie and Grann with the holiday weekend's baking, and find time, somewhere in there, to slip over to the church and give it a thorough scrubbing. Wouldn't do for there to be a speck of dust on the altar or the pews for the Holy Week services that started tonight.

She checked the mantel clock and mumbled a quiet prayer for a nice long nap time today. It was her only hope of—

"Mama! Maaaaaaama!"

Well. Her lips pulled into a smile despite her afternoon schedule being blown to smithereens. At least it was a happy singsong calling her away from housework and not a cry.

Especially since one cry always meant two—but one song meant two too. "Coming, baby girl."

"Mama-mama-mama-mama!"

A chuckle tickled her throat as she climbed the stairs. "I'm coming for you too, baby boy."

They were perfectly capable of getting up out of their matching low-slung beds without her help—they were nearly three, after all. And sometimes they would. When it was in-convenient, mostly. But most days they called to her instead and otherwise stayed put, giggling together, throwing pillows at each other. On those *other* days, they set up a dual wail that sent every gull flying for a mile around.

She didn't mind, truth be told. There was something about wrapping her arms around those two little bodies still warm from sleep and cuddling them close. Something magical about those first cuddles in the morning and after nap time, before they were off to the races again and she to her work. Something precious that she wouldn't trade for anything.

Today she poked her head into their room and found them both on Davie's bed, trying to tie his sheet around his shoulders like a cape. She came in with a grin to help, gathered her hugs and cuddles, and planted a kiss on Evie's head—as fair a gold as a pixie wing, as Grann liked to say—and then on Davie's, which was as dark and curly as her own.

They hopped off the bed in tandem, making a beeline for the door, but she halted them with a mock-stern "Stop. Turn."

They stopped, turned, all but wiggling in their eagerness to get back to the serious business of playing. She planted her hands on her hips and looked from one beautiful face to the other. "Now, what is this weekend?"

Oh, their grins. They about did her heart in every time. "Easter!" they screamed together.

She lifted her brows. "And what does that mean?"

"Job's coming over to play!" Davie bounced on his toes.

Evie shook her head, shoved her brother in the arm. "Jesus. It means Jesus. He raiseded up. Right, Mama?"

Sweet little Evie. Louisa gave her a solemn nod. "You're both right, but that wasn't what I was getting at. What does it mean for today? For Grann and Grandma See and Grandma Ree and Mama?"

Davie huffed out a breath, like it was a personal imposition on him instead of them. "The inn's full," he recited.

"And y'all are busy," Evie added. Then crowned it with another grin. "With *cake!*"

They did have their priorities straight. Jesus and then cake. She restrained her smile and nodded. "So, what are you two going to do this afternoon?"

Together they chanted, "Be good, stay out of trouble, and stay out from underfoot."

"That's right. Now go get your cookies from Grandma See and play on the back porch, okay?" It would last twenty minutes, maybe, before they dashed back inside desperate to share something or show her something or demand mediation on some disagreement that was of the utmost importance to the minds of children. But in that twenty minutes, she could get a pie crust or two rolled out.

She shooed them on their way. And may have let out a groan when she heard the jingle of a pony's harness coming down the lane, through the windows open to the fresh spring breeze. If it was a neighbor, chances were good that they'd offer distraction more than help. And if it was a would-be guest, she'd have to turn them away. They were booked up for the holiday weekend with neighbors' out-of-town family that had come to share the celebration with them.

Or it could be Miss Jackie, Garret's mama, coming by

296

with another letter to share. She always hurried over whenever one came, just as Louisa did in reverse. They made a little celebration of it each time. Word from France, rare and precious. Garret had been there since last summer—he'd signed up just as soon as he'd gotten that *Doctor* before his name and had been serving in a field hospital ever since.

And each letter meant it *wasn't* a telegram sent from the War Department instead. Wasn't word that the front lines had shifted and Garret's hospital had been overrun, doctors gunned down along with soldiers. It was a fear that they could never quite outpace.

Whatever wagon was jingling their way hadn't come into view yet, so Louisa hurried down the stairs. Praying with every step what she always did when thoughts of that ever-stretching war invaded her mind. *Be with Garret, Lord. Protect him over there. Be with Celeste and Maddie, please. Keep them safe and healthy and well wherever they are. Be with Rem's family over in England, where bombs are falling from the sky.*

Bombs from the sky—she couldn't even imagine. Enemies in the skies making something ugly from that beautiful flight that had happened not so many years ago up the coast in Kitty Hawk. Enemies on the land turning God's creation into a mud-filled hell. Enemies now even in one's own body, with that awful flu rampaging over the world. It hadn't come yet to Ocracoke. But it could. There'd been talk of forbidding visitors to the island, stopping even the supply runs to keep their little bubble safe, but that wasn't feasible. They needed those boats that came in and the people who came in on them.

"Louisa, will you see who that is coming up the lane?" Mama called out from the kitchen. "If it's another guest, send them—"

"I know, Mama. I'm going." She peeked into the kitchen first to make sure Davie and Evie were obeying her orders—not that they usually had to be told twice to fetch a cookie. She saw them sign their thanks to Grandma Elsie and then dart out onto the porch, so she turned back to the front of the inn with a smile.

Someone was knocking, which meant it must be a would-be guest. The neighbors all came around the back or shouted a greeting through the screen door. She sighed. Sending people away was never fun, even though they *did* make it a point to know what other places had room.

It wasn't quite warm enough to have the doors left wide for the breeze, so she pulled it open, noted the man in strangely familiar livery standing there, and then looked past him. And nearly fainted in shock.

Edith Culbreth stood on her porch. Edith Culbreth, in a blue silk dress, a fur stole, shiny black pumps, and with a fashionable hat perched on her fashionable head. She stood there, holding her fur in place, holding her spine straight as a mast, and holding her reasons for being there somewhere beneath the placid surface of her face.

Louisa hadn't seen her mother-in-law since the day she left Baltimore. Hadn't had so much as a letter from her in answer to the many Louisa sent with updates on the twins. Hadn't ever received so much as a card at Christmas, yet here she stood now?

Maybe that flu *had* come. Maybe it made people halluci-nate. Maybe that's what this was—fever-inspired delirium.

The servant cleared his throat. "Lady Culbreth for Miss Louisa Adair."

Her fingers gripped the doorframe. "It's Mrs. Culbreth, thank you." Or Miss Louisa, as everyone on the island now called her. But *not* Miss Adair, as Edith well knew. It sent a wintry breeze blowing over her soul instead of the spring one dancing over the porch. She met her mother-in-law's cold gaze without flinching. "Hello, Edith. If you'd sent word you were coming, I'd have saved a room for you."

"I am hardly *staying*." She said it like the very idea was akin to joining the boys in the trenches in France. Unthinkable. Horrific. Filthy. She lifted one over-plucked brow. "I only require an hour's audience."

Louisa stepped aside, holding the door wide. Centuries of Southern hospitality insisted on it, even though she'd have liked to slam the door in her face and send her back to the mail boat.

As if she'd arrived on the mail boat. No, she'd probably come sailing into Silver Lake on some fancy yacht that was taking up all the fishermen's slips now. Inconveniencing the whole village, setting every tongue wagging. They'd all know who it was by the end of the day too. Juicy tidbits like that didn't stay secret for long.

She pasted on a smile, then worked to make it real. How many times had she wished, prayed that she could redo and undo how things had gone between them? Maybe this was her chance. Edith was here, after all. It had to be for a reason.

Shoulders easing, her smile worked its way down to her heart, and she closed the door softly behind her guest, with a nod to the manservant who opted for staying on the porch. "May I take your wrap, Lady Culbreth?"

Edith unfastened the fur, handed it off like she would to a servant, and surveyed the inn's entryway. "Your home is lovely."

Did it sound begrudging? Absolutely. But she said it, which must have cost her. Louisa took it as the peace offering it was as she hung the stole on the coat-tree and then led the way into the main room, grateful she'd already finished the cleaning in here. "Thank you. It's been in the family for generations. Please, make yourself comfortable. May I get you some tea? Or coffee, perhaps?"

She half expected her to refuse, but apparently Edith was playing by the rules today too. "Coffee. Thank you."

It gave Louisa an excuse to vanish for a minute, to dart into the kitchen, knowing her face reflected the entire rainbow of emotions swirling through her as she faced the women she held most dear in all the world.

Mama looked over at her, no doubt to ask who'd been at the door, but went still upon seeing her. "Louisa? Honey, are you all right?"

She didn't know whether to shake her head or nod, only that Mama's concern bolstered her. "Edith Culbreth is here." Four little words that lit an absolute flurry in the room.

"What?" Mama leapt away from the cake batter she'd been stirring, as if to dart straight out to meet the dragon face-to-face. Then she halted, spun, and made for the porch instead. "She'll be wanting to meet the twins—and them looking like little ragamuffins! I'll tidy them up."

Grann had abandoned her bowl too. "She want coffee or tea?"

"Coffee."

"Give her some of them cute little cakes we finished. You put those on a plate, Louisa, while I pour her a cup. Just made a fresh pot."

Bless them, both of them. *All* of them, she amended, when Grandma Elsie slipped to her side, slid an arm around Louisa's waist, and touched their heads together. It was what she always did when she wanted to pray together.

The words were not only silent but still, her hands busy anchoring Louisa. But she didn't need to hear them to know them. To feel them seeping from Elsie's hands into her own body, her soul. To sense them whispering their way straight up to heaven.

When Elsie pulled away, they signed *Amen* together, exchanged a smile, and went on with their tasks.

Petit fours, plated. Coffee, poured. Milk and sugar in their silver dishes added to the silver serving tray. Mama herded the twins up the back stairs, shushing them with every step, and Louisa paused for one final breath. One final prayer. And then swept out with her tray back into the front room and the overdressed blonde who hadn't budged from the chair she'd chosen.

She sat with ankles crossed and to the right, hands clasped in her lap, spine rigid. Like a drawing in a fashion magazine. A paper doll, flat and lifeless—that's how she looked to Louisa's eyes in that moment. No expression on her face. No light in her eyes.

Never in her life had she expected to feel pity for Edith Culbreth. But that's exactly what filtered through Louisa as she slid the tray onto the end table, beside that fresh vase of lilies. Here they were in the holiest of weeks, ready to celebrate the most miraculous of lives. And this woman before her, despite her fine things and high life, looked utterly lifeless.

Louisa sat in the chair across from her. "You must have had a long trip. Is there anything else I can get for you?"

Edith poured a dollop of the cream into her cup and stirred it with the silver spoon. Took a sip, nodded her approval of the blend. "I would like to meet my grandson."

Finally. Three years late, but finally she'd come for the very thing Louisa had been inviting her to do since the moment she announced their births. Never mind that she only mentioned Davie—she'd meet them both, whatever her thoughts on the matter. Louisa smiled. "My mother is getting them both ready right now. They'll be down in a few minutes—they just woke up from their naps." And praise God they'd awoken happy today. No doubt Mama was telling them even now that Grandmama Edith was below, that they'd get to meet her. She'd told them of her, too, just as she told them of Rem, of Uncle Sebastian and Grandpapa Culbreth in England. She'd been assuring them all their lives that their faraway family loved them just as much as their right-here family did.

Maybe it was a lie. But she hoped it was simply a prayer, that the words would become truth through her frequent offering of them to God if they weren't at the start.

Edith took another sip of the coffee, then set the cup on the saucer and both on the tray with nary a clatter. "There is no need to bring the girl. It is only the boy I need to see. You named him David, I believe?"

"David Michael Culbreth. After Rem's father and mine." The reigning David Culbreth wasn't Edith's favorite person, she knew—but the miniature one may soon become just that. He had a charm, that little imp, with his curls and dimples and mischief always ready in his blue eyes. He was clever, too—they both were.

Rem would have been so proud of them. So delighted with them.

Louisa smiled. "I'm afraid you can't see one without the other—they scarcely ever leave each other's side. Sometimes I think they even have a language all their own." Two halves of a whole, that's what everyone in the village said of them. And those two halves had wrapped every single Ocracoker around their little fingers. Even mean old Mrs. Williams smiled when she saw them—and she'd told them to call her Miss Marge, like everyone else did. A courtesy she'd never extended to Louisa, not until her babies had finally won her over.

It was funny. All her life Louisa had thought she wanted to get away, to get her education, to come back to teach so she could earn a real place here. But now those dreams had shifted so fully. They were all she needed, those two little people who had given new meaning to the word *home*.

A muted call from upstairs, then little footsteps raced over the floorboards—but only one set. Mama must have captured one of them, at least. And a moment later, a golden blond head bounced her way into the room.

Evie had waited for Mama to put her pretty new dress on her, anyway, before she made a break for it. And Louisa could only bite back a laugh when her little island princess pranced into the center of the room, did her best imitation of a courtly curtsey, and then bounced on her toes, her excitement unable to be contained.

"Grandmama Edith!" Evie's voice came out high and sweet, all little-girl joy. She pressed her chubby—but clean, praise God—hands to the front of her pink lace dress. "I'm Evelyn Edith—after *you*!"

Edith blinked, and that careful facade she always kept in place cracked a little. Not, Louisa suspected, because Evie was so cute, or because of the name that she'd already known about, but which hadn't apparently made her think she wanted to meet her. No, she'd be seeing what they all did every time they looked at her.

She was Rem, through and through. His hair, the shape of his face. The only difference was that her eyes were Louisa's blue instead of Rem's blue-green. But Edith would see her lost son in that precious face. That was surely what made her draw in a sharp breath. What made a hint of softness creep over her expression. What made a tiny little smile take root on her lips as she said, "Hello there."

It was all the encouragement Evie needed. She flew across

the space between them, ignored Louisa's warning, and clambered right up into Edith's lap.

It wasn't her fault. That's what she did with grandmothers, after all, because the only ones she knew invited her there every chance they got. She lived in a house with women who claimed her as their own, who treasured each cuddle and hug. How was she to know that the silk and diamonds and furs were a fence she wasn't supposed to cross, a sign posted saying *Keep off!*

Louisa held her breath, ready to leap to her baby's rescue if Edith did anything like shove her away. But the hands that jolted in shock at the invasion didn't push—they steadied. Louisa's breath slipped back out. There must be a bit of nurturing in her after all, despite all Rem had told her to make her doubt it.

She even, miracle of miracles, smiled more fully. "Aren't you a darling?"

But Evie didn't grin, as she usually would at a compliment. She cocked her head to the side, fair curls spilling over her shoulder. She reached up, placed her tiny little hand on Evelyn's flawless cheek, and looked deep into her grandmother's eyes. "What's wrong, Grandmama? What hurts?"

"Oh, Evie." Louisa's interjection was nothing but a breath, a whisper too low for even her own ears to hear. She was always doing *that*, too, this girl of hers. Knowing just when a person needed to laugh and when they needed to cry. Seeing the pains they tried to cover. Drawing them out. Trying to heal them with a snuggle and a kiss.

Succeeding more than anybody should.

Edith's eyes took on a bit of a watery sheen. "What makes you think something hurts, little one?"

Evie didn't answer—probably didn't know how she knew. She kept up her study. "You're so sad. Why are you so sad?"

Louisa pressed her lips together. Her daughter, not yet three, saw in about two seconds what Louisa hadn't really noticed until that very moment—the profound, soul-deep sorrow in Edith Culbreth's eyes.

Edith's breath shuddered out, and her lips quivered a bit too. "I am sad, yes. Because I got the most terrible news about my elder son."

Sebastian? Louisa sat up straighter. She'd never met him, hadn't a clue where he was or what he was doing. But she knew Rem had adored him, and so she and the twins prayed for him every night.

"Uncle Sebastian?" Evie sounded as distressed as Edith did. "What happened? Is he hurt?"

"I . . . I don't know." Edith blinked, and a few droplets of that water spilled out onto her cheeks. "He's an officer in the army, you see. In Europe, in the war. And we got word that he's missing in action."

"In the army?" Louisa shook her head. She hadn't been praying as fervently as she would have been had she known that. "Why?"

Edith's eyes slid shut. "Because there was glory to be had. So he had to have it." She turned her face away for a moment, sniffed, visibly regained her composure. Then opened her eyes again and looked not at the angel in her arms but at Louisa. "You see now why I need to meet David Michael."

It took a moment for it all to click into place, actually. She was too busy absorbing that blow—that Sebastian, Rem's brother, was lost. Lost and perhaps dead. The heir to the Culbreth title, the Culbreth estates. And what of the Remington side? Was he heir to that, too, now that Rem was dead? Or was Edgar next in line?

Then her thoughts caught up with what Edith was saying. Rem was gone. Sebastian, lost. That left . . . Davie. Her sweet little Davie, the only male left in the Culbreth line. Her throat went tight.

Mama and Davie chose that moment to clatter down the stairs and into the room. Louisa could scarcely see as her little boy, dressed in the short pants, vest, jacket, and bow tie they'd made for him for Easter Sunday, bowed to his grandmother and let Mama make a more proper introduction than his sister had done. She was too busy watching Edith.

The way she measured him. Weighed him with her gaze. Looked between Davie's hand and Mama's—comparing skin tones? Louisa hated that she was relieved at knowing his was as fair as any other island boy's. He tanned more than most in the summer, but this time of year . . .

Shame on you, Louisa. She wasn't ashamed of her Black family. She wasn't. But she didn't want her children to be judged for it at first glance either.

A prayer she would have to take before the Father another time, for the thousandth time. More pressing was the fact that Edith was asking him all sorts of questions, listening so carefully to his answers. And then she gave a decisive nod and looked to Louisa again.

Her stomach felt like a rock, heavy and hard. Even before Edith said, "He'll do. His accent is atrocious, but that can be fixed at this stage easily enough. How quickly can you have his things packed? He won't need much. We'll have a new wardrobe made and will provide books and toys. He'll be permitted to take a few keepsakes."

Permitted to . . . She expected fury. A quick flash. That same anger she'd felt before at Remington House, when Edith had ordered the staff to steal from her.

The fury Mama apparently felt, given her hiss and the way she pulled Davie back a step.

But Louisa felt only calm. Steady. Solid. She lifted a hand to touch the topaz necklace she never took off and then stood and moved to stand beside Mama and Davie. "I'm sorry about Sebastian, Lady Culbreth, I truly am. And I understand what this means for the family line, and even that Davie must be trained up in ways we can't do here. But not yet."

"He's nearly three." Edith stood, too, Evie scrambling down to keep from being tossed to the floor. Her little girl came and tucked her hand into Louisa's. "High time he be placed with a tutor and taught—"

"Then you can send a tutor here, if you like." She turned her right wrist out, toward her son, and he slid his fingers into hers without a word needing to be said about it. Because that was his side, his hand, and every time she reached, his hand was there. Every time he reached, hers was. They were a unit, the three of them. The six of them. "But he's not going anywhere without me and his sister."

Edith's glare was somehow all the crueler for the tears streaking her cheeks. She ought to understand. She ought to know what a horrible thing she asked. She, who had lost two sons, oughtn't to be demanding someone else's.

But then, Edith had never much cared whether she caused Louisa pain, had she? She stepped forward too. "I am not asking for your permission. I am telling you how it will be."

Now the fire kindled down in that rock in her belly, turning it to a live coal. She gave a squeeze to the hands of her babies and smiled down at each of them. "You two go upstairs with Grandma Ree for a minute, okay? Get those books you love so you can show them to Grandmama."

Davie looked ready to argue, but Evie reached for his hand and tugged on it. "Come on, Davie."

Mama paused between Louisa and Edith, though, on her way out the door with them. She signed, *Need? Yell.*

Louisa smiled. *No, no. One minute.* They didn't need to hear this.

Edith at least waited until Mama had cleared the threshold before starting up again. "He belongs to his family, not just to you. He has responsibilities and duties he must be prepared for. He must learn more than lessons from a book. He must be brought up among the estates he will someday run, taught to love them and care for them. He must—"

"Be burdened by generations of expectation? No. Don't you know, Edith, how Rem *hated* that? How Sebastian did?" Louisa shook her head. "You're not going to do that to him. I won't let you. He can learn it all when he's older—"

"I'm taking him now."

"You are *not*. And there isn't a soul on this island who wouldn't stop you if you tried. He is not *yours*. He is *ours*."

Edith lifted her chin. "You think you can fight me? My family? Our connections?"

The flame fanned higher—but so, too, did the memories. The last time she'd tried to fight this woman, what had it gotten her? Nothing. Absolutely nothing.

It had to be different this time. Somehow. She had to take the higher road, if she could find it. She drew in a deep breath, let it out slowly, indulged in a moment of closed eyes. *Show me, Father. Show me the better way.*

When she opened her eyes again, Edith still stood as she'd been, chin at that patronizing angle. But Louisa, at least, felt calm again. "What exactly is your plan here, Edith, if I refuse? Are you going to kidnap my son? And then what—how are you going to convince that child not to hate you for taking him from all he knows? Will you tell him I'm dead?"

Edith jerked back as if struck. "Don't be ridiculous. But he's only a lad—he'll adapt. Though granted, it will be better for him if you send him willingly. Then he can come back here on holiday, and I won't have to forbid all exchanges. And you'll still have the girl—she's a sweet thing. She'll be enough for you."

Louisa slashed a hand through the air. "No. That's my final answer."

Edith's laugh was so mocking, so bitter, that it didn't even deserve the name. "You're as stubborn as my husband, fool that he is. But this is the best way—the only way. And you do *not* want to fight me on this, Louisa. I promise you that. I'll make your life miserable if you try it. If I'm the only one who cares to preserve this family, then so be it. I'll do so single-handedly."

Listen to her, acting like she was the only one who cared, like her way was the only one worthy of pursuit. Like taking Davie away wouldn't be a bigger misery than anything else she could possibly concoct. Like there was any mountain she could put between them that Louisa wouldn't scale to get back to him, to keep her babies together.

But it was pain that had driven Edith here, to this place. Horror unthinkable. She had to remember that. How was Louisa to know what she would do if faced with the loss of both her children? That called for a bit of grace. Gentleness. That called for looking at Edith like Evie had done, seeing what was beneath, not what was spewing forth.

She stepped forward and clasped Edith's white-gloved hand with her own bare fingers and gave them a squeeze. "You have my condolences, you and Lord Culbreth both. We'll be praying for you, praying that somehow Sebastian comes through, that he's only been taken prisoner or something, that he isn't *gone*. And we will be raising Davie up to be a gentleman, to understand that something more waits for him beyond these beaches. I will see he has the best education, that he would do his daddy proud. And when he's old enough, I'll introduce him to his family in Maryland and England, and he can start learning how to care for the estates."

Edith drew back like Louisa's touch burned her. "*You* will do no such thing. *You* will stay down here on your backward little rock with your mother and *grandmother* and do my grandson the favor of not soiling his future with your association." She sidestepped Louisa, strode from the room, snatched her fur from its hook, and yanked the door open herself.

Louisa stared after her, her words burning a brand onto Louisa's face. *Grandmother.* How had she known? How did she know what Louisa hadn't until Mama and Grann told her? That Grann was blood, not just mammy?

Her fingers curled into her palms. It didn't matter *how* she knew—only *that* she knew. Knew and counted it as such a blight that she would not let Louisa into her family, even by way of Davie and Evie. That's what she'd meant. She'd take them—take Davie, anyway—because he was all of Rem that was left, the only hope of the family line continuing. Perhaps what she'd deemed blighted blood wasn't strong enough in him to be evident. But not Louisa.

"Mama?"

She didn't know how long she'd stood there, staring at where Edith had been, but she looked down at those two precious little faces now as their fingers slipped back into her own. As her own mama filled the doorway, Grann and Grandma Elsie behind her. She looked at her world, and her chest heaved with a sob she couldn't let loose. Not now, not in front of them.

Davie was frowning up at her. "Mama, where did Grandmama want to take us?"

"Not *us.*" Evie sounded close to tears herself. "You. She didn't want me. Didn't want Mama neither."

Davie's face screwed up into pure little-boy stubbornness. "Well, I'm not going without you."

"Oh, babies." She crouched down so she could pull him to her on one side, Evie on the other. "You're not going anywhere without us. Not right now. In a couple years, maybe, we'll go and meet the family. But together. We're only ever going together."

In the long term . . . but more than that. She looked over their heads, to the women in the doorway. And saw that they understood as clearly as she did. These babies weren't leaving their sight.

21

MAY 19, 1918
LONDON, ENGLAND

R em ran with the other wedding guests from the ball-room, out into the streets. Sirens blared in his ears, intermittently drowning out the sounds of the airplanes buzzing overhead, then lapsing away to let the monsters roar again.

The horizon glowed orange with fire—here, there, everywhere.

It should have sparked something in him, shouldn't it have? Desperation. A will to live. Determination to make it home again to Father. But he felt as empty as ever as theatergoers elbowed past him, panicked. *They* were in a hurry to make it to the Tube tunnels, designated air raid shelters as they were. *They* had something to live for beyond the weight of an estate that would die with them anyway.

"Culbreth!" The familiar voice preceded the familiar face by a few seconds. Phillip Camden squeezed through the crowd to Rem's side, his fiancée's hand clasped in his. He was a fellow codebreaker in Room 40 now, but he'd been a pilot before that. No doubt that was why he was eyeing up those planes in the sky like he'd enjoy taking them out one by one. "We're going to the sites already struck to see if we can help. If you're bored . . ."

Rem smiled. "You know, I was thinking that I was. Count me in. Want me to see if Margot's up to the task?"

Camden snorted at the joke—it was her wedding ball the Boche had interrupted, and he didn't imagine either the bridegroom or Margot's brother would take kindly to their enlisting her help. Though he was none too sure she wouldn't volunteer herself and them, too, and perhaps say a prayer of thanks for the premature ending to the ball. "You can ride with us. Come on—we'll see who else we can snag on the way."

It was at least a goal, a purpose. That, he'd found, was what got him through each day. Go to the office, where Room 40 had overflowed its single room years ago and now took up the whole floor. Sit beside the colleagues who had become friends somehow over the years, despite all the times he'd dodged questions or invitations. Select an encrypted telegram from the stack of them, find the appropriate codebook, get down to business. Work until lunch. Mindlessly eat a sandwich. Work more until dinner.

Watch, always watch for one of those *other* telegrams. The ones from Charleville, France. The ones that everyone had learned to simply slip onto his desk for quick decoding.

There'd been two dozen of them, perhaps, over the years. Short. Poignant. With all that desperation he couldn't bring himself to feel anymore about anything else. Every one a cry for help. Rescue. Salvation.

He turned them in with all the others, knowing the brass

wouldn't do anything about them. Couldn't. And he also went to their own wireless set and tapped them onward. Across the ocean. To the Life Saving Station on Ocracoke, North Carolina.

It couldn't actually do any physical good. He knew that. What could Louisa possibly do? But he had to send them. It was the one connection he still had to her, the one thing that lit a bit of life in his veins. Every new message from Celeste reminded him that he was called to something more than mechanical work—he was called to prayer. He was called to do whatever he could for the wife he loved, even if that was to anonymously provide information about her best friend.

But once he trudged home, that was when the purpose began to slip. He'd taken to assigning himself reading. Books he'd always meant to read but hadn't. Books his colleagues recommended on the subjects of interest to them—everything from mathematics to banking to Greek history to archaeological advancements.

Tonight, if he wasn't ready to fall to his bed in exhaustion after the wedding and its ball, he'd been planning on reading more of Lord Sheridan's latest treatise on the Druids. Looked like that would have to wait until tomorrow, if he lived to see it.

A pang of guilt, at least, at that thought. For Father's sake. He had so much pinned on Rem now, with Sebastian still missing. *Please, God. Please deliver my brother back from death. Please.* But it was not enough of a pang to make him turn around.

No, he ducked into Camden's fiancée's car instead, nodding a greeting to the other familiar faces inside—Barclay Pearce and his wife, Evelina. Rem had let them cajole him into joining them at Pauly's Pub for dinner once a month or so, so he knew them both fairly well, along with the rest of Barclay's family.

What surprised him was that they were here, in this car. "I thought you were leading the exodus."

Pearce shook his head. "My sisters had that under control. I want to see the damage done. See what I can do to help."

Camden and his fiancée seemed to be having a debate about who would drive. Miss Denler won and slid behind the wheel while Camden jogged around to the other side. She was a nurse, Rem knew. A logical addition to this expedition, unlike the rest of them. What could *he* really offer to any rescue efforts?

Two hands. A strong back. And a rather unhealthy lack of self-preservation. Could come in handy, really. Best of all, it would be a few hours when he wouldn't have to sit in that too-empty house and pretend he would simply go straight up to bed tonight. He wouldn't pull the photo from his wallet, its edges now so ragged. He wouldn't look at that face he'd never see in life again. He wouldn't wonder what she was doing, where she was, whether she and Garret had children. Whether she was happy.

Pearce leaned toward him after a few minutes of driving. "Any more news of your brother?"

Blast it all. He could never escape any of the black thoughts, no matter where he was. He shook his head. Said another silent prayer.

Sebastian. He'd made it through so much of the war with nothing but a few scrapes. Then he'd led his men in a charge and simply . . . vanished. No one had seen him since. Captured? Possibly. Killed, his body simply not recovered as the lines fell back? Quite likely. They couldn't know, and the not-knowing was destroying his father a bit more each day.

Tonight, he'd actually stopped Rem on his way out the door with a horrible order: "Dance with someone."

Rem had nearly tripped over his own feet at the suggestion. "I beg your pardon?"

He'd looked so tired. Worn. Old. "Perhaps your mother is right, Remmy. Perhaps our only hope of the family living on is for you to remarry."

"No." He'd said it, thought it, felt it, all but shouted it. "Sebastian will come home. The war will end eventually, and he'll be released from whatever prison they're holding him in, and he can marry and give you an heir. He isn't gone. We don't know that he's gone."

Father's shoulders had sagged. "Until the end of the war, then. But if he doesn't come home, what else do we do?"

What else do we do? The question he asked himself every day, every noon, every night. Every moment he wasn't actively working. *What else do we do?* Read, sip at too-weak tea that hadn't seen a sugar cube in ages, eat rationed food that tasted like the mud sucking their men into oblivion. Wait for something to change. *What else do we do?*

Run headlong into bombed neighborhoods, apparently, with some of the only people in the world who accepted him for who he was and didn't expect anything as inane from him as finding another wife when he already had one. Even if she wouldn't admit it any longer.

The car halted in a neighborhood whose streets were littered with glass and whose roofs were ablaze with fire.

Well. He'd never handled a fire hose and didn't know even basic first aid, but he put himself at Miss Denler's disposal and got to work.

It was, at least, something else to do.

OCRACOKE ISLAND, NORTH CAROLINA

Louisa had been to the Life Saving Station a few times, but not enough to know the protocol upon arrival. Should she knock? Call out a greeting? They were expecting her, but that didn't mean that she could just walk in.

"Look, Mama! A froggy!"

Louisa smiled down at Davie. "I see. But let's leave it alone right now, okay? Mama has work to do."

"Can't we stay out here? We'll play with the froggy."

She looked from Davie to Evie, and then over her shoulder. There was no one else out here that she could see, on this stretch of beach broken only by the Coast Guard's station. But that didn't mean no one would come.

That fear had been dogging her every day since Edith's visit. She and Mama and Grann and Elsie had held innumerable hushed meetings about it, plotting and planning ways to keep her babies safe. Grann had even offered to hire a lawyer or a guard for them, and Mama had nodded along like that was even feasible.

Maybe it would come to that—pooling every last resource they had to fight her. But right now, they didn't even know what they'd be fighting. So she'd keep her babies always in sight and try to go on living. "Sorry, kiddo. I don't want you to be in the way if they get called out for a rescue. Inside with me."

Evie's lip pouted down. "Shoulda stayed with Grann."

Yes, they should have. But it had been a tearful wake-up from their nap, and they'd both insisted on coming with *her*. Grann and Elsie had both been under the weather with a spring cold, leaving Mama with all the chores to do in the kitchen, so she'd given in to their pleading. "Now, what did I say?"

They sighed. "That if we come—"

"—no whining."

"We have to be good."

"And look at our book and stay out of the way."

They made good little parrots, though she'd see how well they obeyed in practice when it came down to it. But hopefully it wouldn't take too long to fix the piece of equipment that had been giving the men fits.

And hopefully those men wouldn't hold it against her for fixing the thing when they hadn't been able to manage it. Lips twitching up, she repositioned her tool bag a bit in her hand and mounted the steps.

Thankfully, Herbert O'Neal saw her coming and opened the door for her, smiling a greeting that turned to a grin when he spotted the twins with her. "Well now—I knew Miss Louisa was coming, but I didn't realize she was bringing my favorite twins on the whole island."

Davie laughed and launched himself at Herb's legs. Herb and his new wife, Clara, lived down the lane, beside Miss Marge, so the twins had no compunction about climbing all over him. And he was good with them—good news for the baby Clara would have any day.

"Hey, Herb. Can you point me where I need to go?"

"Oh, I can do you better than that. Johnson appointed me as the official Louisa liaison, with Liam Bryan as backup. Latch on, maties. We'll show your mama to the wireless."

The wireless? Louisa suddenly wasn't so sure Herb should have been bragging on her mechanical prowess to his station chief. "Herb, you do realize I've never worked on a wireless before, right?"

With one of her children attached to each of his legs, he tossed her a grin and started lumbering along a corridor—a clumsy-looking waltz set to a serenade of giggles.

Gracious, the whole station seemed to be coming to see

what the ruckus was about. With smiles, yes, but they couldn't really appreciate the interruption.

Herb certainly didn't look too upset about their presence, though, nor concerned about the very real possibility that she'd fail to live up to his boasts about her. "You'd never worked on a radio until last week at Doxee's, if I recall. But you got it working."

Yeah, but that had been Doxee's old broken set that he hadn't even been able to use since civilian radio was suspended during the war. There'd been nothing at stake. And his radio was not the property of the United States Coast Guard. What if she broke something?

Well, he'd already roped her into it now, so she'd better focus on not making him look the fool to the station keeper. "All right. Let's see what's what."

Apparently the role of "Louisa liaison" involved entertaining her children while she worked, for which she was grateful. The collection of black boxes sitting on the desk, with all their dials and knobs and headphones, was considerably more intimidating than anything of Doxee's. At least someone had left out the manuals that must have come with it.

"Okay." She took a seat at the desk and started by identifying each piece. Type A Cohen receiver. Wireless Specialty Co. receiver—why did they need two receivers? She'd sort that out in a minute. Next was the crystal detector. And finally the ultraudion detector.

Fascinating. She'd read about all these things, and about Marconi's original devices, but she'd never gotten to look inside a machine as complex as this.

An hour sped by while she familiarized herself with the equipment, and then another as she began isolating the possible problems. The twins grew impatient with their books and the games Herb had brought, but someone bought her another half hour of peace with cookies their wife had sent. Evie apparently charmed the station keeper—which might have distracted Louisa, had his laughter not assured her all was well—and Herb even took the kids out for a stroll along the beach when they started getting antsy again.

Time that proved key. She smiled when she flipped the switch just as they were coming back inside and beautiful static crackled in her ears, through the headphones she'd been wearing for the last twenty minutes. "Ah! Got it!"

Maybe those headphones insulated her own voice from herself a little too well, because her words startled the trio. The kids both jumped, making Herb jump in response, stagger a step, bump an overburdened shelf, and send a snowfall of papers flying every which direction.

She whipped the headphones off and dashed into the blizzard. "Gracious, Herb. I'm so sorry!"

He was laughing, though. "Not a worry—not if you got that thing working again."

"Pretty sure I did." She snatched up a handful of papers from where they'd settled. "Though I sure didn't mean to send your files flying. Can I help you order them again?"

He waved that off. "Nothing really to reorder. These are things we've never known what to do with anyway. Messages from somewhere in Europe, but not addressed to anyone, and certainly not for us. They're in some kinda code, but not one of ours."

Code? Her ears perked up at that. It had been years since she'd had any reason to play with codes. She glanced down at the paper in her hands. "Have you tried to crack it?"

Herb scoffed. "The only code I know is Morse, Miss Louisa, and that's more than enough for me. Cracking codes—who does your mama think I am, anyway?" This he directed to the children, who each stood with a haphazard stack of papers in their hands that they'd collected too.

"Herb!" Davie answered with a bounce.

"*Mr.* Herb." Evie, always the polite one, but just as bouncy.

Louisa's gaze skimmed over the words. The numbers. The arrangement, so familiar. And there—a series of numbers that she'd once known so well. How many times had she decoded that very one in Celeste's letters. *P-i-e-r-r-e*, that's what those numbers stood for.

Celeste. These were from Celeste!

Hands shaking, she looked back up at Herb. He'd think she'd lost her mind if she said that out loud. How, after all, would Celeste be sending messages to them here on Ocracoke, all the way from Charleville, behind German lines?

But they were from her, she knew they were. "Don't suppose I could take a look at these?"

Herb looked at her like she'd lost her mind, all right—but in an amused way. "Have at it. Take them with you, if you want. We never do anything with them but shove them up on that shelf there, which clearly wasn't the wisest idea." He took the stacks from the kids with a wink, straightened them, and handed them to her.

She slid them into her bag with the kids' storybooks, prayed her smile looked normal, and hurried back to the inn with her babies.

Her husband was gone. His mother wanted to steal her son. Garret was serving in a field hospital on the front lines.

But Celeste—Celeste, who'd gone silent with the first shots of the war. Was it possible that God was giving Celeste back to her?

22

TODAY

JULY 8, 1942
OCRACOKE ISLAND, NORTH CAROLINA

Sterling slid his fingers into Evie's, even though he had no intention of leaving this room. Not yet. Still, he wasn't about to turn down the invitation to hold her hand in his for a minute, now that he knew who she was. What she was. Why so many mysteries surrounded her.

The only one that remained unanswered was one neither of them could really explain: how he'd ended up on her beach out of all the stretches of sand in the Outer Banks that could have received him. That could be nothing but the divine hand of Providence.

"Hold on a moment. We can't leave all this out like this. It'll scare him off." And it was more imperative than ever that they capture him.

Not only imperative—but possible. They knew Mansfeld would come back here, like he'd apparently done every other night this week. If nothing else, he'd come back for the stash of information he'd been gathering and storing for quite a long time. From all parts of the world.

He had to have brought those European papers with him, all the way across the Atlantic. Sealed in something weather-proof, for them to have survived his weeks hunkered down in the maritime forest.

But why? Spies weren't notorious for traveling with a lot of luggage. One of the lessons Evie's father had taught him was how to encode his messages on the smallest, thinnest slips of paper, using a special shorthand to represent whole words or phrases, so that as much information as possible could be squeezed onto impossibly small surfaces. Slips of paper easily rolled up and hidden in a sleeve, in a shoe, in a belt buckle. Unable to be seen, unlikely to be felt by searching hands. Leaving your own hands free for the skills a very different officer had taught.

These papers, though, would have been easily seen, not to mention felt. This was not traveling light.

Evie gave his fingers a squeeze and then pulled hers away. "Of course. I got ahead of myself. You remember their order?"

And their positions in the drawer. That was his job, what he excelled at—those little details that made a full picture. Like cigarette packs and matchbooks and whatever linked Gustav Mansfeld to Celeste Scarborough Wynnwood.

Like midnight telegrams and photos of manor houses and a barn full of the most exquisite artwork he'd ever seen.

Like his Zodiac washing ashore here, this woman finding him, Celeste's husband doctoring him. His heart trickling her way day by day, steadily if slowly, like water carving its path back to the sea.

God's artwork, that. His mosaic of glass and shell and

human flesh. His symphony of lost friends, enemy torpedoes, and reclaimed hope.

She handed him each newspaper, and he arranged them
into their stacks, arranged the stacks in the drawers. She put
the pillow she'd tossed back on the bed, and he angled it ten
degrees more out of square—sloppy. That was unlike Mansfeld. He must have left the house in a hurry this morning.
Had he heard someone coming? Had he simply overslept?
Or was there something he'd been hurrying to do?

Once he was satisfied that the room—her room, the one
she'd shared three years with Job Farrow—was as Mansfeld
had left it, he held out *his* hand.

And she put hers into it.

A minute later, they'd locked up behind them and aimed
themselves for the doctor's house, the morning hushed and
still around them. He didn't let go of her fingers, even though
he knew any neighbor could look out their window as they
poured their morning coffee and see. Even though it was
the anniversary of her husband's death, and all his friends
had thought her so torn by grief that they'd come to gather
around her. Even though all good sense told him not to get
too attached, because he wouldn't be here much longer.

He held on anyway. Because he'd seen what none of those
Coasties had—that she'd taken off the necklace she'd been
wearing every day since he arrived and likely long before. The
one with that small sliver of blue-green glass dangling on a
dainty chain . . . and a silver wedding band with it. He'd seen
it that morning on her workbench in the barn, sitting there
beside another piece of glass, similar but larger.

He didn't know what that one was, but he'd surmised
that the first was linked to her husband, once he'd seen the
wedding band on the chain. The love of her youth, whom
she'd no doubt carry in her heart forever.

But her hand was in his, and the necklace was off. And she'd told him, of her own volition, who she was. Who her brother was. Why her secrets were no threat.

Maybe God had another piece yet to their mosaic. Sterling couldn't be sure of that—but he knew her hand felt at home in his. And that she might be the only woman in the world who could understand who he was and what he did without his ever having to say a word.

They made their way to the Wynnwoods' house, and Sterling forced his mind off the woman at his side and to the one he'd soon meet. Celeste Scarborough Wynnwood. Aunt Lester. The Celeste from the letters in that trunk in the attic, too, no doubt. "She was your mother's best friend, you said? So not really your aunt."

"No, the title's honorary, like Grandma See."

That brought him up short. "She's not really your grandmother? But you look—"

Her laugh interrupted him. "I know. Our families always found that so amusing. But my actual grandmother, Serena—Grandma Ree—was blond, too, and so was Daddy, before he went gray. Still, I think most people have forgotten we're not *actually* family. Especially after Grandma See moved to the inn during the Great War and then stayed, to help out. She'd been so lonely in this old house."

She patted a fence post as she said it, drawing his gaze to the graceful white house they'd been aiming for anyway. The Wynnwoods' house, he'd thought. Apparently Elsie's house before that.

Another piece in place, though it changed very little. Still, every piece mattered. "She won't mind that we're coming for a visit so early?"

Evie laughed again, this one low and soft. "She's a doctor's wife, Sterling. She's used to interruptions at all hours."

That didn't mean she didn't mind them. But Evie, un-daunted, went straight up to the door and knocked, not even waiting for an answer before pushing the door open and stepping inside. "Aunt L?"

"In the kitchen, *mon petit chou*. I'm making crêpes. Some-one paid Gar yesterday with a cup of sugar and fresh cream."

Sterling hadn't had a crêpe since he was in Paris six months ago. The very mention was enough to remind him that they hadn't sampled any of the abundant gifts the Coast Guards-men had brought for Evie in their rush to investigate her house. Not that he was about to impose—he had no idea how far those extra rations would stretch or the amount of batter Mrs. Wynnwood would have mixed up.

Evie had no such compunction. She all but dashed toward a corner of the house, tugging him along behind her. "Crêpes! I haven't made those in ages. Tell me you have blueberries for them."

They stepped into the kitchen in time to see a statuesque blonde turn with a smile, holding up a bowl of the demanded fruit. "Ask and ye shall receive. I finished the first batch and was going to bring them to the inn, actually. I know it's a hard day for you." Though at that, her gaze dropped to the hand still snug in Sterling's. Her face softened. In relief? He hoped so. "Well. Looks like you brought a guest too. Is this the infamous Sterling?"

In that photo of "all the womenfolk," he'd thought this woman was Evie's mother, given the similar coloring. But seeing them together in reality, with Evie as a woman herself, he wouldn't have made that mistake. It wasn't that where Evie was petite and slender, Celeste was tall. It was more that where Evie was quiet, probing looks, Celeste was bold laughter and even bolder kisses on their cheeks, seeming to take to him as readily as her "niece."

She was dressed casually, but not the sort of casual he'd come to expect on the island. More the type he'd seen on the streets of Paris or London. A bit of the same style Evie had, yes, but even more pronounced, if that was possible.

Evie had introduced him amid all the cheek-kissing, his hand had somehow lost the grip on hers, and now he found his fingers caught up in their hostess's, her twinkling brown eyes looking deep into his face. "You're English."

Hardly any point in denying that. "I am."

"How recently have you been there? And the Continent—have you been to the Continent?"

He nodded. "A few months ago. Paris."

At that, she dropped his hand and took a step back, brow furrowed. "Paris—so recently? Since Hitler took it?"

Evie was sending him one of her probing looks, too, perhaps surprised that he'd set all his cards on the table so quickly. But there was no time for subtlety, not now. He nodded. "On assignment."

"Ah." Her face clouded but then cleared just as fast. She made a shooing motion with her hands. "Sit, both of you. We may as well eat these while they're fresh, *n'est-ce pas?* I'll bring some of the next batch to Grandma."

She urged them into chairs at the kitchen table, set plates before them topped with steaming crêpes, chilled whipped cream, and a generous handful of the blueberries. A few expert motions to fold them, and then she presented them each with a fork. "*Bon appétit.*"

Well. It would be a shame to let them go to waste. He paused while Evie said a quick grace over them and then hurried that first blissful bite into his mouth.

It was like being in Paris all over again. Even with German uniforms patrolling every street corner, it had still been *Paris.* He'd still been able to slip into a little crêperie, place an order, and take his plate to the bistro table outside the shop. He'd been able to sit and eat while the pigeons cooed and the Eiffel Tower presided from on high and an accordion played on some other street corner. "These are fantastic. I can practically hear the street music."

"Is it still playing? Even now?" Celeste pulled out a chair for herself and sat with a sigh. "I cried when I saw the Nazis took the city. Paris, under military control! It's too horrible for words."

"It has dampened the Parisian spirit—but not extinguished it."

She sliced a bite of her crêpe, speared it. "Nothing can extinguish it. The French leaders may not always make the best choices, and they may not put up enough of a fight. But the people do. However they can."

And so they were. But he wasn't here to talk about the Resistance. He was here to talk about *her*. "You've spent a lot of time there."

She didn't look at him now. Keeping her gaze on her crêpe, she nodded. "We spent nearly a year there before the war—my mother and stepfather and me. I was there next soon after the armistice was declared in November. I heard of how when the bells pealed through the fog that day, the whole city poured out onto the streets—or so it seemed. Everyone shouting for joy, flooding the Champs-Élysées with their cheers, throwing their hats into the air."

She should have sounded joyful herself as she spoke of that day and not so . . . tired. Sad. She smiled, but it looked like an echo long faded. Then she blinked, turned the wattage of her smile back up to blinding, and directed it to Evie. "And then the later trips! Shopping and laughing and introducing Evie and Davie and my René and Violette to every French pastry to be found."

"René and Violette?"

She turned the full wattage on him. "Our kids. René is a chaplain in the navy—followed in Uncle Linc's footsteps. And Vi is still attending university on the mainland and volunteering there over the summer."

Another name he hadn't heard yet. "Uncle Linc?"

"My mama's uncle," Evie put in, licking cream from her fork. "He was our pastor for most of my childhood. He's in England at the moment. It was only supposed to be a visit of a few months, but when war was declared, it seemed too risky for any of them to come home. He decided to stay and help Mama with the efforts at Springbourne Hall."

Sterling nodded, letting those details fall into place in the tapestry of these families. Let the picture form. Gave himself a moment to see what new insights they brought or questions they begged.

But that was the thing—they painted a picture both normal and unique. Children serving their country or seeking education, like so many other families. A woman in a kitchen, making pastries with the first bit of cream and sugar she could put her hand to.

But French pastries. Trips to Paris. That was surely outside of what was normal for most Ocracokers. Most people, period.

There was something very much unusual about Celeste Scarborough Wynnwood. And that something must be linked to the reason she'd appeared in Gustav Mansfeld's odd collection of clippings. The question was how to discover what it was.

His gaze flicked to Evie. His method of discovering who *she* was had been more for his own entertainment during the boring weeks of recovery than because it was either efficient or—much as it pained him to admit it—particularly

329

accurate. His usual methods were far more direct. And given that they hadn't time for leisure just now, not if they wanted to catch Mansfeld before he moved again, he would have to go beyond direct questions here and straight to blunt. Shockingly blunt.

That would likely tell him more in her reactions than her mere words. So, he cut another bite of crêpe with his fork, put it in his mouth, chewed, swallowed. And then asked with a smile, "So, Mrs. Wynnwood, why would a German spy be looking for you?"

She froze with the next bite of her own halfway to her lips. Stared at him for a long moment, and then turned an accusing look on her niece as she let her fork clatter back to her plate. *Who bring?* she said with her hands, her face giving the emphasis.

"British intelligence, tracking my opposite number." He said it casually, even tossed in another smile. "A man who came to this country using the name Karl Meyer." He paused, but that name didn't seem to mean anything to her.

He hadn't honestly expected it would. "No? All right. Perhaps his real name will ring a bell, then. Why would a man named Mansfeld be hunting you down?"

Celeste Scarborough Wynnwood went white as a sheet. She pushed away from the table, her mouth open in what he suspected was going to be an insistence that he leave. But her knees buckled, her eyes rolled back in her head, and he barely lunged from his chair in time to keep her from smacking her head on the table.

Perhaps, he granted as Evie scowled at him, that had been a slight miscalculation.

23

YESTERDAY

OCTOBER 10, 1918
NORFOLK, VIRGINIA

Mama? You're squeezing my hand too hard."

Louisa checked her grip on both the little hands clutched in hers. She told herself to smile down at each of her babies. Told herself to make a joke of the anxiety that they'd both no doubt picked up on. Told herself that she wasn't second-guessing—or hundredth-guessing, as the case may be—her decision.

All she managed was the weakest turn of her lips and a marginal loosening of her babies' hands. "Sorry, Evie. That better?"

Evie looked up at her in that way she did, the way that saw more than a three-year-old had any right to see. "You don't wanna go on the trip, Mama?"

Want to? She *had* to. She was the one who had insisted on

331

it. She was the one who'd gone to her own mama and Grann and Grandma Elsie and Linc and begged them to talk her out of it even as she laid out why she had to do this illogical thing.

The problem, though, with being surrounded by so many bighearted, God-focused people was that they actually prayed about it with you, and instead of talking you out of that ridiculous plan, they helped you hatch it.

This was stupid. She'd never been more aware of it than at this moment, as they stood with the other passengers waiting to board that big old steamship in Norfolk Harbor. Bound for England. Across the U-boat–infested Atlantic. With her children. *With her children.*

But what had the alternative been? To leave them here with her family? She might as well rip her own heart out. And besides, Mama had been the one to say that for some reason she thought it was time they be introduced to the Culbreths.

It made no sense. None. But here they were. "Of course I want to, sweetie pie. It's only that I'm a little scared. I've never been on a boat this big."

She didn't mention things like U-boats to the twins. Why scare them with tales of monsters that ate ships like this whole? Or sent them to the bottom of the sea, anyway.

Grann eased up behind her and rubbed a hand over her back. She knew. She knew very well how terrified Louisa was to take this step. She knew how much it was costing her. But she knew why she was doing it too.

The telegrams had been haunting her for months. *Celeste.* She'd been praying every minute of every day for the sister of her heart. Praying and praying and praying. Thanking God that the sheer stack of them meant He'd preserved her life, that she was still there in Charleville. Asking Him to help her to trust Him with Celeste's life.

Then that last telegram had come in two weeks ago, and Herb had rushed it right over to her—the twins having babbled on to him about how their mama "turned all that silly stuff into words from her friend!"

Herb had been doubtful at first. But when she'd shown him the old codebooks that Elsie had brought to Ocracoke with her, when she showed him how they worked on these messages, he'd been convinced.

They'd all been horrible, those telegrams. Cries for help, pleas, anguish tapped into Morse code. But the last one had nearly undone her.

So many are dead. We will soon be among them. Allied victories mean a heavier hand on us. I will be killed soon.

Suddenly, every article about Allied advances and victories, about French territory regained, was cause for fear instead of joy. Dread had settled over Louisa so heavily she could barely move through the days. Celeste had been in danger these four years, yes. Enduring hardships Louisa could scarcely fathom. But something was shifting, something had increased the jeopardy. And what if God had delivered those telegrams to Louisa now because she was meant to act?

"What do you think you could possibly do?" That had been the first question out of Mama's mouth when Louisa brought it up, that logical reaction that had soon given way to prayer.

She didn't know. She still didn't know, not really. All she knew was that those messages had been forwarded to the Life Saving Station from somewhere in London. Which meant that somewhere in London was a friend. Someone had known to send those to Ocracoke. To *her*. Someone had known what they shouldn't have.

She had to find that someone. Somehow. And from there ... Well, she didn't know. Her loose plan was to leave Grann and the twins in the relative safety of London and make her way into France. She'd heard of plenty of gentlewomen ministering to servicemen on the front lines. She'd volunteer with one of them. She'd find Garret. Convince him to help her get to Charleville. Thanks to Grann, she spoke French fluently, which would undoubtedly help her sneak through the French countryside. And with Garret's status as a doctor, they ought to be able to gain access to places usually barred to them.

And then a miracle would have to happen. That's all she could think of that would make this plan work. A real miracle, of the Lazarus or Red Sea sort. Only the God who could raise the dead or part the waters could help her find her lost sister and bring her back whole and well.

But then, that was the God she served.

Of course, something could go wrong. Even when one was following God's illogical plans, things still went wrong. People still died. That was why the current plan would be to leave Grann and the twins with Lord Culbreth. She had to think—hope? trust?—that she'd have a warm reception at either Springbourne Hall or Culbreth House. Not for her own sake, but for Davie's. She didn't trust Edith for a moment to have his best interests at heart, but Louisa *did* want him—both of them—to have the opportunities Rem's side of the family could offer. She wanted them to know the place he'd loved like home. She didn't *want* to leave them there. But she couldn't take them to the front lines. And she knew if she'd left them in Ocracoke, Edith would pounce, probably with high-powered lawyers and court orders that Mama would have no idea how to fight, despite the lawyer of their own they'd retained on the mainland.

Better to take them straight to the lord so in need of an heir.

Soon the crowds of people surged up the gangway and onto the steamer ship *Cascade*. Louisa kept her death grip on the kids' hands, and they certainly didn't complain about it as the mass of people swirled and bumped and pushed. Their trunks had already been checked, their tickets were in Grann's capable hands. They got themselves aboard without any mishap, stayed on the deck long enough to hear that final whistle blow and watch the land retreat from them. Then they found a steward who pointed them toward their second-class cabin and made their way below deck. Once they were inside, Louisa could breathe again.

"Well now. Never did think I'd be on board a ship as grand as this, ready to cross the mighty Atlantic." Grann sat on one of the two small beds and wiggled her fingers in an invitation for whichever twin wanted to come to her lap. Evie accepted, while Davie tested the springs of the other bed's mattress. Her grin looked bright and young and free of reservation.

That must be nice. Louisa had nothing *but* shadows and worry and reservation weighting her bones. But she found a smile. "Well, you're the one we have to thank for the ability to make such a journey."

Money had been the final hurdle Louisa expected to have to sort out. But lo and behold, Grann had simply laid stacks of it on the table. From, she'd said, when they sold the land in Louisiana. She'd been sitting on it all these years, had been ready to use it to pay for Louisa's schooling, but the scholarship had come through, and then . . . well, then the twins had come. Dreams of teaching had given way to the bigger dream and more pressing reality of motherhood.

She didn't regret that lost dream. Not for a minute. She'd gotten to teach these two precious little people for three years now, and God willing, she'd have that privilege the rest of their childhood too. Assuming she got into and back out of France in one piece. So, the money had paid for these tickets, for the lawyer Mama would be meeting with while they were away, for whatever fight they ended up having to bring to Edith.

She would have sunk with a sigh to the bed beside Davie, but a knock came on their door. No doubt someone with instructions on something-or-another. She turned, opened it.

And stumbled back a step in shock when none other than Edith Culbreth pushed into the room, looking fierce and beautiful and with enough anger in her eyes to keep the ship in steam all the way across the Atlantic.

Her mother-in-law slammed the door shut behind her and glared at Louisa without even pretending at a smile. "What do you think you're doing?"

Louisa curled her fingers to her palms. How had she known? How had she known that Louisa was trying to bypass her and go straight to Lord Culbreth? Had she had her watched? Probably had *always* had her watched. And how deep did that go? Did she have someone reading her mail? Spying on her on Ocracoke? Or watching for her to leave? "I don't believe that's any of your business, my lady."

Edith's face flushed red under her rice powder. "How dare you? You're taking my grandson through a war zone, and you say it's none of my business?"

Louisa bristled. "*Both* your grandchildren, actually. And if you knew we were here, then I daresay you already know where we're going."

The flush faded from Edith's cheeks, and in its place came that cool calm Louisa had so hated when they shared a roof. "How did you find out?"

Find out? Louisa's gaze drifted away from Edith to Grann and Evie and Davie, who had opted for the safety of his great-grandmother's side now too. She couldn't be meaning Celeste—couldn't *know* about Celeste and wouldn't care if she did. That couldn't be what she was talking about.

So . . . what was?

It must be something big, if it brought Edith onto this ship, which was already under steam. She'd sworn years ago that she would never cross the Atlantic again. What was big enough to make her do so now?

Louisa folded her arms over her chest and decided that answering how she found out about Celeste was the best possible answer to *any* such question—perhaps the only way that guaranteed her mother-in-law's spies hadn't already known. "Telegrams."

Edith's brows slammed down. "There is no telegraph station on Ocracoke."

No, but there was on the mainland, and telegrams were brought over with the mail—which she knew. If she hadn't considered that as a possible way that Louisa could have found "it" out, it meant that she *was* monitoring Louisa's mail. Which wouldn't be that hard, would it? One mail boat, twice a week. All it would take was finding a person willing to accept a bribe and search each bag for anything addressed to her, either letters or telegrams. But . . . for what purpose?

"Not for civilian use, no. But there's one at the Life Saving Station, and I happen to be friends with a few of the Coast Guardsmen. Let's just say they've received a few intended for me, though it took them a while to sort that part out."

Edith clutched the back of the rinky-dink little chair that matched the tiny desk. Pulled it out. Sat. All without taking her eyes from Louisa. For a moment, she feared the woman might burst into tears. But no.

After a flare of her nostrils as she dragged in a long breath, she simply turned to an ice sculpture again. One that, oxy-moronically, spat fire from her eyes. "And *what*, then? He sends you a few telegrams that eventually reach you, you piece it together, and think you can simply travel to London and pick up where you left off?"

He? Pick up where they left off? Louisa sank onto the second mattress. There were only a few possibilities for who that "he" could be, all in Rem's family. But she had no history to pick up with his father or missing brother. Which left . . . but . . .

God of Lazarus, capable of raising the dead.

Her throat closed off. She couldn't make any reply.

It didn't seem that Edith, with a full head of steam, much needed her response anyway. "It's too late, Louisa. He's moved on—as he thinks you've done. As you both *should* have. The marriage was never legal, which your family certainly knows, given your *Negro* blood." She said it like it was a curse from heaven itself, and aimed her snarl at Grann.

He—Rem? Was that what she was saying? Rem was alive—Rem had moved on? Louisa found her voice. "What do you mean, as he thinks I've done?"

Something of her distress must have come through in her tone, because Edith nearly smirked as she delivered the bare outlines of what she'd done in a series of quick, deadly jabs of words.

The investigation she and Edgar had launched, which she'd mentioned on that dreadful day, but whose results Louisa had never even thought to wonder about.

The bribing of the booking agent to separate their tickets.

But then the part she hadn't known—that Rem's train had been delayed. That he'd missed the *Ignatius* and had to switch his ticket to another vessel. He hadn't known until he reached England what had become of the ship he should have been on, but he'd sent a telegram as soon as he realized.

But Louisa had already been gone. Kicked out, effectively, by Edith, who then received the assurances on her own. And having, by then, the proof that the marriage hadn't been legal, she'd simply let Louisa go on thinking him dead—neat and tidy, that—and informed Rem that Louisa had left in a rage over the investigation and had married Garret.

Louisa's eyes slid closed. Rem—alive, but thinking she'd left him. Thinking she'd run to Garret, who was the one person in the world he'd believe her capable of turning to in such a time.

Rem, who must hate her now, who had moved on.

But he was alive.

She pried her eyes open and found Grann towering between them, rage in every line of her posture. She'd seen Grann frustrated plenty, angry now and again. But never like this. Her words came out in a mixture of French and the Creole Louisa only knew a few words of, but she got the gist—no doubt Edith did, too, given the way she stood toe-to-toe with the woman whose blood she found so inferior.

"I did what I must for my family!" she spat. "To preserve them from a stain that could not be blotted out otherwise. Your granddaughter would have been his *ruin!*"

"Then why did you come for Davie?" Louisa pushed herself back to her feet, even as she noted that the twins had scooted themselves against the wall and were huddling there together, hands entwined. "If we're such a stain on your family line?"

Chin clicking up a notch, Edith looked past Grann to Louisa. "One must have a fallback plan. With Sebastian lost—and Rem hasn't another heir yet. Perhaps he will someday, but we cannot count on that, especially given the bombs falling on London. David ought to be prepared against the possibility."

Or . . . or Rem hadn't "moved on" quite as much as his mother would like. Hadn't remarried. Couldn't produce any other heirs.

Because he surely knew what she did—that what God had joined together, no man had the power to separate.

No *woman* either.

One thing was glaringly clear: She couldn't believe a word Edith Culbreth said. Not knowing the lengths she'd gone to, the people she'd deliberately hurt in pursuit of her own will. Nothing was beyond her.

Louisa went to the door and yanked it open. "I'll thank you to leave our cabin, and not to come here again. You stay on your very lovely first-class deck, and we'll stick to ours."

Edith's eyes narrowed. "Do you really think you can sail to London with your brats and show up at his door? You think he'll take you back after all these years—years he envisioned you with another man? Even if you tell him that was a lie, his heart will have grown cold toward you."

Maybe. Probably. But what did that matter? He was dead, and he'd been brought back to life. Her husband, the father of her children—alive, in London. And if their going there was enough to worry Edith Culbreth that much, then maybe all hope wasn't lost. "Good-bye, Edith."

Her ladyship stormed from the cabin, and Louisa shut the door quietly but firmly behind her—and bolted it. The moment she turned, the children were there, arms coming around her, little faces clouded with confusion.

"What did she want?" Davie.

"Are you happy or sad, Mama?" Evie.

Louisa crouched down, pulled them tight against her, and

340

closed her eyes. Even so, tears surged. Happy ones? Sad ones? Both. Neither.

"Daddy's alive, babies. Daddy's alive. And we're going to see him."

TEN DAYS LATER
LONDON, ENGLAND

Rem shoved his hat on his head, slipped his arms through the sleeves of his overcoat, and, after a moment's hesitation, shoved the decrypt of the latest telegram from Celeste into his pocket. He'd already sent it on to the Coast Guardsmen, already prayed for the thousandth time that it and its sisters would make it into Louisa's hands. Usually he then left the handwritten translations in a drawer of his desk, but this one . . .

There was something different about this one. Something not only urgent and desperate but . . . more. He didn't even know the word to use for it. He only knew he intended to go home, flatten it back out on his desk at Culbreth House, set Louisa's photo beside it, and pray like he'd never prayed before. For his wife. For her best friend. For Sebastian. For all the impossible situations in the world.

He'd grown accustomed to the yawning emptiness in his own life. Perhaps it always chafed like imagined sackcloth, but like sackcloth in the scriptures, he'd decided at some point in the last months that it ought to be a reminder to fall to his knees. Perhaps the cup given him wasn't happiness, but rather holiness. Perhaps he could do as a man of prayer all that he'd failed to do as a man of action.

If those telegrams from Celeste had accomplished nothing else, nothing for her, they'd done that for him.

The autumn air gusted about him as he stepped out of

the Old Admiralty Building and turned toward that familiar pathway through the park. A few of his colleagues exited a step behind him and called a farewell, which he returned with a vague smile. Zivon Marin, the Russian who had joined their ranks not long ago, escorting their photography expert, Miss Lilian Blackwell, home for the evening. Phillip Camden, too, aiming himself toward the nearby hospital to see his fiancée home, as he did every night.

Happy people, even in the midst of war and influenza pandemics. People who had seized light and life amid darkness and death.

He envied them. And yet was so glad they'd found it. That they were proving that though his world had ground to a halt, others still pressed on.

Quick footsteps behind him made him go tense, at least until another familiar form slid into place at his side and angled a grin his way. "Where are you going, Rem? You're supposed to be joining us at Pauly's."

Blast. He'd forgotten all about Barclay Pearce's latest invitation. He'd given up refusing them. Why should he? The evenings he passed with this man's boisterous family in one of London's foulest neighborhoods had proven to be the best distractions to be found. Barclay's sister Willa and her husband, Lukas, played their violins like a couple of virtuosos—Lukas was, in fact, a rather well-known professional. When their other sister, Rosemary, was in Town with her husband, Peter, they always had stories to share about the books he wrote under a nom de plume and the many correspondents he had. And they would share letters from their brother Georgie in France.

Rem always hoped that somehow, even though they weren't in the same regiment, Georgie would have met up with Sebastian. And why not pray it? The God who raised the dead and parted the Red Sea could certainly arrange for a coincidental meeting of their brothers. Stranger things had happened.

But tonight—tonight he couldn't even imagine laughter and meat pies and ten conversations going at once. He could only imagine quiet and this telegram in his pocket and the photo of Louisa. "Sorry, old boy. It slipped my mind and . . . well, tonight isn't a good night."

Barclay frowned, even as he kept pace with him when he turned into the park. "You didn't get bad news about your brother."

He didn't ask it, he stated it. As if he'd have known had such bad news come.

Perhaps he would have. Rem had long ago given up trying to determine *how* Pearce knew all he knew and simply accepted that he did. "No. Someone else."

"Not—is that your wife?"

Rem frowned. He'd shared enough about Louisa with his friend over the years that he supposed it was logical he'd assume that bad news about her would get him down. But he also knew he hadn't had *any* news of her in years, so why would that be his conclusion? "No, it's not about her. Not directly. A friend of hers, though."

"No." Pearce gripped his shoulder, pulled him to a halt, and pointed farther along the path. "That woman, there. She bears a striking resemblance to the one in your dog-eared photo."

He'd kicked himself when one of the photo's corners had folded over—but Lily Blackwell had made him a copy. He had the fresh one in his drawer at home, ready to take this one's place when it finally gave up the ghost. But he hadn't wanted to part with the original, not yet. Not until it crumbled to dust in his wallet.

He finally followed the direction of Barclay's arm with his gaze, out of curiosity if nothing else. He'd seen a few women here and there over the years who made him look twice, but that second glance always proved that it had been nothing but wishful thinking. It was never her. Never would be her.

Though he could see why Barclay would think it, especially given that he'd only seen a photograph. The figure emerging from the autumn mist *did* bear a striking resemblance to Louisa. The same dark curls, the same dusky skin, the same face shape. He couldn't see this woman's eyes from here, but she was even the same height and build, as best as he could tell.

And what Barclay couldn't possibly have known was that she even *moved* like Louisa. That effortless grace, the quick steps that always said she had somewhere to be, something to do, some task waiting. The way her step quickened even more when she spotted him, the way she lifted an arm.

And her voice—the voice that called out "Rem!"—took him straight back to North Carolina, to a summer beach, to the woman who had knit his heart to hers so effortlessly.

He must be hallucinating. That was the only possible explanation. The long hours and sleepless nights had finally caught up with him, just as Father had warned him they would. He'd lost his mind. Had conjured up here on London's streets the very person he most wanted to see.

His figment was running now, tears streaming down her face. Which proved it couldn't be Louisa—Louisa never cried.

But his mind knew that. Why would it make a figment behave so strangely?

"Rem!" she called again. She was close now, so close he could see the blue of her eyes. Catch a whiff, he swore, of salt air and *Louisa*.

His arms opened, because what else was one to do when

344

a vision acted so? And he caught her, held her close. Felt her against him, sobbing into his shoulder.

If this was his imagination, then it was richer than he'd ever imagined. "Lu?" It couldn't be—yet it couldn't *not* be. No one else fit like this in his arms. No one else spoke like she did. No one else held him like she did. "How . . . ?"

"I thought you were dead. On the *Ignatius*. She never told me otherwise."

"What?" His stomach dropped to his feet—then ricocheted, bouncing up into his throat, choking him. Hope? Betrayal? Joy? Agony? All of them. None of them. He loosened his hold a bit so that he could look down at her.

Her beautiful face, streaked with beautiful tears. The face he'd had no right to claim as his own but which he could never close his eyes without seeing. Louisa—precious Louisa. A little bit older, but *Louisa*. His Louisa.

Or—no. Garret's Louisa. But what was Garret's Louisa doing here in his arms?

"My mother? She never told you about the mistake of that telegram?"

"And she told you I'd married Garret, but it was a lie, Rem. I've been home on Ocracoke this whole time, mourning you. I—"

"Wait." Not married to Garret? How—what—when . . . Too many questions to know which to ask. And in that moment, none of them mattered. She was here. His. They were together again. He pried his arms away from her so that he could cup her face between his hands. Looked deep into her eyes until the emptiness filled and overflowed. Until the miracle sank deep into his bones. Until she smiled through her tears, and he knew it was real. "Lu."

He didn't know if he was crying or laughing now, but he dared to press his lips to hers—there on a path through the park in the heart of London—and then crushed her to him again. "You're here. You're really here. And you don't hate me?"

Her laugh was a balm on his soul. "Hate you? How could I hate the one I love with my whole heart? I thought you would hate *me*, thinking me faithless. She said you'd moved on—"

"Never." Where else could there be but with her? "Never. There's only you. There could only ever be you. But if you thought me dead . . . ?"

Oh, her smile. It shot through him like a Paris gun. Shattered him. But put him back together too. "Don't you know, honey? We Adair women love once. With our whole heart. Forever. Especially"—she pulled away a fraction, enough to tuck herself to his side and angle him back toward the path, since their collision had turned them about a bit—"when I had such reminders of you every day."

She held out a hand toward the pathway.

No, toward the cluster of people *on* the pathway. Grann! Come all this way. And Father behind her, a smug smile on his face. No doubt they'd shown up at the house and he'd decided they'd better try to intercept him at the office. And . . .

Two others, so small. Letting loose of Grann's hand even then and running toward that outstretched hand of Louisa's.

Children. *Two* children. One with her dark curls, one with his own golden ones. Both with her blue eyes, full of light and joy and life.

Another collision, full of Louisa's laughter and tiny little voices reaching out to pluck at his heart.

His children. *Their* children. He was a father. All these years he was a father, and he hadn't known it. He was a stranger to his own flesh and blood, and why?

He knew the answer, but anger with his mother would have to wait. Right now, those two sweet little faces were

ROSEANNA M. WHITE

turned up to him with bright smiles, as if they knew him and had been waiting, waiting for this moment.

He didn't know a thing about children. Would probably make a muddle of this. But his knees bent until he'd rested one against the cold, damp pavement. He sank until he was on their level.

Above them, Louisa cleared her throat, which was apparently some sort of prompt. Grinning, the two little darlings joined hands, the boy bowing, the girl curtseying. Together they recited, "Hello, Daddy."

"I'm Davie—David Michael, after Mama's father and yours," his son said. *David Michael.*

"And I'm Evie—Evelyn Edith, after Grann and your mama."

After his mother, even though she'd done her best to ruin everything, to separate them, to keep them apart. Nostrils flaring, Rem sucked in a long breath. "Davie. Evie."

Another bob from both of them, another joint recitation. "How do you do?"

His lips quirked up. A proper *English* greeting. "I don't believe I've ever been better in all my life." Could he embrace them? Would they run the other way, screaming? Go stiff? Start crying? They were only tots, after all. Three years old, by his quick math, barely.

Evie answered the question for him, launching herself at him and giving him little choice but to catch her. He did so with a laugh, opening one arm again when Davie made to follow his sister.

Children. His children. His wife, at his side again. The dead raised. The sea parted.

Evie wrapped her arms around his neck when he made to stand after a long minute, so he simply pulled her up with him, and she anchored herself on his hip like she'd been doing it all her life.

Joy and life and promise and hope. But that telegram still weighed a stone in his pocket. He met Louisa's gaze. "We need to talk about Celeste." He shouldn't ruin the reunion with it, but he knew in his gut they had no time to lose.

She nodded, her hand finding Davie's. "That's what brought us here. I got the telegrams you sent to the station, eventually. I didn't realize you were alive until we were on the ship and your mother confronted us, thinking we'd found out and were coming to you—which I would have been, had I known. Long ago."

He looked to Grann, to Father . . . and to Barclay Pearce, the man who always knew more than he should and could get his hands on things that were impossible.

Pearce was already nodding. "The lady on the other end of those mysterious telegrams of yours, in France? I'll gather the troops."

Rem didn't know who the troops were, but he was all for the gathering of anyone who could help. "Bring them all to my house."

A salute, and his friend took off at a jog back toward the OB.

Rem looked down at his wife's face again. He didn't know what they could do to save her best friend. But God had already given him one miracle today—no, three. Louisa, Davie, and Evie.

He found himself ready to believe He'd deliver another.

24

TODAY

Evie had known Celeste for most of her memory—and even before they'd officially met in London when she was three, Mama's best friend had been one of those people she'd known through all the stories. Like Grandpa Michael, who Grann and Grandma Ree told so many stories about. Like Daddy, who Mama had talked about every day. Like Maddie, who Grandma See would tell her of with signs and writing and photographs. And even, after he joined up and went to serve on the front, Uncle Gar.

Stories had painted the backdrop of her world as a child, more than she'd ever known. Stories had brought to life all the people who mattered to the ones who mattered to *her*. Stories had been reality in her family.

But as she and Sterling got Aunt L settled on the divan in

the living room and she had a little color back in her cheeks, and as her eyes got that distant, haunted look in them when they turned toward the past, Evie realized that there were stories she'd never been told. Stories not deemed appropriate for the ears of a child, no doubt.

Stories no one had thought—or wanted—to pull back out and dust off when she was old enough to hear them.

Stories, perhaps, that no one wanted to relive.

Evie had always known the basics—that Celeste and her mother, Maddie, had been trapped behind enemy lines from nearly the first days of the war. That her stepfather, Pierre, had tried to defend their home against the invading army and had been shot and killed for it. That the whole town of Charleville had been overrun—its mansions, châteaus, and government buildings all taken over by German military command. Its food all requisitioned for the troops, the citizens left to starve. She knew it was ugly. That it had been harrowing. That Maddie had died somewhere in those four misty years of war, and that Celeste had barely escaped with her life.

But the basics weren't what made her aunt's hand shake now as she reached to accept the glass of water Evie held out for her. The basics weren't what made her go so quickly from a robust, healthy woman to someone who looked frail and ill. The basics weren't what put ghosts in her eyes.

Evie exchanged a look with Sterling, not knowing if she was annoyed with him for being so blunt with his questions, or impressed. If she was irritated that he'd never told her the real name of the spy he was hunting, or if it didn't matter. It wasn't as though the name Mansfeld meant any more to her than Meyer had. And it wasn't as though he'd known until that morning that she was, in fact, linked to the organization that had trained him and given him his mission. He probably shouldn't have told her as much as he had.

350

All right, so she wouldn't be irritated—much. Other than over how it affected a woman she loved so fiercely. *That* could have been better handled.

Maybe. Or maybe a subtler approach would have led to Celeste simply going into a French tirade, dismissing him and his audacity, and then taking the time to come up with a sanitized version of whatever the true tale was.

But they didn't need the scrubbed-clean version Evie already knew. They needed the truth. They needed to know why this SS officer was on their island, fixated on *her*.

Celeste took a long sip of water, handed the glass back to Evie, and leaned back against the cushion, her eyes sliding shut. "I never expected to hear that name again."

"Mansfeld?" Sterling pulled a chair close to the divan and offered it to Evie, then grabbed another for himself. To be close to Aunt L, she had to wonder, or to box her in?

Either way, Evie sat. Took her aunt's hands in hers—her fingers cold as ice—and held them.

Celeste shuddered at the name. "He was the one who shot Pierre. The senior officer of those in our neighborhood, the one who had claimed the château for himself and a few aides."

Evie's brows furrowed. Had the description Sterling given her been a lie, along with the name? Because he'd said that Karl Meyer was a member of the Hitler Youth. Which meant he certainly hadn't been old enough during the Great War to be a senior officer.

But he'd also recently told her that he was the son of a general—it must be the general, the father, whom Celeste had known. She held her peace, let the words keep spilling from her aunt's lips without interruption.

"For the first few months, he was civil. Kind, even. He let us stay in the house, didn't force us to the streets as most officers did to the families whose houses they chose. But his kindness had a price." She moistened her lips, opened her eyes. Set her gaze on Evie. "My mother fell ill, that first winter. He said he'd arrange for her to have medicine, that we would both continue to eat—*if*."

Evie's stomach knotted. There was no need to ask a "what" to that "if." Celeste was a beautiful woman, had been every bit as lovely at nineteen. She pressed the fingers held between her own. "That would have been an impossible situation. An impossible choice."

Celeste shook her head. "There was no choice. If I didn't do what he wanted, we'd both die. What did my virtue matter in the face of my mother's life? All my cries for help were going unanswered, no one outside Charleville cared or could do a thing—and those *in* Charleville were worse off than I was. The only friend I had was Angel-Marie, the telegraphist. She helped me send messages out, but we both knew they were cries in the dark. That even if anyone received them and decoded them, there was nothing they could do."

"Wait." Sterling scooted even closer, the consternation on his face only making him handsomer. "You sent messages? To whom?"

Celeste shook her head. "I don't know, exactly. Just before the invasion, there'd been an Englishman visiting the town, and he'd sent a telegram to someone in London. It had seemed to Angel-Marie to be very official, very important. At the time, she whispered to me, so excited, about how she thought he must be a government official, that perhaps it had gone to the Prime Minister himself. I doubt that— but it went somewhere in London, anyway. And, as it turns out, was intercepted by the English Admiralty, along with all other telegrams from occupied territory."

Her eyes met Evie's. "Your father saw them. Decoded

them. There was nothing the Admiralty could do, of course. But he'd sent them on. Here, to the Coast Guard station—or Life Saving Station, as it was called then." Her lips turned up. "And it saved my life. We prayed every prayer we knew as we composed and sent those messages, Angel-Marie and I. We prayed and we tapped them out, and then we waited. Always waited. But no help came.

"Part of me was grateful—Mama had medicine, we both had food. But in some ways, that only made it worse. Everyone knew *why* we had food. What I had traded. Some looked at me with pity, others with judgment."

Evie shook her head. "They had no right to judge."

"Do we ever? But condemnation was the only thing they had left, I think. The only thing that was free to them. Hope cost far too much. Prayers took energy. But hating me was easy. I'd never been one of them—they'd scarcely known me before the war! I was Pierre's upstart American stepdaughter. As targets went, I was a far safer one than the Germans too. They didn't dare spit at or curse the soldiers."

So instead they would take their anger out on the women who sacrificed themselves to feed their families by playing mistress to those officers. Evie had heard some of those tales over the years too—she just hadn't realized it applied to *Celeste*. Aunt L. "I'm so sorry you suffered that."

Celeste's shrug bespoke elegance and breeding . . . but was also underscored with the pure island stubbornness that had led generations of villagers to make their home on a tiny spit of land, despite hurricanes and isolation. *Do your worst,* that shrug said. *I'll survive it.*

They had done their worst, both the Germans and her neighbors. And she had survived it. But it had cost her.

Celeste's gaze dropped to their hands. "I don't blame my neighbors for acting as they did. So many of them were dying of starvation. So many tried to escape to nearby towns and were shot, or died of exposure on the way. Then, in the winter of 1915, Mama died." Her eyes closed again, but tears leaked out. "After everything. It was for no purpose. I tried to get away from him, then, but . . . I couldn't." Her eyes opened again. "He wasn't a monster. He was a man—a lonely man who could never betray any weakness in the eyes of his men. A hard man, yes, and he ran both his regiment and our house with an iron fist. But I think he had some affection for me, at that point. I was the only one with whom he could just be *Max*. Leaving him—I tried, once. Tried to run to Angel-Marie and from there, away. *She* was the one who paid for it. Her parents were killed, both of them. He spared her so that he still had that leverage over me. And then begged me—*begged* me not to 'make him' do such a thing. Cursed me for 'forcing his hand' with her parents." She paused, turned her head away.

Evie could feel the tension of those old memories in her fingers, see it in every line of her face. And she remembered other stories, even older stories. Stories Mama had told her when she was a young woman bemoaning that she had no best friend her age on Ocracoke while Davie had Job, and asking how she and Celeste had become such good friends. "It reminded you of your father."

"That's what he'd always said to my mother. That she'd made him do it, that it was her fault. As if he couldn't control the raising of his own hand. As if Max *had* to shoot Pierre or Claude or Suzette." The shake of her head was fierce. "But I knew he *would*. He would kill my only friend in France. He would kill *me*, if it came down to it, to keep me from escaping and telling the enemy anything about him. He'd let me get close, which meant I was dangerous to him. I could never leave. But I knew how to smile and pretend everything

was all right—I'd learned that at my father's hand. I knew
how to pretend I loved someone when hatred burned deep
inside. I knew how to live one more day, and then the next,
and then the next."

Evie's eyes burned too. No one should have to learn those
lessons. And the hatred, the bitterness—it was poison. Poison Celeste had taken years to heal from, and which even now
could throb like an old wound. Maybe it always would, this
side of heaven. Maybe that final work of forgiveness could
be achieved only in eternity, though Evie knew Celeste had
tried, and tried again, and tried still.

She saw the trying now in the way she sat up straighter,
the way she pulled in a long breath, the way she lifted her
free hand to the necklace she always wore—the gold cross
that Uncle Linc had given her on her first Christmas back
on the island. A reminder of the God who had seen her, had
heard all those cries she sent out into the darkness, and had
made a way for her to come home again.

It was a humbling thing, watching a woman you'd loved
as a second mother pull herself together, pull the tattered
robes of dignity back around the shoulders she'd bared to the
remembered lash. Watch her remember her own brokenness
and reach for the strength she'd found only in the Lord, and
in the family that had waited prayerfully for her return. Evie
prayed now, silently, that Celeste would have the strength to
finish her tale, and that she'd find another level of healing
through the telling of it.

After a moment, Sterling's voice came quietly this time.
Gently. Encouraging. "You were there until the end of the
war?" A mercy, that. Permission to skip all the in-between.
Jump straight to the end.

Celeste nodded and let go of the necklace again. "Charleville was liberated on the tenth of November—just one day

before the armistice. The Germans were in full retreat, and it was chaos. I thought that was our chance, finally, to get away."

"Get away?" Evie tilted her head to the side, unable to contain the question. "Why would you have to get away? Why not wait for him to leave?"

Though her lips turned up, it wasn't a smile. "Because he meant to take me with him."

That was a surprise. From all she'd read, it wasn't so unusual for officers on any side of a war to have a mistress where they were stationed—but it was very unusual indeed for them to want to take those mistresses home again, where most had wives waiting. She glanced over at Sterling, just as he glanced at her. From the slant of his brows, it struck him as odd too. "Take you?"

"Take *us*." Celeste let out a long breath. Shifted. "I don't know why he'd be looking for me now, though. Again. After all these years. He left me for dead that day, a bullet lodged in my ribs."

Sterling cleared his throat. Leaned closer. "It isn't Maximillian Mansfeld who's looking for you, Mrs. Wynnwood."

Now she frowned and sat up straight. "But you said—"

"Mansfeld. But not Max. His son, Gustav."

"Stavi? He's *here*? Looking for *me*?" Again Celeste washed pale, again tears surged to her eyes.

This time Evie didn't have to ask why. It was crystal clear. Gustav Mansfeld wasn't just Max's son—he was hers.

When Sterling couldn't find Evie in the inn or on its porches or at the clothesline, he stepped into the grass, eyes casting first toward the road and then to the barn, where he now knew she'd be bent over silver and glass and shell and art, not tending the hens or the pony that she'd said she and Davie had caught and tamed together when they were ten.

He didn't really need to debate long. Yes, she was certainly the type to watch after her neighbors, to see to their needs, to find solace in serving them. But the sort of storms he'd sensed in her as they walked home, silent, from the Wynnwoods' two hours ago wasn't the kind to be calmed by another person. It was the kind that could only be calmed by quiet and prayer and doing the thing that defined you.

He turned to the barn, hoping she'd had enough solitude. Because the day had already stretched to afternoon, and they needed to have a plan before it leaned into evening.

The shade of the barn was welcome after even that short stint through the sun-glaring heat, and he wiped the sweat from his forehead as he came inside. Times like this, he missed the temperate climes of England. And he heard it got even hotter here as the summer wore on. How did Evie stand it? Or perhaps more to the point, how did Remington Culbreth? Maybe they spent their summers in England, winters here.

He followed the same path he had that morning, past the old rusting equipment, the grain that was stored for the animals, and into the back section. She'd called it her studio, as they walked that morning. It was as much gallery, though, to his eyes. Museum. And she, not only the artist but the loveliest work of art. She was bent over her workbench, tools in hand.

His lips twitched up. What a beautiful, strange combination she was. The practical and the purely lovely. The educated and the hardworking. The aristocrat and the innkeeper. He slid up behind her on silent feet, hoping to steal a glance at whatever she was working on—and of her working on it—before she noticed him.

It was the necklace she'd always worn, the one with the wedding ring sharing the chain. Only that second piece he'd noted that morning was attached now, too, and the band was gone. He wasn't sure how she'd made that silver wire not only hold the glass pieces together but turn them into art, but she'd done it. A swirl, a loop, and the two pieces looked like a reflection, one of the other, in a mirror that had made them grow. Like two pieces nested from one angle, the larger and the smaller; and then when he shifted, like two that were the same, just seen with the advantage of perspective.

"What's the second one?" He breathed the question quietly, right above her ear, when she'd moved the tool away.

She didn't jump. No doubt she'd sensed him as he watched her. "That would be the piece I found right before you washed up on my shore."

"And the first one?"

"The one I found right after Job died."

He let that sink in, good and long. Not that she'd found two pieces. Not that they were, inexplicably, so similar in shape. But that she'd chosen to meld the two.

Past and future? Two halves of her heart?

Did he want half of it? He'd always been the all-or-nothing sort, but the thought of *nothing* when it came to Evie didn't bear thinking about.

She leaned in with her soldering iron again. "I grew up knowing that Adair women love once, forever. Grann and her James. Grandma Ree and her Michael. Mama and Daddy. For almost four years, she thought he was dead—but she never even considered finding another husband. And a good thing, too, since he wasn't. But those were the stories I'd always heard. How fiercely we loved. How true it was. How it lasted a lifetime and beyond, reached right into eternity."

Was this her way of letting him down without ever even

giving him the chance to stretch up? To try? It made the stubborn streak in him flare to life, made his burns ache. He deserved a chance, at least, didn't he? To show her that finding more didn't mean what came before was any less?

She sighed, moved the sea glass a bit, and touched her tool and silver to it again. "So many times lately I've asked myself if I was wrong—if I'd never really loved Job like they loved their husbands. Was there something wrong with me? Do I not love deeply enough? I asked myself if I've betrayed him and them both by not feeling like they did. By wondering if maybe I *do* want to move on." Now she stopped, put the tools down altogether. Turned on her chair and looked up into his face. "I did love him. He was part of my childhood, part of who I was and who I wanted to be. I chose him, chose him over England and balls and landed gentry. That means something."

Because he didn't know how else to answer, he nodded. It *did* mean something—but so did the other part. "There's nothing wrong with you, Evie. *Nothing.*"

She didn't seem to hear him. "Had he lived, we would have grown together, more fully entwined with every year that passed. Had he lived, I would have gone on loving him. We'd have had children, and our family would have been all I needed. All I wanted. I'd have been happy here, forever."

How could he both hate that she was denied that and yet find hope in the way she phrased it all? He nodded again. "Of course you would have."

"But he's . . . *gone*. Death did us part. And he didn't leave me with a family of our own. There were no children to remind me of him every day. And the memories—they're sweet, so sweet. But they're not before my eyes anymore." She scooted her chair away, stood, holding his gaze all the while, so that his heart sped up. "He was real, our love was real. It shaped me into who I am. But it's not my whole story. A piece. An important piece. But not the whole."

Sweet Evie. He lifted a hand, brushed his knuckles over her cheek. "I know."

Her eyes slid shut. "No more hidden pieces, buried in the sand. They need to be seen. How can we ever be understood, be truly loved, if we don't show all our most important pieces?"

Sweet, sensitive Evie, who felt so deeply. How could she have doubted even for a moment her own ability to love? All she was, was love. "Celeste didn't hide that piece from you to keep you from seeing it. She hid it from herself to keep from feeling that pain every day."

"I know." A rushed, hushed whisper. "I know it has nothing to do with me. It was no slight that she never told me. She was protecting herself. A part of herself that she thought was lost forever. Still—I never knew. I consider her children my cousins, but I never knew she had another one, a stranger to us all."

One who was here now. And they had to ask why. Had his father sent him? To what end? Had he only just now realized she'd survived the wound he'd inflicted? Was he so hard a man, so cold that he thought she must be either his or no one's?

"How could you have known?" he asked gently. "She never mentioned it, she said. Not since coming here. No one knew."

"Garret knew, my parents knew. The grandmothers all knew."

"But you were only a child. You were, what? Three?"

"I didn't *stay* three. I should have—"

"She'd gone on living, Evie. By the time you were old enough to be told that story, she'd married Garret. They had children of their own. That was where she was focused—

where she *had* to focus to stay sane. You couldn't have seen, then, that she was still hiding something. It had been too well covered with life. Sands washed over that glass entirely, burying it."

She nodded. And she leaned into his hand. "But then a hurricane comes along and churns it all up again."

"So it would seem. She couldn't have anticipated that."

The corners of her lips curved up. "She should have. That's something every islander knows—there's always going to be another hurricane. Another storm. Everything buried will surface again, and everything you thought would last forever will come down eventually. But you rebuild. You dredge. You keep moving, keep adding new. That's how we go on living."

He leaned a little closer. Wished he could stay there, lost in her gaze, forever. "And you? You're ready to go on living?"

In answer, she turned back to her bench, snatched up the pendant still on its chain, and held it up between them. "I already have. The question, Sterling Bertram, is whether you can accept my complicated history."

Was it? He felt his own lips turn up. "I like complications."

She slid the necklace, not over her own head, but over his. "I can't promise there aren't going to be more storms in my life."

"Fair weather gets boring. I've always liked a good, rousing thunderstorm." Besides, as she'd pointed out, there would always be storms, for everyone. He leaned down until his forehead touched hers. "Seems to me that hurricanes are better weathered together than apart, anyway."

Her hand settled on his cheek, making him aware of the day-old stubble and the fact that her touch had come to mean home to him, sometime between when she nursed him and when he thought she was an enemy. Home and family and all those things he wasn't supposed to be distracted by while he was an agent of His Royal Majesty.

But His Royal Majesty wasn't there just now—and she was. So when she tilted her face up, he caught her lips with his own. And he let that hurricane crash over him. This would come with its own storms.

But he wasn't about to hide from it.

25

YESTERDAY

NOVEMBER 9, 1918
CHARLEVILLE, ARDENNES DEPARTMENT, FRANCE

The short stint in London had not been enough to accustom Louisa to a sea of people instead of water, pedestrians instead of sandpipers and gulls. Being surrounded by towering buildings older than anything she'd ever seen hadn't been enough to make her stop wishing for the beauty fashioned solely by God's hand. Time among Rem's colleagues in Room 40 hadn't been enough to make her really feel like she was anything but a pretender.

But they'd come through. They'd rallied around her, around them, and seemed to take true delight in helping them plot the plan now underway. Lord Culbreth had received her with warmth and grace and had promptly become a doting grandpapa—to *both* the twins, not just Davie. And even the long-overdue confrontation between Rem and his mother hadn't managed to distract them for more than an evening.

Oh, it had been ugly. Accusations and truth and lies and recriminations. Not only between Rem and Edith and Louisa, but with Lord Culbreth in the mix too. It had ended with Edith storming from the house, swearing she'd be back across the Atlantic the moment she could book a ticket.

No one had rushed after her, begging her to stay. Maybe they should have. Maybe God wanted them to forgive, to fix things. Maybe Grann would tell her to pray for Edith just like she'd always told her to pray for Celeste's daddy.

She wasn't ready for that yet. And didn't, frankly, have the space to grant to it. Not now.

Now she was standing, flanked by both her husband and Garret, on a scarred and muddy battlefield gone silent. She'd never seen this land before it became the scene of war, but the smoking hulks of sticks that had once been trees made her whole chest ache.

God's creation, destroyed by man's hatred. It wasn't right. She looked out over that burned and mown-down forest and mourned for it like she'd mourned for the people she'd lost in life.

But there was consolation there. Just as Rem stood now by her side, never truly gone, so too would this wreck of a forest reclaim life. God had created it that way—to rebound from any ruin that man could wreak. To grow again. Thrive again. Cover over the scars with new life. That was what God's creation did, plant and animal and man.

They would survive the devastation of this war, somehow. The scarred men, the abused women, the torn-apart land. They would all go on. All rebuild. All find new life.

New life that might cover those scars but which couldn't obliterate them completely. She knew that too. They'd become part of the earth. Part of the people. Part of the story they'd all tell. The yesterday whose tides would carve tomorrow.

Rem ran his thumb over her knuckles, and it made her miss their babies, safely waiting with Grann and Grandpapa in London. She'd hugged them both until they'd squirmed six days ago. She'd kissed them. Told them to behave themselves and promised to come home as soon as she could, with their Aunt Celeste. She'd promised what she had no idea whether or not she could deliver. But they'd needed the promise.

She'd needed the promise. The hope. The reminder.

On her other side, Garret scrawled one more note onto a clipboard and handed it off to a nurse. He hadn't looked particularly glad to see them when they arrived in his camp last night. She hadn't had to guess as to why. This battle-scarred forest wasn't a sight he'd have wished on her. But his wide eyes when he saw Rem—that had been worth the treacherous road that had led them here.

She'd had her first terrifying and exhilarating ride in an airplane to get across the Channel, courtesy of Rem's friend Camden and an old colleague of his—a duke, of all people, who introduced himself as Stafford, shook her hand like she was his equal, and promised they'd celebrate her safe return with a right and proper dinner party at his country estate, where his wife and children had gone to escape the pandemic.

Camden and Stafford had landed a safe distance from the front, at which point they'd begun the more arduous part of the journey. Equipped with falsified passports and papers that Barclay Pearce had provided—though she certainly couldn't tell by the look of them—they'd made their way slowly to Paris. Shell-shocked, battle-weary Paris. Not the city Celeste had told her of, in so many ways. There was no going to the Louvre or shopping in the boutiques along the Champs-Élysées. There were only soldiers and exhausted civilians and the machines of war everywhere one looked.

She and Rem weren't the first of their number to venture into the unknown world of the front lines, as odd as that was to realize. Margot De Wilde Elton had been trapped in Belgium at the start of the war—but unlike Celeste, she'd gotten out, thanks to the bravery of her brother, the woman who was now his wife, and Barclay Pearce. Barclay, who had traveled again into occupied territory to rescue the man now his father-in-law, a clockmaker who'd been kidnapped because of his mechanical prowess.

Louisa had enjoyed an entire evening in the clockmaker's workshop, admiring the exquisite toys he'd made . . . and mourning that his genius had been put to use for weapons too. But the interrupter he'd designed had helped pilots like Camden and Stafford survive. She couldn't dismiss that.

The best moment of that week, however, may have been when Lily Blackwell arrived with her camera. She took a formal photograph of their family, yes—but it was the others that Louisa loved best. The way she'd captured the twins' joy as they chased falling leaves through Culbreth House's garden. The moment of laughter she'd caught between Grann and Lord Culbreth, who had struck up an unlikely camaraderie. The one she'd snapped of Louisa and Rem looking deep into each other's eyes, marveling. Marveling at the goodness of God to bring them together again. Marveling at all He'd put into place to help them get here, to Celeste. Marveling at the family He'd given them.

She had one of those photos in her bag even now, to hold close. To remind her of why she was away from them, out here in the way of danger. For family. The kind chosen. The kind fought for.

"You really think she's out there? That she'll be killed if

we don't intervene?" Garret, his brows carrying a permanent frown these days, looked out at the mangled forest. She saw the war raging in his eyes—the need to help battling against whatever wounds he still harbored against Celeste from her leaving. The logic that said there was no way they'd really find her clashing against the ream of telegrams and information the Room 40 team had pulled together. Admiral Hall had even had Lily go through her photo archives, looking for any evidence gathered over the years by his undercover agents.

Louisa had *that* photo in her bag, too, the copy of the single snapshot that had made both hope and fear burn in her chest. A photo snapped through a restaurant's wide front window, meant to capture the brass who were dictating so much of the Western Offensive from their command at Charleville. And capture them he had—along with the French mistresses they were dining with.

That was where she'd seen that familiar face. The glossy fair hair. The haunted eyes, masked over with laughter, that she'd seen all throughout her childhood.

Celeste, on the arm of a German officer.

Celeste . . . her stomach round with child.

That must be why she felt herself in such danger now, during a retreat that should have meant freedom. That man who'd claimed her must not want to leave his child behind—but Louisa knew Celeste. There was no way she'd abandon her own little one. She would try to take her child and run rather than be taken back to Germany.

And what would that officer, Mansfeld, do if she tried it?

Louisa nodded in answer to Garret's question. "She needs us, Gar. She and her baby." Her baby wouldn't be a true baby anymore. Given the date on that photograph, he or she would be nearly the twins' age, maybe a few months younger.

Poor Celeste. So many years to have haunted eyes. So many years to live once again with a man who held her life and the life most precious to her in his hands.

Garret's lips made a grim line. "All right. Then I'll go with you and pray I'm only needed as a friend, not as a doctor. But Lulu—it's been ugly. Every town we've liberated . . . the occupation wasn't kind to them."

Hence the Red Cross tents filled with civilians, not just soldiers. Emaciated skeletons covered with skin, barely clinging to life. She nodded. "Our intelligence says the push to Charleville will happen in the afternoon tomorrow. The Germans will know it's coming and be on the retreat. We have to go in at first light."

It would give them the rest of the afternoon today and however much of the night they could use to find Pierre's château, where Celeste was still living, so far as they'd been able to decipher from her cryptic messages. To scout out the surroundings, plan an escape route.

Garret sent his anxious look from her to Rem. "You're really letting her do this?"

A discussion they'd already had no fewer than a dozen times. And though he'd been on the "stay in London" side of that discussion each of those times, he now presented Louisa's own argument. "Louisa speaks the language, which will help us in the town. And Celeste will trust her—she wouldn't necessarily trust anyone else."

At that, Garret's jaw clenched, ticked. He folded his arms over his chest. "She would trust *me*, wouldn't she?"

"I don't know—would she?" Louisa held out her hands, knowing that old exasperation colored her voice. "As far as I know, the two of you parted on a sour note and haven't exchanged a direct word since!"

"It wasn't—" He broke off, spun away, then pivoted back.

"I asked her to stay, all right? To stay with Elsie. I kissed her and told her I loved her and asked her to stay. And you can see her answer."

Her heart broke a little more for her two best friends. They'd only been fourteen. Too young for such declarations, some would say. Too young to make such decisions. But old enough to carry that hurt around for another decade. "Gar, she couldn't leave her mother. They'd been everything to each other for so long."

"You think I don't know that? That I haven't regretted a thousand times putting her on the spot, making it seem like she had to choose?" He shook his head and looked back out to the smoky tree line. "I was a kid. A stupid kid who wanted not to have to say good-bye."

"Maybe that's why her every letter to me said to say 'hello' to you. Ever think about that?"

His shoulders heaved. "She would know me. Trust me. I can do this. You don't have to."

But she *did*. She felt it in her bones, even if she couldn't put words to it. "Together, Gar. You, me, Rem, and Georgie."

Another gift from Barclay Pearce, that last member of their team—his little brother, who'd been serving in France all throughout the war, who knew the forests and the trenches and every path through every town. Who had, apparently, scouted behind enemy lines enough to earn him such a high reputation with his superiors that when Rem had presented their papers to those in command, with *George Pearce as guide* written there, they'd given nods of approval. "If anyone can get you in, it's Pearce," they'd said.

She had to give Georgie Pearce credit—he hadn't even blinked at them out of turn when they were brought to him and introduced. He'd simply shaken each of their hands, nodded, and, when they said they came on Barclay's recommendation, sat down and had them regale him with stories from home. He'd never questioned their purpose or ability.

As they pulled themselves away from the smoky desolation, they found Georgie a few minutes later, checking his wristwatch against the pocket watch of his commander, jotting a few notes in a slender lined book, and looking up to greet them with a smile as boyish as his eyes were old. "Ready?"

Were they? The innkeeper's daughter, the codebreaker, and the doctor, ready to sneak into enemy territory on a rescue mission? Of course they weren't. What did any of them know of clandestine work, aside from the part done at a desk? But they'd be no more ready at any other time. So Louisa nodded, Rem and Garret with her.

He handed a bundle of worn clothing to each of them. "You'll want to put those on. Those clothes of yours will stand out like a sore thumb where we're going. And, Doctor—I don't suppose you can shrink a few inches?"

Garret grinned. "I can slouch."

Slouching wouldn't even begin to make him blend in, but his brawn could be useful. If nothing else, he could play pack mule for the things Celeste needed to bring with her for her and her child.

Please, God, let that be all he has to carry out.

They all changed into the drab, threadbare clothing Georgie provided. And followed him into the remains of the forest, with its eerie quiet, its sting of chemical smells where there should be that of nature, its weird shadows. They walked for what could have been either hours or days, the landscape offering little by way of markers. But their guide never seemed to falter on his path, and eventually they found an *actual* path. And in the distance, a road—of which they steered clear, given the German transport trucks and wagons hurrying along it.

Georgie motioned them behind a grove of trees, still sturdy and tall, and then gestured toward the outline of roofs in the distance. "That's Charleville," he said in a whisper. "You say she's at the Château Challant?"

Louisa nodded. "You know of it?"

Georgie didn't produce his boyish grin now. Just those old, old eyes boring into hers. "Hard to miss. It's right outside town, on the side opposite this one. I daresay it was the first building to be commandeered by the Huns when they invaded. But it being on the outskirts should help us, at least."

Circumnavigating the town without being spotted by the troops clearly in a panic, however, proved a slow and painstaking task. It involved a lot of waiting under cover for the coast to be clear, then dashing to the next stand of trees or abandoned cottage that Georgie had already scouted out for them, then waiting again.

Twilight was falling by the time Georgie led them up that final rise, through the trees, where the music of water laughing along in its banks not only serenaded them but covered the sound of their approach.

She looked across the river, into Belgium. The land that Margot De Wilde and her brother, Lukas, had been born and raised in. The land they'd fled when Germans marched into it in the first days of the war and began systematically dismantling the country's infrastructure. The land into which the Germans would be retreating soon.

Louisa stood there, staring at that river, and saying a prayer that Celeste's feet would not touch Belgian ground. Not today, not tomorrow. Not by force.

"Lu." Rem's voice was barely a breath, a murmur. When

she looked his way, he nodded past the tree line, toward a garden still so carefully tended, despite the destruction of the land they'd crept through. Sleeping but alive.

But it wasn't the plants and fruit trees that had stolen her husband's attention. It was the woman and child in that garden. The woman, tall and blond and both familiar and a stranger. *Celeste.* Clearly, obviously Celeste.

But seven years older. Seven interminable years in which she'd changed and shifted and learned lessons Louisa hadn't. She walked differently. Held herself differently. Even there in a late-autumn garden, she had that same polish that Louisa had so quickly come to hate—resent? fear?—in Edith Culbreth.

"She left us. She's never coming back." How many times had Garret said that, or some variation of it, over the years? Maybe he was right. Maybe the woman she'd become— Celeste Challant—wasn't even the Celeste Scarborough she'd spent her childhood whispering and laughing with. Maybe this sophisticated Frenchwoman wouldn't even *want* to come with Louisa.

Then a familiar sound reached her ears—a little-boy squeal and giggle. And a towheaded tot came running up to that sophisticated Frenchwoman, arms held up, waving something for her to see. A leaf? A dried flower?

And Celeste laughed and scooped the boy up into her arms and twirled him around.

That laughter—it wasn't polished and sophisticated. It was the same laugh Louisa had always known. Too loud, too bold, because it had to be. A laugh determined to drown out the sorrow. The laugh of an island girl in the face of a hurricane.

Louisa slipped her bag off her shoulder, handed it to Rem, and then turned to Georgie with a nod.

His answer was to rearrange the kerchief covering her hair,

hiding its gloss. To press on her shoulders until she stooped enough, and to rub something onto her cheeks to cover the health of her skin and add shadows to create a hollow look. It wouldn't hold up upon close inspection, but from a distance it should suffice. *Please, God.*

Another round of silent nods, and she set off toward the garden at a slow, shambling gait, like that of the villagers she'd seen and studied as they'd skirted Charleville. The clothes Georgie had given her, threadbare as they were, were also several sizes too big, to give her the look of someone who had shrunk *to* her current size from something bigger. Anything else would look suspicious.

In her arms she carried a few scraps of branches that they'd gathered from the riverbank as they walked—supposed fuel for a paltry fire. A reason to be out this far, though, away from the town. A reason to stumble her way along the château's low garden wall.

She was close enough now to hear Celeste talking to the child in her arms in French. Grann had taught it to them both all those years ago, but her accent was different now. Less Creole, more Parisian, if she were to guess.

She called the boy Stavi, and he looked up at her with adoration. Louisa couldn't help but smile. And had no trouble calling her own French words to her lips, as planned. "A handsome child you have."

Would she know her voice, after all these years? It was hard to tell from her reaction. She froze, yes, but Louisa could imagine her doing the same upon hearing *any* friendly voice where she'd come to expect none.

But she didn't stay frozen for long. She turned. And even through the dirt, through the borrowed, too-big clothes, through the kerchief, through the years, recognition lit her eyes like a flame on a winter's night. Her arms held her little boy even tighter, and her eyes darted toward the house. "He is, *oui*," she replied, tone casual. "He takes after his father."

Something about the way she said it, the way she glanced away, made Louisa look toward the house too. Where a window stood open, despite the chill of the air. Where, if she wasn't mistaken, a silhouette moved beyond the curtain.

With slow movements disguised as much as possible by the sticks in her arms, she signed, *M-A-N-S-F-E-L-D listening?*

Celeste knocked a *yes*, hidden from the window by her son.

Aloud, Louisa said, "His father must be very handsome, too, then. You are a lucky woman." It hurt her to say the words, but it was all part of the careful script she'd created. An echo of Jack Scarborough. *"You're lucky,"* he'd always told Maddie. *"Lucky to have me."* A claim that Celeste had echoed in fury in the safety of Louisa's room.

Celeste's larynx bobbed with her swallow, but her voice still sounded normal when she said, "Oui. The luckiest."

Friends here, Louisa signed, and pointed subtly back toward the woods.

The silhouette at the window solidified, pushed aside the curtain that had been veiling him. "You there. Woman. Move on!"

Louisa edged back a step. *"Bien. Au revoir."* All but saying, *I don't want any trouble, mister.* But with her hands, she asked, *Tonight?*

Celeste turned partially away, smiling at her boy. "Come, Stavi, we had better go back inside. We have a busy night planned with Papa."

Her answer, she supposed. Louisa signed, *Morning? Sunrise?*

Celeste nodded toward her son and said, "That's right, mon petit." Even though he'd not said anything.

Louisa didn't dare linger any longer. She trudged away,

heading not for the place where Rem and Georgie and Garret were waiting, but downriver. She'd double back after she was certain Mansfeld wasn't watching, once under the cover of the trees.

Tomorrow. At dawn.

It meant the night dragged by. They didn't dare light a fire, though they could see the flames of many of them dancing through the windows of the château from the many hearths that matched the many chimneys, all belching smoke. To look at the gaily lit house, one would never know that it was filled with officers burning anything they couldn't take—one would simply think it a party. But the scent in the air was not the wholesome smell of woodsmoke, but the kind that carried the bite of ink and who knew what else. Silhouette after silhouette passed before those windows, and now and then a raised voice shouted something crisp and sharp in German.

Only once did Louisa spot Celeste, looking out from a second-story room, gazing toward the trees. Hopeful? Or too anxious for hope? And then—she could scarcely make it out through the night and the distance, but were those signs she was making? Yes.

Baby. Must save.

Louisa wished there was a way to assure her, but any sign she could give her friend would be too easily intercepted by another. So she simply prayed that God would be her assurance, give her peace. Whisper the promise that Louisa wanted to shout. *We'll save him. We'll save him* and *you.*

At long last, the house stilled, engines roaring away from the front, but not until the sky had begun to lighten. Louisa hadn't slept, nor had Rem beside her. But the two more used to the front lines had both nodded off at some point, and they both stirred again as star-pierced black turned gray and then blushed.

She used that first soft light to look over at the face so near her own. Squeezed the fingers that had scarcely left hers all night. Just a few weeks, now, that she'd been greeting him along with each morning. Just a few weeks that his smile had been the first thing she saw in each new day.

It wasn't long enough. Not nearly long enough. She needed months, years, decades, centuries—or at the very least, however much of those God granted them. Together, though. Only, always together. Never apart again, they'd sworn that first night as they cried together over years and milestones lost, as they kissed away the thought of all those lonely days and nights, as they loved away the emptiness.

She lifted his hand now, pressed her lips to his knuckles. Signed, because they didn't dare to speak in the early morning when sound traveled so easily. *I love you.*

He leaned over, pressed his lips to her forehead, her nose, her lips. *I love you.* Silently, they pulled each other to their feet. And then he signed, *Let's go save your friend.*

The four of them crept to the edge of the trees, crouched, waited. Waited. Waited.

A sliver appeared between a back door and its frame, widened, filled with a blessedly familiar figure. Stavi must still be asleep in her arms, because the blanket-wrapped bundle was limp, not offering any help as she struggled to ease the door shut behind her. She had no other bag—probably hadn't dared.

Celeste stepped away from the door, into the garden, her head swiveling as she searched for them.

Louisa stood, knowing that the small movement would be enough to get her attention, and indeed it was. Celeste took one step, two.

Perhaps it was the cold air hitting his face. Perhaps it was the jostling. Perhaps it was a bad dream. Whatever the cause,

Louisa watched the bundle move and then—far worse—heard that familiar just-waking cry of a child who didn't know that Mama was right there.

The cry that split the peace of the morning. The cry that spurred them all into motion.

She wasn't the only one running. She saw Rem and Garret and Georgie all charging in, too, saw Celeste running toward them. She saw another door yank open, saw the figure come out.

She didn't mean to outpace her companions—hadn't known she could. But they were beside her, and then they were behind her, and she was flying over that stretch before the garden wall like it was a stretch of sandy beach. Like she was Jingle, wild and free and unbridled.

The wall didn't slow her down. She vaulted over it as she'd leapt her own garden gate a thousand times.

The air shattered, holes torn in it from behind, from before. *Bullets.* She'd heard her share of them, but somehow the sound of a hunting rifle had never struck the fear into her heart that these pistols did. She ran all the harder, meeting Celeste a few lunges from the wall.

Celeste, who cried out, pain flashing in her eyes and red blooming on the gray of her jacket. Celeste, who shoved the still-crying child into her arms. "Take him!"

Louisa's arms encircled the boy. In that half-second, she had time for a thousand thoughts. How she would pivot, run, leap again. How Garret, surely only a step behind, would scoop up Celeste and carry her. How Georgie, his gun firing and firing and firing, would surely bring down Mansfeld. How they'd have to disappear before other soldiers could swarm.

A thousand thoughts in a half-second. And then pain ripped through her, stole her breath, made her knees crumple.

No. No, she had to get Stavi to safety. She had to turn. Had to run. Had to leap.

Instead she toppled, gasping for breath enough to scream against it when someone tore the child from her arms. *Garret. Georgie. Rem. Let it be any of them, Lord.*

But theirs wasn't the face that loomed over her, that spat on her. Theirs wasn't the boot that delivered a kick to her ribs, right where the pain had latched hold.

Mansfeld. He vanished in the next second, as more bullets came from her friends.

She reached. She tried to stand. She cried out in every language and no language. She rolled, she lunged.

They were gone. *Gone.*

"Lulu."

Celeste's voice was weak, just a rasp. Louisa managed to turn her head and saw the sister of her heart lying on her back, hand outstretched on the ground between them. Louisa reached until their fingertips touched, until the pain screamed from her lips, until her vision blurred. "I'm sorry, Lest. I'm so sorry." She'd failed her. In the moment she needed her most, she'd failed.

Celeste's eyes flickered, searched. Registered the emptiness where there should have been squirming, crying life. Her eyes slid shut. But her fingers moved a bit more, closed around Louisa's, and squeezed. "You came."

Louisa heard the cries of Rem, of Garret. Felt the pound of their footsteps. But all she could see was the expression on Celeste's face. Complete heartbreak.

Complete forgiveness.

Louisa's eyes slid shut. "Of course I came. You needed me."

Arms lifted her, and Celeste's hand raised with her too. And then the darkness closed in.

26

TODAY

JULY 8, 1942
OCRACOKE ISLAND, NORTH CAROLINA

The last light of sunset turned the water of the sound to gold, the clouds to rose, and the day to night, promising Evie Farrow that she would remember this day always—not as the day Job died, not as the day that signaled that eternal march from yesterday into tomorrow, but as the day she looked her own future in the eyes and said, *yes, I'm ready*. As the day she lay in wait for her family's past to come sneaking into her house and make itself known.

She'd lived a lot of years on this tiny little island, a dot in the Atlantic. Home to pirates, home to ships' captains, home to innkeepers and fishermen and Coasties. Home to generations of stubborn people determined to stand, though the sands may shift. To thrive, though the waters may rise. To go on living, though the storms may rage.

Never, in all those years, had she expected to be sneaking up to her own house like an adolescent breaking curfew—before the sun even set. They'd staged the inn with lights ablaze and radio blaring a concert from Glenn Miller, with friends and family gathered to share the feast Job's friends had brought. With Grandma Elsie playing hostess while she and Sterling slipped out, saying they were going to check on Celeste, who'd been feeling under the weather.

They'd gotten a few winks and sly smiles at that—their linked hands not going unnoticed—but no one begrudged them the escape.

An escape that quickly turned to a hurried run through the village. They had to assume that Mansfeld was keeping tabs on them, to know how and when to best avoid them. They also had to assume he never entered the village proper, not during daylight hours.

If he checked on the inn tonight, he would see what looked like a party—and he would assume they were both inside. Meanwhile, they were speeding through the streets he'd never dare to tread, toward the house that he would creep to when darkness provided him cover enough.

They'd already be inside. Evie led the way in even now, as the last rays of sunset burnished the sky, and locked the door behind them. All the windows were already covered with blinds and curtains, to keep the sunlight from fading the items she'd left inside, which meant near-darkness inside, and they didn't dare to turn on any electric lights. Flashlights would have to suffice as they took up the places they'd already discussed.

Evie in the hallway, her hand on the light switch, ready to throw it and illuminate the whole scene the moment Mansfeld came in. She had her pistol in her other hand and knew very well she could look the part of unflinching homeowner.

Sterling, meanwhile, took up position out of swinging range of the kitchen door, in a dark corner where cabinets met wall. A pistol in his hands too.

Lord, may we not have to use them. Please, God, make a way of peace. She didn't know what that way would look like, didn't know what to expect when she looked into Gustav Mansfeld's eyes. Would she see Aunt L there? Or only hatred?

At Sterling's nod, she switched off her flashlight and leaned against the wall, her wall, and replayed all he'd told her that afternoon of their target.

Raised outside Berlin by a stern father and equally stern grandmother. At thirteen, he'd been enrolled in the *Deutsches Jungvolk in der Hitler Jugend*—the German Youngsters of the Hitler Youth. And then the Hitler Youth itself at fourteen. Tall and strong, he'd beaten all his competitors on the field and trounced them in academic circles as well. He'd demonstrated whatever qualities were required to be selected for the SS—Evie didn't really know what those were. Cruelty? Leadership? The ability to get things done? All she knew was that they were Hitler's elite, and Gustav was seemingly the elite of the elite.

Even Sterling hadn't discovered the extent of his training, but it must have been both intense and thorough for him to have been sent out into the world alone as an intelligence operative. On what appeared to be a dual mission—the one that the German command would have given him officially, to coordinate attacks with U-boats. And then this second one, to find his mother. It had to be at the behest of his father, a mission of revenge. Either that, or he thought she was still in possession of something important to him, though they knew not what that could be.

Either way, here. Now. And dangerous.

Either way, his capture would be a coup for the Allies.

Either way, something could go wrong, and it could mean her death or Sterling's or Mansfeld's. It could mean, if he took one or both of them out, a killer on the loose in Ocracoke. Not only a spy but an assassin, then, who would take out anyone in his path as he sought to flee.

It could mean the end of everything. Everything. No more yesterdays remembered. No more todays walked through with determination. No more tomorrows to forge into something new.

If Mama were here instead of trapped in England by U-boats and fighter planes, Evie would ask her if this was what it had felt like that quiet morning in France, when she hid in the forest outside Charleville and waited for the chance to save her best friend. She'd ask if she'd traced the outline of Daddy in the dark and willed all her love into him, willed him to know, if something went wrong, that he was hers forever.

She hadn't spoken those words to Sterling. Not yet. *Tomorrow*, yes, but forever? Two months shouldn't be long enough to know you wanted that with someone. But she did. She knew it. She wanted it. And she prayed to God that they would both live to see this next tomorrow, and the one after, and the one after that, until they melded into that eternity.

There would be separation—how could there not be? He was an intelligence agent, theirs was a world at war. But they could part ways together. Belonging to each other, like so many couples had to do in war. It made a difference, the knowing that there was someone waiting on the other side of today's dangers. It had to.

Though she could scarcely make out Sterling's outline in the darkness, she could feel his gaze reaching through the dark, searching for her as she did for him. She sensed more than saw his hands move, his arms. Could barely see, in the faintest light that sneaked around the drawn curtains, his hand move to his chest, his arms cross that chest, his finger point to her.

She could barely see it, but she knew what he said. The very first sign she remembered learning, the one that Grandma See had greeted them with every morning and sent them to bed with every night.

I love you.

Before she could lift her own arms in reply, there came a creak from outside. The sound of a foot placed carefully on a board too long exposed to wind and sun and rain to be silent. Another creak. And then the scrape of metal against metal, the jiggle of a handle. Her door, swinging open.

She straightened, coiled. One hand on the switch, one wrapped around her derringer. The close of the door. Two footsteps into her kitchen.

She flipped the light, swung into the kitchen doorway, and leveled her pistol, even as Sterling put himself in front of the door, his own gun raised too.

The man between them didn't jump. Didn't curse. Didn't look even a little bit surprised. Hands in the air, he merely slid toward the stove so that he could swivel his head from one of them to the other. And said, in a perfect BBC accent, "Mr. Bertrand. Mrs. Farrow. Good evening."

He looked like René—that was the only comprehensible thought to settle in her mind. An inch or two shorter, but the same sleek, muscular build. The same shiny, golden hair. The same hazel eyes. The same chiseled chin. He looked like the child she'd helped tend and played with, whom she'd watched grow into a man, being just a few years older than he was.

But this man was a stranger. She had to remember that, even if he *did* know her name.

Sterling didn't so much as flinch at the greeting. "Mansfeld. I can't say as this is where I expected to finally meet you face-to-face."

His smile was like Celeste's, bold and brash, like light laughing at the shadows. "You put me in quite a tight spot in London. I thought I was done for, there for a minute. But if I may be so bold—I'm glad you failed that time. Glad I made it here. I daresay you don't regret coming here either, eh, old boy?"

Sterling narrowed his eyes. "God was certainly at work there—but don't think for a moment I'll thank *you* for it."

"Of course not." He turned now to Evie. Hands still up, but there was no surrender in his posture. "But *I* will. Thank you. You have my eternal gratitude."

"*Me*?" She didn't falter—but she did flinch a bit. "For what?"

The smile softened, turned less bold but no less bright. "For taking care of my mother, and of her grandmother. For making my family your own, when I couldn't. For filling her arms until my brother and sister came along."

She didn't mean to lower her gun, and didn't by more than an inch before she caught herself. Still, she knew it was enough of an opening that he could have acted. Could have leapt at her, overpowered her, and what could Sterling have done in that moment? He couldn't fire his gun without the risk of hitting her.

But Mansfeld didn't move.

Sterling saw her falter, too, saw his stillness. He eased half a step closer, no wavering in *his* arms. "Why have you hunted her here? After all this time?"

"Hunted?" Mansfeld breathed a laugh, shook his head. "I suppose it looks that way. And if *track* and *hunt* are interchangeable, then perhaps so. But I assure you that *track* is all I did—and now, because it was the first I could. The first I had the freedom to do so. To find her—my *maman*."

Her gun lowered another inch. Because she saw nothing but sincerity in his eyes. Saw nothing but yearning in his posture. Maybe she was a fool for believing him—Sterling clearly didn't—but when he said *maman*, he sounded . . . he sounded like a lost little boy, desperate for his mother.

"You weren't even four when they took you from her," she said. "You wouldn't remember her."

His eyes slid shut, and his own arms sagged a bit, though he still kept his hands up. "Details, no. But impressions, yes. I remember loving her above all else. I remember the songs she sang to me. I remember knowing that when Father was angry, she was my safe haven. When Father was cold, she was my warmth. I remember missing her and crying for her every day for so long."

For every degree he softened, Sterling had hardened, his jaw now ticking with how tightly he clenched his jaw. He had, after all, chased this agent halfway around the world. She couldn't blame him for doubting his story. "You really expect me to believe that? That you're only here for—for a *reunion*? While German U-boats are patrolling these waters, while your father is leading men across Europe, while—"

"My *father*"—he spat the word—"may be willing to be Hitler's puppet in order to keep his position, his power. But we are not all so blind."

"It was all a show, I suppose. A sham. Hitler Youth, SS—"

"I knew you wouldn't believe me, Mr. Bertram. It's why I've come prepared." He nodded toward the cabinets. "In the silverware drawer, you'll find all the data I was able to gather before I left Germany. Some of it is no doubt out of date, but enough should still be accurate to be useful. I am prepared to turn that and myself over to the Allies."

Now Sterling's eyes narrowed too. "You're defecting?" His incredulous snort was omitted but definitely implied.

And that word finally lit a spark in Mansfeld's eyes and brought his shoulders back up. "I'm an American citizen by birth—it is not *defecting*. It is coming home, to the place my mother always meant me to be. Look, old boy, you can turn me in to the higher-ups. Let them put me on the rack, as it were. All I ask is for a chance to meet my mother first."

"No." Sterling delivered the answer coolly, calmly, quickly. "You'll be interrogated and debriefed—*then* a meeting, if those higher-ups decide you're on the up-and-up."

For the first time since he stepped into her kitchen, Gustav Mansfeld didn't seem to know what to do. His hands fell, then sprang back up. He took a step toward Sterling, quickly retreated again.

"Sterling." Evie lowered her pistol, though she kept her stance tense, at the ready.

He glanced at her for only a second, long enough to see she'd relaxed and countered that with a menacing step forward. "Just because he has a good story doesn't mean it's true, Evie."

She didn't want to argue with him, not in front of Mansfeld—Gustav. He wouldn't easily forgive it. So, she signed instead *You want not, but truth*.

He understood her—that much was clear by the renewed ticking of the muscle in his jaw. But he didn't have the chance to respond. The door behind him opened, forcing him to step out of the way.

Another moment when Gustav could have acted, could have pounced. But didn't. Another moment he stood with his hands in the air when, if he meant to do harm, he could have.

She expected Herb or Cal, one of the neighbors. She expected to have to come up with a good reason for why a stranger who looked like René was in her kitchen, and why she and Sterling had weapons pulled on him.

But it wasn't Herb or Cal. It was Grandma Elsie. And she entered with those all-seeing eyes of hers, looking no more surprised by the scene than Gustav had, though they hadn't told her anything about finding where he'd been hiding and certainly not about linking the man Sterling had been hunting to Celeste.

She took it all in with a glance, closed the door behind her, and slid over . . . to Gustav. Raised her hands, clasped his, and lowered them. Then put herself between him and Sterling.

She didn't need to lift her hands to make any sign. Her stance said it all. *He's mine.*

27

YESTERDAY

NOVEMBER 17, 1918
SPRINGBOURNE HALL, HEREFORDSHIRE, ENGLAND

There were peacocks—peacocks strutting around the grounds, dragging their magnificent tails behind them as if mocking the poor humans who had to create such splendor with silk and satin. And behind them strutted two little angels, with colorful robes unearthed from some long-lost trunk tucked into their belts, trying to imitate the birds. Louisa watched them from her perch on the balcony, shifted on her chair, and debated for a long moment between the pain in her side and the foggy-headedness that the medicine would force on her if she took it.

Pain or fog? Fog or pain? Too many of the last days had been spent under the veil of the medication. But today . . . today she could manage. For now, anyway. She would push the pain aside and watch her babies torment the peacocks, smile at the two men shadowing them to make sure the birds stuck with ignoring them and didn't turn rude, and marvel. Marvel at all God had given her.

She picked up the steaming mug of tea that the house-keeper herself had delivered a few minutes ago, took a sip, and smiled. "How offended do you think the entire country of England would be if I admitted that I prefer yaupon?"

On the chaise beside hers, Celeste snorted. "They may toss you out for good." Of their two nearly matching bullet wounds, Celeste's had actually been the less severe and was healing faster.

But she wasn't *healing*. Not in the way that mattered. Not yet. Though she could say all the right words, there was never a light in her eyes.

Louisa could understand that. But still it hurt worse than the bullet-cracked ribs to see her best friend, her sister, so. She sighed into her cup and slid it back onto its table. So many of the last days had been a blur. Waking up in Garret's hospital tent, then traveling with them back to Paris, where the city was celebrating the end of the war. The end, they said, of all wars.

As if people would ever stop hurting one another. Ever stop stealing what belonged to another. Ever stop separating mothers from their children, sons from their fathers. As if those wounds, once inflicted, would ever cease to fester. As if the festering wouldn't lead to someone seeking revenge.

No. *This* war might be over, but there would be more. She was sure of that. As sure as that there'd always be another hurricane. Forces of nature, both of them.

Even so—just because one person couldn't stop a hurricane didn't mean that you didn't board up your windows. It didn't mean that you didn't seek higher ground. It didn't mean that you let it come, wash over you, and sweep you out to sea without a fight.

They had to fight. Had to fight against those tides, fight to keep their feet on shore. "Celeste."

Her friend looked up, over. Eyes focused, but . . . blank.

She'd said it before, that day. But she had to say it again. And likely again and again and again. "I'm sorry. So sorry. I should have held him tighter. I should have run. I should have—"

"Lulu, stop." She got up, and for a second Louisa thought she'd leave, go back inside, into her room, shut her door. Instead, she moved over to Louisa's chaise and nudged her over, nestled into the space beside her, even pulled Louisa's blanket over her own legs.

Like they were girls again, huddled under the quilt in her room. Whispering long after the lights were out.

She wished they could go back there. No . . . she wished they could go forward. Into something better, something without the shadows of either Jack or Max. She wished . . . she wished for sunshine and summer heat and a respite from the storms. Just for a while.

Celeste leaned her head against Louisa's. "It isn't your fault, Lulu. Don't think for a moment that I blame you. You crossed an ocean for me. Braved a war. Risked your life. I couldn't ask for a better sister."

Louisa reached for Celeste's hand—pampered, elegant, uncallused, so fair—and held it in one of her own chapped, scraped, work-hardened, dusky ones. Such different lives they'd led for the last seven years. But she was right. They were sisters. She gave those fingers a squeeze. "Still. I failed you in the thing that mattered most."

"I never expected you to be bulletproof, Lulu. You did all you could. More than anyone else would have."

390

So why did she still feel so guilty every time she saw that look in her eyes, more haunted than ever? "But it isn't fair. Your arms are empty, and here I am—two kids, and Rem, and all this . . . I don't deserve it. Not while you're hurting so much."

Celeste angled a grin over at her, and it had a hint of the old Celeste. "You offering me one of your kids?"

She couldn't help but laugh at that. "Not for keeps. But you're certainly welcome to borrow one."

It was Celeste's turn to give her fingers a squeeze. "I will. And, Lulu, you *do* deserve it. That husband who adores you, those precious little ones, all this . . . I can't think of anyone who deserves it more. No matter what that horrific mother-in-law of yours says."

Even that could make her smile, now. Edith had already been back in Maryland by the time they made it to Spring-bourne Hall, and apparently she'd been none too pleased to arrive home to word from her legal counsel informing her that Rem and Louisa's marriage had been declared legitimate by the courts of England. That had probably taken some doing on Lord Culbreth's part, but Louisa wasn't going to argue. But her return telegram had simply ordered them to see that David Michael was prepared to step into his role with the Remingtons as well as the Culbreths.

Ice. Disdain. No love. But a promise, at least, that she wasn't going to try to take him from them—how could she, now that they were with Rem? That was all Louisa needed, the peace she'd taken such joy in being able to send home to Mama, along with the news that they'd found Celeste.

Even so, she couldn't imagine her little boy's future. The future they knew, now, was his.

Her gaze drifted outward again, and down. To where Rem and his father stood talking while they kept an eye on the twins. Talking, no doubt, about the soldier who'd shown up at their door last night, cap in his hands and sorrow in his eyes. He'd served under Sebastian. He'd seen him lead a charge. He'd seen him fall, seen the mud pull him down. He'd tried to reach him.

That was the story so many of them would tell. *They'd tried.* Tried to stem the horrors. Tried to stop the tides.

At least they knew. The wondering was over. However chaotic his final moments, Sebastian was at peace now. And his men, that soldier said, held him in the highest esteem. He'd been a true leader. A hero. He'd found that glory he'd wanted.

And at least Celeste knew that Max, whatever his faults, loved Gustav. Her friend had been certain of that, had said it was why he hadn't been willing to part with him. Why he'd tried to force Celeste to come with them. He wanted his son, and he wanted his son to have his mother.

Louisa had been dubious. But Celeste had insisted. Maybe it was the last shred of hope she had. If so, then Louisa would cling to it with her.

If only that was enough to soothe Celeste's aching soul. Louisa covered their joined hands with her free one. "You'll see him again, Celeste. I know you will."

Her sister shook her head, kept her gaze on the peacocks as a tear tracked down her cheek. "I can't—I can't let myself hope that. I can't even think it. He's gone, Lulu. He's just—*gone.*"

Too many were gone, thanks to this war. Gone forever, into eternity. But Celeste's son wasn't. He was alive. In Germany, but alive. That meant there *was* hope. Hope that a mother's love would pull a son back to her. Hope that the world would learn from its mistakes and build friendships where enmity had reigned. There was hope that someday this stitched-together family they'd claimed for themselves would be whole.

She didn't know what it would take, but she couldn't stop believing it. She wouldn't.

But she pressed her lips against the insistence. She'd given her prophecy, praying it was just that. But if hope would hurt Celeste now more than help her . . . so be it. She'd hold her tongue. Never breathe another word of sweet little Stavi. But she'd pray. Every day she would pray.

Yesterday, today, tomorrow. Forever.

28

TODAY

*D*arkness. Everywhere there was darkness—above him, below him, around him, within him, eating him from the inside out.

Sterling Bertrand stood in the middle of an electric-lit kitchen, but even then it seemed he couldn't escape the shadows of night. Darkness still roared, in his ears and around the edges of his vision.

So many years of his life spent hunting this man. Learning everything he could about him, convinced, as were all his superiors, that he was not just *a* threat—he was a threat worth dedicating everything to stopping.

He couldn't have been wrong. He couldn't have been.

He couldn't have been, because that's what brought him here. That's what made him go to Tommie and ask for a tow.

That's what put the *Bedfordshire* on that particular path on that particular morning, into the sights of a U-boat. That's what brought a torpedo cutting through the water, sending that ship and his friend and all those crewmembers to their deaths.

This man, this mission, this hunt had already claimed so much. It couldn't have been for nothing, couldn't have been a mistake. It *couldn't*.

But here he stood, aiming his weapon not at Gustav Mansfeld but at Elsie Neal, who'd planted herself squarely between them and was looking him dead in the eye. Saying without a word, without a gesture, that if he meant to shoot her great-grandson, he'd have to shoot her first.

For one blinding, fire-seared, darkness-covered moment, he considered it—the thing he'd never really considered at all. He considered pulling the trigger and sending that smug SS officer into eternity in Tommie's wake, where God could sort it all out, no matter who was in his way.

No. No. He shook that thought away, dragging in a breath that shouldn't have been so hard in coming. What was wrong with him? Was he really so determined to be right that he'd consider hurting a woman he'd come to love, the matriarch of a family he wanted to join?

He blinked the darkness away in time to see Elsie lift a hand. She twisted her first two fingers to form an *S*, point it at her ear, and move it away—a variation of *silver*, the sign she'd given him for his name.

That was all she said. Just his name.

All she needed to say. Sterling tore his gaze from Elsie and turned it to Evie.

Her derringer was hanging limply at her side now, her eyes watery as she watched from her stance in the doorway. And those words she'd signed still echoed in his mind. *You want not, but truth.* The signs were bare, but he knew the meaning she was getting at—that he didn't want to believe it, and so he was choosing not to. But that didn't change facts.

But he'd never denied the possibility of something, much less the fact of it, just because he didn't *want* it to be so. With his father, with Tommie, even with Evie when he'd thought her an enemy, he'd faced up to it. That one *hadn't* been true, but he'd accepted the possibility, hadn't he?

What made this one different?

He let his breath slowly back out and eased his finger away from the trigger. Pride and guilt. That was what. Mansfeld had been his quest, his mission, his whole life's work. To admit he'd missed something this vital, that he'd been this wrong and it had cost his friend his life . . . what did that say about him?

But what else would it say if he refused to accept what was before his eyes out of stubbornness and pride and shame? What would Tommie say if he were here?

That he'd known the risk. That he'd been on his own mission anyway, one that still would have taken him into those waters on that day. That they couldn't know what would have happened if Sterling hadn't been there—but that he did get to decide what happened now. Whether today would bring more death or perhaps something different.

He lowered his weapon. Didn't put it away, not quite yet. But he lowered it. He couldn't exactly sign with it still in his hands, but he knew Elsie could read his lips without too much effort. "How long have you known?"

A small smile teased the corners of her mouth. *I knew the ways of spies before you were a twinkle in your mother's eye,* she signed.

Mansfeld took a half-step to the side, to see him past Elsie. "She found me two weeks ago. While the two of you were out looking for me, I'd circled round to the inn, thinking to do a bit of surveillance. But she surprised me—sneaky thing that she is." Admiration saturated his tone. "Knew me right away too. It seems I bear a striking resemblance to my brother."

Sterling didn't know a thing about that. But he did know that Elsie saw more than the rest of them—certainly more than he did. He knew that her instincts were right, without fail. And he knew that she, who had chosen to live a life apart from her own family because of the hardship her very existence brought them, wasn't so sentimental that she would choose to believe what she wanted rather than what was true.

Sterling blustered out a sigh and slid his gun back into his holster. These women were forces to be reckoned with. Seemed a wise man would get out of their way, especially since he knew that the brass would probably promise Mansfeld anything he wanted, including amnesty, if he handed over helpful information about the German command. "All right. We'll do it your way, Mansfeld. Your mother first—interrogation second."

He wanted to regret it, even as he spoke it. He wanted to doubt the brilliance of the German's smile. He wanted to think maybe Elsie and Evie were both wrong this time.

But even more, he wanted to witness a circle closed. History rewritten. Hope given wings. He wanted to see truth lived out.

So, he pulled the outside door open again and jerked his head. "Let's get on with it, then. This reunion has been long enough in coming."

Yet Mansfeld hesitated. He dropped his hands, but they certainly didn't look threatening. They looked at loose ends, not knowing quite what to do. "I—are you certain? Now? We could write her a note. Arrange something."

And that—that fear, that insecurity—was what finally

convinced Sterling that Evie and Elsie were both right. That was the look of a boy longing for his mother but afraid to face her. Afraid that she'd reject him. Afraid that all his searching, his years of work to get to this singular point in time, had been wasted.

Elsie turned to face him and lifted a hand, rested it on his cheek. Perhaps she smiled at him. Perhaps she mouthed encouragement. Whatever the case, Mansfeld relaxed. Nodded. And looked more like a composed, unflappable officer again. "All right. Now."

They were a strange party, walking through the dark streets of a sleepy village. The German spy and the deaf grandmother, walking arm in arm. The English spy and the innkeeper, following right behind. Between them, they could speak a half-dozen languages, make codes and break them, list details that normal people had never learned to see.

But they were silent as they made their way through Ocracoke—over a continent, across an ocean, through a torpedoed trawler, to here. This spot. This time.

A light glowed in the window of the Wynnwood house, and a silhouette passed before it, out of sight, back again. Celeste, pacing. Garret, there behind her.

Evie let go of his arm as they neared, dashed past the other two, up to the door. As she'd done that morning, she knocked but then swung the door open, not waiting for an answer. He could see her at that moment as she'd been as a child, he thought—all brightness and light and joy and knowing. Knowing what those she loved needed. Knowing how to help, even when it was just a smile or a touch or a prayer.

More than that this time. This time, as a woman who'd learned so many hard lessons herself, she burst in, but then held the door open and turned back to the rest of them.

Sterling was only a step behind Mansfeld and Elsie. He slid his hand into Evie's, there inside the door, and stopped there with her. Watched as Celeste and Garret both emerged from the front room. Watched as they both looked on the young man who bore such a resemblance, apparently, to one they loved already.

Watched as tears swelled in Celeste's eyes. As she held out her arms. And her son rushed into them, sobbing like the boy he'd been when last they held each other.

They stood there for a minute, then Evie inclined her head toward the night waiting behind the door. "Care for a walk on the beach—or do you think your captive will run away?"

He glanced once more to the knot of family, reunited. Grandmother, mother, father-in-waiting, child. "If he tries anything, Elsie can handle him."

Evie's laughter accompanied them onto the porch, down the steps, onto the sidewalk. She circled her arm around his and smiled up at him, her face silvered by moonlight. "Well, Mr. Bertrand. I'd say your mission is more or less complete. Where do you think they'll send you next?"

Something he'd been giving plenty of thought to that afternoon. He didn't have the answer, of course. But one thing he knew. "Wherever it is, I'm going to suggest a new cover. I think a married couple would make the best sort of agents, don't you? No one would think us anything but lovebirds."

Her eyes danced like the stars. "And they may have a point, at that."

Author's Note

The summer after I graduated from college, I awoke in the early morning hours one day with a story crowding my mind. A story set in my favorite place—the Outer Banks of North Carolina, where I'd married my husband. A story about a wealthy young man from the capital area and a local mixed-race girl he never should have loved. I pulled out my laptop and wrote half of that book in the next three days. A story of that illogical love, of the twins that came from it, of betrayal and second chances and dreams rediscovered. It was a contemporary, that first version, a very different story from what you've just read. But it was Louisa Adair. It was Remington Culbreth. It was Davie and Evie, Serena and Grann.

Years later, I decided to rewrite the book to pitch to publishers, and I called it *Yesterday's Tides*. Still contemporary, and in that version, Rem was an analyst for the CIA. But when I began publishing historical romances, when I started writing about spies and codebreakers and the First World War, when my best friend and critique partner said, "Oo! You should rewrite *Yesterday's Tides* as a historical!" I knew exactly how I would re-set Louisa and Rem's story into "my" era. And so I planted Remington Culbreth in my fictional version of Room 40, and I waited for the chance to tell his story.

My family vacations in the Outer Banks every year, but we've always stayed on the northern islands of Bodie and Hatteras. But always, always I was searching for that perfect village. Where was Louisa from? Where was her mother's inn? I searched and I searched for well over a decade (welcome to the weird dedication of a writer's mind!). Then, one year, we stayed in Hatteras, and I said, "Hey, we should take the ferry over to Ocracoke." We did. And as we drove through that tiny little village, I knew. *This* was Louisa's home.

A couple years later, as I wrestled with how best to tell this story that had been in my heart for so long, I remember thinking, *It's a shame that all the interesting stuff here happened in the Second World War instead of the First.* Then it came—the idea for a timeslip. Evie and Sterling's story in one thread, starting with the U-boats and the sinking of the *Bedfordshire*. Rem and Louisa's story in the other, with its clashes and betrayals and lost friends and Great War. And I knew—I knew this was it, the story it was meant to be. I pitched it to Bethany House a couple months later and nearly wept with joy when they agreed to publish it. Finally, finally this story first imagined in 2004 would have its day!

On May 11, 2021, my husband and I walked from our rental house on Ocracoke, where we were staying so I could do some research, to the British Cemetery. In most years, there would have been a memorial service going on at that very hour, remembering the lost sailors from the HMT *Bedfordshire*, only two of whose names were ever known, including Thomas Cunningham, who left a pregnant wife at home in England. Given the pandemic, there was no memorial that year. Just David and me with some camera gear and phones to record all our impressions, and a few other visitors stopping to pay homage to those fallen friends.

I soaked it in. I took notes. I recorded sounds and images, snapped hundreds of pictures. I visited the island's charming preservation society museum, bought a recipe card for fig cake and a packet of yaupon tea, and listened in on conversations about hurricanes and flooding. I armed myself with information on the "Ocracoke Brogue"—the dialect unique to the island—and spent a lovely hour in the museum's archives, taking pictures of pages and pages of old books and records. Building a world. And best of all, perhaps, was when we took an evening stroll and found the inn. An actual inn, a converted family home, tucked away on the sound. It's now a rental house called the Soundfront Inn, but it had been a working inn in the century past. I renamed it, but that is the house that inspired all descriptions of Louisa's home.

There were indeed stories during WWII about German spies hiding in the woods of Ocracoke. They were dismissed as paranoia, sure, and no doubt that's the truth. But *what if*, I had to wonder. What if there really had been a German agent there? What would his purpose have been? And if there's a German agent, there needs to be his opposite number, hunting him down. And what if that English—because of course he'd be English—operative had been on the *Bedfordshire*? What if he happened upon my inn, and this family who knew more about such things than anyone would expect?

What if Celeste were the linchpin? What if her grandmother was *Elsie*, the deaf child in my final CULPER RING book, *Circle of Spies*, who had carried *that* legacy with her all these years? What if all my worlds collided here and made something new?

That's right—in this story the careful reader will see details of *all* my story worlds, joining together. From the CULPER

RING, we have Elsie herself, and a bit about what it was like for her to grow up in a family to which it didn't look like she belonged, along with a mention of the "godmother" who helped her learn American Sign Language as a child—none other than the heroine of *Circle of Spies*, Marietta. We have her trunk full of espionage history that Louisa and Celeste put to such use here—nothing less than the codebooks and legacy left by America's first spy ring, the Culper Ring, which we saw in *Ring of Secrets* and *Whispers from the Shadows*.

Why, you may ask, was Elsie in possession of it? Because who better to carry on that tradition than a girl whose appearance belied her truth, and whom the world would dismiss and say anything around because of her deafness? I'd always had in mind that Elsie carried the legacy forward into the next century. We may not here learn exactly how she did that as a young woman, but I love that I was able to show how she passed it along to others for the World Wars.

And in Rem's home in England, we have glimpses of all my English-set worlds! It's Justin, my darling Duke of Stafford from *The Lost Heiress*, who joins with Camden in flying Rem and Louisa to France at the end, promising a visit with Brook and the boys once they're safely home. Rem has the joy of getting to know my family of former thieves at Pauly's Pub in Poplar every month—because Barclay is still in Room 40, seeing things people mean to be kept secret, inviting them to join his family. That means entertainment by Lukas and Willa from *A Song Unheard*, and tales of books and pen pals from Rosemary and Peter from *A Name Unknown*. Margot had gotten to observe Rem's growing sadness through the years in *The Number of Love*, and now we get to see her from his point of view. And her wedding, which we first viewed from Zivon and Lily's perspective in *A Portrait of Loyalty*, even got to make another appearance here as Rem joins Camden and Arabelle (*On Wings of Devotion*) and Barclay and Evelina (*An Hour Unspent*) in rescue efforts . . . which meant forgoing his planned evening at home with the "most recent book on Druids" by Lord Sheridan (giving a glimpse of the world from the SECRETS OF THE ISLES series too). And, last but not least, the beloved little brother stationed in France from the SHADOWS OVER ENGLAND trilogy, Georgie, *had* to be their guide here as they move in to rescue Celeste!

But I hope that even if you've read no other book of mine, you'll still be as caught up in this story as I've been for so many years. I pray that you'll have given a moment's thought to the battle that raged off America's East Coast and that cost so many men their lives, and that you'll think, too, about the brave Coasties who worked tirelessly during those years to save whomever they could.

Though most characters in this book are purely fictional, I did pepper in a few historic Ocracokers and draw from some island names too—Farrow, Scarborough, O'Neal, and other last names mentioned briefly in these pages have been around the islands for centuries. Doxee, Fanny Pearl, the Howards, and the Wahabs were all actual people, and Fanny Pearl really did strike up a long-distance friendship with the widowed Barbara Cunningham. Though there were no Evie-made gifts in reality, Fanny Pearl did eventually venture across the Atlantic to visit Barb, long after the war was over, and reported on the visit in the local paper afterward.

I did my best to capture at least a sliver of this beautiful, unique island world, with its figs and yaupon and (historically) sand roads, where banker ponies have traditionally run free over the dunes, and where one of the oldest working lighthouses in America still shines its beacon every night. Where hurricanes and tides have dictated life, but where kindness and hospitality are still the order of the day, just as they were a hundred years ago or more. There is so much rich island history that I could only give the barest glimpse of! From Blackbeard having a lair there to the only Boy Scout troop in the nation that caught their own wild ponies and rode them for all their Scouting expeditions, Ocracoke is a small island with a big heritage.

Many thanks to the Ocracokers who showed me around, answered my questions, and offered true Southern hospitality to me as I researched. Candy, Andrea, Leslie—I so enjoyed talking to each of you! Thank you to Deanna Davidson for helping with the American Sign Language portion of the book. I still can't believe that the day after I was stressing over getting the ASL right, we reconnected in my Patrons & Peers group, and you shared about teaching ASL! My deep and heartfelt appreciation goes out to Toni Shiloh, who yet again agreed to read a manuscript for me to ensure I handled racial issues with the grace and sensitivity they deserve. And as always, thank you to the team of family, friends, and staff at Bethany House who help make each story possible!

DISCUSSION QUESTIONS

1. Evie has a routine she loves and takes comfort in, and yet which is also a burden. Would you want to live the life she's carved out as an innkeeper on a small island? Or would you have preferred the more exciting path she could have followed with the rest of her family? Do you know anyone who seems to have spiritual insight into others' hearts like she does?

2. Louisa has lived her life with questions about herself that her mother and Grann were determined to protect her from. Did you understand their decision to keep the truth from her? Would you have insisted on being told, or buried your questions? Even the questions made Louisa battle feelings of shame and then bitterness toward those who tried to heap that shame on her. What did you think of her struggle? Have you seen a similar struggle play out in your own family or community, whether over race or another quality that inspires prejudice?

3. We all know that the past is what shapes the future, for good and for ill. We also all have things that we

regret, but that we can't wish completely undone because of the good that has come from them. What is an example of this in your life? How do you think things would have been different for Evie and her brother if Edith had behaved differently?

4. Sterling Bertram has to balance his injuries, his mission, and his guilt over his friend's death. Would being in his situation have made you more determined to find Mansfeld or ready to throw in the towel? Should he have been less suspicious of Evie? More?

5. Rem has always resented the responsibilities placed on his shoulders simply because of his birth order, but he also, deep down, wants to live up to the expectations and make his family proud. Jesus captures this human tendency perfectly in the parable of the two brothers—are you more likely to grumble but do what's expected, or to say whatever you must to pacify people but then do what you want anyway? Do you think Rem made the right decision in returning to England to serve during the war?

6. On the invitation for a party my sister was hosting, she instructed her guests to "Be comfy." For some people, that meant yoga pants, and for others, it meant a dress. It's a beautiful difference that we see in Parisian-styled Celeste and Evie, contrasted with Louisa's very practical work wardrobe and the "Sunday clothes" that she hates. What are you most comfortable in? What traditional styles of your parents' or grandparents' generation do you miss? Which are you glad have gone away?

7. Was there anything about Ocracoke that you

learned in the story and were intrigued by? Have you been there? Would you want to visit? Can you imagine living on a small island for your entire life? After the Second World War is over, do you think Evie and Sterling will return to Ocracoke or go to England?

8. Rem discovers that his father isn't quite as demanding and distant as he had thought. Were you surprised by Lord Culbreth? What about his story of failed love with Edith?

9. Were you surprised by the role Celeste ended up playing in the story? What did you think her part was going to be as you read the first half of the book? Hers is a story of struggles, triumphs, and the price we often pay for other people's decisions—a story many victims of abuse live out. What did you think of the sisterhood between her and Louisa? Of how she linked the two halves of the story together?

10. Something I learned over and again as I studied the Great War for my other books is that nearly everything from the Second World War had its roots in the First. Did you know about "Torpedo Junction" and the sinking of the *Bedfordshire*? Or about the English fishing vessels turned into protectors for America's East Coast? Was there anything else you learned about either time period in these pages?

11. Did you prefer one story line over the other? Had you figured out who Evie was before the big reveal?

12. "Adair women love once, forever." To some, the idea of one forever love is incredibly romantic, while others adore a second-chance romance. Louisa and Evie

end up making very different decisions about that, though neither does so without pain. In which direction does your heart lean? Have you been surprised by where life leads you, or someone dear to you, in such matters?

Roseanna M. White is a bestselling, Christy Award–winning author who has long claimed that words are the air she breathes. When not writing fiction, she's homeschooling her two kids, editing, designing book covers, and pretending her house will clean itself. Roseanna is the author of a slew of historical novels that span several continents and thousands of years. Spies and war and mayhem always seem to find their way into her books . . . to offset her real life, which is blessedly ordinary. You can learn more about her and her stories at roseannamwhite.com.

Sign Up for Roseanna's Newsletter

Keep up to date with Roseanna's news on book releases and events by signing up for her email list at roseannamwhite.com.

More from Roseanna M. White

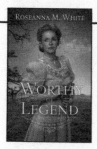

After uncovering a diary that leads to a secret artifact, Lady Emily Scofield and Bram Sinclair must piece together the mystifying legends while dodging a team of archaeologists. In a race against time, they must decide what makes a hero. Is it fighting valiantly to claim the treasure or sacrificing everything in the name of selfless love?

Worthy of Legend • THE SECRETS OF THE ISLES #3

◊BETHANYHOUSE

Stay up to date on your favorite books and authors with our free e-newsletters. Sign up today at bethanyhouse.com.

f facebook.com/bethanyhousepublishers @bethanyhousefiction

OB Free exclusive resources for your book group at bethanyhouseopenbook.com